SNOWBOUND SUSPICION

CINDI MYERS

WYOMING COWBOY SNIPER

NICOLE HELM

MILLS & BOON

First Published in Great Britain 2019
by Mills & Boon, an imprint of HarperCollins*Publishers*
1 London Bridge Street, London, SE1 9GF

Snowbound Suspicion © 2019 Cynthia Myers
Wyoming Cowboy Sniper © 2019 Nicole Helm

ISBN: 978-0-263-27416-5

0519

MIX
Paper from
responsible sources
FSC www.fsc.org
FSC™ C007454

This book is produced from independently certified FSC™ paper to ensure responsible forest management.

For more information visit: www.harpercollins.co.uk/green

Printed and bound in Spain
by CPI, Barcelona

SNOWBOUND SUSPICION

CINDI MYERS

For D'ann

Chapter One

"More snow forecast today for most of the state, with highs in the mid to upper thirties. Parts of the state could see accumulations of another foot, on top of already record amounts of snow this past week. Travel advisories remain active and avalanche danger remains high."

Bette Fuller switched off the radio and gripped the steering wheel more tightly. White flakes drifted down from the gray sky like glitter in a snow globe—so pretty unless you were the shaken-up person in the middle of the flurry. To the growing list of things she didn't like she added incessant snow. And driving in the mountains on narrow, two-lane roads with no guard rails and steep drop-offs. Flashing lights up ahead made her tense her whole body as she eased her Ford Focus past the Highway Patrol vehicle parked on the side of the road. The patrolman stood in the road, motioning traffic past what appeared to be a large boulder in the middle of the road. Bette averted her eyes and shuddered.

Cops. She didn't like them, either, and she was headed for a whole house full of them. If Lacy Milligan hadn't been one of her best friends in the whole world, she would have turned the car around and headed straight back to Denver. But Lacy was her friend, and it wasn't every day a friend got married. Not to mention, catering this wedding was a really big deal. Whether she liked it or not, Lacy was something of a celebrity in Colorado, and the press was sure to cover her wedding to Sheriff Travis Walker. The irony of that matchup made the media salivate—Lacy was marrying the man who had been instrumental in sending her to prison for a murder she didn't commit. The sheriff had redeemed himself by working to get Lacy released, resulting in a story the press couldn't get enough of.

This could be the big break Bette needed to really get her catering business on solid footing. What was a little snow compared with the opportunity to help a friend and advance her career? She had faced down tougher situations than this before. She hadn't always made good choices in the past, but she was a different person now. This time she was going to succeed.

Twenty minutes later, she drove the Ford underneath the welded iron arches that proclaimed Walking W Ranch, est. 1942, and wound her way down the plowed drive—five-foot walls of snow on each side of the single snowy lane. The drive ended in a cleared parking area, a short distance from a sprawling log-and-stone ranch house. Bette shut off the engine and let out a long breath. She'd made it. With luck, that drive would be the worst part of the whole two and a half weeks she would be here.

She climbed out of the car and stretched, unkinking muscles that had been tensed for most of the snowy drive. This was some place Lacy's fiancé—or rather, his parents—had. It looked like something out of a movie, or some Western lifestyle magazine. The front door of the house opened and a man stepped out onto the porch—a tall man in a cowboy hat and one of those long, leather coats with the cape about the shoulders. What did they call them? *Dusters*, that was the word.

The man in the duster raised a gloved hand and bounded down the steps and strode toward her through the still-falling snow. Her heart hammered painfully as she took in his broad shoulders and long stride. He might be dressed like a cowboy, but his attitude was all cop. She had been around enough of them the last few years to be able to spot that particular I'm-in-charge demeanor from across the yard.

"You must be Bette. Travis said you were supposed to be here today." The man stopped in front of her and offered his hand.

Tentatively, she extended her own hand, only to have it engulfed by his leather-clad paw. A tremor of a different kind traveled through her as her eyes met his steely blue gaze and she silently cursed. Of all the really inconvenient times for her to be reminded that it had been a very long time since she'd been this close to a good-looking man.

"I'm Cody Rankin," he said. "Travis and his brother are at work and I guess Lacy is in town, though she should be up here later today. Travis's sister, Emily, is around somewhere, but at the moment, looks like it's just you and me."

Oh, joy, Bette thought, though she didn't say the words out loud. Not that Cody Rankin wasn't a perfectly nice—and perfectly gorgeous—specimen of manhood. She just didn't want anything to do with charming men right now. Especially one who wore a badge. "Are you one of Travis's cop friends?" she asked. Better to get that part of the introductions over with.

"I'm a US marshal," he said. "Though I'm on vacation right now." He nodded toward the trunk of the car. "Can I help you with your luggage? Though I'm not sure where the Walkers have you staying—maybe one of the guest cabins."

"I'll leave the suitcases in the car until I find out where they want me," she said. "But I have a cooler that needs to go into the house." Before she had left Denver, she'd stocked up on fondant, meringue powder, good Belgian baking chocolate and a handful of other ingredients she wasn't sure she would be able to find out here in the boonies.

"I'll get it." He waited while she popped the trunk, then reached in and hefted out the heavy cooler as if it weighed no more than a box of paper towels.

"How is it you know Lacy?" he asked as he led the way up the walk.

She was glad she was walking behind him, so that he couldn't see the way she stiffened at the question. Of course, she had expected it. It was the kind of thing people asked at weddings: "How do you know the bride?" She just hadn't had a chance to think of a good answer. "We met when we were cellmates in prison" wasn't the kind of answer that went over well in polite company, even though it was the truth.

"We've been friends a long time," she said.

He opened the door and led the way into a large great room, fire crackling in a woodstove against the back wall, trophy mounts staring down at them from near the log beams overhead. Bette followed Cody through a paneled door into an equally massive kitchen, the marble-topped island in the center of the room as big as a queen-size bed, stainless appliances reflecting the glow of cherry cabinets. He set the cooler in front of a French-door refrigerator and started to open it. "I'll put everything away myself," Bette said, rushing forward. "Thank you."

He straightened. "Okay," he said, then shrugged out of the duster to reveal a snap-button chamois shirt the color of light brown sugar that stretched over impressive shoulders. Well-fitting faded Wranglers and scuffed brown boots completed the outfit. Her gaze shifted to the gun in a holster on his hip. Discreet, but unmistakable. He put a hand to the gun. "I probably don't need this here," he said. "But habits die hard. I'd feel kind of naked without it."

His word choice created a disturbing picture. She turned away, hoping he wouldn't notice her reaction. "How was your drive from Denver?" he asked. "You're lucky you made it through. The pass has been closed."

"I know," she said. "I've been watching for my chance to get here." She leaned back against the kitchen island, arms folded. "The drive wasn't too bad. Are you in the wedding?"

"One of the groomsmen." He reached past her to pluck a grape from a bunch in a bowl on the island and she caught the clean aroma of shaving cream and fabric softener. "I took vacation to come up here early, thinking Travis and I could hang out before he tied the knot—but he's been working overtime on this serial killer case."

"Serial killer? Here?" Eagle Mountain was such a small town, and so remote. What would a serial killer be doing here?

"You didn't know? It's been all over the news."

"I don't pay much attention to the news." She had been too focused on preparing to come here.

"Three women have been murdered so far—one right here on the ranch." He popped a grape in his mouth and crunched down on it. "Be careful if you go anywhere by yourself."

"I'll keep that in mind."

"I'm surprised Lacy didn't mention it to you, but then, maybe she didn't want to frighten you away."

She met his gaze with a hard look of her own. "I don't frighten easily, Marshal Rankin."

"Aw, call me Cody. We're going to be seeing a lot of each other these next two weeks." He popped another grape in his mouth and crunched. "Now that you've arrived, the time here is going to be a lot less dull."

And just what did he mean by that? "I came here to work," she said. Not only had Lacy hired her to cater for the wedding, she was also preparing food for a bridesmaids' tea and the rehearsal dinner.

"If you need a sous chef, I'm your man." He straightened. "Seriously, I'm bored out of my gourd, with Travis working all the time. I'm not used to being this idle. My job is pretty intense, high-energy stuff—pursuing fugitives, most of whom don't want to be caught."

Bette was well aware of what US marshals did—she wasn't likely to ever forget being tackled by one and dragged, handcuffed, into a waiting car. How long into her visit to the ranch before Cody Rankin figured out her history? One phone call to his office was all it would take to get the whole sordid tale. Or he could just ask his friend Travis. Bette assumed Lacy had told her fiancé about her background. Yet he had agreed to let her come to his home and cater his wedding anyway. Now, that was true love.

A door at the opposite end of the room opened, ushering in a blast of cold air and a tall, angular woman wrapped in a blue wool coat. She stopped short upon seeing them. "Marshal Rankin." She nodded to Cody, then her bird-like eyes shifted to Bette. "Who are you?"

"I'm the caterer—Bette Fuller." Bette started around the island toward the woman, but the woman took a step back.

"I'm Rainey," she said. "And I'm in charge of the kitchen here. I told Travis he didn't need to hire a caterer. I'm perfectly capable of providing anything they need in the way of food—I've been doing it for years. But I guess brides these days want to be able to say they've had their wedding 'catered' by a 'chef.'" She sniffed. "Just stay out of my way when it comes to preparing regular meals. I have all the help I need from my son." She looked back over her shoulder. "Doug! Come in here!"

A man Bette judged to be in his late twenties or early thirties, his head engulfed in a fur cap with earflaps, shuffled into the kitchen, half a dozen plastic shopping bags suspended from each hand. He stopped short when he saw Bette. "Hello," he said, his eyes meeting hers, then darting away.

"This is my son, Doug," Rainey said. "He's been to culinary school and plans to open his own restaurant soon, though for the time being he's helping me here at the ranch. The two of us could have provided anything the Walkers need for the wedding."

Well, Bette certainly didn't have to wonder what Rainey thought about her being here. "I'll try to stay out of your way," she said. "I have some things that need to go in the refrigerator." She indicated the cooler.

"Not in here. Put them in the other refrigerator, in the garage." She jerked her head toward a door at the side of the room. "Doug, show her where to put her stuff."

But Doug had disappeared, the back door slamming behind him.

"I'll show you." Cody shrugged back into his duster, then picked up the cooler. "Nice seeing you again, Rainey," he called over his shoulder. "That omelet you made me for breakfast was divine."

Bette said nothing until they were in the garage, in front of an older-model—but still very high-end—refrigerator. She opened the door and surveyed the contents, which appeared to consist mostly of bottles of beer and a large cardboard box labeled Venison Sticks. Cody reached past her and helped himself to one of the sticks, which resembled a very thin frankfurter. "These are excellent," he said, tearing open the wrapper. "Travis's dad makes them, from venison he harvests himself."

Bette nodded and rearranged some of the beer bottles to make room for her chocolate and fondant. "I can see dealing with Rainey is going to be a barrel of laughs."

"Ignore her." Cody held the top of the cooler open for her. "Lacy and Travis want you here, and that's all that matters."

"Oh, I won't let her get to me," Bette said. "I've dealt with worse." Some of the guards at the Denver Women's Correctional Facility would have made Rainey look like a creampuff. She stowed the last of the items in the refrigerator and shut the door. "Are Mr. and Mrs. Walker around? I'd like to find out where I'm staying."

"They headed to Junction while the pass is open," Cody said. "Rainey might know." He looked doubtful.

Bette laughed. "If it was up to her, she'd put me in a horse stall or something." She shut the lid of the cooler. "No, I can wait until Lacy shows up."

She started to pick up the empty cooler, but Cody swiped it from her. She shrugged. If he wanted to tote her belongings for her, let him. It didn't mean she owed him anything.

Instead of heading back into the kitchen, he led the way out of the garage and around to the front of the house. "Okay if I leave the cooler out here?" he asked, indicating a spot on the covered front porch near the door.

"That's fine." She started to open the door but stilled at the sound of a car approaching. A red Jeep zipped into a parking place near the house. The driver's door flew open and Lacy Milligan, her dark hair in short layers around her face and topped by a pink fleece cap with an oversize pom-pom like the tail of a rabbit, her petite frame wrapped in a white puffy coat that reached to the top of her fur-trimmed boots, raced toward them, arms outstretched.

"Bette!" Lacy squealed and grabbed her friend in a crushing hug. "Oh, it's so good to see you! How have you been? Was the drive from Denver horrible? Oh, let me look at you." She released her hold on Bette and took a step back. "You look fantastic. Oh, I'm so glad you're here."

"You look great yourself," Bette said. She couldn't stop grinning. Just being with Lacy again made her happy.

"I've been trying to make her feel welcome." Cody spoke up from his spot just behind Bette.

"Thank you, Cody," Lacy nodded to him, then turned back to Bette. "I'm sorry I wasn't here when you arrived. With the wedding less than three weeks away things are absolutely crazy. And with the road being closed and Travis working so much—I swear, I'm going to need a vacation when this is over."

She took Bette's arm and ushered her into the house. "I'm going to head over to the stables, if anyone needs me," Cody said, but Bette doubted Lacy heard. She was chattering away about the wedding preparations and the snow and Travis and who knew what else. Bette glanced behind her to watch Cody exit, his duster slung over one arm.

"Leave it to you to make friends with the best-looking single man in the place." Lacy nudged Bette. "It's a good thing you weren't around when I reconnected with Travis. He wouldn't have looked twice at me."

"I'm not interested in catching the eye of any man," Bette said. "That's how I got into so much trouble in the first place, remember?"

Lacy's expression clouded. "You don't hear from Eddie anymore, do you?"

Bette shook her head. "No. And I hope I never do." Hooking up with Eddie Rialto had been the absolute worst decision she had ever made in her life. "I'm staying happily single from now on."

"Oh, men aren't all bad," Lacy said. "You just have to meet the right one."

"You're in love, so you think everyone else should be, too," Bette said. "That's sweet, but I'm here to work—and to spend time with you and wish you well. That's plenty to keep me occupied."

"And I'm so glad you're here." Lacy took both of

Bette's hands in her own and lowered her voice, her expression serious. "Have you met Rainey yet?"

"Oh, yes, I met Rainey."

Lacy winced. "I'm sorry I didn't warn you. She can be a real grouch, but I guess she's worked for the Walker family forever, so I try not to say anything. She wanted to cook for the wedding herself, but thank goodness Travis backed me up when I said I wanted to hire you."

"I really appreciate your giving me this chance." Bette squeezed Lacy's hands, then released them. "But tell me the truth—how many people know about me? How many people know the two of us met in prison?"

"Travis knows, of course. And his parents. I had to tell them. And his brother, Gage, probably knows. I don't think he and Travis have any secrets. But it doesn't matter. They know you served your time and paid for your mistakes, and that you're making a fresh start. They admire you for it, the way I do. And really, what can they say? I was in prison, after all."

"You were innocent," Bette said. "And Travis proved it. You never did the things you were convicted for. But I was guilty. I did help rob a bank."

"You made a mistake and you paid for it," Lacy repeated. "That doesn't mean you're a bad person."

Bette let out a breath, trying to ease the tension in her neck. "I'm glad Travis and his parents were so understanding." She glanced toward the door. "Not everyone would be."

"If you're thinking of Cody, I'm sure he doesn't know," Lacy said. "And Rainey doesn't know, so don't worry about her. Did you meet Doug?"

"We were introduced. He didn't stick around long."

"Just so you know, he has a record, too. He's supposedly reformed, but frankly, he gives me the creeps. Rainey won't hear a word against him, though, so if I were you, I'd have nothing but good things to say about her darling boy. You'll get on her best side that way."

"Does she have a best side?"

Both women laughed. Lacy put her arm around Bette. "We have you staying in one of the guest cabins," she said. "It's adorable, plus you'll have your privacy. Come on, I'll show you. And then I want a nice long visit, so I can hear all about what you've been up to."

Chapter Two

Cody leaned over the stall to run his hand along the rough velvet of the mare's shoulder, and smiled as the animal nuzzled at his shirt pocket. "Sorry, girl, I don't have any treats for you today," he said. He'd have to remember to bring a few horse nuggets or a carrot with him next time he visited the stables.

The mare lost interest and turned away to pull hay from the rack on the wall and Cody sat on the feed bin across from the stall. He inhaled deeply of the oats-and-molasses aroma of sweet feed and the still-green scent of hay, and tried to quiet his racing mind. He'd been spending a lot of time here since coming to the ranch. The stables were a quiet place to think. Or maybe *brood* would be a better word. He wanted to be out there, tracking down and apprehending fugitives, getting bad guys off the streets. Instead, his supervisors had forced him into taking vacation. One screw-up and they thought the answer was time off, but they were wrong. He needed to be back out in the field, proving to them and to himself that he could still handle the job.

He hadn't minded so much about the forced leave at first—he'd figured this would be a good chance for him and Travis to catch up before the wedding. They could go ice fishing, or maybe elk hunting. Cody could help with work on the ranch. Instead, Travis was neck-deep in the hunt for a serial killer, and Cody could do nothing to help. Sure, his friend had taken pity and let him sit in on a few briefings, but Cody had no jurisdiction and, really, no experience figuring out who committed crimes. As a US marshal, his job was to find the suspects after they had been identified.

At least he wouldn't be the only outsider at the ranch now. Bette Fuller had been a nice surprise. Somehow, when Travis had talked about the caterer, Cody had pictured an older woman—maybe someone who looked like Julia Child. Instead, a curvy blonde with the most amazing blue eyes and a full mouth that smiled with a hint of a challenge had emerged from the snowstorm to make life on the ranch a whole lot more interesting.

She hadn't exactly warmed up to Cody. Was Bette so cool to him because he was a cop, or a man—or both? Never mind—he liked a challenge, and they had a couple of weeks to get to know each other better. And if they did hit it off, she was from Denver, and so was he. This could be the start of a fun friendship.

He stood. Time to head back to the house. Bette and Lacy should have had enough time to swap girl talk, and maybe he could find out from Lacy what was up with Travis. As he exited the stables, the scent of tobacco smoke drifted to him. He followed the smell around the side of the barn, where he found Doug Whittington, huddled out of the wind, with a half-smoked cigarette. "Hello, Doug," he said.

The young man jumped and made as if to hide the cigarette behind his back. "Too late for that." Cody joined him in the L formed by the stables and the tack room. "I don't care if you smoke—just don't set the barns on fire."

"Don't tell my mother," Doug said, then took another long drag. In his late twenties or early thirties, he had close-cropped brown hair and freckles. Cody had never seen him smile, and probably hadn't exchanged a dozen words with him in the week since he had arrived at the ranch.

Neither man said anything as Doug finished the cigarette. He threw down the butt and ground it into the snow with the heel of his boot. "Who's that girl?" he asked. "The one who showed up today."

"You mean Bette?" Was Doug asking because he was interested in the pretty newcomer? Cody couldn't blame the guy, though he didn't think the sullen cook was the type to catch the eye of someone like Bette. "She's catering the wedding."

"Yeah, but who is she? Where's she from and who decided she should come here?"

"She's from Denver and she's a friend of Lacy's."

"Did you know her in Denver?"

"No. Why did you think that?"

"The two of you seemed friendly, that's all."

Cody laughed. He wouldn't have called his interaction with Bette exactly friendly. "Are you worried she might take your mother's job?" he asked. "I don't think that's her intention at all."

Doug rolled his shoulders. "Just wondering. How long is she going to be here?"

"The wedding is in two and a half weeks, so I imagine she'll be here at least until then."

"Just wondering," he said again, then stuffed his hands in his pockets. "I gotta go."

He shuffled off through the snow, away from the house. He was an odd duck, Cody thought, but then, it took all kinds. He headed back to the house and found Lacy and Bette seated before the fire. "Cody!" Lacy greeted him with her usual enthusiasm. "We wondered where you had gone off to."

"I thought I'd give you two a little time alone to catch up," he said. He took a seat at the end of the sofa on one side of the woodstove, opposite Bette.

"So considerate," Lacy said. "Have you been bored out of your mind up here by yourself? I hope not."

"I'm okay," he said. "How's Travis? Any word on how the case is going?"

Lacy shook her head. "I saw him for a few minutes this afternoon, but you know him—he doesn't like to talk about cases. He did say he'd try to make it home for dinner."

"Being a cop's wife isn't for the faint of heart," Cody said.

"Oh, I know that." Lacy waved off his concern. "But I love Travis as much for what he does as for who he is. I like that he's so committed to doing what's right. If he wasn't, I'd still be sitting in prison."

Cody still marveled that Travis had ended up marrying a woman he had arrested for murder. Three years after her conviction, the sheriff had discovered new evidence that proved Lacy was innocent, and he had thrown himself into seeing that her conviction was vacated. After she was freed, he had enlisted her help to find the real murderer. Talk about an unlikely love story.

"I can't believe there's a serial killer in Eagle Mountain," Bette said. "Lacy, why didn't you tell me?"

"I didn't want to scare you off," Lacy said. "Call

me selfish, but it's true." She leaned toward her friend. "You're not scared, are you? You don't need to be. I can't think of anything safer than being here at the ranch, with two lawmen in residence, now that Cody is staying here. And Gage is up here all the time, too."

"I'm not afraid," Bette said. "Though Cody said one of the women was killed here on the ranch."

Lacy frowned. "Well, yes, but that doesn't mean it was someone from here. We were having a scavenger hunt. People were spread out all over the place, so the killer could have sneaked onto the property at any time. But if you make it a point not to go anywhere by yourself, you should be fine."

"I'm happy to accompany you if you need an escort," Cody said, but the offer only earned him a sour look from Bette.

The door from the kitchen opened and Rainey emerged, bearing a large silver tray. Cody rose to help her, but she shrugged him away. "I can get it," she said, as she set the tray on the low table in front of the sofa. "I thought you might like something to snack on before supper."

"Oh, it looks delicious," Lacy said, scooting forward and helping herself to a cheese puff.

Rainey remained tight-lipped. "Have you seen Doug?" she asked. "He's disappeared and it's time for him to help me with supper."

"I saw him a few minutes ago, out by the stables," Cody said.

"Probably smoking a cigarette," Rainey said. "He does that when he's upset."

Cody stuffed a sausage roll into his mouth, using it as an excuse not to comment.

"I can help you if you like," Bette said. She started to stand. "Just tell me what you want me to do."

"I can manage fine on my own," Rainey said. "I've been doing it for years. I'm sure you're the reason Doug is staying away. You've upset him."

"What have I done to upset him?" Bette asked, but Rainey was already walking away, back to the kitchen.

"I'm sorry she's being so rude to you," Lacy said. "I can talk to Mr. and Mrs. Walker if you like. I'm sure they would speak to her."

"No, don't say anything. I don't want to cause trouble." She stood. "I think what I'd like to do is freshen up before dinner. And I want to check out that cute cabin where you've put me. I didn't see much when we dropped off my luggage."

Cody stood. "Let me walk you out. My cabin isn't far and I should probably clean up before dinner, too."

"I don't think that's really necessary," she said.

"Humor me," he said, lifting her coat off the pegs by the door.

"Let him go with you," Lacy said. "I mean, you're probably perfectly fine, but until Travis catches this killer, it probably doesn't hurt to be overly cautious."

If looks could kill, Cody thought Lacy might have been at least injured by the glare Bette sent her, but she allowed Cody to help her into her coat, and she stalked out the door in front of him.

Cody followed, not trying to catch up with her, more amused than insulted. He half suspected Lacy of doing a little matchmaking, trying to throw the two of them together, but it probably didn't hurt for the women to be a little more careful until the murderer was caught.

Bette had been assigned the first in a row of four

log guest cabins arranged alongside the creek, past the horse barns. Cody's cabin was next to hers, the other two reserved for wedding guests due to arrive later. Someone—one of the ranch hands, probably—had shoveled the stone walkway leading to the cabin, which, if it was like Cody's, consisted of a single large room and attached bathroom, and a small covered porch with a single chair and small table.

The sun had set, casting the world around them in gray twilight, but a light shone over the door of Bette's cabin. She stopped at the bottom of the steps leading up onto the porch. Cody halted behind her. "What is it?" he asked, then followed her gaze to the door. There, in bright red paint, someone had scrawled the words *Go Home!*

ONCE SHE WAS over the initial shock of seeing the message on her door, Bette was more angry than frightened. "I guess we know what Doug Whittington was up to when his mother couldn't find him," she said, starting up the steps, her key in her hand.

"Don't touch the door." Cody took her hand as she was reaching for the knob.

She glared at him. "What? You think you're going to find fingerprints? And then what? I don't think a nasty message is exactly a major crime." She pulled out of his grasp, inserted her key in the lock and shoved open the door. Not waiting to be asked, Cody followed her in—not that that surprised her. He was in full-on cop mode, on the case. Except there was no case.

"You don't know that Doug did this," he said.

"Unless his mother took a break from preparing dinner and ran out here with a can of red paint, my money is on Doug. No one else here is so anxious for me to leave." She looked around the room, but clearly nothing had been disturbed. Her unopened suitcases stood by the bed, which was still neatly made, a blue-and-yellow patchwork quilt draped across it.

"I'll talk to him," Cody said.

"No." She grabbed his wrist, squeezing hard, making sure she had his full attention. "Don't say anything. The best way to deal with this kind of harassment is to ignore it."

He set his jaw in a stubborn line and his eyes met hers—denim-blue eyes a woman could get lost in. Clearly, he wasn't a man who ignored anything. "If I tell him to lay off hassling you or he'll have to deal with me, I think he'll stop," he said.

"Your job is not to protect me," she said. "I'm perfectly capable of looking after myself."

He took a step toward her, so that the front of his duster almost brushed against her puffy coat. He was breathing hard, and she realized she was, too. She was torn between wanting to slap him and wanting to grab his shoulders and pull him down to her in a kiss. Her hormones were jumping up and down, shouting, "Big, sexy man—must have," trying hard to drown out her brain, which was pleading that she had more sense than this.

Cody's gaze shifted to her lips and she wondered if he was thinking the same thing—a dangerous thought that had her releasing her hold on him and stepping back, until she bumped into the bed. "You need to leave," she said, her brain momentarily getting the upper hand.

"Yeah, I probably do." He stepped back also, though

his eyes remained locked to hers. "Just promise me if anything else happens—something more than annoying messages—you'll call for me. My cabin is next door." He nodded to his right.

"Sure." She hugged her coat more tightly around her body. "But nothing is going to happen. This is kid stuff."

"What are you going to do about the door?"

"I'll find something to clean the message off the door before anyone sees it."

"Or you could show it to the Walkers and let them know what's going on."

"No. I don't want to do anything to upset them. They've got enough on their hands, between the wedding and this whole serial killer thing. I mean, it can't be that easy, having two sons out hunting a murderer."

Cody wanted to argue—she could practically see the words building up in his head. She braced herself to reply, but instead, he turned and took hold of the doorknob. "Have it your way. But remember—I'm right next door if you need me."

He left and she dropped onto the bed, struggling to control her racing heart. Great. He was next door. Entirely too close for comfort. He had no idea, but Cody Rankin was a lot more dangerous to Bette's well-being than Rainey and her son.

Chapter Three

Bette couldn't decide if the dinner of roast beef, potatoes au gratin, green beans almandine and home-made rolls was designed to impress her with Rainey's prowess in the kitchen, or if it was simply the way the Walker family ate every evening. Add in the gleaming oak table, polished silver and dishes she guessed were hand painted, and the place screamed laid-back luxury. "Everything is so delicious," she said, determined to give credit where credit was due.

"I wish Travis and Gage could have been here," Mrs. Walker said, as she passed the dish of potatoes.

"They said they were sorry to miss eating with us, but they think they have a break in the case," Lacy said.

"I hope that means they're close to catching the murderer," Mrs. Walker said.

"And without another woman dying," Mr. Walker said.

Silence descended on the table, broken only by the clink of ice in glasses and the scrape of forks on china.

"Not the most cheerful topic of conversation," Travis's sister, Emily, said, slicing into her roast.

"One of the hazards of living with law enforcement," Cody said. "Lacy will get used to it."

"Oh, I am," Lacy said. "I think it's interesting, actually."

Mrs. Walker turned to Bette. "I hope you're finding the cabin comfortable."

"Oh, yes," Bette said. "It's beautiful. I'm going to really enjoy staying there."

"Well, if you need anything, just let me know," Mrs. Walker said.

"Maybe some more cleaner." Seated next to her, Cody whispered the words under his breath. Bette kicked him in the shin. She had refused his offer to help scrub the painted message off the front door, but it was true she had used most of a bottle of cleaner and probably ruined a bath towel cleaning everything up. Someone looking closely would probably still be able to see the shadow of the words, but tomorrow she planned to make a wreath or something to hang on the door to cover them up. She had gotten to be pretty crafty, all those years behind bars.

"If I wasn't staying here, you could have had my room," Lacy said. "Though you'll probably appreciate the privacy of the cabin."

"I thought you had a place in town," Bette said. She remembered Lacy's excitement over the apartment she had rented from a friend.

"I do, but Travis persuaded me that I should stay here until the wedding."

"He didn't like the idea of you living alone while this killer is on the loose," Mrs. Walker said. "And I don't blame him."

"It's very sweet of you to take me in," Lacy said. "My room is very nice."

"We thought about putting you in one of the cabins," Mr. Walker said. "But we didn't want to make it too easy for Travis to sneak off to see you. It's good for young men to have a challenge."

Lacy blushed bright pink, while the rest of the table burst into laughter.

The door from the kitchen opened and Rainey entered. "Does anyone need anything?" she asked, surveying the table.

"Everything is delicious," Bette said. "I'll have to get your recipe for the roast—it's so well-seasoned."

"I don't give out my recipes," Rainey said.

Bette kept a smile on her face. She wasn't going to let this old bat get her down.

"My favorite is the potatoes," Cody said.

"Doug made those," Rainey said.

"So I guess he made it back in time to help you with the cooking after all," Cody said.

"I told you, he was just out smoking." She turned on her heels and left them.

"I'm afraid Rainey's feelings are a little hurt that Travis and Lacy didn't ask her to cater the wedding," Mrs. Walker said. "I tried to explain we didn't want to burden her with so much work—and that it meant a lot to Lacy to have her friend do the job. I'm sure she'll calm down soon. In the meantime, I hope you won't let her bother you, Bette."

"Of course not." Bette took a sip of her water, aware of Cody watching her. Honestly, did he have to sit right next to her? She couldn't make a move without being aware of him. When he reached past her for the rolls, his arm brushed hers and a tremor shuddered through her. So annoying. Tomorrow, she'd suggest she trade places at dinner with Lacy or Emily. Or maybe she could stick Travis next to his friend.

"What's next on the wedding agenda?" Emily asked.

"The bridesmaids' tea is Saturday," Lacy said. "Now that Bette is here, we can finish planning that."

"It sounds very formal," Cody said.

"It's just a chance for us to dress up and eat lots of fancy finger food," Lacy said. "I wanted something different from a bar crawl."

"There aren't many bars to crawl to in Eagle Mountain," Emily said.

"That's not going to stop the men." Lacy looked down the table to Cody. "Gage told me he's planning to kidnap Travis and force him to attend his bachelor party Saturday night."

"If the roads stay open, he's booked a hotel in Junction," Cody said. "If not, we'll make do with Moe's Pub."

"I'm rooting for Moe's," Lacy said. "There's no way they can get into trouble there, with half the town watching them."

Rainey returned and began clearing the table. "Where's Doug?" Cody asked. "Doesn't he usually help you with that?"

"He wasn't feeling well," Rainey said. "I sent him to lie down."

"Let me help." Bette stood and began gathering the plates on her side of the table.

"There's no need for that," Rainey said. "I can manage on my own."

"I want to help," Bette said.

Cody stood and began collecting dishes also. "I'll help, too," he said.

The two of them followed Rainey into the kitchen. "Put the dishes in the sink and then go sit down," Rainey directed. "I don't like a lot of other people in my kitchen while I'm trying to work."

"I'm the same way," Bette said. "You know just where everything is and how you want to do things, and it's annoying to have to keep stopping and telling other people what to do."

Rainey glared at her, but Bette kept smiling.

"I don't think your plan to win her over with flattery and kindness is going to work," Cody whispered as they made their way back to the table.

"Maybe I'm not trying to win her over," Bette said. "Maybe I'm trying to drive her crazy. Crabby people hate it when their enemies are nice to them."

A few moments later, Rainey entered the dining room, carrying a large apple pie and a carton of vanilla ice cream. She set them in the center of the table. "You can serve yourselves," she said.

"None for me." Lacy stood. "I have a wedding dress to fit into."

"Thank goodness, I don't." Bette picked up the knife and prepared to cut into the pie. "Who wants ice cream?"

Mrs. Walker declined, but everyone else wanted dessert. Bette dished up the pie, while Cody took charge of the ice cream. When everyone was served, Bette sat back and took a bite.

"What do you think?" Cody asked.

"It's very good." She took a small spoonful of ice

cream. "A little sweeter than I like, and a dash more of cloves would have been a good addition—but very good."

Lacy, who had left the room, returned, phone in hand. "I just had a text from Adelaide Kinkaid." She glanced at Bette. "She's Travis's office manager."

"Is something wrong with Gage or Travis?" White-faced, Mrs. Walker half rose from her chair.

"They're both fine," Emily said. She studied her phone screen. "Adelaide says they've made an arrest in the Ice Cold Killer case."

"The Ice Cold Killer?" Bette asked.

"That's what they're calling the serial killer," Emily said. "Apparently, he leaves behind little cards—like business cards—that say 'ice cold.'"

"Who did they arrest?" Mrs. Walker asked, settling into her chair once more.

"I texted back that question," Lacy said.

The phone pinged and Lacy swiped the screen. Her eyes widened. "She says they arrested Ken Rutledge."

"Who is Ken Rutledge?" Cody asked.

"He's a schoolteacher," Lacy said. "He lives in the other half of the duplex where Kelly Farrow—the first murder victim—lived."

"So he's the serial killer?" Emily asked.

Lacy shook her head. "Adelaide doesn't say. She just says Travis arrested Ken and Gage and Dwight are driv-ing him to the lockup in Junction tonight."

"Well, she can't say, can she?" Emily asked. "But if Travis arrested him—and he's really connected with the case—then he must be the murderer."

"This whole situation has been horrible," Mrs. Walker said. "But I hope it's over now."

"I do, too," Emily said. "In any case, I know I'll sleep better tonight, knowing a killer is behind bars."

"Speaking of sleeping..." Bette pushed back her chair. "I'm going to say good-night now. I still have to unpack, and I've had a very long day."

"The drive from Denver is enough to wear anyone out," Mrs. Walker said.

"I'll walk you to your cabin." Cody stood also.

"I don't need an escort," Bette said.

She could see in his eyes that he wanted to protest, but she didn't give him a chance. She hurried to hug Lacy, said good-night to the others and quickly made her way to the front door. To her relief, Cody didn't follow.

As she took the shoveled path toward the cabins, she told herself she really didn't have to run away from Cody Rankin. He was just another man, and she was a strong enough woman to resist his attractions.

Maybe she should go ahead and tell him she had a record. As a cop who devoted his life to putting away people like her, that information was sure to make him keep his distance.

CODY WAITED UP with the Walkers until Travis came home. The Rayford County sheriff looked as sharp-pressed and alert as always, though Cody recognized the fatigue in his eyes.

"Well?" he asked, once Travis had shed his coat and kissed Lacy.

"Well what?" Travis asked, his arm around Lacy.

"Is Ken Rutledge the Ice Cold Killer?" Lacy asked.

"Probably not—though we're still tracing his movements around the time of all the murders."

"If he's not the killer, why did you arrest him?" Mrs. Walker asked.

"He attacked Darcy Marsh."

"Darcy is a local veterinarian," Emily told Cody. "She and Kelly Farrow were business partners."

"But you don't think he's the serial killer?" Mrs. Walker asked.

"We're not ruling that out completely." Travis moved past them, toward the fire. "I really can't talk about the case—except I'm wondering how you all already know about the arrest."

"Adelaide texted me," Emily said.

"Of course she did." Travis settled onto the sofa.

"She wanted me to know you were all right," Emily said. "And it's not as if something like that is going to stay a secret very long. I imagine most of the town knows about it by now."

"I imagine they do," Travis said, without anger.

"Did you have anything to eat?" Mrs. Walker asked.

Travis shook his head. "I'll get something in a minute. Right now, I just want to rest and warm up."

"What's the weather like?" Mr. Walker took a seat across from his son.

"It's snowing again. I told Gage and Dwight to hurry to get the evidence we collected to Junction. If one of the avalanche chutes on Dixon Pass lets loose, they'll have to close the road again."

"You'll be in big trouble if two of your officers get trapped on the other side of the pass," Cody said. "You might even have to deputize me."

"Only as a last resort," Travis said. He didn't smile, but Cody caught the glint of humor in his eye.

"Bette arrived this afternoon," Lacy said. "She's in

the first guest cabin. Poor woman was exhausted from the drive." She squeezed Travis's arm. "I can't wait for you to meet her."

"I'm looking forward to it," Travis said, though he didn't sound very enthusiastic. In fact, to Cody's ears, his friend sounded like a man who was telling his fiancée what she wanted to hear, not what he necessarily felt.

Rainey appeared, carrying a tray, which she set on the coffee table in front of Travis. "I've been keeping this warm for you," she said. "Eat it now before it gets cold." Before he could reply, she had turned and fled.

"I see Rainey is in one of her moods tonight," he said. He leaned forward and picked up a fork.

"Her nose is out of joint because Bette is here," Lacy said. "But honestly, Bette is the nicest person in the world. If anyone can win over Rainey, she can."

"She doesn't have to win her over," Travis said. "She just has to ignore her and cater the wedding."

"Oh, Bette will do a good job," Lacy said. "A wonderful job. And she really appreciates us giving her this chance. It means a lot to her."

"Happy to help." Travis focused his attention on his plate. "I'm starving."

Mr. and Mrs. Walker said good-night, as did Emily, leaving Lacy and Cody alone with Travis. He was wondering if he should leave the couple to themselves when Travis said, "It would make it easy on everyone if Ken Rutledge turns out to be our killer. But I really don't think he is."

"What happened tonight?" Cody asked. "That is, if you think you can talk about it."

"I can talk about it to you." He turned to look at Lacy.

"You know I won't say anything to anyone," she said. "And this is your life. I have to be a part of it."

Travis nodded and looked thoughtful as he chewed, then swallowed. "Someone has been harassing Darcy since Kelly was killed," he said. "Someone ran her off the road, and someone attacked her and Highway Patrolman Ryder Stewart while they were skiing yesterday. Apparently, Rutledge was trying to frighten Darcy into turning to him for help. I think he saw his opportunity when Kelly and Christy O'Brien were murdered, but he went too far."

"You say he attacked Darcy again tonight?" Lacy asked.

"He kidnapped her. Ryder spotted the damaged snowmobile at Ken's duplex and figured out he was the man who had attacked him and Darcy. He found them at Darcy's house and rescued her."

"Why do you think he didn't kill the other women?" Cody asked.

"He has alibis for two of the killings. Pretty solid ones. And while he was willing to admit everything he had done to Darcy, he's adamant that he didn't have anything to do with the murders. We'll see." He pushed his empty plate away and stretched his arms over his head. "I need a shower and bed," he said.

Cody stood. "Good night. See you in the morning."

After the warmth of the fire, the cold hit him like a slap. He hurried along the path to the cabins, his breath fogging in front of his face, snow squeaking under his boots. As he neared the first cabin in the row—Bette's cabin—movement on the little porch caught his eye. He stopped and stared at the dark shape near the door of the cabin. He moved off the path and took shelter behind a tree. The shape on the porch didn't flee or move toward him—maybe it hadn't seen him coming.

No lights showed behind the cabin's drawn blinds. Bette was probably asleep, unaware that someone was outside her door—and clearly up to no good. Stealthily, using the cover of the trees, Cody moved closer to the cabin. The shape on the porch shifted slightly but didn't leave its position by the door. The shadow wasn't tall enough to be someone standing—Cody thought the man was crouching by the door, perhaps trying to jimmy the lock.

Reaching the end of the porch, Cody didn't hesitate. He made a flying leap and tackled the lurker, forcing him to the ground.

"Let go of me, you creep." An elbow thrust hard into his ribs, followed by nails raked across his face. "Get off of me!" The voice—definitely not a man's—demanded.

Cody couldn't get off fast enough. The beam of a flashlight blinded him. "Cody Rankin!" Bette said. "What do you think you're doing?"

Chapter Four

Cody held up a hand to shield his eyes and took another step back from an enraged Bette. "I saw someone on the porch and thought they were trying to break into your cabin," he said.

"I couldn't sleep and I was sitting out here, enjoying the moonlight." She gathered what appeared to be the quilt from her bed around her. A knit hat covered most of her blond hair, and thick gloves on her hands had probably prevented her from doing more damage to his face.

"It's zero degrees out," he said. "Who sits outside in that kind of weather?"

"It's not bad if you're wrapped up," she said.

He was feeling more foolish by the minute. "I'm sorry," he said. "I didn't hurt you, did I?"

She lowered the light so that it was no longer shining in his eyes. "You scared me half to death, but I'm not hurt. What about you?"

He rubbed his side. "My ribs are going to be sore for a few days, I think."

"Serves you right. Who appointed you my personal protector, anyway?"

"I was on my way back to my cabin and I saw someone lurking on your porch. Someone I didn't think should be there. And protecting people is what I do."

"No, you pursue them."

"I pursue bad guys as a way of protecting law-abiding citizens," he countered.

"Well, you can stop pursuing me."

He started to argue that he wasn't pursuing her, but he was tired of standing out here in the freezing cold. "I'm going to bed," he said, and limped past her.

"You are hurt!" She touched his shoulder, stopping him.

"I've dealt with worse."

"Sure you have, tough guy." She wrapped both hands around his biceps. "Come inside and let me have a look. You might have broken ribs."

He let her lead him into her cabin. Inside, warmth wrapped around him like a cocoon. He sank into the single armchair while she went around turning on lights. She dropped the quilt back onto the bed and divested herself of hat and gloves, revealing herself dressed in knit leggings and a long sweater that clung to every curve. "Take off your jacket and pull up your shirt so I can check your ribs," she said.

He took off the jacket, then took off the shirt, as well. When she turned toward him again he was standing beside the chair, naked from the waist up, and enjoying seeing her flustered. "I didn't tell you to get undressed," she said, avoiding his gaze.

"It's easier this way." He held his arms out to his sides, wincing only a little from the effort.

She moved closer and, after a brief hesitation, felt gently along his rib cage, where a faint bruise was already starting to show. Now it was his turn to be unsettled, the silken touch of her hand sending a jolt of desire straight to his groin. He shifted, trying to get comfortable in an impossibly uncomfortable situation.

She looked up, her eyes soft with concern. "I'm sorry. Did that hurt?"

"No." He took a step back. It was either that or pull her into his arms and kiss her until she was as hot and breathless as he felt. Or until she punched him in the mouth for presuming too much. He reached for his shirt. "I'll be fine," he said. "A little sore, but I guess that's no more than I deserve." He turned away, trying to hide his arousal. "I'll just use your bathroom, then say good-night."

In the bathroom, he splashed cold water on his face and practiced deep breathing until he had himself under control. Unfortunately, every breath pulled in the soft, feminine scent of Bette's perfume, which did little to lessen his arousal. For whatever reason, Bette Fuller checked every box on his list. His head could tell him to play it cool and keep his distance, but his body was determined to go full-on caveman.

He looked around for a towel on which to dry his hands and wipe his face. Finding none, he opened the cabinet beneath the sink. He spotted a stack of hand towels, but as he reached for one, his hand knocked against something. Crouching and peering into the cabinet, he spotted a paintbrush—and a can of red paint.

The same crimson color that had been used to paint the warning message on her cabin door.

BETTE PACED WHILE Cody was in the bathroom, trying desperately to cool down and calm herself and act like a sensible woman instead of some sex-starved maniac.

The sight of Cody Rankin, all six-pack abs and muscular chest, was one that would haunt her dreams—and her fantasies—for no doubt years to come. She wouldn't have been surprised if she had seared her fingers touching him—he was that hot.

And she was in so much trouble if she even thought about fulfilling the fantasies he inspired. She had lost her head over a man like this before, and he had come close to ruining her life. She didn't put Cody in the same category as Eddie, but he had the same potential to distract her from her goals and make her act recklessly.

The door to the bathroom opened and he emerged—fully dressed and looking grim. Obviously, she had injured him worse than she thought. She straightened. She wasn't going to feel remorse over that. He deserved a little pain for tackling her like that.

She expected him to head for the door, but instead, he sat in the chair again. "Tell me a little more about yourself," he said. "How, exactly, do you know Lacy?"

She frowned. She was tired, it was late and this was no time for a get-to-know-all-about-each-other conversation. Then again, she had been looking for a way to put some distance between herself and this sexy cop. The truth was sure to do that.

She sat on the end of the bed and pulled one end of the quilt across her lap. "We were cellmates in prison." She kept her head up, defiant. She wasn't proud of what she'd done, but she wasn't going to deny it, either.

He blinked. Clearly, he hadn't expected that one. She waited, then he asked the question she had known would come next. "What were you doing in prison?" he asked.

"Ten years for robbing the bank where I worked as a

teller," she said. "Though I was paroled early because I was such a model prisoner."

His eyes narrowed. "So you admit you're guilty."

"Oh, yes. There were five of us—four of us were caught. I was the person on the inside. It was the stupidest thing I ever did and I don't intend to so much as jaywalk from here on out."

"You robbed a bank," he repeated.

"The man I was living with at the time was the one who waved a gun around and demanded the money—I only silenced the alarm and let him out the back door. That made me just as guilty, of course."

"Why did you do it?"

"Because I was stupid. Over a man." She stood. "That's a mistake I won't make again, either."

"Does Travis know about this?"

"Of course he does. And his parents. I wouldn't ask them to invite me into their home without being honest about my past. I appreciate the chance they're giving me to start over. Their trust really means a lot."

He rose also and stood looming over her—still sexy, but also menacing. She had to force herself to stand firm and not shrink under his cold gaze. "I hope their trust isn't misplaced," he said.

"It isn't," she said, licking her suddenly dry lips.

The lines around his eyes tightened. "Just know, I'm going to be keeping an eye on you," he said.

Delivered in another tone of voice, the words might have been a sexy come-on. But Bette heard only warning behind the words—the words of a cop to a suspect. Though she had achieved her goal of putting emotional distance between herself and Cody, her success left a heaviness in her heart. She supposed part of her had hoped Cody Rankin would be different—able to for-give, even if he couldn't forget.

CODY LAY AWAKE for several hours that night, trying to make sense of that paint can and brush under the sink in the bathroom of Bette's cabin. Surely she would have mentioned finding them there when she pulled out the cleaner and towels to clean the paint off the door.

But she wouldn't have mentioned them if she had known all along the paint was there—known because she had put it there herself, and used it to paint that message. But why? So that he would see it and feel protective?

No—that wasn't her game. She definitely didn't like him hovering too close. And she hadn't put the mes-sage there in order to make a fuss with the Walkers—she had refused to mention the incident, and had made him promise not to, either.

But he couldn't assume her motives were those of most law-abiding people, he reminded himself. She had a record. She had admitted to the bank robbery with scarcely a trace of shame. Oh, she had made all the right noises about having learned her lesson and intending to go straight, but how many times had he heard that kind of talk before? Just because she had big blue eyes and a sweet, sincere manner—and a body that made it difficult for him to think straight—didn't mean they shouldn't all be on their guard around her. If she was concocting some scam to cheat his friend or his friend's family, she was going to have Cody to deal with—and he'd make sure her punishment was swift and sure.

On this disturbing thought, he fell asleep, and woke at dawn, stiff and sore. After a hot shower, he walked up to the ranch house, thankful that he didn't run into Bette. He found Travis alone in the dining room, eating breakfast. "Where is everyone?" Cody asked, helping himself to coffee from a pot on the sideboard.

"We're the early birds," Travis said.

Cody sat, moving gingerly still.

"What's up with you?" Travis asked. "You take a fall or something yesterday?"

"Something like that." Cody changed the subject. "What do you know about your caterer, Bette Fuller?" he asked.

Travis frowned. "Why do you ask?"

"She told me she and Lacy were cellmates—that she served time for bank robbery. She admitted it outright."

"Lacy says she was led astray by her boyfriend, a longtime felon named Edward Rialto."

"Do you believe that?"

"It happens." Travis spread jam on a slice of toast. "And I did check on her—she didn't have so much as a traffic ticket before the robbery."

"She said they caught all but one of the people involved in the robbery," Cody said.

"That's right. The getaway driver evaded capture," Travis said. "Apparently, the car he was driving struck and killed a pedestrian while the gang was fleeing from the bank. He's wanted for vehicular manslaughter as well as bank robbery. The others refused to identify him."

"Including Bette?" Continued loyalty to her "gang" didn't sound good to him.

"She said she had only seen him once, for a few minutes, that they hadn't been introduced and she couldn't identify him."

"Convenient." Cody scooped up a forkful of eggs. "I know I don't have to tell you to be careful, but I'm going to play the role of concerned friend and tell you anyway."

Travis set down his coffee cup and studied Cody. "What's wrong? Has Bette done something, or said something, that's disturbed you?"

Cody thought about mentioning the can of paint and the message on Bette's door, then thought better of it. He had no real proof Bette had put the message there herself, and no motive for her to have done so. Right now, Travis and his parents had accepted having a convicted felon catering the wedding. Cody had no grounds for upsetting them. "No, I just wanted to know more about her. What are you up to this morning?" he asked.

"I'm going to stay here this morning, catching up on paperwork. Gage texted me late last night—he and Dwight made it back to town about two in the morning. I've got two other deputies on duty, and I'll go into the office about noon."

"Do you have other suspects for the murders?"

"Not really." Travis pushed back his empty plate and held his coffee mug in both hands. "There are a few possibilities, but no one who lines up for everyone. The only connection the women have is that they were all in their twenties or thirties, and they all lived here in Eagle Mountain." He pushed back his chair. "There's still a lot to sift through. We'll find him."

"Let me know if there's anything I can do to help."

"Sure. What are your plans for the day?"

"I thought I'd go ice fishing, over on Lake Spooner."

"Sounds good. If you catch enough, maybe we can have a fish fry. There's a bunch of fishing gear in the tack room, if you want to borrow any. I think there's even an ice auger in there." He pushed back his chair. "I'd better get to work. Talk to you later."

AT BREAKFAST HER first morning at the ranch, Bette waited anxiously for Cody to appear. Not that she was looking forward to seeing him again after their tense parting the night before, but since he was the only person who knew about the message that had been painted on the door of her cabin, he was the only one she could confide in now.

This morning, while getting ready for a shower, she had retrieved a towel and washcloth from beneath the bathroom sink and been startled to discover a paintbrush and a can of red paint. She had even cried out, as if she had encountered a snake under there. She was positive the paint hadn't been there earlier, and she wasn't sure what to do about it now. She hated the idea that someone had come into her cabin while she wasn't there, but she didn't know if she should say anything to the Walkers. Cody might not be her friend, but he might have some idea about what she should do.

"Good morning!" Lacy greeted Bette with a hug and walked with her to the breakfast table, where Mr. and Mrs. Walker and Emily were eating.

"Good morning," Mrs. Walker said. "I hope you slept well."

"I was fine," Bette said. No sense revealing she had lain awake for hours, fretting and furious about Cody Rankin. In the cold light of day, it seemed foolish to waste any time thinking about a man like that.

"Glad to hear it." Mrs. Walker smiled. "I know you and Lacy are working on plans for the tea this morning. You're welcome to anything in the house you need in the way of furniture or decorations or ingredients. Just help yourself."

"Thanks," Bette said. "That's very generous."

Mr. Walker checked his watch, then pushed back his chair. "We'd better be going," he said to his wife.

She laid her napkin beside her chair and stood. "We'll see you girls later."

"I have to go, too," Emily said. "I have a conference call."

"I thought you were off school for winter break," Lacy said.

"I am. But research projects don't stop just because school isn't in session. I need to meet by phone with my colleagues about a research grant."

"Emily is an economics graduate student at Colorado State University," Lacy said when she and Bette were alone.

"How is school going for you?" Bette asked as she added cream to her coffee. She recalled her friend had used part of the wrongful conviction settlement money she had received from the state to finance her education.

"I'm only just starting out, but I'm loving it so far," Lacy said. "I'm really looking forward to being a teacher."

Travis joined Bette and Lacy as the women were finishing up their breakfast. Bette had seen pictures of the sheriff before—his efforts to clear Lacy's name, and their subsequent engagement, had made the pages of the Denver paper. But in person he was both more handsome, and more forbidding, than she had imagined. Certainly he welcomed her warmly enough, but it was clear he was tired, and probably distracted by his case.

"You're up early," Lacy said, after the introductions had been exchanged and Travis informed them that he had already had breakfast. "You've been working some long hours lately."

"I'm going to stay around here this morning and catch up on some paperwork," he said. "There are too many interruptions at the office."

"Good idea," Lacy said. "Have you seen Cody this morning? He wasn't at breakfast with everyone else."

"He said something about going ice fishing," Travis said.

Or maybe he's avoiding me, Bette thought. But the marshal didn't strike her as a man who avoided much of anything.

CODY FINISHED HIS breakfast, then collected his coat and his car keys and headed to the tack room. No sign of Doug Whittington stealing a cigarette this morning. He found the fishing gear and selected what he'd need and loaded it into the RAV4 he used as his personal vehicle.

The day was sunny, though bitingly cold, the sky free of clouds and a blindingly bright blue. The road to the lake had been plowed, only a thin layer of snow left in place. Dark evergreens crowded close to the side of the narrow track in a wall that looked almost impenetrable. He passed a pair of cross-country skiers and waved, then turned onto the narrower Forest Service track that led to the lake. This road hadn't seen a plow, but enough traffic to the lake and backcountry ski trails had packed it down so that Cody's RAV4 had little trouble navigating.

Just before he reached the lake, he spotted a silver Hyundai pulled to the side of the road ahead. He passed it slowly. It appeared to be empty, but this was a funny place to park. The snow around the vehicle was churned up, as if several people had been walking around it. He drove on, but something about the vehicle nagged at him, so he decided to go back.

He parked across the road and about fifty yards away from the Hyundai and walked slowly toward it, keeping to the center of the road until he was even with the driver's side door. Then he approached cautiously and peered inside.

A woman stared up at him from the passenger seat, as dead and lifeless as a store mannequin.

Chapter Five

After breakfast, Lacy and Bette moved to the sun-room, just off the main room, to plan the bridesmaids' tea to be held that Saturday. Windows on three sides sent sunlight streaming over plank-wood floors and an overstuffed sofa and two chairs in a faded floral print. Despite the bitter cold outside, the room felt warm and inviting. Bette brought along her planner, menu suggestions, pictures of possible table settings and a notebook for jotting down ideas, and spread these over the massive coffee table.

"You're so organized," Lacy said as she flipped through the pictures of place settings and centerpieces. "I'm very impressed."

"I want to do as professional a job for you as I'd do for anyone," Bette said. "It's very hard to start a new business when you don't have a lot of experience to show. That's why I really appreciate you and Travis giving me this chance."

"I promise to post lots of glowing reviews everywhere—and to recommend you to everyone I know," Lacy said. She put her hand over Bette's. "But I'm not doing this out of the kindness of my heart. I'm doing it because I want a great caterer for my wedding, and I know that's you."

"How do you know?" Bette asked. "The only things I've catered on my own are a couple of birthday parties and a bridal shower. And you weren't there for either one of them."

"But I've eaten your cooking," Lacy said. "And it's wonderful."

Bette couldn't keep back a snort of laughter. "You ate things I cooked in the prison kitchen." Once the warden learned that Bette had culinary training—she had been attending culinary school at night and working weekends for a caterer when she was arrested—he'd seen to it that she was moved to the kitchen. "That's not a great compliment."

"Your food was so much better than anything else they served," Lacy said. "I knew if you could work magic in that setting, you'd be fabulous when let loose on your own."

"I've been doing a lot of practicing since my release," Bette said. She was a good cook, and she had a gift for making occasions special. All she needed was a chance to prove herself—and Lacy and Travis were giving her that chance. She angled one of her notebooks so Lacy could see it. "Here are some menu ideas. If you want a traditional high tea, you'll want scones, with jam and clotted cream, fancy tea sandwiches and a variety of little cakes—maybe petit fours. Those always look so elegant. I could do chocolate-dipped strawberries, if I can get the berries, and there are lots of sandwich choices."

"It all looks wonderful," Lacy said, scanning the lists of dishes and their descriptions.

"How many people will be at the tea?" Bette asked.

"Let's see." Lacy sat back and began counting on her fingers. "There's my mother and Travis's mom, and my maid of honor, Brenda. She's married to one of Travis's deputies, Dwight Prentice. A second marriage, so it was a small ceremony, at Dwight's family's ranch over Thanksgiving. You haven't met her, but she's a dear, dear person."

She held up a fourth finger. "Then there's Maya Renfro—Gage's wife. She kept her maiden name. They had a quick ceremony, too—they ran off to Vegas one weekend without telling anyone. And she'll be bringing her niece, Casey, who is five. Casey is my flower girl, and she's so excited about it. So Casey makes five."

She held up a sixth finger. "Travis's sister, Emily, is one of my bridesmaids, of course." A seventh finger went up. "And last but not least, Paige Riddell. She used to run a bed-and-breakfast here in town, but after it burned down she decided to move to Denver. Her brother and her boyfriend live there—he's a DEA agent. I guess that's all—seven adults, if you include me, and one child."

"A lot of cops in the wedding party," Bette said.

Lacy laughed. "Yes, can you believe it? But I've found out when you hang out with one cop, a lot of his friends are cops, so that becomes part of your life."

"Besides Cody and I assume Gage, who are Travis's groomsmen?" Bette asked.

"There's Ryder Stewart—he's with the state highway patrol. And Nate Hall. He's with Parks and Wildlife."

"A park ranger?" Bette asked.

"Not exactly—a wildlife officer. I guess that's what they call game wardens these days."

So, lots of men with guns who were used to being

in charge. "No chance of anyone getting out of line with so many law enforcement officers at the wedding," Bette said.

"When I first got out of prison, it made me nervous to be around so many men in uniform," Lacy said. "But it doesn't bother me now. Travis's friends are all really nice."

"You were innocent and they all know it," Bette said. "They can't look at me the same way."

"Don't say that!" Lacy squeezed Bette's hand again. "Travis was happy to have you here."

"Travis wanted to please you. And maybe, because of his experience with you, he's a little more forgiving than some. Not everyone feels that way." She thought of the cold expression in Cody's eyes last night.

"Has someone said something to upset you?" Lacy asked. "What is it?"

"I told Cody Rankin last night about my record," Bette said. "He wanted to know how I knew you and I figured I might as well come out with the truth. It would be easy enough for him to find out."

"How did he take the news?" Lacy asked.

"About like I expected. He's suspicious, wondering if I'm up to something. He doesn't trust me."

"He doesn't know you," Lacy said.

"I don't care if he doesn't like me," Bette said. "As long as he doesn't hassle me."

Lacy regarded her friend kindly. "I know it can be very hard to start over on the outside when you have a record," she said. "But it will get easier, you'll see. Your business will be a success, and while you might have to tell employers about your conviction, there's nothing that says your new clients ever have to know. In a few years you'll look back on your time behind bars as something awful that happened to someone else."

"Maybe." She picked up her pen. "Now tell me which sandwiches you want for your party, and which of these petit fours and cookies you want to serve. I'd suggest three types of sandwiches, three varieties of cookies and one petit four, or two cookies, strawberries and a petit four, or—"

"Enough!" Lacy held up her hands in surrender. "Too many choices." She scanned the lists again. "Why don't you tell me your favorites and we'll go from there?"

Thirty minutes later, they had a menu plan and a decor scheme. They decided to hold the tea in this sun-room and in addition to tea, they'd have champagne cocktails. The decor would be "winter wonderland," with lots of snowflakes and lace and little fascinators for everyone to wear in their hair in lieu of hats. "This is going to be so much fun," Lacy said.

She left to keep a hair appointment, and Bette headed for the kitchen, to see what ingredients were available, and what she would need to buy. List in hand, she pushed open the door to the kitchen. Rainey leaned against the counter, a cup of coffee in hand, a frown on her face. She straightened when Bette entered. "What do you want?"

"I'm making the refreshments for Lacy's brides-maids' tea this Saturday." Bette walked to the refrigerator and swung open the door. "I wanted to see what ingredients were already on hand, so I'll know what to buy."

"Don't think you're going to go raiding my kitchen for what you need," Rainey said. "If you need any-thing, go buy it."

"I can certainly do that." Bette closed the refrigerator. Mrs. Walker had told her to help herself to flour, butter, sugar and anything else she needed, but Bette wasn't going to fight this battle. And she could understand that, if Rainey had purchased supplies with the intent to make certain meals, it could throw a wrench in her plans if Bette came along and used up all the butter in baked goods, for instance. Later today, she'd go into town and shop, and store everything either in her cabin, or in the garage refrigerator.

The back door opened and Doug slouched in. He looked different this morning, a hoodie pulled over his head, shoulders slumped. Rainey stared at him. "What do you think you're doing, coming in here looking like that?" she asked. "You haven't even shaved."

Doug rubbed his chin, the scratchy sound setting Bette's teeth on edge. "I thought I'd grow a beard," he said.

"I won't have one in my kitchen," Rainey said. "They're nasty."

Bette decided she had heard enough and retreated to the living room. She chose a chair by the fire and began to make a long shopping list. She hoped she could find fresh strawberries in Eagle Mountain in January. Real clotted cream was probably out of the question, but she could make her own.

The sound of boot heels on the hardwood floor behind her startled her, and she looked up to see Travis, in full uniform, crossing to the door. So much for sticking around the house to do paperwork.

He noticed her sitting by the fire. "Hello, Bette," he said. "Did Lacy abandon you?"

"She went to get her hair done. But I have plenty to keep me occupied, seeing to the tea this Saturday."

He nodded and slipped into his heavy black leather coat, with a shearling collar. He looked troubled. "Is everything all right?" Bette asked. Maybe he was going into work early because something had happened.

He frowned, as if unsure whether to say anything to her or not. "They've found another body," he said, after a moment. He opened the door. "I have to go."

He left, the door shutting softly behind him. Bette sagged back in her chair and stared at the flames dancing in the woodstove. Another body. Another victim of the Ice Cold Killer. The knowledge made her sick, and a little frozen inside.

Chapter Six

Cody stood with Travis and wildlife officer Nate Harris on the side of the road, as two EMTs carefully removed the woman's body from the Hyundai. Nate, a tall blond native of Eagle Mountain and another of Travis's groomsmen, had been patrolling in the area when the call went out requesting assistance. The men stood hunched against the cold, hands shoved into the pockets of their coats. "I was in this area yesterday and this car wasn't here," Nate said. "In fact, mine were the only tracks on this road then."

"I passed a couple of cross-country skiers on the county road," Cody said. "This road had obviously been driven on—I assumed by other fishermen headed to and from the lake."

"There's better fishing on Lake Monroe," Nate said. "This one doesn't get that much use."

The medical examiner, a portly man dressed in camouflaged snow boots that came almost to his knees, an ankle-length duster and a wool cap with ear flaps, stood to one side, chin tucked to his chest as he watched a crew of EMTs remove the body from the vehicle. Travis had introduced him as Butch Collins, a retired local doctor who filled the role of county medical examiner.

When the ambulance doors had shut, Butch moved over to join the three lawmen. "You know, when I took this job, they told me if I had to go out on one call a month for an unattended death, that would be a local record," he said. "This murderer seems determined to keep me busy."

"Any estimate on the time of death?" Travis asked him.

"I'd say she was killed last night," Butch said. "Maybe in the lab I can get a better idea, but she had been there long enough for the tissues to freeze."

"The low was minus nine last night," Nate said.

Butch nodded. "This looks the same as the others to me."

"Hands and feet bound with duct tape, throat slit," Travis said.

"Did you find one of the killer's calling cards?" Cody asked.

Travis took an evidence pouch from his coat pocket and held it so that Cody could see the white, business-card-sized rectangle of cardboard, with the block-print words ICE COLD. "It was tucked in her coat pocket," Travis said, stowing the evidence pouch back into his jacket.

Nate looked up and down the narrow road, snow-shrouded evergreens crowding in close on each side. "Not much traffic out here this time of year," he said. "The road dead-ends at the lake. There aren't any houses or campgrounds along the way. Fishermen use it, sometimes skiers, but no one would be out here after dark in the winter. No reason to be."

"So what was she doing out here?" Cody asked.

"Maybe she wasn't here," Travis said. "Maybe the killer drove her here."

"And walked out?" Cody asked.

"Or was driven out," Nate said. He turned to Travis. "Didn't you tell me once that you think the killer might have an accomplice—or rather, there are two men working to kill together?"

"That seems the most likely scenario to me," Travis said. "Two men working together would have an easier time subduing the women and killing them quickly. Several times the bodies have been found in remote places, which points to someone transporting them there, then leaving in another vehicle."

"Is it twice as hard to find a pair of killers?" Cody asked. "Or twice as easy? You'd think there would be more evidence with two people. More clues."

"You'd think," Travis said.

"Tell me about the other killings," Cody said. "Were the circumstances of those similar to this?"

"Similar," Travis said. "Kelly Farrow was the first—a local vet. A really vivacious, pretty woman. She had only been in Eagle Mountain four months. A highway patrolman found her car up on Dixon Pass—Ryder Stewart. I think you've met him before. He's in the wedding, too."

"I remembered Ryder," Cody said. "Was the car like this—on the side of the road?"

"It had been buried by an avalanche and Kelly's body was inside. That night, the second woman was killed. Christy O'Brien. She had actually driven the wrecker that pulled Kelly's vehicle out of the snowbank."

"Did the killer know about that connection?"

"I don't know. The third woman, Fiona Winslow,

died four days later, on my family's ranch," Travis continued. "We were having a scavenger hunt. She and Ken Rutledge—the man we arrested yesterday—were partnered for the hunt. They had a disagreement and she decided to leave him and join some girlfriends who were hunting as a team. She never made it."

"Rutledge couldn't have killed this woman," Cody said. "Not if he's in jail."

"He's still there," Travis said. "I already double-checked."

"Having someone killed on the ranch hits close to home," Cody said. "Do you think that was intentional?"

"Maybe. Leaving those cards is a way of taunting law enforcement. So would a killing right under my nose, so to speak."

"Who else was at the party?"

"Lots of people. There were a couple of college guys who came to town to rock climb and got trapped by the storm. They knew Emily from school and she invited them out. They were top on my suspect list, but I saw them yesterday at the gas station and they said they were headed back to Denver."

"Worth checking that," Cody said.

"Oh, I will."

Cody studied the draped figure on the gurney. "So this is the fourth victim."

"I was hoping the killer or killers took advantage of the break in the weather and left town," Travis said. "But I guess we couldn't be so lucky."

The license plate on the car had been issued in Denver—the prefix told Cody that much. "Who was she?" he asked.

Travis consulted a small notebook. "Lauren Grenado," he said. "Her license information has an address in Denver. We found paperwork in the car that seems to indicate she's staying at a condo here in town."

"Is she married? Have kids?" Cody asked.

"The paperwork lists the rental in the name of Adam Grenado. I'm guessing that's her husband. We need to check at the condo and find out."

"I don't envy you that job," Cody said.

"I was hoping you'd come with me," Travis said. "I've called Dwight to stay here and finish processing the scene."

"I'll stay, too," Nate said.

"Then will you come with me?" Travis asked Cody.

Cody didn't hesitate. His friend needed backup, and Cody was more than qualified for the role. "Sure, I'll come."

Travis exchanged a few words with Gage, then signaled that Cody should follow him. They drove around the barriers and headed into town. Travis was on the phone for most of the drive—probably giving instructions to his deputies, and maybe checking in with Lacy. Cody wanted to call his own office, to find out what was going on—what he was missing during his forced time off. But he doubted anyone would tell him anything, and he might have to endure another lecture about how he needed to get his head clear and de-stress. No one seemed to realize how stressful it was to be out of the action so long.

Travis signaled a turn onto a road that skirted town and passed the high school. Three teenagers with snow shovels labored to clear the walkway in front of the school. Travis slowed and rolled down his window. Cody followed suit. "How's it going, boys?" Travis called.

"It's going okay." The tallest of the three spoke, a blond in an expensive down jacket and mirrored sunglasses. The other two boys looked up, their expressions unreadable.

"Keep up the good work," Travis said, and drove away.

Cody parked behind Travis on the street in front of a row of cedar-sided condos, probably purpose-built to rent to summer residents and winter tourists. He joined Travis beside his SUV. "Those boys back at the school," Cody said. "Community service?"

"Yeah. They were involved in a series of pranks that got out of hand. They were near the place where the second murder occurred and I was hoping they might have seen something that could help us, but they say no." He consulted his notebook. "Lauren Grenado was in 2B."

They climbed the stairs to the second floor and knocked on the door labeled B. Beyond the door came the sounds of a television, then someone's approach. The young man who opened the door wore a T-shirt and sweats, his light brown hair uncombed and the shadow of a beard across his jaw. He blinked at them, a little bleary-eyed. "Yes?"

"Adam Grenado?" Travis asked.

"Yeah." He squinted, as if trying to bring them into better focus. "Is something wrong?"

"We need to talk to you for a few minutes. It would be better if we came in."

"Oh, okay. Sure." He opened the door wider and Cody and Travis filed past. Adam rushed forward to sweep a pile of jackets off a chair and pick a blanket up off the floor. The room smelled of stale food. Adam grabbed the remote and muted the television. "What's going on? Is this about Lauren?"

"What about Lauren?" Travis asked. Cody sat back. He saw his role as an observer. He'd let Travis do all the talking.

Adam sank onto the sofa. "She left yesterday," he said. "We had a fight. I guess we got pretty loud. If some of the neighbors complained…" He let the words trail away and shook his head.

"Where was she going?" Travis asked.

"She said she was going out for a drive—that she needed to think."

"You'd had a fight?"

"A disagreement. I wanted to take some money her folks gave us for Christmas and buy a boat, but she didn't think we should do that."

"Where is she now?"

"I don't know. She isn't answering her phone." He picked up a cell phone from the end table beside the sofa and studied the screen. "When she didn't come back last night I tried calling and texting—after a while I'd decided she must have gone back to Denver. She did that to me once before—left me stranded without a vehicle."

"So you haven't been worried about her?"

"A little. But mostly I'm angry. Like I said, she's pulled this kind of thing before—she can be very impulsive."

"What did you do last night when she didn't come back?" Travis asked.

"I got drunk and went to bed." He shrugged. "I'm not proud of it, but that's the truth. Why? What's with all these questions?" The first sign of fear shadowed his eyes. "Is something wrong? Has Lauren been in some kind of accident or something?"

"I'm sorry to have to inform you that your wife is dead, Mr. Grenado."

He stared at them, eyes gone glassy. "No." He shook his head. "No. She can't be dead. She was fine when she left here last night."

"She apparently died last night. Marshal Rankin found her this morning, in her car on a remote Forest Service road." He nodded to Cody.

Adam shook his head. "No. That can't be. How did she die? Was there an accident?"

"No," Travis said. "She was murdered."

The echo of the word hung in the air, stark and ugly.

Adam stared at them a few seconds more, then buried his head in his hands and began to weep, great, racking sobs that shook his body. Travis and Cody waited a moment, then Travis said. "Mr. Grenado, we need you to pull yourself together so you can help us find who did this."

He nodded, and after a visible struggle, sat upright, though his voice broke when he spoke. "Who would do something like this?"

"What did you do after your wife left here last night?" Travis asked. "Did you follow her?"

"No. I stayed here." His eyes widened. "You don't think I—I would never hurt Lauren. I loved her. Sure, we had had a fight, but we did that sometimes. It didn't mean anything."

"So you were here all night?"

"Yes. I told you."

"Is there anyone who can prove you were here all night?" Travis asked.

"No. I mean, I guess you could ask folks in the other condos if they saw me leave. But I don't have a car. Lauren has it."

"Do you know anyone else who might want to hurt her?" Travis asked. "Have you noticed anyone suspicious hanging around the condo, or following you while you were out?"

"No. Nothing like that. Lauren didn't have any enemies." He scrubbed his hand across his face. "Is this that serial killer? I thought I heard something about a serial killer. Did he kill my wife?"

"What do you know about the serial killer?" Travis asked.

"Not much. We're on vacation, so we haven't been following the news. But we were in a restaurant the other night and someone said something about this guy who had killed three women around here." He frowned. "He had a funny name—you know, how the press always tags these guys with nicknames. Like people would forget them if they didn't have a catchy handle."

"The Ice Cold Killer," Travis said.

"That was it. Did he kill my wife?"

"We don't know, Mr. Grenado," Travis said. "Do you know of any reason your wife would have been out on a deserted Forest Service road last night? Would she have gone there to meet a friend, maybe?"

"No. Lauren didn't know anyone here."

"Why did you come to Eagle Mountain?" Travis asked.

"We wanted a getaway, somewhere in the mountains. And the rates are good this time of year."

"What have you been doing while you're in town?"

"Just, you know—relaxing. We went out to eat. We

rented snowmobiles and took them out one day." He shrugged. "We were just hanging out."

"And you didn't see anyone suspicious or encounter anyone who made you nervous?"

"No." His face crumpled again. "What am I going to do?"

"Do you have a family member you can call to come help you?" Travis asked.

He nodded. "My brother. He lives in Denver, but I know he'll come."

Travis stood. "I can send someone from my office to wait with you until he comes."

"No." He rose also. "I'll be okay. Am I supposed to do something else, about my car and about…about Lauren's body?"

"Someone from my office will call you later today with that information." Travis handed him a business card. "If you have any questions, or you think of anything else that might help us, call me."

"Okay. I will."

Travis waited until he and Cody were at the curb again before he spoke. "What do you think?" he asked.

"He's really grieving and logistically, I don't see how he could have done it." Cody glanced around the parking lot. "You'll verify he and his wife only had one vehicle here. And then there's that business card."

"Information about that card has been in the paper."

"So you're thinking this could be a copycat killing?"

"It could be, but I don't think so." Travis looked back toward the building. "I think Lauren Grenado went out alone at night and the killer saw her and took the opportunity to kill her, then drove her to that remote location, thinking it would be a while before anyone found her."

The burden of these killings showed on Travis's face. Cody knew he took each death personally. "I've asked the Colorado Bureau of Investigations to send some help," Travis said. "Now that the road is open, someone should be able to get through."

Cody nodded. "You've been hung out on your own until now. It's a lot for a small department to handle."

"Still, it's my county. There aren't that many people here—I should have been able to handle it."

Cautioning Travis not to be so hard on himself wouldn't do any good. He was wired to take responsibility—it was one of the things that made him a good sheriff. "Tell me what I can do to help," Cody said.

"Right now I need you to go back to the ranch and let everyone there know what's going on. Tell the women especially to be on their guard. They probably shouldn't drive anywhere alone. I already talked to Lacy."

"All right. But if there's anything else, you know I'm here."

Travis stared down the quiet street, snow mounded on the sides of the road, no sign of activity in the surrounding homes. If not for the knowledge of what had happened near here, it would be an idyllic scene of winter peace. "The killer is here, too," Travis said. "And I need to find out where, before he kills again."

Chapter Seven

The town of Eagle Mountain might have been a village in the mountains of Switzerland or Austria—Victorian buildings lining narrow streets in a valley below snow-capped peaks. Glittery snowflake decorations adorned light posts along the town's main streets, and storefronts advertised winter sales. Bette guided her car slowly through town, struck by the jarring discordance of such horrible violence taking place in such a peaceful setting.

It hadn't taken long for news of the latest murder to spread through town. As Bette guided her grocery cart down the aisles of Eagle Mountain Grocery, she overheard customers discussing the murder, speculating on the identity of the latest victim and the motives of the killer. Most people seemed to think the woman who was killed was a visitor to town, since no one knew of any local who was unaccounted for.

Weather and news that the highway remained open were the next most popular topics of conversation, though some people were of the opinion that the town's reprieve wouldn't last. "Those avalanche chutes above the pass are full to bursting and all this sunshine is making them more unstable," one woman said to a friend as they perused the selections in the dairy case. "I'm stocking up while I can, before the snowslides start and they have to close the road again."

Bette selected several pounds of butter and two cartons of cream, then steered her cart toward the center aisles. As she had feared, good strawberries weren't to be had this time of year in the mountains, so she had switched her menu to chocolate-covered dried fruit. She was trying to decide between apricots and cherries when an attractive woman with streaked blond hair approached. "Excuse me, but are you Bette Fuller, the caterer?"

"Yes," Bette said, cautious in spite of the woman's friendliness.

"I'm Brenda Prentice." The woman offered her hand. "I'm Lacy's maid of honor. It's so good to meet you. Lacy has told me so much about you."

How much? Bette wondered. Did Brenda's friendliness mean she didn't know about Bette's past—or that she knew and had decided to give her the benefit of the doubt? Bette hoped it was the latter, but she knew better than to expect that. "It's good to meet you, too," she said, shaking Brenda's hand.

"It was so kind of you to come all this way to cook for the wedding," Brenda said. "I know it means a lot to Lacy."

"I was happy to do it." In her opinion, Lacy was the one who was being kind.

"I'm looking forward to the tea this weekend," Brenda said. "Such a clever idea to do that instead of a girls' night out at a bar."

"It was all Lacy's idea," Bette said. "But it should be a really fun party. Lacy said you're married to one of Travis's deputies."

"That's right. Dwight Prentice. We went to high school together, but it wasn't until after my husband died that we connected again."

"Lacy mentioned you're a newlywed."

"Yes. She still hasn't forgiven me for cheating her out of being a bridesmaid in a big, fancy wedding." She shifted the package of salad she carried to her other hand. "I'd better get back to work. I only swung by to grab something for lunch. See you on Saturday."

"It was good to meet you."

Bette took her time completing her shopping. Brenda had been very nice—exactly the sort of woman she would have pictured as one of Lacy's best friends. If Bette and Lacy hadn't been thrown together in prison, she doubted they would have ever made a connection at all. Lacy came from a conventional family in a small town. She had always been loved and protected and, even after she had been convicted of murder, her family and friends had stood by her.

Bette was a city girl from a broken home. She had been on her own since she was seventeen, and had never had much support from anyone. It didn't take a psychologist to see that was why she had fallen so hard for Eddie. He had not only promised to love and protect her, he had made her believe he couldn't do anything without her by his side. When he told her of his dream of opening a garage, she had believed every word, because she had always wanted to open her own catering business. When he proposed robbing the bank where she worked to get the money to make those dreams come true, she had hesitated only a few hours before he made her believe it was the right thing to do.

She had had years since then to regret her decision,

and to see how Eddie had manipulated her. He had never had any intention of opening a garage, and the people he had introduced to her as friends of his who wanted to help had only been criminals like him, out for their share of the take. All Eddie's flattery and lovemaking had been a lie. He had singled her out for attention because she worked at the bank, and he recognized her as someone he could manipulate.

It was a good thing for her the police had caught the robbers. If her arrest hadn't halted her brief criminal career, there was no telling where she would have ended up. Now, thanks to Lacy and people like her, she at least had a chance to live her dream.

She paid for her purchases and loaded them into her car, then drove slowly through town. She had no desire to live in a sleepy place like Eagle Mountain, but she could enjoy visiting here. She hoped she would have the chance to come back in the summer or fall and explore the surrounding mountains more.

Reluctantly, she turned the car and headed back toward the ranch. She didn't look forward to the inevitable confrontation with Rainey when she went to unload the groceries she had purchased. She wasn't anxious to see Cody again, either, though she needed to talk to him about the paint she had found in the bathroom. And she needed to come up with a way to keep intruders out of her cabin.

Her mind full of these thoughts, she didn't notice the vehicle coming up behind her until it was on her bumper. The dark SUV raced up behind her, the insistent blare of the horn shattering the peace of the quiet countryside. Alarmed, Bette steered her car as far over to the side of the road as she could safely go. The vehicle surged up beside her and she took her foot off the gas, anxious for it to pass. Instead, the car stopped in the road, and the driver got out. She had an impression of black—black pants, black gloves, black coat with the hood pulled up to hide the driver's face. As he raced around the car toward her, she pressed down on the gas, determined to drive away, but the tires spun in the soft snow. The man, whose face she still couldn't see, beat his hands on her closed window. Bette groped for her phone, to call for help. Then the window shattered. A large rock hit the side of her head, then the door opened and the man dragged her out, into the snow.

SNOW HAD STARTED falling again by the time Cody headed back toward the Walker ranch. Flakes whirled toward his windshield in a mesmerizing onslaught and his SUV plowed through already-forming drifts across the road.

So much for his fishing trip. Maybe he'd try again in a day or two, and this time, he'd ask Bette to go with him. It would give him a chance to question her about the paint and about her intentions toward the Walkers, without an audience to overhear.

He didn't see the car on the side of the road until he was almost on it. Snow drifted over the vehicle, which listed in the ditch like a boat taking on water. He braked hard and turned on his wipers in an attempt to clear the snow from his windshield. No movement in the other car, but the vehicle looked familiar. With a jolt, he realized it looked like Bette's Ford.

He punched the button to turn on his emergency flashers and stopped in the road, then bailed out of his RAV4 and trudged down into the ditch and around the car. The driver's side door was open, snow sifting over the upholstery. A large rock rested in the driver's seat. Cody stared at it, trying to make sense of the sight. Fields and woods lined this stretch of road, not rocky cliffs. For that rock to get there, someone must have thrown it.

And where was Bette? Had she gotten her car stuck in the ditch and decided to walk to the ranch for help? But that didn't explain the rock.

"Bette!"

The silence swallowed his shout. He stepped back, intending to set out to look for her. His foot struck something soft and yielding.

Something that groaned.

Bette lay in the ditch, snow sifting over her still body. Cody knelt beside her and felt for a pulse at her neck. Relief flooded him when he found the steady beat and felt the warmth of her skin. "Bette, wake up." He tapped her cheek with the back of his hand.

She groaned and rolled her head away from him.

He pulled out his phone and called 911. "There's been an accident on County Road Seven," he said. "About a mile from the Walking W Ranch. A woman is unconscious."

The dispatcher promised to send an ambulance and a sheriff's deputy. Cody pocketed the phone and examined Bette more closely. Blood oozed from a jagged cut over her left temple, but he could find no other injuries. She groaned again. Cody squeezed her hand. "Bette, it's me, Cody. You're going to be okay."

Her eyes fluttered, snow caught in her lashes. "What happened?" She stared at him, her gaze unfocused, tense with pain.

"I don't know," he said. "I found you here, in the ditch beside your car. You must have been on your way back to the ranch."

She moaned and tried to sit up, but he pressed her gently back down. "The ambulance is on its way," he said. "Don't try to move."

"I'm cold," she said.

Of course she was cold—lying in the snow. Cody stripped off his coat and laid it over her. "The ambulance will be here soon," he said, hoping the words were true.

"What happened?" she asked again.

"Something hit your head. I think a rock. What do you remember?"

She closed her eyes. "I can't remember. I was at the store, talking to a nice woman—Brenda. I bought some butter and cream." She shook her head, wincing. "I can't remember."

"It's okay. Don't worry about it."

"My head hurts."

"I know. It will be all right soon."

She didn't try to talk after that. Had she passed out again? Should he try to wake her? Her hand in his was so cold, a chill he could feel even through his gloves. He gathered her other hand between his palms and chafed them both gently. Her nails were short and she wore no rings—maybe jewelry got in the way of cooking. She had long, slender fingers and delicate wrists. He pressed her palms to his cheek—the skin was like satin and smelled faintly of roses.

She moaned again, and he quickly lowered her hands and tucked them beneath the coat he had draped over her. It didn't feel right, to be studying her this closely while she was unaware. Where was that ambulance?

"Cody?" she asked.

"I'm right here."

"Did you come to arrest me?"

He stiffened. "Arrest you for what?"

"That's what you do, isn't it? You arrest people."

She stared at him, but he had the sense she wasn't really seeing him. "Only if they've broken the law," he said. "Have you broken the law?"

"That doesn't matter, does it?" she said. "You think I'm bad, and I'll never be able to make you believe I'm good." She closed her eyes again.

"Bette?"

She didn't answer, only moaned and shook her head.

The distant wail of the ambulance broke the winter silence. Cody stood and trudged out of the ditch, into the road to flag it down. It parked in the road behind his RAV4 and a middle-aged man and a slightly younger woman climbed out. "Emmett Baxter," the man introduced himself as and shook Cody's hand. "This is Joan Anderson." He indicated the woman, who was taking a large plastic tote from the rear of the ambulance. "What have we got?"

"I'm not sure." Cody led the way around the car. "She's got a head injury."

They knelt in the snow, one on each side of Bette, and opened the medical tote. Cody moved to the bumper of Bette's car, trying to get a sense of what had happened here. He could barely make out the tracks where her car had left the road and gone into the ditch. He wasn't trained in assessing traffic accidents, but he couldn't see any skid marks—no churned earth or deep ruts to indicate she had skidded off the road. Yet surely she wouldn't have deliberately driven into the ditch.

He moved to the front of the car. Except for the broken driver's side window, the vehicle appeared undamaged, though the snow might be hiding some ding or scrape that would tell a different story. Had someone sideswiped her and driven away? Had someone stopped after she had gone into the ditch and, instead of helping her, had thrown the rock through the window and dragged her out of the vehicle? The idea sent a chill through him that had nothing to do with the temperature.

Emmett stood and Cody walked back to join him. Bette was sitting up now, a bandage over the cut on her head. "How are you feeling?" Cody asked.

"I've been better, but I'll live." She looked more alert, though still in pain.

"Do you remember anything more about what happened?" Cody asked.

"No. It's all…just a blank."

"Short-term memory loss isn't uncommon with a head injury," Joan said. "Or with any kind of trauma, really."

"Will my memory come back?" Bette asked.

"Maybe. Maybe not," Joan said. "I wouldn't worry too much unless you start noticing bigger gaps."

"We can take her to the clinic in town, but they can't get her to the hospital," Emmett said. "Dixon Pass is closed again. Chute number nine let loose about half an hour ago. It'll be twenty-four hours, at least, before the road opens. More, if it keeps snowing."

"I want to go to the ranch," Bette said.

"I can take her," Cody said. "There are plenty of people who can look after her there."

"What about my car?" Bette asked.

"We'll get a wrecker, or maybe one of the ranch trucks, to pull it out later," Cody said.

"I'll need my purse and the groceries I bought."

"I'll get them." Emmett moved toward the vehicle, but stopped short when he saw the broken window and the rock. "What happened here?"

He started to reach in for the rock, but Cody caught his arm. "Don't touch anything," he said.

"What, you think someone did this deliberately?" Emmett asked.

"I don't know. But don't touch it. Just get her purse off the passenger seat." He scanned the interior. "The groceries must be in the trunk."

He took the keys from the ignition and pressed the button to unlock the trunk. He and Emmett were retrieving the grocery bags when a black-and-white sheriff's department vehicle parked behind the ambulance and Travis Walker got out. "I heard the call on the scanner, figured I'd better see what was up," he said. He looked over as Bette, leaning on Joan, came around the front of her car. Cody read the relief on his face and realized the sheriff had been worried the victim might be his fiancée, Lacy. "What happened?" Travis asked.

Bette shook her head. "I'm not sure," she said.

"The head injury is hampering her memory of the events," Joan said. She steered Bette over to Cody's vehicle and helped her into the passenger seat.

Travis walked around to the side of Bette's car, where Emmett was packing up the last of the medical supplies. "Looks like someone broke the window with that big rock in the driver's seat," Emmett said. "She must have been sitting in the seat at the time and the rock hit her on the side of the head."

Travis studied the broken window and the rock. "Where is this somebody now?" he asked.

"Bette was the only one here when I showed up," Cody said. "I didn't pass any other cars after I turned on the county road."

"Neither did I," Travis said. "And there aren't any houses between here and the ranch." He looked at Bette again. "She really doesn't remember anything?"

"She says not. It's a pretty nasty gash on the side of her head—she was unconscious when I got here."

"Good thing you showed up when you did," Travis said. "She might have frozen to death before anyone found her."

Cody had been trying not to think of that. "I need to get her to the ranch," he said. "But someone should take a closer look at the car."

"I'll take care of that," Travis said. "The snow is going to make finding tracks almost impossible, but I'll do what I can."

"Thanks."

He returned to the RAV4 and started it up, then turned the heater to high. "You doing okay?" he asked Bette.

"I'll be fine." She stared out the window, not looking at him.

What had she meant, when she had said he thought she was bad? It wasn't true. She made it sound as if he passed judgment on everyone he met, putting them into categories—bad and good. If he did do that, he wouldn't know where she belonged. She had a bad past, and he couldn't say he entirely trusted her, but it wasn't fair for her to say he had made up his mind about her.

When they reached the house, no one else seemed to be around. Cody helped Bette out of the car, his grip firm, yet gentle. "I'll be fine," she said, pulling away from him. "I'll just go to my cabin and lie down for a while." She tried to turn away but almost lost her balance.

"I think you'd better come into the main house for a little while," he said. He put his arm around her. "Let me help. You don't want to fall and bust open your head again."

She gave in and let him help her into the house. He settled her into a chair near the fire. "Thank you for your coat," she said, returning it to him.

He hung the coat on a peg by the door, then returned to sit beside her. "How are you feeling?" he asked.

"I wish people would quit asking me that."

"You'd better get used to it. How are you feeling?"

"I have a pretty bad headache," she admitted.

"Do you remember any more about what happened?" he asked.

"No." Her eyes met his, her expression troubled. "I'm sorry, I can't."

"There's no need to apologize."

"Hello, I didn't hear you come in." Emily came in from the other room, smiling, but her smile vanished when she noticed the bandage on Bette's head. "What happened to you?" she asked.

"I'm not sure." Bette touched the bandage gingerly. "Cody found me on the side of the road, in a ditch."

"Cody! What's going on? Did you call Travis?"

"He's still on the scene. Bette has a head injury— maybe a mild concussion. She can't remember anything.

I thought it would be a good idea for her to stay where someone can be with her until we're sure she's okay."

Emily sat beside Bette and took her hand. "You need to see a doctor."

"I called for an ambulance and the paramedics treated her," Cody said. "They couldn't take her to the hospital because an avalanche has closed the pass again."

"I didn't want to go to the hospital, anyway," Bette said. "I'm sure I'll be fine, once I get a little rest. I just wish I could remember what happened. The last thing I remember, I was in the grocery store. I met Brenda—such a nice woman."

"But how did you hit your head?" Emily looked to Cody. "You say you found her in a ditch?"

"Her car was in the ditch and she was lying in the snow beside the car," he said. "The driver's side window was busted out, and a big rock sat in the driver's seat. The rock probably hit her in the head when it went through the window."

"A rock?" Bette stared at him. "But how did it get there? I mean, I always see the road signs that say watch for falling rocks, but I never dreamed one could come through the window like that."

"This wasn't a falling rock," Cody said. "It happened in an area of open fields and woods. There isn't any place near there that a rock could have fallen from."

"Are you saying someone *threw* the rock at her?" Emily asked.

"We don't know," Cody said.

"Who would do something like that?" Emily asked.

He didn't see any point in trying to answer that question. "You might fix her some tea or something," he said. "She was lying in the snow who knows how long and she's probably still chilled."

"I'm sitting right here," Bette said. "If I want tea, I can get it myself."

"I'll get it." Emily stood. "I could use a cup myself."

She left them. Bette glared up at Cody. "Don't you have something to do?" she asked.

"I'm doing it."

"I don't like you hovering over me."

He leaned toward her and lowered his voice. "Want to tell me about the red paint I saw in your bathroom last night?" he asked. He hadn't planned to question her about the paint right now, but why not take advantage of the opportunity?

She gasped. "What were you doing snooping around in my bathroom?"

"I was looking for a towel and I saw the paint and a brush. The same color paint that was used to write that message on your door."

"Why didn't you say something to me about it then?"

"Why didn't you say something to me?"

"Because I didn't know it was there—not until this morning." She clutched at his arm. "I swear that paint wasn't there before last night. Someone—probably the same person who put that message on the door—must have come in while I was out and put it there."

"How did they get in? You locked your door, didn't you?"

"Of course I did, but mine might not be the only key."

"I'll ask the Walkers if there's another key."

"Don't." She drew back. "And don't look at me that way."

"What way?"

"As if you think I'm guilty of something."

"If you're not guilty of something, why don't you want me talking to the Walkers?"

"Because I don't want to worry them over something so stupid. It was just a childish message painted on my door."

"But who wrote it, and why?"

"My guess is someone who doesn't want me here. Someone who wants me to, as the message said, go home."

"I guess Rainey is at the top of that list. And maybe Doug."

"Probably. But it doesn't matter. I'm not going to leave, and there's no sense making a fuss. That's probably what they want. When they realize I'm going to ignore them, they'll have to give up."

"I'd think the Walkers would want to know if one of their employees is harassing a guest," Cody said.

"They have enough to worry about right now, with the wedding and the snowstorms and the serial killer," Bette said. "I can look after myself. Promise you won't say anything to them."

"All right. I won't say anything."

"Won't say anything about what?" Emily returned, carrying a loaded tray.

Cody stood and relieved her of the tray. He handed one of the steaming mugs on it to Bette and took one for himself. "I asked Cody not to say anything to Rainey and Doug about my injury," Bette said. "I don't want Rainey using it as an excuse to push me out of her kitchen."

"She's bound to hear about it from someone." Emily settled next to Bette with the third mug of tea. "And she's not going to push you out of the kitchen. We won't let her."

"Still, it would be better if you just don't mention me to her," Bette said.

The door opened and Travis came in, followed by Lacy. "Come sit by the fire," Emily said. "The two of you must be frozen."

The couple shed their coats, then Lacy sank into a chair across from Bette. Travis remained standing. "I was on my way home when I saw Travis on the side of the road, with your car," Lacy said. "He told me what happened. How are you feeling?"

"I'm fine." She looked up at Travis. "Did you find anything to tell us what happened?"

"Have you remembered anything that happened?" Travis asked.

"I'm sorry, no. I'm trying to remember but..." She shook her head. "I don't even recall leaving the grocery store and getting into my car."

"I'm having your car towed to the station so we can take a better look at it there," Travis said. "If you need to borrow one of the ranch vehicles in the meantime, just ask my mom or dad. They'll be happy to lend you whatever you need."

"I shouldn't need to go anywhere for a few days, at least," Bette said. "I stocked up on supplies today. By the way, I need to bring them inside and put them away."

"I'll take care of that in a minute," Cody said.

"There's something else you should know." Travis took an evidence pouch from the pocket of his coat. "We found this in the ditch near the car."

Bette took the packet from him and frowned at the contents. "Duct tape?"

A chill went through Cody. The Ice Cold Killer had used duct tape to bind the hands and feet of his victims.

"Did you have any duct tape in your car that might have fallen out when you got out?" Travis asked.

"No," Bette said. "It's not something I've ever owned."

He tucked the evidence pouch back into his pocket. "I need to get this over to the station. I just stopped by to see how you were doing."

"I'm going to be fine," Bette said. "Thank you."

"I'll get those groceries out of the car," Cody said. He followed Travis out the door. On the front porch, the two friends stopped. "Did you find any of the killer's calling cards?" he asked.

"No," Travis said. "Just this roll of duct tape. It looks brand-new. I'm not even sure any tape has been used off the roll."

"Maybe the killer ran out and needed more."

"There are only a couple of places in town that stock the stuff," Travis said. "I'll be checking with them." He shoved his hands in his coat pockets. "It's snowing pretty hard, but I got out of the cruiser several times and walked the roadside on the way back to the ranch. I didn't see any signs where a vehicle might have turned off the road—no tracks or depressions in the snow or broken plants or anything."

"Cars don't vanish into thin air," Cody said.

"They don't," Travis agreed. "If whoever attacked Bette didn't turn off and he didn't turn back, that means it came here, to the ranch. And it means he's still here."

Chapter Eight

The idea that Bette's attacker could be here at the ranch put Cody on high alert. "What do you need me to do?" he asked.

"I need you to help me search the ranch," Travis said. "We'll check all the outbuildings and anywhere someone could possibly stash a vehicle."

"Sure. Do you suspect someone at the ranch—an employee or somebody else?"

"Right now, I suspect pretty much everyone."

Cody retrieved Bette's groceries from his RAV4 and stashed them in the garage refrigerator, then he and Travis set out across the ranch.

"If this was the Ice Cold Killer, he's getting pretty reckless," Cody said as he and Travis made their way toward the stables.

"He killed Fiona Winslow in the middle of a party," Travis said. "Anyone could have come upon him at any time. I think that's part of the thrill for him."

"What are we looking for, specifically?" Cody asked, as they stopped behind a trio of vehicles parked near the stables. All three were covered with snow—in one case the vehicle, an older-model sedan, was almost buried in a drift.

"I'm looking for anything that looks like it's been driven in the last two hours," Travis said.

"It's been well over an hour," Cody said. "The engine probably won't be warm."

"No, but we should be able to tell if it isn't covered with snow. We can rule out your car, mine and Lacy's, but anything else we find, we'll take a very close look at the driver."

For the next two hours, they trudged through the snow, knee-deep in places. They peered into sheds and walked up narrow tracks that led into the woods. What few vehicles they spotted had clearly not been moved since the snow started. Travis questioned a few ranch hands, but all denied seeing any strange vehicles—or even any familiar ones. "Not much call to go out in a storm like this," one man said. "Especially with Dixon Pass closed."

By the time they made it back to the house, the sun was setting, and Cody's fingers and toes ached with cold. "Let's check around back here and we'll call it a night," Travis said, leading the way around the side of the house.

"The killer really has nerve if he's stashing his car this close to the house," Cody said, but he trudged along behind his friend, toward the back door, and the beckoning warmth of the kitchen. They had almost reached that warmth when Travis stopped. "What is it?" Cody asked. He followed his friend's gaze toward the shadows at the edge of the glow from the light shining through the kitchen window. He could just make out the bumper of a car.

He followed Travis over to the car and the sheriff played the beam of his flashlight over the windshield and hood. A scant half inch of snow coated the vehicle, compared with the much thicker coatings they had found on the other ranch vehicles. Travis directed the light to the ground around the car. "Does it look like there's less snow behind the back wheels to you?" he asked.

"That's harder to tell," Cody said. "Maybe. Whose vehicle is this?"

"It belongs to Rainey." He switched off the flashlight. "Let's see what she has to say."

"I'm going to be fine," Bette said, struggling to keep all trace of annoyance out of her voice. Lacy and Emily meant well, fussing over her like two mother hens, but she was beginning to feel a little smothered. They had plied her with tea, ibuprofen, blankets and offers of chicken soup and a hot water bottle, and they didn't want to let her out of their sight, even to go to the bathroom. She pushed aside the blankets and pillows and stood. "I'm going to go check on the groceries Cody put away, and then I'm going out to my cabin. I'm going to take a shower and go to bed early, get a good night's sleep and I'm sure I'll be fine in the morning."

"Shouldn't someone check on you during the night?" Lacy asked. "I mean, aren't you supposed to wake up someone with a head injury periodically, so they don't go into a coma or something?"

"If anyone wakes me up out of a sound sleep I can't be held responsible for the consequences," Bette said.

"You can't blame us for being worried about you," Lacy said.

"I know," Bette said. "And you're being really sweet, but I'll be fine. I'm feeling much better now. I hardly even have a headache." Not exactly true—her head still hurt a lot. But she wasn't going to let on about it or they would insist on taking turns waking her up all night to make sure she didn't die. And if they did that, the only lives that would be at risk would be theirs.

Lacy and Emily exchanged looks. Bette was sure they were going to argue with her. Before they got the chance, she headed for the kitchen.

Rainey looked up from the pot she was stirring on the stove. "What do you want?" she asked. "I'm in the middle of fixing dinner."

"I don't need anything from you," Bette said. "I'm just going through to the garage."

Once safely in the garage, she switched on the light and pulled open the door to the refrigerator. As she had expected, Cody had shoved both bags full of groceries on top of the cases of beer, not bothering to sort out what required refrigeration and what didn't. Sighing, she pulled out the bags and took out the dried fruit and several other items that didn't need to be kept cold. She would store these in her cabin until she needed them. She wouldn't give Rainey an excuse to complain that Bette's supplies were taking up space in her pantry.

She closed the refrigerator, hooked the bag of groceries to take to her cabin over one wrist and returned to the kitchen—and almost collided with Cody.

He reached out to steady her. "What were you doing in the garage?" he asked.

"I needed some things from the refrigerator." She looked past him, to where Travis stood with Rainey. Neither of them looked happy about something. Travis was scowling and Rainey was hunched, arms folded tightly across her chest.

Rainey glanced at Bette, then looked back to the sheriff. "I always park my car back there," she said. "I don't see what business it is of yours. If your parents have a problem with it, they can tell me themselves."

"I don't care where you park, Rainey," Travis said. "I asked you when the last time you moved the car was."

"Why do you need to know that?" she asked.

"Just answer the question, please."

"Yesterday," she said. "I ran some errands in town and it's been parked there ever since."

"Are you sure?" Travis asked.

"Of course I'm sure," she said. "What is all this about?"

"I noticed there isn't much snow on the car," Travis said. "Not as much as you'd expect if it had been sitting there over twenty-four hours."

Rainey hunched her shoulders more. "Doug cleaned it off for me. I don't like letting snow pile up on it too high. Then it's that much more trouble to clean off. So he swept it off for me."

"When was this?" Travis asked.

"I don't know. Sometime after lunch."

"Where is Doug?" Travis looked around the kitchen. "Shouldn't he be helping you with supper?"

"He wasn't feeling well, so I sent him to his room to lie down. I think he might be coming down with the flu or something."

"I'll need to talk to him," Travis said.

"Why? He hasn't done anything wrong."

"Then there won't be any problem with him answering some questions for me."

"What kind of questions?" Rainey demanded.

"He's a grown man," Travis said. "I think he can speak for himself."

Rainey uncrossed her arms and whirled to face him. "Do you think that badge gives you the right to pick on him?" she shouted. "Just because that woman lied about him in court and he had to go to prison, you think you can blame anything that happens around here on him. When you've invited someone else into your home who is so much worse. You ought to be ashamed of yourself, Travis Walker."

"Rainey." His voice carried a sharp edge of warning.

Bette shrank back, half hiding behind Cody as Rainey turned on her. "She's the one you ought to be questioning," she said, pointing to Bette. "She robbed a bank, and she's probably planning to rob you all blind as soon as you turn your backs."

Rage fogged Bette's vision. How dare this woman accuse her of wanting to harm people who had been so kind to her. If anyone had dared to say something like that to her in prison, she would have lit into them then and there. Fighting meant losing privileges, maybe even having time added to your sentence. But that was better than losing face. If some of those cons learned they could take advantage of you, they would make your time behind bars a living hell.

This isn't prison, she reminded herself. This was a respectable home, and Bette was here to do a job. She wouldn't let this spiteful woman take that from her. So she held her head up and forced herself to move into the middle of the room. "The sheriff knows I'm happy to answer any questions he has," she said, finding and holding Rainey's gaze. "Now, if you don't mind, I'm going to say good-night. It's been a trying day."

She was halfway across the yard, cold wind freezing the tears that streamed down her face, when Cody caught up with her. "Hey," he said, taking hold of her arm.

"Leave me alone," she said, wrenching away from him.

"I'm going to walk you to your cabin," he said, falling into step beside her.

"I didn't ask you to be my bodyguard," she said.

"No. But someone has threatened you twice in the last two days—and this morning you might have been killed. I'm not going to ignore that, even if you are."

She didn't know what to say to that, so they walked without speaking the rest of the way to her cabin, their footsteps crunching on the snow. "No messages on the door," he said as they climbed the steps to the little porch. "That's good."

"Everything looks fine." She faced him, key in her hand. "All right, you saw me here, you can go now."

"Not until we make sure everything inside is all right." He took the key from her and inserted it into the lock.

She followed him into the room. Everything looked as she had left it. "Everything's fine," she said. *Just— go*, she thought.

But he didn't leave. "I'm sorry about what happened back there, in the kitchen," he said. "But it was all on Rainey. Travis will see that, too. She was upset about him questioning her, so she tried to create a distraction."

Bette sat on the side of the bed. "What was all that about the car?" she asked. "Why was Travis questioning her?"

"We were looking for the car driven by whoever attacked you," he said. "Neither of us passed another vehicle between the turnoff for the country road and your car. If your attacker didn't travel that way, the only other direction he could have gone was toward the ranch. When we looked at cars on the ranch, Rainey's was the only one we found that looked as if it had been cleared of snow in the last few hours."

"Rainey hates me, but forcing me off the road and attacking me with a rock?" Bette shook her head. "She doesn't strike me as the type. She'd rather spit in my soup, or spread rumors behind my back—or announce to everyone that I'm a bank robber and I can't be trusted." That moment in the kitchen when everyone had turned to look at her still stung.

"What about Doug?" Cody asked. "Do you think he was the one who attacked you?"

"I don't know." She curled her hands into fists. "I honestly don't remember anything from the time I was standing in the grocery story with Brenda, until I woke up with you shaking me. It's frightening, having a chunk of your life just missing that way."

"But you can't say Doug wasn't the one who hurt you?"

"No. I guess Doug could have done it, but why?"

"He has a record," Cody said. "He served time for beating up his girlfriend. He put her in the hospital."

"Not exactly a comforting thought, but I can't see why he'd want to hurt me," Bette said. "We haven't said more than half a dozen words to each other since I got here."

"He could have hurt you out of some misguided attempt to protect his mother," Cody said.

"Oh, please!" Bette grabbed a pillow and hugged it to her stomach. "I know Rainey resents my getting to cater the wedding, but it's not like she's out of a job.

She's still doing what she's done for years, doing the cooking for the ranch. After the wedding I'll be gone and she'll still be here. That isn't a good reason to physically hurt someone. The petty harassment—sure, maybe she'll make me miserable enough and I'll leave. But violence?" She shook her head. "It's not worth the risk of getting caught."

"Is there someone else who might be a threat to you, then?"

"Who? I know it's a cliché for someone to say she doesn't have enemies, but honestly, I don't."

"What about your ex? The one who talked you into robbing the bank?"

"He's still in prison."

"Do you know that for sure?"

She frowned. When she had first been released, she had been almost obsessive about keeping tabs on Eddie. Lately, that obsession had faded. "The last time I checked was six months ago, but yes, he was still serving his sentence."

"A lot of cons have connections outside prison—people who are loyal to them who will do things for them, like check up on an old girlfriend to make sure she doesn't say something she shouldn't."

"But he's in prison. Nothing I say can hurt him worse," she said.

"There was one member of the gang who was never caught," Cody said.

"So you did check up on me."

His expression remained cool. "Are you really surprised?"

"No. I guess I'd have been more surprised if you

hadn't. So yes, the guy who drove the getaway car was never caught."

"You didn't testify against him." A statement, not a question. Oh, yeah, he had gotten all the details, hadn't he?

"I didn't know anything to testify," she said. "I saw him for a few minutes exactly once, and I don't remember anything about him."

"Does your ex know that?"

"Yes. He was the one who made sure I knew as little as possible. He said it was for my protection, but it worked both ways. The less I knew, the less I could testify to."

"All right, so you don't know who the getaway driver is—but he probably knows you. Maybe he's come after you to shut you up."

"That's pretty far-fetched." She held up her hand and began counting off the reasons. "One—how does he know I'm in Eagle Mountain? Two—when did he get here? There was only, what, a two-day window when the pass was open so he could follow me here. And three—and this is the biggest reason I think you're wrong—it's been nine years since that robbery. What are the chances that he's still out there walking around? He probably committed other crimes and is locked up for one of them."

"Maybe he was like you—a dupe for your ex. The near miss scared him into going straight."

"In which case, why would he throw all that away to shut me up?"

"If you identify him, you ruin his life. He might have a good job now, a wife and a family. Those things are worth taking risks for."

"But this is a crazy risk. And really foolish. Because I don't know anything."

"All right," he said. "But until we find out who's behind these threats, I'm going to be keeping a closer eye on you than you may like."

"Why? Why do you even care?"

"Let's just say it gives me something to do. I can only take so much shoveling snow and chopping firewood."

"What are you doing here at the ranch anyway?" she asked.

"I'm one of the groomsmen."

"Yeah, but the wedding is two weeks away. Why are you here so early?"

He studied her for a long moment, silent.

"It's a simple question," she said.

"But it doesn't have a simple answer." He stared at the floor, then let out a long, slow breath. "I told you before I'm on vacation, but that's just the polite word for it. Actually, it was more of a forced leave."

"What happened?" she asked. "Did you screw up? Shoot someone you shouldn't have?"

He winced, and she wanted to take the words back. "I'm sorry," she said. "I shouldn't have assumed."

"It's okay. I'd rather you said what you were thinking than try to tiptoe around my feelings. I've had enough of that."

She waited for him to say more. The silence stretched, until she became aware of the gentle sigh of his breath and the brush of the denim of his jeans when he shifted in the chair. "I was on a job," he said finally, his voice low and tight, as if he was forcing out the words. "Routine stuff—pursuing a fugitive with a warrant. The guy was wanted for sexually molesting his ten-year-old niece. Nice, upstanding citizen—a banker. A girls' soccer coach, so there was a question of whether other girls were involved. Basically, I thought he was scum, but I would never have let him know that. I did my job—tracked him down at a friend's cabin where he had gone in a pretty feeble attempt to hide from the cops. I gave him my usual spiel of how he should come with me quietly."

He closed his eyes, and she sensed he was replaying the scene in his head. "He had a gun. He was waving it around. One of those cases you hate, because the way he was holding the gun, I could tell he wasn't really going to shoot me. He was trying to commit what we call suicide by cop. But I wasn't going to let that happen."

He opened his eyes again. "It's a matter of pride for me that when I go after someone, I bring them back alive ninety-nine percent of the time. I knew I could handle this guy. I wasn't in a hurry. I had all the time in a world to talk him off the ledge, get him to put the gun down. There are rules for handling these kinds of things and I knew how to follow them to reach a good outcome."

He fell silent again, the lines around his eyes so deep, the hunch of his shoulders that of a man in pain. "What happened?" she whispered.

He licked his lips. "He didn't know the rules. I was right that he didn't want to shoot me. Instead, he shot himself. Put the barrel of the gun in his mouth and pulled the trigger. He was looking me right in the eye when he did it."

She put a hand to her mouth to stifle the cry she couldn't keep back.

Cody shook his head, like a boxer shaking off a blow

to the chin. "It rattles you, something like that. But I knew I could deal. I told my boss the best thing for it was to get back out in the field, but he didn't see it that way. He ordered me to take time off—to get out in nature, to see a counselor if I needed. But not to come back on the job until February."

"So you came here."

"I couldn't just sit around my apartment. And Travis is a great guy for giving you perspective. You might not see it, but the man is beyond calm in a crisis. I figured he and I could hang out, go fishing, I could work on the ranch. But he's tied up chasing a killer, and I'm going crazy." His eyes met hers again. "That's where you come in."

"So I'm going to be your distraction."

"Oh, you're a distraction all right."

He stood and moved toward her. There was nothing subtle about his stance, or the look in his eye. She felt that look like a bottle rocket straight to the middle of her chest, the heat of the explosion radiating down through her middle to pool between her legs. Something pulsed between them, and her gaze shifted from the almost painful fire in his eyes to his lips, the bottom one a little fuller than the upper, the black shadow of whiskers above the upper lip.

He took the pillow from her and tossed it aside, then pulled her up to face him, one hand at her waist, the other beside her left breast as his lips crushed hers. She returned the fierceness of that caress, kissing him as if her next breath depended on it, opening her mouth and tangling her tongue with his, wanting—insisting—on having all of him, right this minute.

It was a long time before he dragged his head up,

breaking contact and staring into her eyes with a look
that was equal parts desperation and defiance. "If you
want me to leave now, I'll go," he said, his voice a rough
growl that scraped across her nerves. "But you'd better
be sure it's what you want."

"What do you want?" she asked. It wasn't a question
so much as a dare.

"I think you know that." His lips closed over hers
again and she surged up, her whole body bowing toward
him, her hands clutching his biceps, fingers digging
into his taut muscles. He grasped her hips and ground
against her, leaving no doubt of his desire.

Her need for him thrilled and frightened her. Some
small voice in the back of her mind said she was being
too reckless. It was too soon. She hardly knew this
man. He—

She told the voice to shut up and grabbed the hem of
the fleece pullover he wore and shoved it upward. Then
they were tearing at each other's clothes with an urgency that would have destroyed less sturdy garments.

She pulled him down to the bed on top of her, then
he rolled until she was straddling him. She laughed at
the heady feeling. "What's so funny?" he asked.

"Haven't you ever laughed simply because something
felt so good?" she asked.

"I don't know. If I ever did, it's been a while."

"Then I'll have to see if I can change that." She slid
down his body and took him in her mouth, surprising
a gasp from him. He caressed and kneaded her shoulders as her mouth worked on him, then he dragged her
back up to meet his mouth with hers. "Let's not end this
too soon," he said, with some effort. His gaze searched

hers. "Are you sure you're up to this? I forgot you had a pretty hard blow to the head."

"I read an article once that said sex was better than painkillers for getting rid of a headache," she said.

The slow, sexy smile he gave her could have melted chocolate. "Then I'll do my best to make you forget the pain," he said. It was his turn to surprise her, as his skillful fingers delved and fondled. When he began licking first one breast, then another, she squirmed against him. "Do you like that?" he asked.

"No, I hate it. Can't you tell?"

In answer, he drew the tip of one breast into his mouth, while his fingers moved more deftly.

Her climax rocketed through her, fierce and freeing. She collapsed against him and he held her—rather tenderly, she thought, which made her blink back foolish tears. She propped herself up on her elbows and met his gaze. "It's, um, been a while," she said, almost sheepishly.

"I'm a very lucky man," he said. He flipped her over on her back and moved between her legs.

She grasped his shoulder. "Wait."

His eyes met hers, and she saw the moment he recognized the problem. "We don't have any protection," he said.

"Hmm. Then we'll have to work around that."

She started to slide down the bed, but he pressed her back against the pillows. "Wait a minute," he said, and got up.

He disappeared into the bathroom and returned seconds later, a gold foil packet held aloft. "Where did that come from?" she asked.

"The medicine cabinets in these cabins are fully

stocked," he said. "The Walkers think of everything for their guests' comfort."

"I didn't see those before," she said.

"You weren't looking." He parted her knees and knelt between them. "I was."

She wanted to ask him what he meant by that but was distracted by the sight of him sheathing himself. And then he was moving into her, and she didn't want to think about anything for a while. She only wanted to lose herself in the sensation of being filled and surrounded and uplifted by this man.

Such a wonderful feeling.

And a dangerous one. But she didn't want to think about the danger now. She'd have all kinds of time for thinking later.

Chapter Nine

Bette untangled herself from the bedcovers the next morning, aching in body and mind. Her head hurt and her muscles ached, but worse than that, her emotions felt bruised. Cody had stayed long into the night, making love with such tenderness and ferocity, before slipping away some time very early this morning. What was it about him that made her want to be so reckless? He had given her probably the best night of her life, but this morning she was no more certain about where she stood with him than she had been at this time yesterday.

She dressed and emerged from the cabin into a world frosted in white. Sunlight sparkled on the drifts of snow that covered everything, transforming woodpiles and old machinery into glittering confections. The air was so sharp and clean it hurt to breathe. She felt energized with every inhalation. She found Emily, Lacy, Travis and Cody in the dining room, digging into an egg-and-ham casserole that smelled mouthwatering. "How are you feeling this morning?" Lacy asked. "Does your head hurt?"

"Only a little. I feel fine." A little beat up, perhaps, emotionally and physically, though for long moments last night she had forgotten all about her headache, or anything else. But all the closeness and compatibility that had come so naturally last night in the intimacy of her cabin felt a lot shakier and out of reach here in the real world. She poured coffee, avoiding looking at Cody, though she was as aware of him as if he were the only person in the room.

"I'm so glad," Lacy said. "I had to make myself not go out there in the middle of the night, just to make sure you were okay."

Bette was glad she had her back to the table as she served herself from the buffet. Her cheeks burned with the memory of what Lacy might have found if she had decided to visit the cabin last night. "I'm glad you restrained yourself," she said. "I was fine." Though *fine* was a poor word to describe what she had been feeling last night—*elated*, *transported*, even *awed* would have been better choices.

"I have something fun for all of us to look forward to," Emily said. "Gage and I have decided we should have an old-fashioned sleigh ride to take advantage of the snow. Dad agreed we could use the old sleighs that are in the barn—he and Mom are out there now, checking the harness."

"When did you and Gage decide this?" Travis asked.

"Yesterday. He telephoned the ranch, wanting to talk to you, but you were in the kitchen with Rainey, so he and I got to talking. Casey has been begging to go on a sleigh ride ever since he showed her that album of family pictures that Mom gave him. We figured with all this snow, now is the perfect time."

"When is the sleigh ride?" Travis asked.

"Tonight, after supper," Emily said. "We'll hook up both sleighs and ride over to the little line shack in the south pasture. We can have hot chocolate and maybe s'mores." She nudged him. "Don't look so stern—it will only be for a few hours, and it will be a nice break from all the tension. We've all been feeling it, you know— not just you."

"It sounds like fun," Lacy said. "Romantic."

"Very romantic," Emily agreed. "We'll have lots of fur robes and blankets for snuggling under, and Gage promised to bring a flask of peppermint schnapps for spiking the hot cocoa."

"That sounds like Gage," Travis said drily.

"Oh, you're going to enjoy it," Emily said.

"I wouldn't dream of disobeying orders." Travis kept a straight face, but Bette didn't miss the sly look he sent Lacy across the table.

Lacy sat up straighter, her cheeks only slightly pink. "It does sound like lots of fun. I'll be looking forward to it. In the meantime, I have a Skype meeting with the wedding planner this morning." She looked around the table. "What are the rest of you doing today?"

"I'm working here for a while, then heading to the office," Travis said.

Cody made no comment, eyes focused on his plate. Bette had the strong impression he was pretending not to have heard Lacy's question—when, really, he didn't want to answer it. "I'm a little concerned about how a couple of my recipes will turn out at this altitude," she said. "I thought I'd make some test batches, in case I need to tweak things."

"I've talked to Rainey," Travis said. "She shouldn't give you any trouble."

"Thank you." Bette settled in the chair across from the sheriff. He really had been so kind to her—Lacy was lucky to have found a man who was so perfect for her. "If they turn out well, we can use them for more refreshments for tonight."

"Any idea when the road might reopen?" Cody asked.

Travis shook his head. "They'll be working this morning to clear the avalanche chutes."

"What does that involve, exactly?" Bette asked.

"They use dynamite, or sometimes a grenade launcher, to explode the snow out of the chutes and create a slide—an intentional avalanche," Travis said. "All the snow ends up on the highway and they have to haul it off. There are twenty-four chutes in that section of highway, so clearing them can take several days. And there's more snow in the forecast."

"Why don't they build another road?" Bette asked. "It's crazy to have a whole town full of people who can't go anywhere every time it snows."

"The road usually only closes for a few hours, maybe half a day, at a time," Lacy said. "Some winters it doesn't close at all. This winter is just particularly bad."

"There's nowhere to put another road," Travis said. "Not without spending hundreds of millions of dollars to blast through mountains. And it would probably be subject to avalanches, too. The people here are used to it. They know how to cope." He slid back his chair and stood. "I need to get to work."

The rest of them finished breakfast and left the table one by one, until Bette was the only person left. She lingered over coffee, wanting to give Rainey time to finish the dishes and clear out. She wasn't afraid to confront the cook, but it would be easier on everyone if she didn't have to.

About ten o'clock, she retrieved the ingredients she

needed from her cabin and returned to the kitchen, relieved to find it empty. She pinned up her hair, then slipped her apron over her head, some of the tension draining from her body as she did so. She smiled to herself as she began assembling the tools and ingredients she needed. This was the best therapy. So many times, when her life had felt out of control, she had found solace in the kitchen. Mixing, kneading, stirring, basting—here she was ruler of her own domain, a magician who had the power to conjure beautiful things from simple ingredients.

She went into the garage to get the cream and butter she needed for the tea cakes. She found the butter immediately, but where was the cream? She moved items around and even looked to see if somehow the carton had slipped behind the cases of beer. But the cream simply wasn't there. She shut the door, confused. Had the cream been left behind when Cody transferred the groceries from her car to his? No—she was sure it had been there last night when she rearranged everything.

She returned to the kitchen and began opening doors and searching everywhere for the missing cream. She was being silly—there was no reason the carton would have ended up anywhere in these cabinets. But she couldn't shake the compulsion to look.

And then she found it, sitting on a middle shelf in the kitchen's walk-in pantry, next to a jar of roasted peppers. The carton was warm in her hand, and before she even opened it, she knew it would be spoiled. Disgusted, she dumped the contents in the sink, rinsed the carton and tossed it in the recycling bin. She knew she hadn't put the cream in the pantry, which meant someone else had—probably Rainey or Doug.

A shadow passed in front of the window. She looked out and spotted Doug, shoulders hunched, hood pulled over his head. She grabbed a coat from a peg by the back door and shoved her feet into a pair of women's snow boots—no doubt Rainey's. Let her complain about Bette borrowing her coat and boots and she'd get more than an earful in return.

She found Doug huddled next to a tall stack of split firewood, cupping his hand around a cigarette to light it. "Doug!" she called.

He jumped and almost dropped his cigarette. "What do you want?" he asked, half turning away from her.

"Someone took a quart of cream from the garage refrigerator and put it in the pantry to spoil," she said. "Did you or your mother do that?"

He blew out a stream of smoke, which hung in the cold air between them. "You probably did it yourself. I heard you got hit in the head. It probably made you loopy."

She took a step closer; he moved a step back. "What do you know about that? Did you hit me in the head?"

"Why would I do that? I never laid eyes on you before you showed up here."

"So why do you and your mother hate me?" The answer to that question was behind all this, wasn't it? "It's not like I'm trying to take your jobs," she continued. "I'm just catering the wedding of a friend. Then I'm going to go back to Denver and you'll probably never see me again."

"You should just go back now." He flicked ash into the snow.

"You're the one who painted that message on my door, aren't you?" she asked.

"I don't know what you're talking about. I just think it would be a lot less trouble for everyone if you went home now."

"Since the pass is closed, that's impossible. But why do you care if I'm here or not?"

"Who said I cared?" He dropped the cigarette on the snow and ground it out with the heel of his boot. "If you've got a beef with my mom, take it up with her."

"I'll do that. Where is she?"

"She went to her room to lie down. Said she had a migraine. You won't get anywhere talking to her right now." He left, moving along the edge of the woodpile and staying as far from her as possible, keeping his head down.

Bette stared after him. What was up with this guy? He wouldn't even look at her.

She returned to the kitchen and shed the coat and boots. She'd make do without the cream today and go into town tomorrow to buy more. For the moment, she would leave Rainey alone. She wouldn't get anywhere if the woman really did have a migraine. Instead, she would focus on baking, and getting ready for the bridesmaids' tea. Those were things she could control, in a world where so much was out of her hands.

CODY WALKED BY the kitchen, refusing to give in to the temptation to go in and talk to Bette. He could hear her in there, opening and closing doors, rattling bowls and pots. He imagined her, focused on her work, the scents of vanilla and cinnamon clinging to her, mingling with her own sweet essence, the memory of which made him hard.

He hadn't gone to her cabin last night intending to

take her to bed, but he wasn't sorry he had. She got to him. He hadn't talked to anyone about what had happened on his last assignment—not even the shrink his bosses had made him see—before last night. He had been certain that he didn't need to talk about it. Talking didn't do anything but pull the scab off the wound.

But telling Bette had been easy somehow. Once he had made up his mind to talk to her, he had *wanted* her to know. He didn't feel the need for barriers with her. He couldn't say that about many other people. Last night had been powerful, but he wasn't sure what it meant for the future.

Hell, he didn't know if he even had a future. He might as well admit that, if only to himself. He didn't know if he would have a job waiting for him when he reported back to the US Marshals Service in February. He had heard rumors of budget cuts and restructuring for months now. An officer they saw as "damaged" would be first in line to be let go.

He needed to work—to prove he could still do the only job he had ever really wanted. With this in mind, he knocked on the door of Travis's home office, half of a suite of rooms he occupied on the ground floor, just off the kitchen. "Come in," the sheriff called.

Dressed in his sheriff's department uniform, as if at any minute he might be called out, Travis sat behind a scarred wooden desk in a small, cluttered room that resembled, in many ways, the cramped space he had claimed at the sheriff's department in Eagle Mountain. Cody stepped in and closed the door behind him and Travis looked up from a laptop computer, but said nothing.

"What can I do to help?" Cody asked.

Travis pushed the laptop to one side. "Aren't you supposed to be on leave?" he asked. Cody had told his friend some—but not all—of what had happened.

"I'm not an invalid," Cody said. "I need something to do and you need help. Deputize me or something." He sank into a cowhide-covered armchair across from the desk. "Besides, with the pass closed, you're not going to be able to call in help from the state. I'm the best you've got."

"Then I'd better not turn down your offer," Travis said.

"So what can I do? Is there someone you want me to interview? Something you need researched?"

"You've spent more time with Bette than I have— what's your feel for her?"

Cody had an immediate, intense image of heated, satiny skin sliding beneath his fingers. He kept his face stony, betraying nothing, hoping Travis wouldn't notice how tightly he gripped the arms of the chair. "What do you mean?" he asked.

"Is she really reformed?"

"She seems serious about her catering duties, and I haven't found any evidence of wrongdoing." He didn't see any need to mention his suspicions about the painted message on her door. As evidence of a crime, it was pretty weak, especially since she'd refused to say anything about it to the Walkers.

"There's a *but* at the end of that sentence," Travis said. "But what?"

"But she has a record. And bank robbery is a pretty serious crime." He couldn't forget that, no matter what else he thought about her.

Travis nodded.

"Why are you asking me about her?" Cody asked. "Do you know something about her I don't?"

Travis sat back, hands clasped over his stomach. "Have you considered the possibility that no one attacked her?"

"What do you mean? Someone threw that rock and hit her in the head."

"She could have driven the car into the ditch, then gotten out, picked up the rock and thrown it through the window herself. We didn't find any blood in the car."

Cody frowned. What Travis described was certainly possible. "Why go to all that trouble?" he asked. "And it doesn't explain the head injury."

"We only have her word for it that it was a bad enough injury to cause memory loss," Travis said. "The EMTs weren't able to x-ray her, or perform any other tests. The cut didn't require stitches. Maybe she bashed her own head."

Would Bette do something like that? Then again, was it any more far-fetched than his suspicions that she had painted those words on her door? Some sick people worked to call attention to themselves, even if it meant hurting themselves. "Again—why?" he asked.

"I don't know." Travis frowned. "I'm not saying that's what happened. I'm just trying to look at all the possibilities."

"Then why not focus on the most likely scenario—that she was attacked by the Ice Cold Killer and something scared him off?"

"What scared him off?" Travis asked.

"Maybe my arrival."

"You didn't see a car. We never found a car or any sign of one."

"Did you talk to Doug Whittington?" Cody asked. "He could have driven his mother's car."

"I talked to him," Travis said. "He said he was sleeping in his room all afternoon. His mother vouches for him."

"I think Rainey would lie to protect her son," Cody said.

"Maybe. But I can't find anyone who remembers the car not being parked near the kitchen yesterday, or anyone who saw Doug in Rainey's car. Rainey's story about having him brush the snow off her vehicle so it wouldn't pile up is plausible."

"Then maybe it was someone else," Cody said. "There was a big time gap between when I found Bette and when we started looking for a vehicle. Time enough for someone to hide a vehicle where we couldn't find it. And we were hampered by the snow. This Ice Cold Killer has done a good job of eluding detection so far."

"This doesn't fit the pattern of his other victims," Travis said. "They were subdued and bound fairly quickly, especially in the case of Fiona Winslow. Yet he didn't even have time to get any tape off the roll we found. And the whole deal with the broken window and the rock—it's sloppy. It doesn't feel like the same man."

"Maybe he felt rushed. Maybe he's getting desperate."

"There are too many *maybes* with this case."

"What do you think we should do?" Cody asked.

"Nothing right now. But keep your eyes open. Let me know if you notice anything suspicious."

"I will." He didn't need an excuse to watch Bette closer, but Travis had just given him a reason to take the job even more seriously.

Chapter Ten

"Oh, it's lovely weather," Lacy sang as she stepped out onto the front porch, arm in arm with Travis.

"For a sleigh ride together with you!" Bette joined in. The sleighs stood ready in the drive—old-fashioned wagon boxes with curved sides, painted bright red and hung with silver bells that glinted in the light from the lanterns hung at the four corners of the sleighs. The horses—two teams comprising four big draft horses hitched to each sleigh, their manes and tails combed and braided—stood between the shafts of the sleighs, their harness also hung with bells, which rang out with every shake of their heads or stamp of their hooves.

"Right this way." Gage, a red scarf wound around his neck above the collar of his shearling jacket, ushered the group toward the sleighs. "Find a seat on one of the benches in the sleighs," he instructed. "There are plenty of blankets for keeping warm, and a few buffalo robes, too."

Bette hopped up onto the wooden crate that served as a step into the sleigh. Someone reached up to steady her and she glanced back to see Cody, his hand at her back. "Where did you come from?" she asked. She had looked for him when she had first stepped onto the porch and hadn't seen him anywhere.

"I'm sticking close." He joined her in the sleigh and took her arm to pull her to the bench at the very back.

She opened her mouth to protest that she didn't necessarily want to ride next to him, but who was she kidding? The thought of snuggling under a buffalo robe with this man made the prospect of this evening even more pleasant. He slid in next to her and pulled the heavy covering over them. Bette sank her gloved fingers into the thick, black fur of the robe, smiling at the sensation of softness and warmth.

"You're in a good mood tonight," Cody said.

"Baking always puts me in a good mood," she said.

"All kinds of lines come to mind about cooking something up with you," he said. "But for now, I'll resist."

"You'd better." But she took his hand underneath the robe.

"More coming aboard!" Gage declared, and assisted a petite young woman, the tips of her dark hair dyed a bright blue, into the sleigh, followed by a little girl dressed all in pink, from the pom-pom of the knit hat pulled over her blond braids to the toes of her snow boots.

"That must be Gage's wife, Maya, and her niece, Casey," Bette whispered to Cody.

"I think you're right," he said.

The little girl's fingers flew, and Bette realized she was using sign language. Gage responded in kind, and said, "I've got a seat saved for us right up front so you can see the horses." He settled her on the front bench between himself and Maya, and tucked a blanket securely around her.

In addition to Gage and his family, Bette's sleigh contained Mr. and Mrs. Walker. Lacy and Travis rode with Dwight and Brenda Prentice and Emily in the sleigh ahead of them. Though only a few days ago the presence of so many law enforcement officers would have made Bette uncomfortable, she was more at ease with them now. She could even admit their presence tonight made her feel a little more secure.

A ranch hand, swathed in a long leather duster, climbed aboard to take the reins of their sleigh. "Giddy up!" he called, and with a jolt, they surged forward, then glided smoothly over the snow. Casey laughed and clapped her hands and Bette felt like joining in. There was something magical about floating over the snow on a cold night, the stars overhead like diamond dust, so bright and sharp that if she reached up she feared she might cut herself.

"There you go, smiling again." Cody leaned close and spoke in a low voice. "Makes me suspect you're up to something."

"I'm always up to something." She watched him out of the corner of her eye. "I thought you knew that."

He let go of her hand, but only to slide along her hip, his fingers coming to rest between her thighs. "So am I," he said.

She looked away, lifting her face to the rush of icy air across her cheeks, aware of the strong beat of her pulse in time to the jingle of the sleigh bells, of the skitter of sensation across her skin as Cody languidly rubbed his thumb up and down the seam of her jeans. For so many years in prison she had kept herself numb, pretending feelings like these didn't exist. If you didn't let yourself feel, then you couldn't hurt. Pretending that avoiding emotion made her stronger was a habit she had carried into life after she was freed. How quickly Cody had proved that belief to be a lie!

"Oh, it's lovely weather!" Emily sang out, and the others joined in to sing "Sleigh Ride"—slightly off key, but with great gusto. Cody's voice, a tuneful baritone, mingled with Bette's clear alto, and she thought how well they sounded together.

Almost too soon, the sleighs stopped before a flat-roofed log cabin, the windows outlined with white lights. A cowboy came out to meet them, and everyone piled out of the sleighs and trooped into the cabin, which glowed with the warmth of a wood fire and half a dozen lit oil lamps.

Two cowboys passed out tin cups, then came around the room with kettles of hot chocolate and ladled the hot drink into the cups. Another man served platters of the tea cakes and cream puffs Bette had made that afternoon.

The young woman with the blue hair approached with the little girl. "I'm Maya," she said, offering a hand. "And this is Casey."

Casey held out one of the cream puffs and signed with her free hand. "She says she really likes the cream puff," Maya said. "I told her you made them."

"I did." Bette smiled at the little girl. "Tell her I'm glad she likes them."

"And you must be Cody." Maya turned to the man beside Bette. "Gage has told me about you and I know you've been staying at the ranch, I just haven't made it up there since you arrived."

"I'm pleased to meet the woman who could put up with Gage," Cody said.

"Don't say that." Gage joined them. "I'm the underdog in my own house now. These two team up on me all the time."

"Excuse me if I don't feel sorry for you," Cody said, grinning at Maya.

"That's a beautiful ring," Bette said, nodding to the silver band on the third finger of Maya's left hand. "May I see?"

Maya held out her hand. The filigree band sparkled with brilliant pink and blue stones. "I wanted sometime simple, so Gage had it made. All the materials are from Colorado. The stones are Colorado rhodochrosite and aquamarine."

"It's gorgeous," Bette said.

"You should see the rings Travis and Lacy picked out," Maya said. "Gage and I went with them to pick them up."

"Sometimes my brother has good taste," Gage said. "Or maybe I should say Lacy has good taste."

"If you're saying something about me, it had better be good," Lacy said, as she pushed in between Gage and Cody, Travis right behind her.

"I was just telling them about your wedding rings," Maya said. "How beautiful they are."

"I'm really happy with them." Lacy looked at Travis. "You should show them to them when we get back to the ranch house."

Travis's brow furrowed. "Isn't that bad luck?" he asked. "To see the rings before the wedding?"

"That's the wedding gown," Lacy said. "And I want them to see them."

"All right," Travis said.

Emily joined them. "Everyone having a good time?" she asked.

"We are," Bette said. "This was a great idea."

"It was mine," Gage said.

Emily punched him. "It was not. It was mine."

"It was your idea to have a party," he said. "I suggested the sleighs."

"All right, I guess I'll give you that."

His expression sobered. "It's good to have a night off…from everything else."

A shiver ran up Bette's spine. For a little while, she had forgotten about the killer who was preying on women in the area. She imagined the thought of him seldom left Gage's and Travis's minds.

Maya slipped her arm into Gage's. "No work talk," she said. "We agreed."

"That's right." He raised his arms over his head and began clapping. Everyone turned to look at him. "Finish up the snacks, people," he said. "Part two of the evening's festivities are about to begin."

"What are we going to do now?" Bette asked, handing her cup to the man who came to collect it.

"Party games," Emily said. "You have your choice of cornhole or bowling." She held up a small beanbag and a plastic bowling pin.

Groans rose from around the room. "Don't be sticks in the mud," Emily said. "This will be fun." She began dividing them into teams. Bette found herself assigned as one of the cornhole players. The object was to pitch a small beanbag into a hole on a slanted board set up at the other end of the room. Cody was nowhere to be seen. *Coward*, she thought, as she hurled her first beanbag toward the game board, only to have it land in the floor only halfway to the target.

"I'm horrible at this!" she complained a few minutes later, after her third miss in a row. She gladly relinquished her beanbag to the next person in line and looked around for some avenue of escape.

Cody had emerged from hiding. He grabbed her hand and pulled her toward the door, where he helped her into her coat and slipped on his own. "Where are we going?" she asked.

"Just to get some fresh air." He glanced back toward the game players. "Unless you're dying for another turn at cornhole."

"No!" She zipped up the coat and slipped her hands into her gloves.

Outside, the first blast of icy air made her catch her breath and made her wonder at the wisdom of being out here. But when Cody set off around the side of the cabin, she hurried to catch up with his long strides. "Where are we going?" she asked. "It's freezing."

"I brought you out here to get warmed up."

"Cody, that sentence doesn't even make sense."

"Oh, no?" He pulled her to him and lowered his lips to hers.

She returned the kiss, slipping her arms inside his open coat and around his back. She loved that he was taller than her, but not too tall—exactly the right height for kissing. "Are you warm yet?" he asked, smiling down at her.

"I don't know." She wiggled against him. "Maybe you should try again."

He kissed her again, and she willingly lost herself

in the bliss of that moment, floating on a mix of desire and contentment and anticipation.

A burst of noise several minutes later made them jump apart. Cody glanced over her shoulder toward the front of the cabin, where light spilled onto the snow from the open front door. "I think everyone's getting ready to leave," he said.

"I guess we'd better go with them," she said.

"Or we could let them leave behind us and spend the night here by ourselves," he said.

"Right. But I didn't see a bed in that cabin, did you?" she said. "And the few chairs I spotted didn't look that comfortable."

"Home it is, then."

They loaded into the sleigh and Cody put his arm around Bette as they settled onto the back bench. She leaned her head on his shoulder and closed her eyes, half drowsing in his warmth and the magic of the moment. She wanted to sear times like this in her memory, stamping them over recollections of darker times in her life, when such bliss had seemed utterly unreachable— happiness so far from her grasp she couldn't even fantasize about it. Her life was so different now, and she never wanted to take even one moment for granted.

Back at the ranch house, everyone gathered in the great room, saying their goodbyes. "Don't go yet," Lacy said. "I promised to show you the rings. Travis, would you get them right quick?"

The sheriff headed out of the room and Lacy turned back to her guests. "We found this jeweler in Cheyenne who does these incredible Western designs—mostly belt buckles and things like that, but he does wedding rings, too. We had them made from the gold from melting down my grandmother's wedding ring and rings from both Travis's grandparents."

Travis rejoined them, but empty-handed. His face wore a pinched expression. "What's wrong?" Lacy clutched his arm. "Where are the rings?"

"I had them in the top drawer of my dresser," he said. "They're gone."

TRAVIS'S ANNOUNCEMENT SHIFTED the mood in the room. Everyone fell silent, looking at each other. Cody looked, too, examining the faces of those around him. Did anyone seem unsurprised by this news? Did anyone look guilty?

Lacy, white-faced but trying to maintain her composure, clutched Travis's arm. "Maybe they fell behind the dresser," she said. "Or you accidentally put them in another drawer."

Travis shook his head. "They were there this morning when I got dressed. Now they're gone."

"You mean someone came in and stole them?" Travis's mother stared at her son.

"I don't know, Mom," he said. "I don't know what else could have happened."

"It couldn't have been any of us," Maya said. "We were all together at the sleigh ride."

"It might have happened earlier today," Travis said. "The last time I saw the rings was this morning."

"This house is full of cops," Emily said. "You ought to be able to figure out who did it." She turned to the others. "In the meantime, the rest of you should go on home. Thank you for coming."

She and Lacy helped usher people out the door. Maya took Casey and Brenda with her, and Gage promised to catch a ride home later with Dwight. Then the law enforcement contingent—Travis, Gage, Dwight and Cody—gathered in a corner of the room. "I think you can rule out family," Dwight said. "Your mother and father and Emily, and, of course, Lacy wouldn't have any reason to take the rings."

"Maya and Brenda only came to the sleigh ride," Gage said. "They're out."

"All the employees have been with the family a long time," Travis said. "I'm not saying one of them didn't do it, but I can't think why."

"Doug Whittington hasn't been here that long, has he?" Cody asked.

"He has a record," Dwight said. "Though not for theft."

"There's someone else here who has a record," Gage said. "For robbery."

A chill ran through Cody. "I don't think Bette—"

"You don't know she wouldn't," Gage said. "None of us really know much about her. And she was working in the kitchen all day—right next to Travis's rooms."

Cody nodded. Gage was right. He couldn't let his personal feelings for Bette cloud the fact that on paper, at least, she looked like the ideal suspect. "How do you want to handle this?" he asked.

"I'll talk to Doug first," Travis said. "I think just you and me. He knows both of us, so that may put him more at ease."

"Do you want Dwight and me to talk to Bette?" Gage asked.

"Wait," Travis said. "Let's see what we hear from Doug first."

They found Doug and Rainey in the kitchen, washing cups and plates brought over from the cabin. Rainey turned when Travis and Cody entered the kitchen, but Doug remained hunched over the sink. "What can I do for you two?" she asked.

"We wanted to talk to Doug for a bit," Travis said. He crossed the room and opened the back door. "It won't take long."

Rainey dried her hands and started to remove her apron. "Just Doug," Cody said, and looked hard at the young man. It was a look that had induced many a suspect to be more cooperative, and it worked on Doug, as well. The young man tossed his dish towel on the drain board and followed Travis out the door, Cody close behind.

Outside, the cold bit through Cody's fleece pullover and jeans, and he noticed Doug was already shivering. Maybe that was part of Travis's plan. Instead of sweating the truth out of Doug, he planned to freeze it out of him. "What do you want?" Doug asked.

"Have you been in my room today?" Travis asked.

Doug blinked. "Your room? You mean your bedroom? Here?"

"Yes. Have you been there?"

Doug shook his head. "No. I never go in that part of the house. I mean, why would I?"

"Have you seen a couple of rings I had in there?" Travis continued. "Gold wedding rings."

"No. I told you, I don't go in there. I keep to the kitchen and the dining room and my room. Mom was real clear about that when I moved here."

"Have you seen anyone else in or near Travis's room?" Cody asked.

"Is something missing?" Doug asked. "Is that why you're asking all these questions?"

"Have you seen anyone near Travis's room?" Cody asked again.

He hesitated, then said. "I think I saw that Bette woman. Not in your room, but in the hall just outside of it."

He was lying. Everything in his manner—the shifting eyes, the defensive hunch of the shoulders, as if he was expecting a blow, told Cody his words were a lie. Did Travis see it?

"What time was this?" Travis asked.

"I don't know. This afternoon. She was supposed to be in the kitchen, baking. Mom had told me to stay out of her way. So I thought it was strange she was in the hall in that part of the house."

"Where were you when you saw her?" Cody asked.

Another long pause. "I was just, you know, crossing the great room. I thought I might have left my gloves in there."

"Why would you have left your gloves in there if you never go in there?" Cody asked.

Doug flushed. "I didn't say I never go in there."

"Thank you, Doug. You can go back in now."

The young man left them. As soon as the door closed behind him, Cody turned to Travis. "He's lying," he said.

"Maybe." Travis turned and walked around the side of the house.

"Where are you going?" Cody asked, hurrying after him.

"Let's talk to Bette."

The light over the door to her cabin was lit, and Bette

opened the door within seconds of Travis's knock. She was very pale, her lips in a tight line, and she wouldn't meet Cody's gaze. "Come in," she said. "I've been expecting you."

The two men filed in. Bette sat on the edge of the bed—just as she had last night. Cody took the same chair he had used last night, too, while Travis remained standing. "We're asking everyone what they know about the missing rings," the sheriff began.

"You asked Doug," she said. "Now you're asking me. That's not everyone. Just the people with prison records."

Travis didn't react to this accusation. "Do you know anything about the missing rings?" he asked.

"No. I'm not a thief. The bank job—that was one time. And it was stupid. Something I'll regret the rest of my life. But it doesn't matter to you how many times I say I'm sorry, does it? People like you are going to blame me for the rest of my life." Her voice broke on the last words, and Cody had to curl his fingers into his palms to keep from reaching for her. He pushed away the emotion here, freezing it out. Bette wasn't his lover right now—she was a suspect.

"Someone said they saw you near my room this afternoon," Travis said.

"Who said that?" she asked. "Rainey or Doug? They both hate me. They'd say anything to get me into trouble."

"Why do they hate you?" Travis said. "You didn't know them before you came here, did you?"

"No," she said. "Lacy said Rainey was upset that she wasn't chosen to cater the wedding, so maybe this is all part of that resentment. Some people are like that, building grudges into rage."

"I've known Rainey a long time," Travis said. "She gets upset at people, but she's not a liar."

Bette said nothing, merely stared at him.

"Were you in my room at any time today?" Travis asked.

"No," she said. "I've never been in your room. And I didn't take the rings. I didn't even know about the rings."

"Lacy didn't mention them to you when the two of you were talking about the wedding?" he asked.

"No," she said. "I mean, I assumed there would be rings, but we never discussed them."

"Beyond their monetary value, they have a great deal of sentimental value," Travis said. "Especially to Lacy."

"I know. But I didn't take them. I wouldn't do something like that. I would certainly never hurt the person who is my best friend in the world."

"Do you know anyone else who might have taken them?" Travis asked. "Have you seen anyone suspicious in the house?"

"No. I'm sorry, I don't."

Travis glanced around the cabin. "Do you mind if we take a look?"

"You want to search my cabin?" She stood, face flushed, eyes bright with tears. "You mistrust me that much?" This last question was directed at Cody.

"You don't have to submit to a search," Cody said. "But doing so is the quickest way to establish your innocence."

"Oh, sure, because you couldn't just believe me or anything simple like that." She threw up her hands.

"Go ahead. Rifle through my belongings. You won't find a ring."

The look she gave him made Cody feel black inside. Whatever the two of them might have started last night, it had ended now. He turned away, to Travis. "Where do you want to start?"

Chapter Eleven

They found the rings in Bette's cosmetic case, the box wrapped in a piece of tissue and stuffed beneath tubes of lipstick, mascara and eyeliner. When Travis showed it to her, she went so white Cody poised to catch her, thinking she might faint.

She shook her head. "No." She covered her mouth but couldn't hold back a sob. "I swear on my mother's grave, I don't know how that got there." She looked at Cody. "You believe me, don't you?"

His throat hurt as he tried to get the words out that she needed to hear—that yes, he believed her. Of course he knew she wouldn't take the rings.

But he had spent years training to believe what was right before his eyes. He dealt daily in evidence and rules of law based on hard facts, not emotions. So, though his heart wanted him to say the words, it couldn't overrule his head.

Travis slipped the ring box into his pocket. "Are you going to arrest me?" Bette asked.

"As long as the pass is closed, you can't go anywhere," Travis said. "I don't want to upset Lacy, so for now we'll leave this, while I investigate further."

She sank to the bed again, face buried in her hands.

As Cody followed Travis out of the cabin, her sobs hit him like blows. He didn't even feel the cold as they walked toward the house, but when Travis stopped on the porch and turned to him, Cody said, "If that was the right thing to do, why do I feel so awful?"

"Do you think she took the rings?" Travis asked.

"It doesn't matter what I think," Cody said. "We have a witness who said he saw her outside your room this afternoon, and we have the rings in her possession."

"And we have her record."

"Yeah. And we have her record."

Travis pulled out the ring box and looked at it. "I don't think she was faking her shock when we found the ring box."

"Maybe she thought she'd hidden it too well," Cody said.

"It was a lousy hiding place," Travis said. "And she could have put up more of a fuss about us searching. She's been in the system, so she knows her rights. She could have insisted we get a warrant. But she didn't."

"She's right that Doug and Rainey resent her," Cody said.

He nodded. "But if she didn't take the rings, how did someone get into her room?"

"Is there more than one key to those cabins?"

"Yes. There are at least two—maybe three," Travis said.

"Do a lot of people know where they're kept?"

"They're in my dad's office," Travis said. "But it isn't locked. Anyone could get in there."

"This isn't the first time someone may have been in Bette's cabin while she wasn't there," Cody said.

"Oh?"

Cody glanced at the cabin door. "Can we go inside to discuss this? I'm freezing out here."

Travis blinked. Cody thought his friend probably hadn't even noticed the cold until now. "Sure. We'll go into my office."

"Travis!" Lacy called from her seat by the fire when he and Cody entered. He waved her off and led the way across the room to his office.

Cody sank into the cowhide-covered chair and let the warmth of the room wash over him. Travis sat behind the desk. "Bette thinks someone has been in her cabin before?" he asked. "Why didn't she say anything to me or my parents or Lacy about this? How do you know about it?"

"She didn't want to upset your family," Cody said. "She felt they had enough to worry about, what with the upcoming wedding and a serial killer running around. Also, I think she didn't want to call attention to herself or get any kind of reputation as a complainer or a troublemaker. She didn't tell me that, but that's the impression I get."

"That answers part of my question," Travis said. "When did someone go into Bette's cabin, and how do you know about it and I don't?"

"It happened the first night she was here," Cody said. "I walked her to her cabin—mine is the one next to hers. Someone had painted the words *Go Home* in red paint on her door. She washed it off before anyone else could see, and she made me promise not to tell anyone."

"That's still outside her cabin," Travis said. "You said someone was inside."

"I'm getting to that," he said. "The next night I walked her back again, and this time, I went inside.

While I was there, I used the bathroom, and when I opened the cabinet to get a towel to dry my hands, I saw a can of red paint and a brush there."

Travis waited, a skeptical look on his face. "I didn't say anything about it to her," Cody said. "I even played with the idea that Bette had painted the door herself, but I couldn't figure out why she would do something like that. If it was a ploy to call attention to herself, it failed, because I was the only one who saw."

He shifted in the chair. "Later—after her accident, when we were talking—I asked her about it and she said she hadn't seen the can of paint in the cabinet until she was getting ready to take a shower the next morning. She thinks someone was in her cabin while she was out—someone who had a key."

Travis considered this. "So that same someone could have taken the rings and planted them in Bette's cabin, knowing she would be a suspect in the theft, because of her past."

"Right," Cody said. "Except who would do that, and why? Would Doug and Rainey really go to so much trouble to get rid of her? Would they take such personal risk just so they could cater your wedding? It doesn't make sense."

"No. Is there anyone else who might want to get rid of Bette?"

"Whoever attacked her on the road," Cody said.

"If that's the case, her attacker wasn't the Ice Cold Killer," Travis said.

"Did your investigation of Lauren Grenado's murder turn up any new evidence?" Cody asked, grateful for a momentary shift of focus.

"Nothing so far." Travis sat back, the chair creaking

underneath his weight. "The business cards are generic cardstock available at pretty much any office supply or craft store and online. The printer is a laser printer—we don't have the expertise to determine a particular brand. The duct tape, again, is a brand that is sold by the millions in hardware stores and home improvement centers. We checked with the stores here in town that sell it, but their records haven't turned up anyone suspicious making a purchase. We've turned up some hairs and fibers from the vehicles, but we're still waiting on test results from the ones we were able to get to the lab before the road closed. No fingerprints. No DNA. No other physical evidence to speak of."

"Is this killer that skilled, or just that lucky?" Cody asked.

"Maybe both," Travis said. "I'm still hanging on to my theory that we're looking for two people, not one. The speed of the crimes points to that. It takes time to subdue and secure a conscious victim and, except for Fiona, the evidence points to the women being conscious until they're killed. Fiona was hit on the head with a rock, but that may be because it was the most public of the killings, and therefore necessitated silencing her immediately."

"And no suspects?" Cody asked.

"There are always suspects," Travis said. "I have a couple I want to interview again tomorrow, if you want to come with me."

"Yes." Cody sat up straighter. He had been dying to have more of a role in the case.

"I'd be interested in getting your perspective on these guys," Travis said.

"What are you going to do about Bette?" Cody asked.

"You two are friends," Travis said. "Talk to her. Feel her out on this theory that someone planted the ring. See if she can come up with possibilities."

"I'll talk to her," Cody said. Though he doubted the friendship they had been building could ever be repaired after tonight. She thought he had betrayed her.

Part of him thought that, too.

"I THINK IT would be better if I didn't cater your wedding," Bette said to Lacy as she pulled her aside after breakfast the next morning. She had lain awake half the night agonizing over what she should do. Travis was willing to let her walk around free for now, but his accusations had cast a pall over what was supposed to be a happy occasion.

"What are you talking about?" Lacy stared at her, confusion filling her hazel eyes.

"After what happened last night, I don't think it would be right for me to have a role in the wedding." Bette twisted her hands together, determined to remain businesslike and not upset her friend more than she had to. "Travis doesn't trust me and I would never, ever want to come between you two."

"What are you talking about, silly?" Lacy took Bette's hand and pulled her down onto the sofa beside her. The two were alone in the great room. "What makes you think Travis doesn't trust you?"

"He thinks I stole your wedding rings."

Lacy's eyes widened. "He does not!" Lacy put her arm around her friend. "He found the rings last night," she said. "He'd misplaced them, that's all."

Bette couldn't look at her friend. Travis must have

told Lacy that lie to protect her. He certainly hadn't done it to save Bette.

"I don't want anyone else catering my wedding," Lacy said. "Besides, you've worked so hard already. Those cream puffs and tea cakes you made yesterday were divine, by the way. I know people don't come to weddings for the food, but my guests are going to be blown away by your dishes. Besides, where do you think I'd get a caterer this close to the wedding?"

"Rainey and Doug could do it."

Lacy snorted. "Please! If I wanted to serve steak and potatoes and apple pie, they'd do a fine job. But I don't want that."

"Travis would probably like it," Bette said.

"He'd love it. But he'll like your food, too. He's not as hidebound as he comes across sometimes."

Last night in her cabin, the sheriff had been as unbending as steel. Obviously, Lacy knew another side of him.

"Come on," Lacy said, patting Bette's back. "You need to get away from the ranch for a while. Let's go to town and poke around in some of the cute shops and have lunch."

"All right," Bette said. "While we're there, I need to stop by the store and get some more cream."

"Didn't you just buy some?" Lacy asked. Before Bette could reply, she laughed. "I probably shouldn't have eaten so many of those cream puffs last night— cream puffs, indeed. They'll probably go straight to my hips. Let me get my purse and we'll go right now. I'll meet you by the car."

Bette trudged through the snow to her cabin, torn over what to do next. She had thought to spare her friend pain by resigning from the catering job and quietly fading away. She could find some place in town to stay until the pass opened again. She would have to let Travis know her new address, of course. Otherwise, he might think she was trying to leave town to escape charges.

Was he going to press charges? Should she try to find a lawyer to represent her? The idea dragged at her like a lead coat. She had thought she was past ever having to deal with lawyers and courts and prison again. Yet here she was, being sucked right back into that life. Maybe the real reason so many people returned to prison wasn't that they went back to a life of crime, but because everyone around them assumed they were guilty whenever anything bad happened.

She tried to push these worries aside and focus on having a good time with Lacy. As her friend drove, she chattered happily about the upcoming bridesmaids' tea, the wedding, honeymoon plans and all the things that should capture a bride's attention. Bette listened and nodded and faked enthusiasm. Whatever happened, she was determined it wouldn't spoil Lacy's happiness. She believed Travis wanted that, too, which meant he would do what he could to avoid making a big scene. For now, she would try to be thankful for that small consideration.

Eagle Mountain, with its beautiful setting and access to hiking, skiing, Jeeping and other outdoor activities, catered to tourists. The town's main street was lined with shops selling everything from antiques to climbing equipment to T-shirts. Bette and Lacy spent the morning admiring the clothing in the boutiques and the decorative items in gift shops. Bette even purchased a ceramic chicken designed to hold a recipe card or ingredients list in its beak. She hoped after she left here the item would remind her of her friend—and not the sad way they had parted.

As they headed into the Cake Walk Café for lunch, Lacy hugged Bette. "I'm so glad you could be here for my wedding," she said. "You are one of the dearest people in the world to me. I don't know if I would have survived those years in prison without you."

Bette returned the hug, struggling for composure. "You would have survived," she said. "You're a lot tougher than you look."

Inside, they took a table by the window, looking out onto the town's main street. Tall berms of snow formed a wall on each side of the pavement, and long icicles hung from the eaves, the sun highlighting intricate ice crystals. Under happier circumstances, the effect would have been magical.

After they had ordered, Bette said, "I always knew you were innocent of the charges against you."

"How did you know?" Lacy asked.

"The man who died—your boss?"

"Andy Stenson."

"He was stabbed, right?"

Lacy nodded.

"I couldn't see you doing that—ever," Bette said. "You're just not that type. You don't have a hair-trigger temper. You don't get frustrated easily. If you didn't like your boss, you would quit and find another job. You wouldn't kill him."

"No, I wouldn't."

Bette picked up the paper cover from the straw in her glass and began tying it in knots. "I don't mean to bring up a painful subject," she said. "But what Travis did to you—accusing you of murder and sending you to prison—it was so awful."

"Yes."

"You used to talk about how much you hated him. And now it's easy to see how much you love him. What happened to change that?"

Lacy traced a line of condensation down the side of her water glass with one finger. "I guess I learned to see past my anger to Travis himself," she said. "To the kind of man he really is. He arrested me not because he disliked me personally, but because he believed at the time that it was the right thing to do. A man had been killed and he believed the man's family—his widow, Brenda—deserved justice. That's not just an abstract term to Travis. He really believes in it. Which is why, when he found evidence that proved I was innocent, he did everything in his power to see that I was released, and the real killer apprehended."

The tender expression on Lacy's face when she spoke of her fiancé made Bette feel teary again. Or maybe that was just her general state of mind today. She touched her friend's hand. "You're a very lucky woman."

Lacy nodded. "I am."

Bette frowned. "Did you say the murdered man's widow was Brenda? Is that Dwight's wife?"

Lacy nodded. "Brenda Prentice was Brenda Stenson. It's kind of crazy, all the connections. But that's part of life in a small town."

"And she never held her husband's death against you?" Bette asked.

"I don't think so." Lacy squeezed her hand. "Forgiveness is a really powerful thing."

After lunch, they headed to the grocery store to buy

the cream Bette needed. As they headed up an aisle from the dairy section toward the cash registers, they had to squeeze past a tall gray-haired man, his shoulders hunched. He turned to look at them and Bette gasped and stepped back.

The man grinned. "Hello, Bette," he said. "Somebody told me you were here in town. Small world, isn't it?"

Bette grabbed Lacy's hand and pulled her toward the cash register. She all but threw her money at the startled clerk and hurried out of the store.

Lacy caught up with her in the parking lot. "What was all that about?" she asked, a little breathless.

"Let's just go." Bette tugged at the handle of the locked passenger door on Lacy's car.

"All right." Lacy unlocked the car and slid into the driver's seat.

Bette leaned back against the seat, trying to control her breathing. She watched the exit of the store to see if the man followed them out, but he did not.

"Who was that back there in the store?" Lacy asked as she turned onto Main Street. "Why did he frighten you?"

"I knew him as Carl. Just Carl. No last name." She shook her head. "He was a friend of Eddie's. He was one of the bank robbers."

"Oh," Lacy said, the one syllable full of understanding. "What is he doing in Eagle Mountain?"

"I don't know."

Lacy pulled the car to the curb and stopped. "I guess I understand why seeing him would have been a surprise, but why are you so terrified? I mean, you're trembling."

Bette clenched her hands in her lap. "I guess I—he

was a really good friend of Eddie's. I thought, maybe Eddie sent him after me."

"Why would Eddie do that?" Lacy asked.

"Eddie threatened to kill me if I told the police anything about the robbery and any of the people in it," Bette said. "Of course, I testified at my trial about what I knew. Everyone but the getaway driver had already been arrested and the police had more than enough evidence to convict them. Nothing I said added to that. But Eddie might not have seen it that way."

Lacy turned off the car and unbuckled her seat belt. "We need to tell Travis this right away," she said. "That man may be the one who attacked you the other day."

Bette looked over and realized they were parked in front of the sheriff's department. The last person she wanted to see right now was Travis Walker. But Lacy was right. Carl might be the key to the whole crazy mess she was in.

Chapter Twelve

"Tell me about these guys we're going to talk to," Cody said as he rode with Travis toward town. All the coffee he'd drunk at breakfast in an attempt to be more alert after a sleepless night had left him wired and jittery. He welcomed this expedition to interview two suspects as a distraction from thoughts of Bette.

"Alex Woodruff and Tim Dawson," Travis said. "They're undergraduates at Colorado State University, where Emily is doing her graduate studies. She knows them casually. Their story is that they came up here to ice climb and got stranded when the road closed earlier this month. They're staying at a vacation cabin that belongs to Tim's aunt."

"Does their story check out?" Cody asked.

"I didn't have any luck getting in touch with the aunt, but the cabin is registered to her. They are students and they do climb."

"Why are they suspects in the murders?" Cody asked.

"They can't account for their whereabouts when the first two women—Kelly Farrow and Christy O'Brien—were killed. They were at the ranch the day Fiona Winslow died. I want to ask them what they were up to the night Lauren Grenado was murdered."

"There are two of them and you think two men are responsible for the murders," Cody said.

"I don't have enough evidence to get a warrant to search their property, or to request hair and DNA samples to look for a match to what we've got," Travis said. "All I can do is keep a close eye on them."

The cabin where the students were staying was outside town, on a snow-packed Forest Service road. When Travis pulled up to the square log building with a rusting metal roof, it was clear the driveway hadn't been plowed since the last storm. The windows of the house were dark and no vehicle sat under the attached carport. "Looks like no one's been home in a while," Cody said.

"Let's take a look."

Crossing to the house meant post-holing through thigh-deep snow. Cody followed Travis, instinctively taking up position behind and to the right of him, one hand on his Glock. The house might look deserted, but someone inside could be watching their approach, ready to ambush them when they got closer.

But no gunfire or other noise greeted them as they stepped onto the porch. The shades were drawn over the windows and the door locked. Cody looked around. Snow had settled and crusted over the firewood pile and an old bucket that sat overturned near the carport. "I don't think anything here has been disturbed in a while," he said.

"They must have gone back to Fort Collins when the road opened up." Travis turned away and headed back toward his SUV. "I'll contact the university and the police in Fort Collins and double-check with them."

Back in the SUV, Travis put the vehicle in gear and turned back toward town. "Depending on when they left town, they couldn't have killed Lauren Grenado," he said.

"That place looks like it's been empty more than a couple of days," Cody said.

Travis nodded. "On one hand, it's good to rule out innocent men."

"On the other, it bites not having a good suspect for the murders," Cody said.

"I need to stop by the office, if you don't mind hanging out there awhile," Travis said.

"No problem." Cody stretched. "I'm desperate enough for work I'll even fill out reports for you."

As they approached the sheriff's department, Travis said, "That looks like Lacy's car parked out front."

"What did she say when you told her about the rings?" Cody asked.

"I didn't." Travis sighed. "I knew it would upset her terribly if I told her about Bette, so I pretended I had found the rings in another drawer. I don't like to lie to her, but I couldn't think what else to do."

"You don't know that Bette took the rings."

"I don't. And maybe because of what happened with Lacy—that wrongful conviction—I'm more inclined than most to give a person the benefit of the doubt. There are a lot of things about what happened last night that don't quite fit."

He drove around behind the station and parked, then he and Cody entered through a back door. Adelaide met them in the hallway. "Sheriff, Lacy and—"

"Thanks, Addy. I saw Lacy's car out front. I assume she's in my office." He moved past the older woman.

Cody nodded to Adelaide, and followed Travis into his office.

He stopped short when he saw not only Lacy, but Bette, seated in front of Travis's desk. Both women looked upset about something.

Travis moved behind his desk. "Close the door," he said to Cody, then turned to Lacy. "What's wrong? Has something happened?"

Lacy looked to Bette. She pressed her lips together, as if debating whether to speak, then said, "I saw a man in the grocery store just now—one of the other bank robbers. It...it frightened me. I don't know why he's here."

"What this man's name?" Travis asked.

"Carl. I just know him as Carl."

Travis turned to his laptop. As he typed, Cody watched Bette, willing her to look at him. But she kept her head down, staring at her clasped hands in her lap.

"Carl Wayland," Travis said after a moment. "He was released from the Englewood Federal Correctional Facility six months ago. This was his second conviction for armed robbery, and he has a record of a few other lesser crimes—auto theft, one count of menacing. He took a plea bargain in the bank robbery case, thus the lighter sentence."

"What is he doing in Eagle Mountain?" Lacy asked.

"What do you think, Bette?" Travis asked.

Bette shook her head. "I don't know."

"Did he recognize you also?" Travis asked. "How did he behave?"

"Oh, he recognized me. He smiled and said someone had told him I was here." She looked ill. "I don't know, it just struck me as if...as if he had been looking for me."

"Do you think he's the person who attacked you on the road?" Cody asked.

"I don't know. I still can't remember anything about that attack."

"Did he say anything else?" Travis asked. "How long he's been in town, where he was staying—anything?"

"No. I didn't give him a chance to say anything else. I just left."

"Have you been in touch with him, or with anyone else who was part of that robbery, at any time since your release?" Travis asked.

"No! I don't want anything to do with any of them."

"Have any of them tried to contact you? Any phone calls? Letters? Other encounters?"

"No. Never."

Travis angled the computer toward the women to show a mug shot of a man in his fifties with thinning gray hair and a wispy gray goatee. "Does he still look like this?" he asked.

"Yes," they chorused.

"He was wearing a black leather jacket," Lacy said. "And jeans."

Travis swiveled the computer back around. "I'll find him and try to learn what he's doing here."

Lacy took Bette's hand. "Come on," she said. "Let's go back to the ranch. Travis will take care of this now."

Bette rose and the two women left the office. When they were gone, Travis looked up from the laptop again. "What do you think?" he asked Cody.

"I think Bette is terrified of this man. And I think she's telling the truth."

"I think so, too." He stood. "Come on. Let's go see if we can find Carl."

"He's not going to admit it if he is after Bette."

"No. But we might be able to warn him off. A con with a record like his might think twice about going after a woman who's under the protection of a couple of cops."

"I like the way you think." He followed Travis back outside, the image of Bette's terrified white face haunting him. In all the time they had been in the office together, she had never once looked at him. It was as if he no longer existed for her. That hurt worse than if she had stabbed him in the heart.

WHEN BETTE AND Lacy returned from town, Lacy insisted on going over the seating list for the wedding reception, as well as reviewing the menu for both the reception and the bridesmaids' tea. Bette knew her friend was trying to distract her from her worries, and she was grateful for the attempt, but nothing could make her forget for long the shock of seeing Carl standing in the aisle in the grocery store in Eagle Mountain.

What was he doing here, unless he had somehow followed her? A man like Carl wouldn't have any business in a small town like Eagle Mountain. She kept going over and over the events of the day she had been attacked. Had Carl been in the grocery store that day, too? Had he followed her back to the ranch?

But if Carl was targeting her, why would he do so? The bank robbery had occurred almost nine years ago. Bette had been out of prison eight months. If Eddie had been serious about exacting revenge for her testimony at his trial, surely he would have acted long before now.

Still, it seemed too much of a coincidence that Carl should be in Eagle Mountain, just when so many bad things had happened to her. Had Carl stolen Lacy's and Travis's wedding rings and hidden them in her cabin? She shook her head. That didn't make sense, either. Carl would have kept the rings for himself. From what she remembered, he had a taste for theft. He had even bragged about things he had stolen, the way other men might boast about their times in a marathon or deals they had closed at work. Then again, theft was Carl's work. As far as Bette knew, he had never held a legitimate job—something he had in common with Eddie, though she hadn't realized it at the time.

She was still pondering all this when Travis and Cody returned to the ranch. Everyone else had finished supper, so the two men ate the food Rainey had saved for them and recounted their afternoon's work. "We tracked Carl to the motel in town," Travis said. "But by the time we got there, he had checked out."

"He registered under the name of Charlie Fergusen and paid cash," Cody said. "But the clerk recognized him when we showed her his photograph."

"She says he checked in two days ago," Travis said. "Shortly after the road closed. He said he was passing through and got stranded."

Bette's heart sank. "If he's not at the motel, where is he?" she asked.

"Is the road open again?" Lacy asked.

"Nope." Travis finished the last bite of roast beef. "Which means he found somewhere else to stay. Maybe he heard we were looking for him."

"Or he figured since Bette and Lacy saw him, it was time to hide out," Cody said.

"Every one of my deputies has his description and photograph and will be watching for him," Travis said.

"So do all the ranch hands. He won't get near the ranch without us knowing."

"Thank you," Bette said. "I… I don't know what to say. If I brought this trouble to you and your family—"

"You didn't do anything wrong," Travis said. "If this man intends to cause trouble, that's on him." His eyes met hers. "You're my guest and my wife's friend. I'm going to make sure you're protected. I'm sorry if I didn't make that clear before."

Bette read the determination and sincerity in his eyes and in that moment thought she knew what Lacy saw in this serious, quiet lawman. She nodded and turned away, aware as she did so of Cody watching her, just as he had watched her in Travis's office. He was serious and quiet, too, but harder for her to interpret than the sheriff. How could he have made such passionate love to her one night, and stood by saying nothing while Travis accused her of taking those rings? Whatever feelings he had for her, they weren't enough to overcome his suspicions—or his desire to look good in front of his friend. He wasn't that different from Eddie, really— the kind of man who would always put his own best interests ahead of any woman.

Chapter Thirteen

Bette returned to her cabin after breakfast the next morning, and found Cody waiting on the front porch.

He rose from the chair where he had been sitting. "I wanted to talk to you," he said.

She did not want to talk to him. What could she possibly say to him? When he refused to defend her to Travis, she had known what people meant when they talked about a broken heart. It had felt that way, that night in her cabin, a great, tearing pain in her chest.

"You shouldn't be here," she said. "I don't have anything to say—" She stopped, the incongruity of his presence here hitting her. "How did you get in here?" she asked. "I locked the door when I went to breakfast."

He held up a key, identical to the one in her hand. "There are at least three of them for every cabin," he said. "In a box in the drawer of Mr. Walker's desk, where anyone can help himself."

She shut the door behind her and sat on the side of the bed, while he once more took the chair she had almost begun to think of as his. "Why do they have so many keys?" she asked.

"When they built the cabins, they had the idea to rent them out to tourists—sort of a cowboy guest ranch," he said. "They had multiple keys made so that they could give out more than one if, say, a couple stayed in a cabin, and in case someone lost a key."

"How did you find out about the keys?"

"I asked Travis. And I told him about the paint on your door and the paint you found in the bathroom. I know you didn't want me to say anything about that, but I wanted him to know it was possible someone got into your cabin—using a spare key—and planted those rings there."

She eyed him warily. Cody had actually defended her? And Travis had listened? "Did he believe you?"

"He was open to the possibility."

Do you believe me? But she had too much pride to ask the question. "So I know how you got in," she said. "What are you doing here?"

"I came to ask you to go ice fishing with me."

She definitely hadn't seen that one coming. "Ice fishing?"

"Yes. There's a lake on Forest Service land near here that Nate Hall assures me has good fishing. We can use one of the snowmobiles to get there." He actually looked excited about the idea.

"Why would I want to go ice fishing?" she asked. "With you?"

"It's a beautiful day. And I don't want to go fishing by myself."

"Then ask Travis or one of the ranch hands to go with you." She folded her arms across her chest. "Or is this your idea of keeping an eye on me—trailing after me like you trail after one of the fugitives you intend to apprehend?"

He flinched, but she couldn't feel very victorious

about the hit. Sitting here with him, in such familiar postures, made her ache for what they had had between them. How perverse was it that she could hate him— and at the same time want to jump his body? She stood. "You need to leave."

He stood also, but instead of moving toward the door, he moved toward her. "Look," he said. "I'm sorry about the other night. You don't want to hear it, but I am."

"You didn't even try to defend me!" She couldn't keep the words back, or the venom behind them. "You stood there while he accused me of a horrible betrayal of my best friend, and you wouldn't even look at me. And you helped him paw through my things, as if I was some common criminal—because that's all that I am to you."

"Bette, no." He took her by the arms. She tried to pull away, but he held on, gentle, yet unyielding. "Look at me," he said.

She looked, and was surprised to see pain in his eyes. "I'm a cop," he said. "It's what I do. What I've trained to do for years. That night, I wasn't here as your lover, I was here as a cop. I had to put aside emotion and consider the evidence as dispassionately as possible."

"So I didn't matter at all—only the evidence."

"That's what I've been taught." He slid his hands down, until they encircled her wrists, his touch burning into her. "But I learned something important that night."

She couldn't help it, he mesmerized her. This must be what the mouse felt before it was swallowed by the viper. "What did you learn?"

"That I'm not the stone-cold, by-the-book cop I always thought I was. You do matter. And it didn't make any difference what my brain told me when I looked at the evidence, my heart shouted something different.

That's why I told Travis about the paint, and went looking for the key."

She wanted to believe him, more than she had ever wanted to believe anyone. Her gaze shifted to his lips, and she leaned in closer, wanting to feel their touch, to taste him, to breathe him in and...

She pulled away. "I don't know if I can trust you," she said.

"I understand that. But come fishing with me today anyway."

"Why?"

"Because you're smart. And I'm smart, too. And I think the two of us can figure this out. Whoever put those rings in your cabin wanted to get you into trouble. I figure if we spend some time away from the ranch and all the tension here, just the two of us doing something mindless like fishing, it might come to us how and why they did it—and maybe even who."

He released her wrists and stepped back. "The Walkers are having a new lock put on your cabin today," he said. "With only one key, which they'll give to you. It would be a good idea if you got away for a few hours so they can do the work."

"So I guess I might as well come with you," she said. "But just so you know—fish are the only thing you're going to catch today."

The lines around his eyes tightened, and she wondered if he was trying not to laugh at her. "Understood."

APPARENTLY, ICE FISHING required donning a pair of thick insulated coveralls and round-toed insulated rubber boots that made prison uniforms look like high fashion, and a helmet that weighed as much as a Thanksgiving turkey. "Are we going fishing or visiting the moon?" Bette asked when she was thus dressed.

"You don't want to get cold, do you?" Cody asked.

"Why would anyone want to do anything where you have to dress like this?" she asked, as she climbed onto the back of the snowmobile he had parked in front of her cabin.

"Because it's fun."

"Standing around a hole in the ice waiting for a fish to get hungry enough to eat a worm does not sound like my idea of fun," she said.

"Sure it is." He climbed on the snowmobile in front of her and punched the button to start the engine. It roared to life, shaking every part of her. "Hang on!" he shouted over the rumbling noise, then they shot forward.

She clung to him, her heart in her throat, but after a few hundred yards she began to relax a little and enjoy the sensation of racing over the snow. Cody whooped and steered the machine through the trees, which sped by in a blur of white and green. They roared up an incline, then plunged across an iced-over creek. It was like riding a motorcycle, only better, since they didn't have to follow a road. They could pick any path they liked over the deep snow, though she realized after a while that Cody was following orange markers blazed on the trees.

Half an hour or so later, he slowed the machine. He gestured toward a frozen lake in the distance, the ice a blue mirror reflecting the surrounding evergreens. After a few minutes, the lake disappeared from view. Cody halted the snowmobile in a clearing. Bette's ears rang in the sudden silence. They climbed off the snowmobile and removed their helmets. "You know how they say getting there is half the fun?" she asked.

"Yeah," he said.

"I think in this case, it was all the fun." She grinned. "That was a blast."

"You've never been on a snowmobile before?"

"No."

"Then after we're done fishing I'll take you the long way home."

"I want to drive," she said.

"No." He pocketed the keys. "You just told me you've never even been on one of these things before."

"I'm a quick learner. Besides, how hard could it be? They rent them to tourists."

He opened a compartment on the back of the snowmobile and took out some disassembled fishing poles, a tackle box, two plastic buckets and what looked like an oversize drill. He fitted the sections of the poles together, handed the poles and tackle to her, then shouldered the drill and picked up the buckets. "What is that thing on your shoulder?" she asked.

"Ice auger. We just have to hike through those trees and up that little rise to reach the lakeshore." He strode toward the trees and she tromped through the snow after him. As the woods thinned, the lake came into view once more, heavy snow on its shore giving way to thick ice. Out on the ice, Cody lowered the auger. "As soon as I drill a hole with this, we can fish," he said.

"Excuse me if I don't stand around watching," she said. She returned to shore and began following a trail around the edge. Hoofprints in the snow showed where deer had walked along the edge of the lake, perhaps searching for open water to drink. She couldn't see the snowmobile from here, which made her feel all the more isolated. When she had gone some ways, she turned and looked back toward Cody. He was attacking the ice with the auger, all his concentration on the task.

I'm a cop. It's what I do. What did that mean—to be a cop? If someone had asked her that question a year ago, when she was still in prison, she would have said cops went after people who committed crimes—and a lot of people who didn't. She would have pointed out that cops too often locked someone up because it was easy to make a case against them, and that they were more interested in cadging free doughnuts from the coffee shop than finding out the truth.

There were still some cops like that, she believed. But there was another kind, too. Travis had worked hard to get to the truth and free Lacy, long before she fell in love with him. His brother, Gage, seemed to be a man who tried to do what was right.

Then there was Cody—who had refrained from killing a desperate man, only to have that man commit suicide right in front of him. The pain she had seen in his eyes when he had told her that story, and the pain she recognized when he had apologized to her, had been real, mirroring her own hurt. She believed he was trying to see past the evidence and his training to her innocence. But was that going to be enough?

He set aside the auger, then spotted her and motioned her to come back to him. She retraced her steps around the pond and out onto the ice. He handed her a fishing pole, then turned one of the buckets upside down and set it beside the hole. "Make yourself comfortable and drop your line in," he said.

She sat on the bucket and plopped the end of the

weighted line into the water, where it sank out of sight. Cody sat on the other bucket beside her. "Isn't this fun?" she said, heavy on the sarcasm.

"It's a beautiful day," Cody said. "We're out in the fresh air, we might catch some fish for supper and we're alone."

Right. Alone at last. "Then let's talk about who stole those wedding rings and put them in my cabin," she said.

"Almost anyone at the ranch could have taken the key from Mr. Walker's desk and let himself into your cabin," Cody said. "Just as many people had access to Travis's bedroom, where he kept the rings."

"It would be easier on everyone if the thief wasn't someone on the ranch, but an outsider," Bette said. Another reason suspicion had focused on her.

"Someone like Carl Wayland," Cody said.

"Yes, but I don't see how Carl—or Charlie, or whatever name he's going by these days—could have slipped into the house unnoticed, taken the key and the wedding rings and stashed them in my cabin," she said. "There are always too many people around. Besides, why carry out such a complicated plot to implicate me?"

"I agree," Cody said. "I still think Doug or Rainey is the most likely candidate for that, though I can't think why. Even given that they're jealous of you, or want to cater the wedding themselves, that kind of behavior doesn't make sense. They risk too much for too little gain."

"I agree," Bette said.

"Is there someone else who wants you away from the ranch, but is being more subtle about it?" Cody asked. "Do you have an ex-lover among the ranch hands? Or someone you double-crossed in prison who wants to get back at you? Are you the long-lost daughter of the duke who has come to claim her birthright and the family fortune?"

She laughed. "I guess those theories made as much sense as anything I can come up with."

His expression grew more serious. "Let's put aside the ring theft for a while. What about the person who attacked you with the big rock on your way home from town? Still no memory of that?"

"No. I'm wondering if I should try being hypnotized or something. I can't remember anything."

"But it could have been Carl?"

"Yes," she said. "That attack strikes me as more his style."

"Why would he want to hurt you?"

"He was friends with Eddie. Eddie swore he'd kill me if I gave the police any information about the gang or the robbery."

"So you think maybe Eddie sent him here to make good on his threat?" Cody asked.

She shifted the fishing pole in her hand. "I don't know. That doesn't make a lot of sense to me, either. By the time the police arrested me, they already had everyone but the getaway driver, and I didn't know anything about him. Nothing I told the police made things worse for Eddie. I never talked to him again after the day of the robbery, but he could have easily gotten a message to me if he wanted to threaten me again or remind me of his promise. I've been out of prison eight months and nothing has happened to make me feel like I'm in danger."

"Until you showed up here." He sat forward on his bucket. "I think I got a bite."

A few seconds later, he was scooping a large trout into a net and depositing it on the ice between them. "Dinner," he said, and grinned at her.

While he took care of the fish and rebaited his hook, she thought about Carl. "When I saw Carl in the grocery store, he didn't seem surprised to see me," she said. "Maybe that's because he did come to Eagle Mountain to look for me."

"Was a lot of money taken in that robbery?" Cody asked. "Maybe Carl thinks Eddie gave the loot to you and he wants his share."

She shook her head. "The bank got all the money back. The police caught Eddie and the others before they even had a chance to divide it up."

"Why didn't they catch the driver?" Cody asked.

"I guess he wasn't at the apartment the afternoon the police showed up. I really don't know, since I wasn't there, either. They arrested me later, after they learned of my relationship with Eddie. They already knew someone had shut off the alarm system and left the back door unlocked." She hung her head. "You don't know how many times I've regretted doing those things. I knew they were wrong, but Eddie had persuaded me the ends justified the means. I was so stupid."

"You paid for your mistake," he said.

"I did." She gripped the fishing pole tighter. "I've worked really hard to build a new life for myself, and I wouldn't risk throwing all that away by stealing a couple of wedding rings—especially rings that belong to a woman who's done everything she could to help me."

"I believe you," Cody said.

She stared at him. "You're willing to overlook the evidence and take my word for it?"

"I'm not overlooking the evidence," he said. "The rings were hidden in an obvious location. You're not that dumb. If you had taken them, you would have locked them in your suitcase or tucked them under the eaves or, I don't know, sewn them into your bra. You wouldn't have put them where we could find them so easily."

"Maybe I believed you wouldn't look," she said.

"You let us search your cabin without a warrant. Even an innocent person might not have done that. Again—you're not stupid."

"Thank you. I think."

"I convinced the Walkers not to tell anyone about the new lock on your cabin," he said. "They're going to leave the spare keys in the desk, just like before, and Travis is setting up a hidden video camera in the office, focused on the desk. If anyone comes to take the key again, we'll catch them."

"Then I hope they do come," Bette said. She cleared her throat. "And thank you. You're going to a lot of trouble to clear my name. Travis, too, I guess."

"We want to catch the right person," he said. "The worst thing that can happen, as a law enforcement officer, is to find out you helped put an innocent person behind bars. It makes you doubt everything about yourself and the job."

"I guess I never thought about that," she said. "I only saw things from the point of view of the innocent person—someone like Lacy."

"Sometimes cops are victims of their own zeal to close a case," he said. "Or we get fooled by the evidence. It can happen easier than you think."

"Has it ever happened to you?"

"No. And knowing it can happen makes me more careful." His eyes met hers. "I don't want you to be my first mistake."

She looked away, warmed by his words, but too unsure to speak. She wanted to believe Cody had her best interests at heart, but she had learned the hard way that her hormones could overrule good sense. She didn't want to make the same mistake again.

She cleared her throat and turned to him. "Why a cop?" she asked. "I mean, why would you want a job that puts you in contact with so many dangerous, unpleasant people?"

"Why did you want to be a caterer?"

"Because I like to cook, I like parties and it's something I'm really good at."

"It's sort of the same thing with me." He pulled up his line and checked the hook, then lowered it into the water again. "I started out wanting to be a lawyer. I liked the idea of putting away criminals, and television shows and books make it seem really glamorous. By the time I graduated and started prepping to take the bar exam, I'd figured out it was a lot duller than most people know. Then I met a guy who worked for the US Marshals Service and he told me they were hiring, and that with my law degree, I'd have one up on a lot of candidates. I decided to apply, maybe do the job for a couple of years before I took the bar exam." He shrugged. "I got hooked and never looked back."

"Do you ever think about doing anything else—maybe taking the bar?" she asked.

He hesitated before answering. "I never used to," he said. "Now... I don't know. Maybe someday. I guess seeing somebody blow his brains out right in front of you gives you a different perspective on the job."

She put her hand on his arm and kept it there. "I guess law enforcement needs people like you," she said. "But you'd probably make a good lawyer, too."

"The path we choose when we're young doesn't have to be the one we stay on our whole lives." His eyes met hers, and she had the sense of seeing the real man, with no defensive screens. "People can change."

He was telling her he believed she had changed, and her heart felt too big for her chest as the idea sank in. This hard-nosed cop was telling her that—maybe—he was learning to see past the mistakes she had made.

Maybe even into a future where a woman like her and a man like him might be together.

BY THE TIME the sun began sinking behind the trees, Cody and Bette had caught five good-sized fish. He cleaned them and packed them in snow in one of the buckets, then they gathered their gear and headed back toward the snowmobile.

They were still a few dozen yards from the machine when Cody halted, frowning. Bette set down the tackle box and followed his gaze toward the snowmobile. "What is it?" she asked.

He shook his head and started forward again. Twenty yards farther on, Cody stopped again and set down the auger and the bucket of fish. He motioned for Bette to stay back and he approached the snowmobile.

The snow around the machine had been churned up. The snowmobile's hood lay in the snow a few feet beyond them, and Bette could see wires sticking up out of the engine compartment. Cody carefully circled the machine, then scanned the area around them. "What's wrong?" Bette called when she could bear the tension of his silence no more.

"Someone's wrecked it," he said. "On purpose." He gestured toward the dangling wires. "They've cut the wiring harness."

"What are we going to do?" she asked.

He pulled out his phone and took photographs of the damage, and of the ground around the snowmobile. "No service," he said, checking the screen. "We'll have to walk back."

She looked past the snowmobile, at the faint track they had made getting to this place. "How far is it?" she asked.

"About five miles." He moved the bucket of fish and the auger closer to the snowmobile, and took the poles and tackle from her to add to the pile. "Come on," he said. "We'd better get started if we want to make it back before dark."

Chapter Fourteen

The trek back to the ranch was brutal, post-holing through snow up past the knees. They hadn't traveled half a mile before Cody was sweating inside the thick insulated coverall, and the rubber boots that were fine for snowmobiling and fishing felt as if they weighed ten pounds each. Bette was having a hard time, too, though she didn't utter a word of complaint. He tried to break trail for her, but that didn't make the going much easier.

He had remembered to grab a water bottle from the snowmobile, and he stopped after what he judged to be the first mile and handed it to her. She drank deeply and returned it to him. "How do you know we're headed in the right direction?" she asked.

"I'm following our path here, and the blazes on the trees." He indicated the orange plastic diamonds affixed to tree trunks at regular intervals.

She nodded. "So, is this just another prank to annoy me—like the message on my door?"

"The lake is on National Forest land," Cody said. "It's possible someone came along and decided to mess with the snowmobile—malicious mischief."

"Why didn't we see them—or hear them?"

"I think they parked in the woods and walked in,"

Cody said. "We were out of sight over the hill, and the sound wouldn't necessarily have carried that far. They wouldn't have had to make a lot of noise."

"Maybe I'm being paranoid, but I think this was directed at me," she said. "It kind of fits with a pattern of harassment."

"Would Carl do something like this?"

"I have no idea. Maybe. I didn't know the man. I didn't want to know him."

"When Travis finds him, he can follow up on his alibi for this afternoon."

"If he finds him," she said.

He stashed the water bottle in one of the pockets of his coat. "Come on. Let's keep walking." But before he could take even another step forward, something whistled past his ear, followed by the distinctive popping sound of weapons fire.

"Get down!" He shoved Bette into the snow and threw himself on top of her, as bullets continued to strike around them. "Into the trees," he said and shoved her forward. Scrambling in the deep snow, they headed for a stand of fir, fifty yards to their left, away from the direction of the shots. They moved clumsily through the thick snow, clawing their way toward cover as bullets continued to rain down. Cody tried to keep himself between Bette and the shooter, staying low to present a smaller target and moving erratically when possible. They had almost reached cover when the impact of a bullet propelled him forward. Burning pain radiated from his shoulder as he fell, but he kept moving, crawling after Bette, into the trees. They lay at the base of one of the evergreens, gasping.

Grimacing, Cody raised up enough to unzip his coverall and draw his Glock, though the movement cost him. His right shoulder felt as if someone had rammed a hot poker through it, and he could feel blood dripping down his back.

"You're hurt!" Bette stared at his shoulder, her face almost as white as the surrounding snow.

He sat back against the tree, keeping his weight on his good side, and closed his eyes a moment, gearing up for what he knew he'd have to do next.

Bette crawled up beside him. "Let me see," she said.

He angled his body so that she could look. "I think the bullet is still in there," he said. "How much blood is there?"

"Not as much as I would have thought," she said. "It's more seeping than gushing. That's good, I think."

He nodded. It was good—as long as the bullet hadn't nicked some internal artery. But he didn't think so. "How are you at first aid?" he asked.

"I can put a Band-Aid on a boo-boo," she said. "I think this requires more than that."

"If I was the kind of man who carried a clean white handkerchief everywhere, we could use it as a bandage," he said.

She studied the wound again. "I guess what we're looking for is something clean that can soak up the blood and protect the wound from dirt, right?"

"Right."

"Then I have something." She turned her back to him and unzipped her coveralls. A few deft movements later, she pulled out her bra and dangled it in front of his face. "It's padded and it's mostly cotton. And it's clean."

He choked back a laugh. "You're amazing, you know that?"

"I'm practical. It's not the same thing. Now turn around."

He grit his teeth and cried out only once as she doused the wound with the rest of the water from their bottle, then twisted and wrapped the bra into an awkward bandage. "It looks ridiculous, but I think it will serve our purposes," she said. "Now what?"

"Now we try to find a way out of here," he said. The gunfire had stopped, leaving the area silent—the unnatural silence after violence has intruded.

Bette followed his gaze to the open area they had just crossed. "He was waiting for us," she said in a ragged whisper. "Watching us. He let us get away from the snowmobile, out in the open, and when we stopped, he tried to kill us."

"It looks that way." Cody checked his gun to make sure it was loaded—it was always loaded, but this gave him something to do with his hands, since whoever had put them in this situation wasn't close enough to strangle.

Bette closed her eyes, then opened them again. "This is crazy. I just need to find Carl and ask him what he wants. That's what I should have done in the grocery store that day, instead of running away."

"Maybe this isn't Carl," Cody said.

She stared at him. "You don't think it's Doug? Or Rainey?"

"Maybe it's the Ice Cold Killer."

"He's a serial killer. He ambushes women and cuts their throats."

"He didn't cut your throat," Cody said. "You're unfinished business." The more he thought about it, the more it made sense to him. Yes, the attack on Bette hadn't been the killer's usual style, but that might be a sign that he was getting desperate. Coming unhinged. Considering that it took a kind of mental imbalance to become a serial killer in the first place, was it so far-fetched to think that could progress into an obsession with one particular woman? "Maybe he's been waiting for another chance and thought this was it."

"So what do we do now?" she asked. "Lie here and wait for him to come after us?"

"I think we wait and see what he does next."

"I am not going to lie here and let him pick us off like shooting fish in a barrel," she said. She started to rise but wasn't to her feet yet when a bullet hit the tree trunk above her head, sending bark flying.

With a yelp, she flattened herself on the ground once more. "Okay, I guess that was stupid," she muttered.

Cody studied the landscape beyond this stand of trees. A small rise, slightly above and to the left, would provide good cover for the shooter. "I think he's in the rocks up there," he said, indicating the spot. "I don't think he can see us here, but he probably knows he hit me. He's waiting to see what we do next."

"Can you shoot him from here?" she asked.

"No. He's using a rifle. My handgun isn't going to do us any good unless he gets closer." He nudged her. "Let's start moving back, deeper into the woods. He won't be able to get a clear shot at us, and he may have to expose himself to come after us."

They crawled backward twenty, then thirty feet, to the banks of a frozen creek that wound through the trees. Cody moved awkwardly, trying and failing to protect his wounded shoulder, so that by the time they reached the creek, he was dizzy from pain. When he could speak, he said, "If we move along this creek, we'll be headed toward the ranch, but we'll still have cover."

"It's going to take all night to get back to the ranch, crawling on our hands and knees," she said. "And you need a doctor."

Cody didn't tell her they probably didn't have all night. A killer who had followed them to the lake, sabotaged their snowmobile, then waited patiently for them to provide clear targets wasn't going to stop his pursuit now. All Cody could do was try to make the task more difficult for him. Keeping in the shelter of the trunk of a large fir, he rose to his knees, then stood. All remained silent. "Come on. It will be easier walking."

They moved alongside the creek, climbing over snowbanks and skirting deadfall. No one fired on them, but Cody had the sensation that they were still being watched. Was the shooter waiting for them to emerge into the open again?

And then they were almost out of cover, the woods giving way to a broad meadow, snow like icing over a sheet cake. He stopped ten yards from the last tree. "We can't cross that," Bette whispered.

Cody scanned the surroundings, looking for the shooter's vantage point. He saw half a dozen possibilities. He needed to draw the man out, make him show his hand. He had no chance if he didn't know where the shots would come from. But Bette was right—stepping into that open field would be suicide.

"When we don't come back for supper, someone from the ranch will come looking for us," Bette said. "They knew we were coming here to fish."

It was anyone's guess how long that would take. By himself, Cody might have hazarded more direct action, but he couldn't risk Bette. "Then I guess we wait," he said.

He made himself as comfortable as possible—which wasn't very comfortable, his back to a tree, the gun in his right hand, trying to ignore the throbbing pain in his left shoulder and arm. Bette sat beside him, one hand on his thigh. She kept glancing at his injured shoulder. "What?" he asked, the tenth time she looked.

"The blood is seeping through," she said.

"I hope it wasn't your favorite bra," he said.

"If you'd ever had to wear one, you'd know there is no such thing," she said.

"I think I can speak for most men when I say you never have to wear one on our account."

A twig snapped, and they both sat up straighter. His hand tightened on the Glock.

"Maybe it's just a deer," she whispered.

A bullet thudded into a tree five feet in front of them. "Last time I checked, deer didn't carry rifles," Cody said, as he urged her to the ground. He peered around the trunk of the tree. Was that movement there, behind those rocks? He fired, and shards of rock flew from a boulder at the front of the grouping, followed by a volley of gunfire in their direction.

He flattened himself on the ground over Bette. "You're crushing me," she said, her face in the dirt.

"Better flattened than dead."

"And people say chivalry is dead."

"If I could get a little closer, I'd have a better chance of hitting him," he said.

She clutched his arm. "No. He'll kill you."

"Not if I'm careful."

"No," she said again. "Don't leave me."

"I won't." He realized he couldn't. If the gunman did kill him, she'd be left helpless. The shooter fired sporadically for the next ten minutes, with Cody returning fire. Then the hammer clicked onto an empty cylinder. He sagged to the ground behind the tree again and tried to move his left hand toward the spare ammo clip on his belt. It was impossible.

"What are you doing?" Bette asked.

"I need you to get the ammo clip off my belt," he said.

She fumbled a little, but managed to unfasten the clip. "Aren't you Mr. Prepared?" she said.

"Aren't you glad I am?"

"Oh, I am." She levered herself up and kissed him, hard. "I'm very glad."

The roar of an engine—more than one engine, Cody decided—broke the stillness that had followed the last volley of gunfire. Headlights swept the edge of the forest. Breaking twigs and muffled steps announced the shooter's retreat. Cody waited, heart pounding painfully. Beside him, Bette breathed raggedly.

"Cody! It's Travis! Are you okay?"

"In here!" Bette stood and waved, then moved toward their voices. Cody closed his eyes and sagged against the tree. They were safe. For now, anyway.

Chapter Fifteen

"Travis, I've never been so glad to see anyone in my life." Bette grabbed the sheriff by the arm and dragged him toward the tree where she and Cody had been sheltering. "Cody's hurt. He needs a doctor right away."

"What happened?" Mr. Walker strode up behind his son.

"Someone sabotaged our snowmobile, so we had to walk out," Bette said. "Then they started shooting at us. They hit Cody." They had reached the tree.

Travis knelt beside Cody. "Hey."

Cody scowled at him. "Hey yourself. About time you got here."

"Bette said somebody shot you."

"Rifle shot. It didn't bleed too much."

"Let me take a look." He helped Cody sit forward, and he shined the light on the bloodstained bandage. He frowned. "What is that you've got on there?" he asked.

"A padded bra," Bette said, her tone daring him to say something about it.

"Any idea who was doing the shooting?" Travis asked.

"Never got a look at him," Cody said. "He fired on us first in the open, then followed us in here. He had us pinned down while he was shooting from behind those rocks." He gestured toward the shooter's location. "I kept him from getting any closer, then you scared him off."

"I need you to wait here while I take a look," Travis said.

"I'm not going anywhere."

Mr. Walker stayed with them while Travis went to investigate the rock outcropping. "When you didn't show up for supper, we figured your snowmobile might have broken down," Mr. Walker said.

"Someone cut the wiring harness," Cody said. "It shouldn't be too hard to fix."

"I'm not too worried about that machine right now, son," Mr. Walker said. He turned to Bette. "How about you? Are you okay?"

"I am now," she said. "You arrived just in time."

The approaching beam of Travis's flashlight signaled his return. "I didn't find much," he said. "Some impressions in the snow. We'll come back in the morning and take a better look. It's getting too dark to track anybody right now."

"Whoever it was is probably long gone," Cody said.

Travis handed his father the flashlight and moved to Cody's other side. "Can you walk?" he asked.

"I can walk," Cody said. With Travis's help, he staggered up. Bette followed, Mr. Walker bringing up the rear. Travis helped Cody onto his snowmobile, then Bette climbed on behind his dad.

The return trip to the ranch had none of the joy of the morning's journey. Bette held on to Mr. Walker, teeth chattering as icy wind buffeted her, her gaze fixed on the dark shadow of Cody's back on the snowmobile just ahead.

As they neared the ranch, Travis slowed. "We've got a phone signal now," Mr. Walker called over his shoulder. "He's phoning ahead for help."

Fifteen minutes later, they arrived at the ranch house, where a small crowd waited to greet them. "An ambulance is on the way," Travis said. "Let's get inside, where it's warm."

Bette climbed off the snowmobile, stiff with cold. She tried to move toward Cody, but Lacy put her arm around her and steered her toward the house. "You're half-frozen," she said. "Come in here by the fire."

"Cody—" Bette looked over her shoulder.

"I've got Cody," Travis said. "Go inside."

Too worn out to argue, Bette let Lacy lead her into the house and help her out of the bulky helmet, coveralls and boots. She sighed with relief as Lacy tucked her under a blanket in a chair by the fire. A few second later, Cody came in, leaning on Travis's arm. But he balked at sitting on the sofa. "I'm not going to bleed on your furniture," he said.

Mr. Walker brought a chair from the dining table and Cody lowered himself gingerly into it. His face was gray, tight with pain. Bette hurt, looking at him, but she couldn't tear her eyes away. She couldn't forget the way he had lain on top of her, protecting her body with his own. "Where is the ambulance?" she asked.

"It's coming," Lacy said.

"What happened?" Emily asked. "Travis didn't give a lot of details when he called."

"Someone wrecked the snowmobile, then started

shooting at us," Cody said. "He had us pinned down behind a tree when the cavalry arrived and scared him off."

"Who would do something like that?" Emily asked.

"If I knew the answer to that, I sure wouldn't be sitting here right now," Cody said.

The strident wail of the ambulance stopped all conversation. Mr. Walker went outside to direct them and moments later two paramedics came in and began examining Cody.

Lacy handed Bette a mug and pulled a chair closer to her. "Are you okay?" she asked. "No wounds or frostbite or anything that needs seeing to?"

"No, I'm fine." She sipped the mug, which turned out to be hot chocolate, heavily laced with peppermint schnapps. Soothing warmth spread through her.

"That must have been terrifying," Lacy said.

"Yes." The fear still hadn't left her. They both might have been killed. No. She couldn't think about that. They were safe. They were going to be okay.

Cody let out a sharp cry and she had to set the mug on the table beside her, her hands shook so violently. Then the paramedics helped him onto a waiting stretcher and draped blankets over him.

Travis came and bent over Bette. "They're taking him to the clinic in town to have the bullet removed," he said. "I'm going to go with him. Is there anything else you can tell me about the guy who shot at you?"

She shook her head. "We never saw him. Cody said he had a rifle. He followed us for a while. I think he was waiting for us to come out into the open again, then he came in after us. I don't know who he is, I swear."

"Doug and Rainey both served supper tonight," Travis said. "So it wasn't them. We're still trying to find Carl Wayland."

"Call us after Cody comes out of surgery," Lacy said.

"I will." He kissed her goodbye and left.

"Drink your chocolate," Lacy said. "I'll bring you something to eat."

"I don't think I could eat," Bette said.

"Then I'll bring it and you can pick at it."

After she left, Bette leaned back in the chair and closed her eyes. She had thought the events of the afternoon would replay in her head but instead the image that came to her was of Cody, bringing up that first fish and giving her a look of triumph—the kind of look friends would share.

The kind of look she thought she would like to see over and over again. For the rest of her life.

CODY CALLED THE sheriff's department the next morning just after eight. Adelaide answered and when Cody said he wanted to speak to the sheriff, she informed him that Travis was still at the ranch, probably eating breakfast. "He was out on a call very late last night," she said.

"I know," said Cody. "I was that call."

"Marshal Rankin, is that you?" Adelaide asked. "How are you doing?"

"I'm sore and grumpy and don't intend to stay in this clinic one minute longer than necessary."

"I don't know what you expect the sheriff to do about that."

"I want him to come get me and take me back to the ranch. But since he's not there—Adelaide, everyone knows you really run that department. Can't you send a deputy over to get me?"

"This is a sheriff's department, not a taxi service."

"I'm an officer of the law, so consider it an inter-agency favor." No response. He resorted to begging. "Please, Adelaide. They don't even make decent coffee in this place and I had to threaten the nurse to get her to bring me my clothes."

"I'll see what I can do."

Ten minutes later, Gage walked into the clinic. He grinned when he saw Cody, who was sitting on the edge of the narrow clinic bed, his shoulder swathed in bandages. "I figured your shirt was trashed, so I brought you this." He held out a Rayford County Sheriff sweatshirt. "Size extra-large, so it should fit over those bandages."

"Thanks." Cody stood and began struggling into the shirt. Gage moved over to help him. "Let's get out of here," Cody said, when he was dressed.

When they were in the cruiser, Gage handed him a large cup of coffee. "Adelaide sent this," he said.

"Bless her." He popped the lid and drank deeply.

"She said you were a real bear on the phone. Want to tell me why?"

"Oh, I don't know. Having a divot taken out of my shoulder and trying to sleep in that clinic on that narrow bed, and nobody telling me anything about what is going on—I think that would put anyone in a bad mood."

"Normally we send gunshot victims to the hospital in Junction," Gage said. "The clinic isn't really set up for surgery. And from what I hear, you were lucky. The bullet just missed shattering your shoulder blade."

Cody grunted and drank more coffee. He began to feel more human. "How is Bette?" he asked.

Gage glanced at him. "Was she shot, too?"

"No. I just… I just wondered how she's doing."

"I haven't heard. You can ask her yourself when you get to the ranch. I called and let Travis know you were coming."

"Any sign of Carl Wayland?"

"Nope. But unless he hiked out, he's still here. Last avalanche on the pass took out a bunch of power lines—poles and line strung all over the highway, under about ten feet of packed snow and rock. It's going to take a while to fix that mess."

Another grunt from Cody. That seemed to be the best he could do at the moment. His shoulder hurt like the devil, but he had refused the pain meds the doctor had prescribed, not wanting to fog his brain. He had lain awake in the early morning hours, replaying everything that happened yesterday. But no matter how many times he went over the puzzle, he couldn't find the missing pieces. That, more than anything, had put him in a bad mood.

At the ranch, Travis came out to meet him, followed by Bette and Lacy. Cody refused Travis's offer of assistance and got out of the car under his own power. He caught Bette's eye and nodded. He was all right. And he was going to make things all right for her.

"Should you be out of the hospital?" Lacy asked.

"There is no hospital," he said. He moved past her. "I can mend here as well as anywhere."

"You look like you're in pain," Bette said, coming alongside him.

"So do you," he said. "What's your excuse?" He winked, to let her know there was no heat behind the words, no matter how gruff they may have sounded. That earned him a smile.

"I'd better get back to work," Gage said. "And I've got a bachelor party to see to."

"I don't think now is a good time for that," Travis said. "We should put it off."

"Moe is closing down the whole pub for us," Gage said. "It won't kill you to take a few hours to say good-bye to single life with your friends."

"Neither you nor Dwight had a bachelor party," Travis said.

"Right. So we're really looking forward to yours. It's too late for you to back out now."

"Besides, you have to get out of the house so we women can have our party," Lacy said.

Gage glanced at Cody. "If you feel up to it, you're still welcome to come," he said. "Since you probably can't drink, you can be our designated driver."

"I'll let you know," Cody said.

When Gage had gone, Travis joined Cody by the fire. "Dad and I went out to the lake again at first light," he said. "We were able to follow tracks we think were the shooter's to that rock outcropping, back to where it looks like he parked a snowmobile. But then we lost him."

"What about your wrecked snowmobile?"

"Dad doesn't think it'll be too hard to fix. We brought home the fish you caught—frozen solid in that bucket."

"Guess we'll take a rain check on that fish fry," Cody said. He pulled a plastic bag from his pocket. "I brought you something."

Travis studied the smashed piece of metal. "The bullet they took out of you?"

"They got a few bone fragments, too, but I didn't think they qualified as evidence." He nodded to the bag. "It's pretty distorted, but you can tell it's a .225 round."

"Maybe it will help, if we ever find anybody to pin this on." He pocketed the bag. "What does the doctor say about your shoulder?"

"I didn't smash my shoulder blade. I didn't slice an artery and bleed out—which I already kind of figured. Didn't tear any major ligaments. Chipped some bone, damaged some muscle. I need physical therapy and for the rest of my life I'll know when a snowstorm is on its way." He blew out a breath. "Two months off work, at least. Maybe three."

"That bites."

"Yeah, well. Maybe I'll take up a hobby."

"I have to go," Travis said. "I'm determined to track down Carl Wayland today."

"I hope you do."

Travis started to walk away, then turned back. "About this party tonight. You really don't have to come."

"Are you kidding? I wouldn't miss it for the world."

BETTE SPENT THE rest of Saturday morning in the kitchen, preparing the food for the tea that evening, glad to have something to keep her busy. She was pulling a sheet of petit fours out of the oven when Rainey came in. Bette braced herself for some criticism or complaint. "What are you making?" Rainey asked.

The question surprised Bette. Rainey sounded genuinely interested. "These are petit fours for Lacy's bridesmaids' tea," she said. "They don't look like much right now, but they will after I decorate them."

"I guess those girls really go for that fancy food,"

Rainey said. "I never learned how to do all that. All I know is plain cooking."

"Every meal I've had here has been excellent," Bette said, truthfully. "I imagine you make exactly the kinds of meals the family loves."

"Oh, yeah. Cowboys like plain food that'll stay with them when they're working all day," Rainey said. "Still, it might be nice to know how to do fancy stuff."

"You could learn," Bette said. "You already know how to cook, so it wouldn't take you any time at all to pick up a few new techniques. I could even show you if you like."

"Maybe. Though I don't know if I'd have time. They keep me pretty busy around here."

"I imagine you were glad to have your son come and help you," Bette said.

"I was. Except…"

"Except what?"

"He hasn't been all that much help since you came." She gave Bette a sideways look. "I was hoping you could tell me why."

"What do you mean?" Bette asked.

"It took me a while to figure it out, but it finally come to me—Doug is afraid of you. That's why he avoids you so much."

"Afraid of me?" She stripped off her oven mitts and faced Rainey. "Why would he be afraid of me?"

"I was hoping you could tell me."

Ah. Maybe this explained Rainey's uncharacteristic friendliness. "What makes you think Doug is afraid of me?"

"Just the way he acts. I know my boy. What I can't figure out is why."

"I don't know what to tell you," Bette said. "I haven't done anything to him, I promise. I mean, what could I do?"

"Well, he's always had some strange ideas," Rainey said. "But he's a good boy. He's made some bad choices, but he's promised me he's going to do better."

"Then I hope he will," Bette said. The timer dinged and she pulled the last tray of petit fours out of the oven. "These need to cool before I decorate them. The oven is all yours if you need it to prepare lunch."

"Oh, I made a stew and sandwiches," Rainey said. "We'll be fine."

"I think I'll go see if Lacy needs any help with the decorations for tonight," Bette said. She still wasn't that comfortable with the older woman.

She was crossing the living room when Cody hailed her. "Bette!"

She turned to find him moving toward her. He still wore the sweatshirt over one arm, leaving the other arm free. "Can you help me with something in my cabin?" he asked. "It's supposed to be a surprise for Travis, so I can't really tell Lacy or his folks."

"I'd like to," she said. "But I was going to see if Lacy needed any help with the decorations for her party."

"Emily is helping her," he said. "It sounded to me like they have everything under control."

"All right." She was curious to know this big secret of his.

They collected their coats and crossed to Cody's cabin, which was the twin of Bette's. The only real difference was a large stuffed cow that occupied the chair beside the small table. It was easily three feet long and two feet tall. "Where did you get this?" she asked, hefting the brown-and-white plush beast.

"Gage got it somewhere," Cody said. He slipped out of his coat, then helped her with hers. "This was all his idea—it's a gag gift, for the party tonight."

"You aren't going to the bachelor party, are you?" she said.

"Why not? I can suffer there as well as I can here, and at least there I'll have distractions."

She scowled at him.

"You're cute when you're disgusted with me," he said.

She launched the cow at him. He caught it by one hind leg, grinning. She couldn't help but grin back. "What am I supposed to help you with?" she asked.

He set the cow on the table and picked up a set of deer antlers. "We have to tie these to the cow's head."

"Why?"

"According to Gage, when Travis was twelve, his father and his uncle took him on his first deer hunt. Travis was so nervous and excited he ended up shooting a neighbor's cow. He spent all summer working to pay for that beef."

"Travis did that?" She had a hard time imagining the straight-arrow sheriff ever coloring outside the lines, even as a kid.

"Gage swears it's true."

"And, of course, his brother never let him forget it," she said.

"Of course." Cody picked up a spool of brown ribbon. "I bought this. I figured we could use it to tie on the antlers—but that's kind of hard to do one-handed. And you probably tie a better bow than I do, anyway."

"I ought to tie a bow around your neck," she said, as she took the spool from him.

"Why? Because I led you into an ambush?"

"No! Do you really think I blame you?"

All the teasing and laughter had left his eyes. "I'm trained to track people. I ought to know when some-one is tracking me."

"You had no reason to believe anyone would follow us," she said. "Much less attack us. It was a fishing trip. And I was having a good time until the shooting started."

"Me, too." He reached out with his uninjured arm and pulled her closer, then kissed her. She sank into that kiss, the tension of the past few days easing. She had missed this—she had missed him.

He raised his head and looked into her eyes. "Do you know what one of my favorite memories of yes-terday is?"

"What?"

"When you sacrificed your bra to bandage my wounds."

She laughed. "You would say that."

He shaped his hand to her breast, a mock look of disappointment pulling down the corners of his mouth. "You're wearing a bra now."

"I have more than one."

"I'll buy you a new one." He slid his hand around to her back and deftly undid the clasp. "Something low-cut. With lace."

"I might have guessed." The last word came out in a rush of breath as he pulled down the neck of her sweater to expose the tops of her breasts. He began kiss-ing his way along them. "Cody, what are you doing?" she gasped.

"This." He pulled the sweater lower, and dragged his tongue across her nipple. "And this." He addressed the other breast.

"But, um, you're wounded," she said.

"Not where it counts." He unzipped her jeans.

"I'm worried I'm going to hurt you," she said.

"Sex is a great pain reliever," he said. "I think you told me that once."

He was definitely making it hard for her to think straight. Then again, what did she need to think about? She wanted him, and she was more than relieved to be with him again. Making love seemed right. Healing. She slid both hands under the sweatshirt he wore, skimming the taut muscles of his stomach and over his chest. "Let me help you undress."

"Best idea you've had in five minutes."

She helped him out of his clothing, with a minimum amount of pain on his part, and multiple apologies on her part. "Maybe we shouldn't do this," she said, after she managed to get the sweatshirt off over his head.

"We definitely should," he said, and slipped his hand inside her panties to persuade her.

"All right, we should," she agreed, a little breathless. She moved toward the bed, then stopped. "Should you lie down, or should I?" What would hurt less for him?

"I have an idea." He grasped her hips and backed her toward the bed, which, like the one in Bette's room, was an old-fashioned iron-framed model that sat high off the floor. With her sitting on the edge of the bed and him standing, they lined up perfectly.

"Oh." She wrapped her legs around his hips. "Good idea."

He leaned over and reached for the condom packet

on the bedside table. "I see now you didn't really want help with that cow," she said. "You planned to seduce me." She took the packet from him and tore it open.

"I still need help with the cow." He kissed the side of her neck. "Later."

She took the condom from the packet and reached for him. "Allow me."

"There are…definitely…some advantages…to being one-handed," he breathed as she rolled on the condom. Then he wrapped his arm around her and drew her to him, kissing her fiercely.

The man knew how to kiss—deftly setting every nerve on fire with the pressure of his lips or the sweep of his tongue. She reveled in the feel of him in her arms, tracing the line of his spine with her fingers, cupping his firm ass. She let out a sigh when he slid into her, and opened her eyes to stare into his as he began to move. She grasped his hips and met him stroke for stroke, watching as passion etched deeper lines on his face and darkened his eyes. Then he raised her legs, tilting her back slightly, and her breathing grew ragged and her vision blurred. She was dimly aware of the bed knocking against the wall, and her own rising cries as a powerful climax shook her. Cody gripped her more tightly and drove harder, until he came with a shout.

They fell back together on the bed. Bette rolled over and he slid up beside her. "Careful of your shoulder," she cautioned.

"What shoulder?" he breathed.

They lay, not speaking, for a long time. She trailed her fingers through his hair, eyes half-closed. "Did you ever think you'd be involved with a former bank robber?" she asked.

"No." He lifted his head to look at her. "Did you ever think you'd take a US marshal as your lover?"

"Never."

"What's going to happen to us?" he asked.

"Someone is trying to hurt me—maybe kill me," she said. "This isn't a great time to talk about the future."

"Call me an optimist," he said. "I think it is."

"Since when is any lawman an optimist?"

"Since I met you." He kissed her cheek. "You have me believing all kinds of improbable things."

Improbable. That's exactly what they were. Yet here they lay, together, and in spite of the fact that her life might be in danger and she didn't know what she should do next, she was happier than she had ever been.

Chapter Sixteen

"I can't believe how beautiful everything turned out."
Emily stepped back and admired the array of white-
clothed tables, each with a centerpiece of white lilies
and silver plumes. The buffet table featured similar arrangements, as well as carved-crystal snowflakes and
drifts of glittery fake snow.

"Most of the decorations were Lacy's idea," Bette
said. "I stuck to what I know best—food."

"And what food." Emily lifted the plastic wrap off a
tray of silver-and-white-frosted petit fours. "They look
so good—you don't mind if I take just one, do you?"

"Go ahead," Bette said. "But just one."

Grinning, Emily chose a petit fours and bit it in half.
The delight on her face transformed into a grimace. She
spit out the cake, choking.

"What is it?" Bette asked. "What's wrong?"

"The cake!" Emily stared at the mangled pastry in
her napkin. "I don't mean to criticize but—did you taste
these?"

"No. I mean, I did taste the batter, and I sampled the
frosting—they were fine."

"This one wasn't fine."

Bette pulled another cake from the tray and bit into

it. The bitterness brought tears to her eyes. She spit it out and looked around for water, but there was none. "Someone has done something to my petit fours!" she wailed. She scanned the buffet table. The finger sandwiches and cream puffs were still in the refrigerator. She wouldn't put them out until after the guests arrived. But the scones, chocolate-dipped apricots and hazelnut shortbread were already arranged on the table, covered with plastic wrap. "We'd better taste everything," she said. "The refrigerated food, too."

Looking doubtful, Emily followed Bette down the table. They sampled cakes and scones and cookies, and by the time they reached the end of the table, Emily was smiling again. "Everything else is delicious," she said.

Bette remembered Rainey's interest in the petit fours, and how she had left the cook alone in the kitchen with the cakes while she went to Cody's cabin. She turned and raced toward the kitchen, Emily in pursuit. "Where are you going?" Emily called.

Bette burst into the kitchen. Rainey looked up from the dishes she was washing. "Is something wrong?" she asked.

"You know what's wrong." Bette crowded the other woman against the sink. "What did you put in my petit fours?"

Rainey's eyes widened in fear. "What are you talking about? I didn't touch your petit fours."

"I left you alone with them and you put something in them," Bette said. "You wanted to embarrass me in front of Lacy and her guests, so you ruined them."

Rainey leaned away from her. "I swear I didn't."

"Taste this!" Bette shoved a cake at the older woman. Hesitantly, Rainey took the cake and put it in her mouth. She immediately made a face and spit it out. "That's horrible! It tastes like pine cleaner."

"Bette." Emily tugged on Bette's arm. "I think Rainey is telling the truth. Why would she doctor your cakes that way?"

"If she didn't do it, her son did." Bette glared at the cook. "Has Doug been in here this afternoon?"

Rainey hesitated. "He helped me with lunch," she said after a pause.

"Did you see him messing with the cakes?" Bette asked.

"No. I swear I didn't." She swallowed. "He asked me about them, and I told them they were petit fours for the party tonight, and that you were coming back later to frost them."

"Was he ever alone in the kitchen after that?" Bette asked.

Rainey looked panicked. "Maybe," she said. "But why would he ruin your beautiful cakes? And try to ruin Lacy's party? He likes Lacy."

"But he doesn't like me," Bette said. "And you said he's afraid of me. He would like me to leave here."

Rainey hung her head. "He was in here alone while I cleared the table. When I came back, he was acting funny. He left before we had even finished the washing. He told me he had something he needed to do."

"Where is he now?" Emily asked.

"In his room, I guess," Rainey said.

"We'd better talk to him," Bette said.

Rainey led the way up a set of back stairs, to a room at the rear of the house. She knocked on the door, but there was no answer. "Doug?" she called. "Doug, it's Mom. Please open the door."

Silence. Rainey frowned. "I can't think why he's not answering."

"Is the door locked?" Bette asked.

Rainey tried the knob. It wouldn't turn.

"We'll have to wait until he comes back or wakes up," Emily said.

"No we don't." Rainey reached up and took a cotter key from atop the door frame. "All the doors around here unlock this way."

"I always forget about those," Emily said.

Rainey slipped the angled bit of metal into the hole beneath the doorknob and they heard the lock pop.

Doug's room was dark and crowded, the blinds drawn and items piled on the floor, the bed and every flat surface—clothing, shoes, magazines, video games—and on a bookshelf by the door, a bottle of pine cleaner and a syringe. Bette stared at the items. "He must have injected the cakes with this," she said. "He could have even done it after I iced them. If he used just a little bit you wouldn't even be able to tell what he had done by looking."

Behind her, Rainey began to weep. "Why would he do something so horrible?" she sobbed. "Why would he ruin your beautiful cakes?"

The woman's distress moved Bette. She was angry about the ruined petit fours, but Rainey was devastated. "I don't blame you," she said. "Doug is responsible for his own actions."

"What are you going to do about the party?" Rainey asked.

"We have plenty of other food," Emily said. "I'm betting the sandwiches and cream puffs are all right."

"But the cakes—you have to have cake at a party,"

Rainey said. She sniffed and wiped her eyes. "I can help you make more. I'll do whatever you need me to do."

Bette considered the offer. "We don't have time to make more petit fours."

"We could make cupcakes," Rainey said. "They don't take long, and you could decorate them all fancy."

Bette nodded. "Cupcakes are a good idea." Not as impressive as petit fours, maybe, but the women would like them. She patted Rainey's arm. "Come on. Let's get to work. We have just enough time before Lacy's guests arrive."

"SURPRISED TO SEE you here, Cody," Dwight said as he entered Moe's Pub that evening and spotted the marshal at the end of the bar with Travis and Gage. "How are you feeling?"

"About like you'd expect someone to feel who's been shot and carved up." Cody wrapped his hand around a glass of iced tea. He would have preferred a stiff whiskey, but before leaving the ranch he had reluctantly taken one of the pain pills the doctor had prescribed and he knew better than to mix narcotics and alcohol.

"You could have stayed back at the ranch," Travis said.

"He didn't want to miss seeing you attempt to cut loose and enjoy yourself," Gage said.

Travis looked as if he wanted to cut something, all right. Or someone. "What's the plan for this evening?" he asked.

"I wanted to hire dancing girls, but you nixed that idea," Gage said.

"There are no dancing girls in Eagle Mountain," Dwight said. "What's plan B?"

"Plan B is to buy the groom a beer." He signaled to Moe, who was behind the bar. He slid over a pint and Gage handed it to Travis. "Then we have a little gift for you."

Cody and Bette had eventually gotten around to attaching the antlers to the stuffed cow—they poked out of the top of the shopping bag he handed to Travis. The sheriff set aside the pint glass and accepted the bag with the stoicism of a man who has resigned himself to eating a live worm. He pulled the cow out of the bag and his cheeks pinked. The rest of the men, who had already heard the story behind the gift, guffawed. "You never got a trophy from your first deer hunt," Gage said. "So we thought you deserved one now."

"You can hang it over the fireplace," one of the groomsmen, Ryder Stewart, said.

"Very funny." Travis set the cow aside and stood. "How about a game of pool?"

Someone put money in the jukebox, and most of the men teamed up to play pool at the two tables at the back of the room. Cody remained at the end of the bar, sipping tea and wondering if he would have been better off staying home. Gage slid onto the stool next to Cody. "You should have been the one to have a bachelor party," Cody said. "You would have enjoyed it more."

"Oh, Travis is having a good time." They watched as the sheriff bent over the pool table and lined up his cue. "He's a shark and this lets him show off his skills, plus I'm going to make sure he drinks more than he should. He needs to forget about this serial killer business for a while."

"Is he getting a lot of pressure from the town to solve the crime?"

"Eagle Mountain's new mayor thinks Travis hung the moon—but he doesn't need to apply any pressure. My brother is good at doing that himself."

"It's a tough case," Cody said.

"It is. We can't catch a break, and meanwhile, this guy goes around murdering more women." He set down his beer. "This conversation is too depressing. We need to talk about something else."

"Such as?"

"Such as—what's up with you and that pretty blonde caterer?"

"Bette."

"Yeah. Bette." Gage gave him the look of a cop interrogating a suspect. "Travis said you went to bat for her pretty hard over those stolen rings. You don't think she took them."

"Travis doesn't, either," Cody said. "Not really."

"Travis said she was pretty upset about you getting shot," Gage said.

"The guy was shooting at her, too. That would upset anybody."

"She was the first person you asked about when I picked you up this morning."

Cody sipped his tea. "Why are you interested in my personal life?"

"I'm a nosy guy. It's a good quality for a cop."

"Go nose into someone else's life."

Gage stood. "Maybe I will."

The door to the bar opened and a man stepped in. He scanned the room, taking in the half a dozen men playing pool and the two at the bar. A tall man with hunched shoulders, he had a few wisps of gray hair about his balding head and a ragged gray goatee. Moe moved from behind the bar. "This is a private party," he said. "Didn't you see the sign on the door?"

"It's okay, Moe." Cody put up his hand. He motioned to the newcomer. "Come on in. I'll buy you a drink."

The man hesitated, but apparently the prospect of a free drink won him over. He shambled to the bar and took the stool a few down from Cody. Moe had just served him a beer when Travis and Gage joined them. Travis slid onto the stool beside the man. "Hello, Carl," he said.

The man flinched. "Are you talking to me?"

"Carl Wayland, right?" Travis asked.

"I don't know anybody by that name." He turned his attention to his drink.

"How about Charlie Fergusen?"

"I'd better go." The man stood, but Gage put a hand on his shoulder. "Stay a minute and talk to us."

Carl looked around. All the men had gathered at the bar now. Dwight and Ryder still carried pool cues. "What is this?" he demanded. "Can't a man come in out of the cold and have a drink?"

"What are you doing in Eagle Mountain, Carl?" Travis asked, his tone genial.

"None of your business."

"Where are you staying since you checked out of the Eagle Mountain Inn?" Cody asked.

"Again—none of your business." He hunched over the bar and sipped his beer.

"Where were you yesterday afternoon?" Travis asked. "From, say, three o'clock until seven?"

Carl remained silent.

"What about Wednesday morning?" Cody asked. "Where were you then?"

Carl shoved back from the bar. "I gotta get out of here. It stinks too much of cop in this place."

He moved past Travis and Gage, but Cody blocked his exit. "Bette Fuller doesn't want to see you," he said. "If you come anywhere near her, I'll have you back in jail, charged with harassment."

Carl grinned, showing a broken incisor. "Bette is an old friend," he said. "A real nice girl. When you see her, you tell her I said hello." He pushed past Cody and out the door. Cody started to follow, but Travis held him back.

"I just want to get a look at his car," Cody said.

"Dwight is taking care of that," Travis said. "He's going to follow him and see where he's staying."

Of course Travis would have thought of that. Cody sat on the bar stool again.

Travis's phone rang. He answered it, turning slightly away from Cody and speaking low. Then he pocketed the phone and looked around the room. "Gage!"

Every head in the room swiveled toward the sheriff. There was no mistaking the urgency in his voice. Gage came over. "What's up?" he asked.

Travis voice was rough with strain. "There's been another woman killed," he said. "They found her in her car near the high school."

"To Lacy!" Maya held a glass of champagne aloft in a toast. "A wonderful friend who is going to be a beautiful bride, my future sister-in-law and a woman who knows how to throw a great party!"

"To Lacy!" the others echoed.

"Speech! Speech!" someone called.

Cheeks flushed with happiness—and maybe a little

from the champagne—Lacy stood. "Thank you all so much for coming tonight," she said. "It's been so special for me to get to spend this time with all my favorite women in the world." She spread her arms wide, as if to give them all a hug, and they clapped.

Lacy gestured to the one vacant place at the tables. "I'm so sorry Paige wasn't able to be here. Everyone keep your fingers crossed that the highway opens again before the wedding."

"I ate her share of the refreshments," Emily said, to more laughter.

"Wasn't the food fantastic?" Lacy said. She held up her champagne glass. "I want to propose a toast to my friend Bette, who made this scrumptious feast."

"Thanks to Rainey, too," Bette said. "She helped a lot with the cupcakes." Together, Rainey and Bette had baked carrot cake and devil's food cupcakes, decorated with cream cheese or buttercream frosting, and decorated with hand-piped snowflakes.

"And now I have something else for you all," Lacy said. She beckoned to Bette, who came forward and began handing out little white boxes tied with silver ribbon. "These are just little thank-yous to all of you for being in my wedding. I appreciate each of you so much."

A beaming Casey held aloft the little crystal snowflake on a silver chain that Lacy had chosen for her.

The other women oohed and aahed over the jewelry they received while Bette rearranged the refreshment table, consolidating the food so it looked less picked-over, and removing empty trays and platters. There wasn't that much left, a sign that the women had enjoyed everything. Fortunately, the petit fours were the only casualty of Doug's tampering.

"Bette, come up here," Lacy said.

Bette turned, surprised. Lacy had retrieved a white gift bag from somewhere. "I have something for you, too," she said. "You didn't think I'd leave you out, did you?"

Feeling a little self-conscious, Bette walked over and accepted the gift bag. "Open it!" Emily called.

The bag contained a large box wrapped in silver paper. Bette lifted the lid of the box and gasped. "Lacy!" She lifted out a pristine chef's smock, her name in dark blue lettering on the left breast pocket. Beneath this was a pair of checked chef's pants. Tears stung Bette's eyes as she stroked the fabric.

"I remembered you saying how one day you wanted a real chef's outfit," Lacy said.

Yes, Bette had said that. But these items, the cut and quality of them, had been out of Bette's reach when she had so many other expenses associated with starting her catering business. "They're beautiful," she said.

The friends hugged, then retreated to the kitchen with the boxes. "That's a really nice gift," Rainey said, admiring the chef's coat. "You'll look real professional in them." She nodded toward the party. "Travis found himself a really nice young woman. I wasn't too sure at first, but then it goes to show I can be inclined to misjudge."

"I think we all do that," Bette said. She had misjudged Rainey, mistaking her insecurity for animosity and her concern for her son as involvement in his wrongdoing.

"Doug still hasn't come home," Rainey said. "It's not like him to be away so long. I guess he knows he's in big trouble over those petit fours."

"I had to tell Lacy what happened," Bette said. "And I'm sure she'll tell Travis. It's up to them what happens next."

Rainey nodded. "I wanted him here because I wanted to keep him out of trouble," she said. "I thought away from the city, he'd have less temptation. And this would be a good job to have on his résumé. I guess you know how it is—when you have a blot on your record, people never want to look past it. They don't even give you a chance."

"I know." Lacy had given Bette a chance—her wedding planner had already talked to Bette about catering another wedding for a client in Denver, and with a few more jobs like that, and good references, she would be on her way.

"The problem is, a young man who's used to the city life gets bored here in the country," Rainey continued. "There's not enough for him to do. And it's always been hard for Doug to make friends. He told me recently he ran into someone he knew from Denver, who was visiting Eagle Mountain, and that seemed to cheer him up. But I worry, you know? Maybe if his father had stayed around to be a good influence on him he would have had an easier time of it. Or if I'd stayed in Denver to keep a closer eye on him, but as soon as he was out of school, he was anxious to be out on his own, and the opportunity came to take this job with the Walkers—I didn't feel I could pass it up. They've been so good to me—I hope they don't blame me for what he's done."

"I'm sure they won't." Bette squeezed the older woman's arm. "I'll make sure they know you didn't have any part in this," she said.

Rainey sniffed and turned away. "They're still talking and eating in there," she said. "You have time to put your gift in your cabin. You don't want those nice things getting dirty. And really, I can handle cleaning up after them myself. I'll box up the leftovers and we can deal with the rest in the morning."

"Thanks. But I shouldn't be gone long." Bette grabbed her coat from the pegs by the back door and stepped outside. The moon was almost full and provided plenty of light for the walk to her cabin. The old snow crunched underfoot, but new flakes were beginning to fall, like a sifting of powdered sugar over an already-iced cake.

She reached the cabin and shifted the box to one arm so she could dig out her key. The new one the Walkers had given her when they changed the locks was attached to a key chain with a rabbit's foot—maybe they hoped this key would be luckier for her than the last one. She grabbed hold of the key chain and started to pull it out when a strong arm wrapped around her neck and dragged her back. She dropped the bag that contained the chef's outfit, the contents spilling across the welcome mat in front of her door. She tried to shout, but the arm around her neck tightened. "Hello again, Bette," a familiar voice growled in her ear. "Or should I say, goodbye."

Chapter Seventeen

Anita Allbritton was a short, plump woman of about forty, with strawberry blond hair and round, tortoise-shell glasses. She taught business technology and computer science at the high school, and worked summers at the local Humane Society thrift store. She drove a burnt-orange Toyota Yaris, and was discovered in the front seat of this vehicle in the high school parking lot by a parent who was picking up his son from a sleepover.

"I recognized Anita's car and thought it was odd it was parked way out on the edge of the lot like that," the very agitated man told Travis and Cody, who had insisted on coming with the sheriff to the scene. "I stopped to see if there was any kind of note or obvious sign of trouble." He swallowed, struggling for composure. "I couldn't believe when I looked inside and saw... saw..." He shook his head, unable to go on.

What he had seen was Anita Allbritton laid across the front seat of her vehicle, her throat cut and her wrists and ankles bound with duct tape. Travis had found the Ice Cold Killer's card in the ashtray of the car, and a bloodstain beside a dumpster behind the school that he thought indicated the kill site. The car itself was clean of evidence.

"It almost looks like it was just vacuumed," Gage said, studying the vehicle's gray carpeting. "Do you think he did that—took the time to vacuum it out?"

"Maybe." Travis looked around the lot. "There are no lights this far out. No games or other activities tonight. Not a lot of traffic on the road. The killer may have felt he could take his time, be more careful. It was just chance that the parents decided to meet here to pick up the kids from that birthday sleepover. Just chance that the dad drove over to take a look."

"You don't think he's the killer?" Gage asked.

Travis shook his head. "He had his two children in the car with him. We'll confirm the time he left his house with his wife, but I'm pretty sure it will check out." The man had been devastated by the discovery, and had vomited on the edge of the parking lot. Fortunately, by the time Travis questioned him, he had pulled himself together and was anxious to get his children away from there.

Deputy Jamie Douglass, an attractive young woman with long dark hair worn in a bun beneath the regulation Stetson, joined them. "I talked with the Delaneys," she said. "They're the parents who met Mr. Karnack here to drop off his son, Colin. They didn't even notice the car parked over here. They live on the other side of town. They chose the high school as a good place to meet because it's halfway between the two homes."

Travis surveyed the area. The school was flanked on three sides by empty pasture. Across the street the school district's bus barn and maintenance sheds were deserted. "There's a neighborhood behind the bus barn,"

Travis said. "Start knocking on doors over there. Maybe someone was driving by here and saw something."

"Yes, sir." Jamie shoved her hands into the pockets of her Sherpa-lined leather jacket. "I'm sorry I had to break up your bachelor party with something like this," she said.

"You weren't interrupting anything," Travis said. "Whenever I'm not working on this case, I'm thinking about it—and dreading the next call about a dead woman." He looked at the Yaris. "It was only a matter of time. We aren't even managing to slow him down."

"Maybe we'll catch a break this time and someone saw something," Jamie said. "I'll get right on it."

"What can I do to help?" Cody asked, when she was gone.

"Go back to the ranch," Travis said. "Tell the women at Lacy's party to spend the night there. We have plenty of room. I don't want any of them out driving around tonight. And I'll feel a lot better if there's at least one cop there with them."

"Of course." Cody hesitated, then said, "Don't let this eat at you. You're doing everything you can to catch this guy—he's just not giving you anything to work with."

Travis studied the toes of his boots. "They tell you in the academy not to take the job personally. Maybe that works in the city, but in a small town like Eagle Mountain, everything is personal. I knew almost every one of these victims—some better than others, but they're all my responsibility. I wasn't just hired by the town—the citizens of this county elected me to do a job. There's no way to do that job except by taking it personally."

"It's why you're good at it," Cody said.

Travis swore—something Cody had never heard him

do. "I'm not good at it right now," he said. "If I was, I would have caught this guy—or guys—by now."

There was no sense arguing about it, Cody thought. In Travis's position, he would feel the same way. Though he could have told Travis that sense of responsibility wasn't limited to small-town cops. As much as Cody had tried to deny it in the weeks since it had happened, he felt responsible for the man who had killed himself in front of him. The man might be the worst kind of criminal—one who preyed on young children. But Cody's job had been to bring him to justice. When the guy pulled the trigger on that gun, he had cheated his victims and their families of that justice. He had prevented Cody from doing his job.

The drive to the ranch on the narrow mountain road seemed to take forever. Snow was falling again, and the cold seeped through Cody's clothes and the layer of bandages to his wound, until he felt like a giant was gripping him with strong fingers and squeezing, hard. The pain pill he had taken before the party had long since worn off. All he could do was grit his teeth and clench the steering wheel with one hand and keep pushing forward.

At the ranch, the women were gathered in the living room, donning coats and exchanging hugs. They stopped talking when Cody walked in and turned to look at him. "Cody, you're white as a sheet," Mrs. Walker exclaimed. "Come sit down before you fall down."

He shook his head. "Ladies, I have some news," he said. He looked for Bette in the crowd but didn't find her. She was probably in the kitchen, cleaning up after the party. "I'm afraid there's been another murder, a teacher from the school."

"Who?" It was Maya who spoke. She pushed her way to the front of the group. "Cody, please tell me," she said. "You're talking about one of my coworkers."

"Anita Allbritton." He looked at them sternly. "That information doesn't leave this room. The sheriff hasn't had time to notify her family."

"Poor Anita," Maya moaned. "How horrible."

"Travis wants you all to stay here tonight," he said. "We'd feel better if you weren't out on the roads tonight."

"Of course," Mrs. Walker said. "We have plenty of room."

"It'll be like a slumber party," Lacy said. "We'll find night things for you to wear—and we still have a couple of bottles of champagne and more food."

They moved away from the door, removing coats and talking all at once about this latest turn of events. A group clustered about Maya, asking about Anita, while Emily and Brenda conferred with Lacy and Mrs. Walker about sleeping arrangements. Cody interrupted them. "Where's Bette?" he asked.

"In the kitchen, probably," Lacy said. She smiled. "The party turned out so wonderful. It was a real triumph."

"I'll let her know what's going on," he said and made his way to the kitchen.

Rainey was alone in the room, arranging leftover sandwiches in plastic storage containers. She looked up at his arrival. "Hello," she said. "What can I do for you?"

"Is Bette here?" he asked.

"No, she isn't. She left a little while ago to put something away in her cabin and she hasn't come back yet. I told her I didn't mind cleaning up after the party and I guess she decided to take me up on the offer."

"That doesn't sound like her, leaving you to do the work," Cody said.

"Well, no, it doesn't. But maybe she was tired. She worked really hard today." She yawned. "So did I."

"I'll stop by her cabin and check on her," Cody said. He moved past her to the back door, quickening his pace as he stepped into the snow. He told himself the latest murder had raised his anxiety level, but he couldn't shake the sense that something was really wrong. By the time he could see the row of cabins ahead, he had broken into a painful jog, every movement jarring his injured shoulder.

The scene didn't look right. Something was scattered across the porch of Bette's cabin. He bounded up the steps and stared at the gift bag, a box wrapped in torn silver paper, and what looked like a top and a pair of pants spilling across the doormat. A gift? But what was it doing here?

He stepped over the items and pounded on the door. "Bette! Bette, it's me, Cody!"

He pressed his ear to the door but heard nothing inside. He tried the knob, but the door was locked—and Bette was the only one with a key to the new lock.

He forced himself to step back, to slow down and examine the scene objectively—to think like the cop he was. He studied the items strewn across the doormat. They hadn't been placed—they had been dropped. Bette had been standing here in front of the door, maybe searching for her key, and something had made her drop the package. Surprise? Fear?

He retraced his path to the steps and studied the snow illuminated in the moonlight. The snow here was churned up, then dug into grooves. A struggle, then someone being dragged backward, the person's heels digging in. Heart pounding, he followed the marks until they stopped, beside the track from a vehicle.

He squatted down and studied the impressions, still fairly clear despite a light dusting of snow. Deep tread on wide tires. But not car or truck tires. They were too close together. They were tractor tires—or no, tires of one of the utility vehicles used around the ranch for everything from hauling hay to plowing snow to herding cattle.

That meant that whoever took Bette was probably still on the ranch. Cody pulled out his phone and called Travis. "I'm here at the ranch and Bette is missing," he told the sheriff. "Looks like someone grabbed her on the front porch of her cabin. I found the tracks of what looks like a utility vehicle. I'm going to follow them."

"Wait for me," Travis said. "I can be there in thirty minutes."

"I don't have time to wait," Cody said. "The snow is covering the tracks fast." And he didn't know what whoever took her planned to do with Bette. He might already be too late. "Where is Carl? Is Dwight still with him?"

"Dwight followed him to a rental out of town, then he returned to help process the scene at the high school."

Carl could have hurt Bette. "I have to go after them now," Cody said.

"Get one of the ranch hands to go with you," Travis said. "Or more than one."

"I don't have time to go looking for people," he said. "Besides, it's Saturday night. They might not even be here. They're probably in town, or visiting family or friends."

Snow was falling harder. "I have to go," he said. "You can track me when you get here." He ended the call and stowed his phone, then pulled his coat more tightly around him and set off across the snow, following the line of treads that led over the pasture.

BETTE LAY ON the floor of the old cabin where the sleighing party had gathered. Was that really only two days ago? Duct tape tightly bound her hands and feet, and a bone-deep chill had seeped in, so that her teeth kept chattering—or maybe that was just fear.

Carl sat on an upturned section of log across from her. "I bet you never thought you'd see me again," he said. He chuckled, a sound like an accordion with a hole in the bellows. "Get it, 'Bette'?"

"Why are you doing this, Carl?" she asked. "What did I ever do to you?"

"Oh, it's nothing personal, sweetheart. I'm just doing a favor for an old friend. He needs you out of the way before you open your big mouth."

"You mean Eddie." She'd known it, hadn't she? As much as she told herself she had nothing to worry about, that Eddie wouldn't waste any more time on her, she'd been fooling herself.

"Eddie?" Carl laughed again. "Not him. He's dead."

"Dead?"

"Yeah. Got knifed in an alley one night just a couple weeks after he got out." Carl shrugged. "Guess he crossed the wrong guy."

"I don't understand," she said. "If you're not doing this for Eddie…"

"You don't think I have more than one friend?"

Stamping footsteps on the porch interrupted him. The door opened and Doug Whittington came in, brushing snow off the shoulders of his coat. "We could have picked a better night for this," he said.

"Doug, what are you doing?" Bette asked.

He scowled at her. "What do you think we're doing? We're going to slit your throat, stick you in your car and drive you out to some deserted road. By the time the cops find you, Carl and I will be safely tucked in our beds—innocent lambs who don't know anything about what happened to you."

"You're the Ice Cold Killer?" She hated the way her voice shook on the words.

"No!" Doug shook his head. "But that's who the cops will think did you." He felt around in his pockets and handed Carl a small white card. "This is why I was late. I had to wait until the coast was clear so I could sneak into the Walkers' home office and print this."

Carl showed Bette the card, which read "Ice Cold." "It's genius, right?" he said.

"It's a stupid catering job!" she said. "That's not worth killing me over."

He walked over to her and stood looking down. "You really don't know who I am, do you?" he asked. He picked up one of the kerosene lanterns and held it closer to his face. "Sure I don't look familiar?"

She stared, recognition washing over her like a

bucket of cold water. "You drove the getaway car," she whispered.

"Bingo." He set the lantern down. "I couldn't have you telling the police that, could I? They don't just want me for my part in the bank robbery—they want to hang me for the murder of that pedestrian. It wasn't my fault the dope walked out in front of me!"

"But I didn't remember it was you!" she said. "I couldn't have told the police anything."

"You'd have figured it out soon enough," Doug said. "I couldn't keep avoiding you all the time. Not with my mom nagging me about helping her more in the kitchen, and you always popping in and out of there. It's your own fault we're having to take such drastic measures, you know."

"What do you mean?" she asked.

"I tried to warn you off," he said. "I left that message on your door—I even hit you in the head with that rock. I thought you'd believe you'd narrowly escaped being the Ice Cold Killer's next victim and you'd want to get out of Dodge, wedding or no wedding."

"You stole the wedding rings and planted them in my room," she said.

He frowned. "I thought the sheriff would carry you off to jail and that would be the last we saw of you. It was really tempting to keep those rings for myself, but I figured that was working a little too close to home. But then that marshal had to stick his nose in things and I finally accepted that I wasn't going to scare you off. I was going to have to do something more drastic."

"That's where I come in," Carl said. "A job like this works better with two people."

"So he called you to come out and help kill me," she said.

"Not exactly," Carl said. "I actually looked him up. I wanted to see about doing another job together. He told me about his problem with you and I offered to help him out."

"Which one of you tampered with the snowmobile and shot at Cody and me?" she asked.

"That was me," Carl said. "I should have just picked you off while you were sitting out there on the ice, but I wanted to make it a little more fun. I almost had you, too. A few more minutes and the marshal was bound to run out of ammo, then I would have closed in for the kill." He frowned. "Too bad I didn't finish off the marshal when I had the chance. I would have liked to have taken out a fed."

Bette looked at Doug. "You're being stupid," she said. "You'll never get away with this."

"Who are you calling stupid? I'm the only one involved in that bank job that didn't get caught. I've been walking around free while you did eight years. Besides, Travis and his buddies think I'm just some jealous punk. They think poisoning your fancy cakes is as malicious as I get." He reached down and took her arm. "Come on. We need to go."

He lifted her by the arms, while Carl hefted her legs. They carried her out to the utility vehicle and dumped her in the bed. She had to lie with her knees to her chin to fit. "This snow is perfect," Carl said. "It will cover up our tracks. Did you get her car keys?"

"I got them," Doug said. "I had to break the back window to get in. The key I had for the door to her cabin doesn't work anymore. They must have changed the locks after the business with the rings."

"I told you that was never going to work," Carl said. "You should have just kept the rings for yourself. That gold is worth a lot these days. We could have melted it down and no one would ever know."

"Yeah, well, it's too late now." Doug climbed in beside him. "Let's get this over with."

Carl started the vehicle and it jolted forward. Bette tried to sit up. If she could lean out over the back, maybe she could fall out.

And then what? It wasn't as if she could run away, or even crawl, trussed up as she was. She closed her eyes and tried to pray. Surely someone from the ranch house had missed her by now—Lacy, or even Rainey. What time would Cody and the others return from Travis's party? Probably not until late. Too late for her.

"What the—!" The vehicle skidded sharply to the right as gunshots sounded. Bette flattened herself to the bed of the cargo area, flinching as a bullet thudded into the side of the vehicle.

"It's that marshal!" Doug shouted. He—or maybe Carl, Bette couldn't be sure—returned fire.

"Come on!" Doug shouted. "He's on foot. He can't catch up with us."

"I'm going as fast as I can," Carl said. "It's not that easy in this snow."

Another bullet struck the vehicle, this time hitting the tailgate, inches from Bette's curled legs. She had to let Cody know she was in here, before he accidentally shot her.

Grunting with the effort, she sat up, praying Cody would see her. She looked back and spotted him, pounding after the utility vehicle, his gun in his uninjured hand. But he was no longer firing. He had seen her; she was sure of it.

The vehicle jounced over rough ground, throwing her back against the tailgate. One of the men fired at Cody, but the shot was wild. She wondered if they were even aiming—if it was possible to aim in the wildly careening vehicle.

She jolted against the tailgate again, and one side of the latch popped. Sitting up again, she braced herself against the side of cargo bed and slammed both feet into the other end of the latch. It gave way and, afraid of losing her nerve if she waited, she rolled out of the vehicle.

She hit the ground hard, but the thick snow provided some cushion. She forced herself to keep rolling, despite the pain of every movement, trying to put as much distance between herself and her two captors as possible.

Cody stopped her, dropping to his knees beside her. "I'm here," he gasped, trying to catch his breath.

She lay still, tears freezing on her cheeks. "What are they doing?" she asked.

"They're coming back."

"They'll kill us," she said.

"No." He crouched in front of her and fired toward the approaching vehicle. They returned the fire, but as before, their shots went wild. Cody kept firing, a rapid burst of staccato reports. Bette closed her eyes and waited—for what, she wasn't sure.

And then she realized the sound of the utility vehicle's motor was fading. And Cody had stopped shooting. "They're running away," he said.

He holstered his weapon, then found a knife and began cutting away the layers of tape around her wrists and ankles. He helped her sit up, rubbing her hands between his own to restore her circulation. She cupped his face and kissed him. They held each other for a long moment, neither of them speaking.

"Come on," he said finally. "Let's get out of here before we freeze to death." He stood and helped her to her feet, then, leaning on each other, they started walking toward the ranch house.

Travis and Gage met them when they were halfway home, pulling up on snowmobiles. "Carl Wayland and Doug Whittington are in one of the ranch utility vehicles," Cody said. "I'm pretty sure I wounded both of them. They had kidnapped Bette and they tried to kill both of us."

"They were going to kill me and make it look like another murder by the Ice Cold Killer," Bette said. "Doug even printed up a business card on your home office printer."

"We need to go after them," Travis said. "Can you make it back to the ranch house?"

"Go," Cody said. "We'll be fine."

By the time they reached the house, Bette was shaking with cold and Cody's breath hissed through his teeth with each step. The man had just gotten out of the hospital this morning—how had he even found the strength to come after her?

The women who had attended the party descended on them with blankets and steaming mugs of cocoa and hot water bottles, then Lacy shooed them all away. "Don't bombard them with questions," she said. "Let them catch their breaths."

Bette and Cody huddled together on the sofa. When

Bette had finally stopped shaking, she asked, "Do you think Travis and Gage will find Carl and Doug?"

"They'll find them," he said.

"Doug admitted he wrote that message on my door," she said. "And he stole the rings and planted them in my room. And he was the one who attacked me that day on the road. Carl was the one who tampered with the snowmobile and shot at us."

Cody sipped his cocoa. "Why did they go after you?" he asked.

"Doug was the getaway driver in the robbery. The one who killed that pedestrian. I didn't recognize him, but he had never let me get a really good look at him. Once I saw him in good light, I realized who he was. He was afraid I'd turn him in and he'd go to prison for robbery and for killing that man."

"Where does Carl come in?"

"He came to town to ask Doug to do a job with him. I think he meant another robbery. Doug told him about me and they decided they needed to get rid of me. Permanently."

She laced her fingers in his. "Thanks to you, that didn't happen."

He turned to look at her. "I think I'm going to have to take you into protective custody," he said.

Her heart skipped a beat. "What are you talking about?"

He brought their linked hands to his lips, kissing her knuckles. "One of my jobs as a US marshal is witness protection," he said. "I think I need to put you under my protection. Permanently."

She caught her breath. "You're going to have to speak plainer than that, Marshal."

"I'm asking you to marry me," he said. "I love you and tonight I learned that I don't really want to live without you."

She thought of him, facing down that vehicle racing toward him, bullets flying. He had done that to protect her. To protect what they had found together. "Can a US marshal marry someone with a criminal record?" she asked.

"I don't care if they can or not," he said. "I want to marry you. If you'll have me."

"I'll have you." She kissed his cheek. "But your job—"

"I'm on leave for at least three months, with my injured shoulder. And since I've come here, I've been thinking. Maybe it's time for a change."

"What will you do if you're not a marshal?"

"I have a law degree. All I have to do is pass the bar and I can study for that while I recuperate. What would you think of being married to an attorney?"

"Defense or prosecution?"

"Prosecution. I can leave law enforcement, but I can't leave putting away criminals."

"Fair enough."

He squeezed her hand. "So your answer is yes?"

"Yes. I'll marry you." She kissed him, then couldn't stop smiling. "You know, I have a fabulous recipe for wedding cake."

"I can't wait to taste it."

"By the time we caught up with Carl and Doug, they were ready to surrender," Travis said over breakfast the next morning. "They had wrecked the ute and were both freezing, and bleeding pretty heavily." He glanced at

Cody, who sat across from Travis at the table, next to Bette. "You hit Doug once and Carl twice. None of the shots were serious, though Carl has a broken arm. I've got two deputies guarding them at the clinic. As soon as the doctor will release them, we'll lock them up in our holding cell until we can transfer them to Junction."

"We found that business card on Doug," Gage said. "Too bad we couldn't get them for the Ice Cold murders, too."

"They couldn't have done those murders," Travis said. "Carl was talking to us at Moe's when Anita was killed. He was in Denver when Kelly and Christi died, and Doug was here at the ranch."

"How is Rainey taking the news about Doug?" Lacy asked.

"She's stoic," Travis said. "Blaming herself, I think."

"I imagine she's heartbroken," Bette said. "He's really all she has. She told me she raised him pretty much on her own after his father deserted them."

"I'm glad he's gone," Lacy said. "Poisoning those cakes was downright creepy, and then when I learned all he did to you—well, it was horrible."

"We caught him on camera taking the spare key to the old lock on your cabin yesterday afternoon," Travis said. "And we have the gun Carl used when he shot at you two. We shouldn't have any trouble sending both of them to prison for a long time, on multiple counts."

"Any news on Anita's murder?" Cody asked.

"No." Travis poked at his eggs with a fork, his expression glum. "All we can do is keep looking."

"You'll find the killer," Lacy said. "If anyone can, you will."

"Spoken like a loving bride," Bette said.

"Of course." She looked at each of them in turn. "I'm not being callous, but in spite of this killer, we have a wedding to prepare for," she said. "In the midst of so much tragedy, it's especially important to hold on to the joyous occasions."

Bette lifted her glass of orange juice. "Here, here," she said.

Lacy's smile grew sly. "I hear you have some joyous news of your own," she said.

Bette looked at Cody, who cleared his throat. "Bette and I are going to be married," he said.

"Congratulations," Travis said. "Though it's no surprise."

"No?" Cody asked.

"I figured you were pretty much gone after that first day." He glanced at Lacy. "I know the signs from personal experience."

"We haven't set the date yet," Bette said. "It will be after we're settled again in Denver, but you'll all be invited to the wedding, I promise."

"If I were you, I'd wait until that shoulder heals," Gage said. "Be a shame to have to deal with that on your honeymoon."

"I don't know about that." Bette rubbed Cody's uninjured shoulder. "This way, I have the upper hand. Not a position I've ever been in with a US marshal."

"Watch yourself," Cody said. "Even with one hand tied behind my back—so to speak—I can get the best of you."

"I don't know about that," Lacy said. "It looks to me as if Bette has pulled off one last heist."

Cody's eyes narrowed. "Oh?"

Lacy laughed. "Yeah, you goof. Clearly, she's stolen your heart."

Everyone around the table groaned, but Cody's eyes met Bette's, and she thought she could never get tired of looking into those depths, figuring out what made this man tick. "Guilty as charged," she said. Lacy was right. In spite of all the tragedy around them, it was important to celebrate the things in life worth hanging on to. Like the kind of love that gave you infinite second chances.

* * * * *

WYOMING COWBOY SNIPER

NICOLE HELM

For opposites who attract.

Prologue

Dylan Delaney considered the scene around him an atrocity: Carsons and Delaneys of Bent, Wyoming, not just mingling in the same yard but celebrating.

Celebrating the marriage of his sister—an upstanding, rule-following sheriff's deputy with too good of a heart—to a no-good, lying, cheating, *saloon-owning* Carson.

The fact his sister looked so happy as she danced with her newly pronounced husband was the only reason Dylan was keeping his mouth shut. That and a well-stocked makeshift bar in the Carson barn that had been transformed into a wedding venue for Laurel and Grady.

Dylan had been bred to hate Carsons and what they represented his whole life. Delaneys were better than thieving, low-class, lying Carsons—and had been since the town had been founded back in the eighteen hundreds.

Dylan's siblings had always been too soft. Though Jen had held strong with him, Cam and Laurel were growing even softer in adulthood as they mixed themselves up with Carsons.

Romantically of all things.

Dylan had prided himself on being hard. On being *better*. Half his siblings had been happy to ignore the calling of the Delaney name, but he'd used everything he had in him to live up to it.

If it felt hollow in the face of his sister happily marrying Grady Carson, he'd ignore it.

"Worried about your precious bloodline, Delaney?"

Dylan sneered. Normally, he wouldn't. Normally, he'd be cool, collected and cuttingly disdainful of Vanessa Carson even breathing the same air as him, let alone addressing him. But the liquor was smoothing out just enough of his senses for him to forget he never engaged with the Carson he hated the most.

"Aren't you worried about catching a little law and order? Ruining that bad-girl reputation of yours?" Dylan smiled, the way he would have smiled at a dirty child who'd just smeared mud over his freshly dry-cleaned suit.

She wore the same shade of black as his suit, but not in a sedate cocktail dress that might have befit a wedding. He'd have even given a pass to a funeralesque sundress, because it was a rather casual affair all in all, and it felt like a funeral on his end.

But no. Vanessa wore tight leather pants and some kind of contraption on top that flowed behind her like a cape down to her knees. It knotted in the front above her belly button. A little gold hoop dangled there, mocking him.

He was so attracted to her, it hurt. He hated himself for that purely animalistic reaction that he'd always, *always* refused to act on. He'd dealt with cosmic jokes his whole life. This was just another one to be put away and ignored. He was stronger than the cosmos. Had to be.

She flashed a grin meant to peel the skin off his face. "My bad-girl reputation is rock-hard solid, babe." She sauntered around Dylan and the makeshift bar, then started looking through the collection of bottles and cans.

The hired bartender blinked at her, clearly caught off guard and having no idea what to do despite making a living from serving drunk and rowdy wedding guests. "I can get you what you—"

"No worries." She nudged the bartender away and rummaged around, then poured herself an impressive and possibly lethal combination of alcohol. She lifted her cup in Dylan's direction, which was when he realized he'd been watching her. She drank deeply.

"If that was for my benefit, color me unimpressed," he muttered, looking away from that long slender neck and the way long wisps of midnight-black hair danced around her face.

"Baby, I wouldn't do anything for your benefit, even if you were on fire," Vanessa said, her voice a smooth purr.

He refused to let his body react. "Someone's going to be carrying you out of here if you drink all that."

She laughed, low and smoky. It slithered through him like—

Like nothing.

"I could shoot you under the table, sweetheart."

"Wanna bet?" he muttered, forcing himself to stare ahead even though he could feel her come to stand next to him.

She laughed again, the sound so arousing he wanted to bash his own head in.

"I know you didn't just say that to me, Delaney. You're not that stupid."

Which poked at all the reactions he kept locked far, far away. Apparently the rather potent drinks he'd been downing in swift succession were the key to unlocking them. "I'll repeat it, then. Want to bet?" He enunciated each word with exaggerated precision as he turned to look at her.

She smirked, somehow a few inches shorter than him even though she always seemed to take up so much space. "Oh, I'll take that bet. How much?"

He named a sum he knew she couldn't possibly afford.

She rolled her eyes and waved a dismissive hand that glinted silver and gold with an impressive array of rings, including more than one in the shape of a skull or dagger.

He despised her. Every inch of her. Which he drank in against his will.

"Delaneys love to flaunt their money."

He flashed a wolfish grin, enjoying far too much the way her eyes narrowed as if preparing to ward him off. *Good luck, little girl.* "Chicken?"

Some little voice in the back of his head reminded him of propriety. Reminded him of his place in Bent and the fact that getting in a drinking competition with Vanessa would only end in embarrassment and trouble. It went against everything he believed and stood for, and he should just walk away.

He stood where he was and ignored that voice.

When he woke up the next morning, definitely not in his own bed, ignoring that voice was the last thing he remembered.

VANESSA WAS DYING. From the inside out. So, so many bad decisions made last night. But it was her brother's fault for marrying a Delaney. That she was sure of.

She groaned, rolling over in bed as her stomach roiled in protest. She'd had her fair share of hangovers, but this one was truly something.

And now she was hallucinating.

Had to be. Because there was no way on God's green earth that Dylan Delaney was in her bed.

No *Delaney man* was *naked* in her bed, in the middle

of her apartment above her mechanic shop. She looked to the left. There was her little kitchen, the hall with the bathroom door. She looked to the right, at the door to the stairs down to the shop, and in that line of vision was clearly a man.

As she blinked at that shape of a man next to her, it was Dylan's dark eyes that widened and sharpened. It was every gorgeous plane of Dylan Delaney's face that went very, very hard.

Vanessa closed her eyes tight, counted to ten in a whisper. It had to be a dream. It had to be an alcohol-induced mirage. It had to be anything but the truth.

But when she was done counting, Dylan was still there.

"Apparently bad dreams do come true," Dylan said, his voice all delicious rough gravel.

Get yourself together. Nothing about Dylan Delaney is delicious.

She watched, horrified, really she was horrified and not intrigued at all, as he flung the covers—*her* covers—off of him and stood, clearly having no compunction about being *naked in her room*.

With jerky movements, he pulled on his pants from last night. Last night. She'd…

"You can't tell anyone." If she'd been feeling better she would have kept that inside. Ignored the panic and held on to the upper hand. But she was *dying*, and she'd apparently slept with Dylan Delaney.

She remembered nothing. Nothing about last night beyond the wedding ceremony where her rough-and-tumble brother had promised himself forever to goody-two-shoes Laurel Delaney. A *cop*.

Beyond that, everything got fuzzier and fuzzier until…

Best kiss of your life.

Ha! She'd been drunk. How would she have known?

Dylan gave her one smoldering look—enough her heart started pumping overtime and her whole body seemed to blaze with heat. She could almost, *almost* picture them together, feel his big rough hands on her—

But Dylan Delaney, a bank manager, did not have rough hands. She was hallucinating. And was that a *tattoo* on his chest that disappeared as he pulled his shirt on and began to button it?

"Who on *earth* do you think I'd tell about this horrifying lapse in judgment?" he said disgustedly.

It didn't sting, because she felt the same way. Except *lapse in judgment* was way too tame. *Catastrophe of epic proportions* was more appropriate.

A catastrophe she would also blame on Grady, because if he hadn't married a Delaney, she wouldn't have gotten drunk enough to *sleep* with one.

Dylan was now completely dressed, and she was still naked in her bed. *Naked.*

"We'll both forget this ever happened," Dylan said. No. He demanded it, like she was a peon to be ordered about. But even she couldn't work up contrariness at his tone when *this* had happened.

"I don't even know *what* happened. We didn't really…" But he'd been naked, and she was naked so…

"I don't remember either. So we'll just say we didn't."

"But—"

"We didn't," he said firmly, patting down his pockets. "I have my wallet. No keys."

"Surely neither of us were stupid enough to drive."

"Surely neither of us were stupid enough to have someone drive us *together* anywhere." He sighed, running an agitated hand through sleep-tousled hair. He did not look like his normal slick self. He was disheveled and…

Appealing.

No, not that.

"Hate sex is a thing," she blurted, feeling unaccountably out of control and nervous. Which did not make any sense, but she couldn't seem to straighten herself out. It had to be the hangover and all the booze still in her system.

He scowled, and Vanessa didn't understand why her eyes wanted to track the small lines around his mouth or note the way dark stubble dotted his chin where it had been smooth last night.

There was something compelling about him. She'd admit it now and regain some of her control. They were polar opposites, and sometimes when polar opposites got drunk enough, they ended up attracting.

She'd swear off alcohol for the rest of her life right here, right now.

"Hate sex is not a *thing*. Not for me it's not."

"Apparently for drunk you it was."

He pinched the bridge of his nose. "I'm leaving. We'll never speak of this again. And if anyone saw us…"

"We lie," Vanessa supplied for him.

He seemed startled by that word, but what else was there to do?

Eventually, he gave a sharp nod. "Through our teeth." He turned and strode out her apartment door.

Vanessa stared at the ceiling, hoping she never, ever remembered what had transpired and willing herself to forget about it for good.

Chapter One

Four months later

Vanessa Carson was not a coward. In her entire life, she'd never backed down from an insult, a challenge or a fist. She'd faced all three of those things practically since she'd been born, and yet none of it held a candle to this moment.

She sat in the driver's seat of her ancient sedan in the back parking lot of Delaney Bank. She preferred her motorcycle but... Without thinking the movement through, she placed her hand over her stomach. It was starting to round, just a little bit. No one else would notice, but she could tell. It wouldn't be long before other people would be able to tell, as well.

The morning sickness had been hell, but it seemed to dissipate more every day. She'd taken to eating better, and she'd sworn off alcohol for different reasons ever since that night. Her doctor said she and baby were healthy as a horse.

Luckily, she was surrounded by clueless men for the most part, so no one in her life had any idea. She was convinced it was paranoia that on more than one occasion she'd caught her cousin-in-law or new sister-in-law staring at her with a considering gaze when she did something like eat a veggie plate or pass on another hit of caffeine.

Paranoia or not, she had to face the music before anyone actually put the puzzle together. Had to. Before the music told him itself.

You are not a coward.

She repeated those words with every step toward the bank. She had never once stepped foot in Delaney Bank, would have rather chewed her own arm off—or simply driven the twenty-plus minutes to Fremont whenever she needed a bank.

But this wasn't about asking for a loan or sullying the white halls of such an upstanding establishment run by the Delaneys. It was about the very unfortunate truth.

She was going to have Dylan Delaney's baby.

For a few weeks she'd considered running away. Disappearing. Grady would likely try to find her, with her cousins Noah and Ty not far behind him. But it would have been possible if she'd played her cards right. Eventually, they'd have given up on her. Maybe.

But Bent was her home. Her life. Her mechanic shop was everything she'd built her life on. She'd paid in blood, sweat and tears for it. She wasn't ever going to let a Delaney scare her into running away.

Your baby is half Delaney.

She paused at the corner of the bank building. Ruthlessly, she reminded herself Dylan wouldn't want anyone to know that any more than she did. He'd agree to her plan. He had to. He'd *never* risk his reputation just to be a part of his baby's life.

Which was why she had to tell him. He'd be spiteful if he found out some other way. She needed this to be quick, easy and painless. Which meant she couldn't just stand here.

She heard a noise from behind her and turned to see a back door opening. Dylan stepped out, looking perfectly dapper in a suit with a briefcase clutched in his hand. He slid sunglasses onto his face in defense of the setting sun, his dark looks tinged with gold in the fading light.

She'd never understood her reaction to him—a tug, a *want*. No matter how much she knew she did not want the uptight, soft banker boy, something deep inside of her begged to differ.

Luckily, she was a smart woman who knew when not to listen to stupid feelings. She just needed to explain to him how things were going to be, and be done with him for good.

"Dylan."

He startled, as if he recognized her voice instantly and how incongruous it was at his precious bank. He immediately scanned the lot before turning his gaze to her.

When he'd seen there was no one else around he took a few steps toward her, suspicious and uncomfortable, but not sneery. She would have preferred a little sneery to get her back up.

"Vanessa," he said, his voice cool and clipped, though not nasty.

"Dylan. We need to talk."

He raised an eyebrow. Such a disdainful look, and yet she didn't feel that same animosity from him she'd always had when they'd been growing up. They'd avoided each other even more carefully than usual since Laurel and Grady's wedding, which was hard to do in a small town when your siblings were married. But they'd done it.

Still, there'd been a cooling of antagonism on both their parts. Perhaps they now knew a little too well where unchecked dislike could lead. Being apathetic worked a heck of a lot better.

But she wished he'd be nasty, so she could be angry and defensive instead of so nervous she felt sick.

This is better. You can be calm and collected and show him he's not the only one with some control.

"We really need to talk," Vanessa repeated when he said nothing. "Privately."

Again he scanned the lot and seemed satisfied no one lurked in the dusky shadows. "Follow me."

He used a key card on a pad outside the door he'd come out of, then pulled it open and gestured her inside. She went, chin too high and sharp, shoulders back and braced for a fight.

But it wouldn't be a fight. It would be a quick, informative conversation, and then she'd walk right out of the bank with this awful weight off her shoulders. She wouldn't run her mouth. She'd just say it plain.

He stepped inside, the door closing behind him with a definitive slap. With a nod, he moved down the hallway, leading her to another door—this one glass. Inside was a fancy office. Evidently his, since his name was printed on the glass.

"You know, in my shop I don't have to put my own name on the door to my office."

"I'm guessing, in your shop, you're not entertaining wealthy clients in your office."

She flashed him a hard-edged grin. "You'd be surprised who likes me doing the oil change on their car."

His lips pressed together. She couldn't help but remember him not as the slick, suited businessman who stood before her but as the rumpled, slightly shaken man she'd woken up with that morning all those months ago.

He set his briefcase down and took a seat behind the big, gleaming desk, then ran a hand over the lapel of his suit jacket. He looked impossibly elegant. He wasn't like his siblings. They were the down-home noble type. Laurel the cop, Cam the former marine and Jen the shopkeeper.

Dylan had style—with an edge to it. She didn't know why he stayed in Bent when he was clearly meant to be somewhere a lot more posh than this nowhere Wyoming town.

She didn't know why she had this odd memory of his hands on her feeling *right*.

Just insanity and liquor, she supposed.

"What did you need to discuss?" he asked in the cool, detached voice he'd almost always used on her. Even when they'd been in the same class in first grade, he'd spoken like that to her at the age of seven. Like he was inherently better.

It should have put her back up, but all she could do was stare at him behind his big desk, looking imposing and important in this big, fancy bank office.

She swallowed as an unexpected emotion swamped her. Regret. It was a shame the way her baby had been conceived because this whole Delaney legacy belonged to him or her too.

Money. The kind of reputation people slaved a lifetime to never live up to. The baby wouldn't even have to deal with being the first commingling of Carson and Delaney. Laurel and Grady would always take whatever heat people blamed on a foolish curse, because they'd promised to love each other in front of God himself.

Not everyone in town took the feud between the Carson and Delaney families as seriously as she did, and not everyone in town believed the old tale that if a Carson and Delaney ever fell in love, the town itself would be cursed to destruction.

A story passed down from generation to generation

since the Carsons had accused Delaneys of stealing their land back in the eighteen hundreds.

Enough people believed it to make it a *thing*.

The fact Bent hadn't immediately crumbled or been struck by lightning didn't soothe the most superstitious. They were still waiting for it. As for Vanessa, she was more of a take-life-as-it-comes type of girl. She'd deal with a curse if there was one, and she wouldn't be surprised if life went on as it always had.

"I know you're not here for the view. Or a repeat performance," Dylan said, shocking her out of her reverie.

Repeat… She clamped her jaw shut so it wouldn't drop. No one ever turned her off-center like this.

It was the baby softening all her edges. Which was fine and dandy, once she'd done her business. She was determined to be a good mother—the kind hers had never been—where her kid came first and foremost. And not one man was going to ruin that for *her* kid. She'd soften every last edge, sand off her tattoos and cut out her own swearing, drinking, idiot tongue if it meant giving this baby the kind of idyllic childhood she'd never had.

Which meant no strife with the father of the baby, even if Vanessa didn't plan on him being involved.

The best way not to have any strife was to be quick and to the point. She took a deep breath in and let it out, forcing herself to meet Dylan's dark, imposing gaze.

"I'm pregnant."

THE WORDS LANDED like a blow, the kind that had your ears ringing and your eyes seeing stars. Even as Dylan's brain scrambled to make sense of those two simple words, he desperately held on to his composure.

In business, composure was everything.

This wasn't business.

Pregnant. Baby. She was telling him she was pregnant and that meant…

He opened his mouth to speak, though he wasn't sure what it was he meant to say. No words or sound came out, anyway.

"I'm not asking you for anything," she said clearly. Her gaze was calm, direct, but he saw the way she clutched her hands together in her lap. For a woman like Vanessa she might as well have been shaking in her boots. "I'd rather—"

"Yes, I can imagine all you'd rather," he muttered. He glanced at her stomach where her hands were clutched. There was no evidence a child grew there, but one did and it was his.

His.

His heart squeezed as if gripped by some iron outside force, a mix of panic and awe. Mostly panic, he assured himself.

"But if I didn't tell you, you'd figure it out and assume. So I'm telling you. You don't need to worry or do anything. I'll keep your part in this a secret and raise this baby myself." Her hands squeezed harder, and he couldn't seem to bring himself to lift his gaze from them to meet hers.

"Yourself," he repeated stupidly.

"Yes. I'm capable. Maybe I don't look like the most maternal—"

"I'm not challenging you, Vanessa," he snapped, looking away from her hands. Her eyes were storms of a million things. Things he didn't want to consider.

But she was pregnant with his child. *His* child.

Hell.

"Regardless," she said, sounding surprisingly prim. "I

wanted to be clear that I'll be taking care of everything. As long as you don't yap, we'll be fine."

"Fine," he echoed. Fine. This was not fine.

She began to stand.

"Where the hell do you think you're going?"

She raised her eyebrows. "Home. I told you what I had to say and—"

"And you think I'd just step back and ignore the fact I have a child? You honestly thought you'd make your little announcement and that would be it?"

Her eyes went cool, the nervousness in her clutched hands gone as they came to rest on the arms of the chair. "Obviously, I considered you'd be obnoxious, but I held out hope you'd understand that yes, that's it. Because it's a Carson child."

He stood, pressing his hands to the shiny surface of his desk in an effort to center himself and leash his anger. "Half Delaney."

She folded her arms across her chest and gave him one of those patented Vanessa Carson, *you-are-a-bug-to-be-scraped-off-my-boot* looks. "Are you suggesting we cut the baby in half?" she asked dryly.

"I'm not suggesting anything. You're not giving me time to suggest anything. You've dropped your bomb and now seem to think you're going to waltz out of here and leave me to deal with the fallout."

"I believe that's usually how bombs are dropped," she replied. She was back to herself. Sharp, dismissive and oh so sure she was better than him.

But she hadn't been for a few minutes, and she was carrying his baby. His child.

A living, breathing *human being*.

He sat back down. The weight of it floored him. "I

can't… How long? It'd be…" He did the math. "You've been sitting on this for a while."

She shrugged. She wore jeans and a long-sleeved T-shirt. Heavy black boots. Even with her tattoos covered, she looked like trouble. She always had. He didn't know why he'd think pregnancy would change it.

He focused on her. On the gleaming silver skull ring on her thumb. The way her hair seemed all that much blacker against the fair, freckled skin of her cheeks. Sharp edges with surprising hints of vulnerability.

And she was carrying his child.

She sighed heavily. "Look, I don't know what you think sitting there staring at me is going to accomplish, but this is how things are going to be. I have the kid, tell people the father's some random out-of-towner. I live my life and you live yours."

"Knowing your child is mine."

"Consider yourself a sperm donor."

"I will not," he said, managing to keep his voice as even as hers. It was a hard-won thing. "I don't know if you're trying to be difficult or if it just comes naturally, but this is not a *small* thing. It's a huge, bomb-sized thing."

"You seem pretty calm and collected to me," she muttered.

"Years of practice," he said through clenched teeth. The lies he'd told and the things he'd seen. Yes, he'd had *years* of practice in how to appear calm when he was anything but. In control of a world that would not bend to his will—here in Bent or out there where he'd lived his secret life.

Now this. He wanted to be angry, but every time it spurted up, this strange weight settled over him. *Calm* wasn't the right word for it. There was something like a flash of her, from that night. Something he should re-member and couldn't. A softness. A rightness.

He shook it away, but he couldn't shake away the re-alization he didn't have a choice here. She thought he could walk away, turn his back on his own child, and he wouldn't in a million years.

Which meant he had to find common ground with the one person in this whole town—and possibly world—he wasn't sure he could.

There had to be common ground here though, whether he liked it or not. They had to find a compromise.

Something had changed that night, and not just the life it had created. The animosity between him and Van-essa had dulled. Or maybe it was watching Laurel and Grady these past few months. No matter how much grief they got from the town or Dad, they laughed and smiled and…didn't care. Something had changed inside of them so they didn't care.

Dylan had made a child. It was time to not care. "Van-essa."

The distinct sound of a gun being fired jolted them both. It had come from the front. Dylan was on his feet in seconds.

"Stay here," he ordered.

"Stay *here*?" Vanessa repeated incredulously. "You can't… Was that a gun?"

But he was already striding out of his office. He made it not even halfway down the hall before he heard foot-steps behind him.

He whirled on Vanessa. "I told you—"

"Was that a gun? We should call someone! Why are you running toward it?"

He didn't have time to explain, but she could call. "Go back to my office, lock the door from the inside and dial

911. Tell them you heard two shots fired in the lobby. One employee inside, not sure about customers. Go."

He nudged her back toward the office.

"Aren't you coming with me?"

"I have to make sure Adele—"

Two masked men slammed through the door from the bank lobby. It was a robbery. Possibly the stupidest of all crimes in this day and age. Surely Adele had hit the alarm and these two men would be caught before they even tried to leave.

Dylan glanced down at the assault rifles they each carried. Unless they'd shot her first. He felt the horror move through him, but quickly pushed it aside. Compartmentalized and assessed the situation.

Two armed robbers in front of him. The Carson woman, pregnant with his baby, behind him.

And he'd thought it was going to be your average Monday.

Chapter Two

Vanessa tried to think, but unfamiliar panic tickled the back of her throat. Masked men with guns. She'd faced a lot of bad crap in her life, but this was a first. Fear had turned her body to lead.

"Office," Dylan said under his breath. He didn't look back at her, just ordered her to move.

But she couldn't. She was rooted to the spot by a mind-numbing panic that barely allowed her to suck in a breath. The guns. She wasn't usually rendered useless by the sight of guns. She'd shot her fair share, sometimes even carried one, and had been in the presence of them her whole life.

But these were so big, and they looked more military than recreational. She was sure she and Dylan were dead where they stood, and all the fight she was so certain she had in spades deserted her.

"Who are you?" one of the men demanded, gesturing his gun toward her. "Supposed to be one," he muttered to the other man. "Boss promised us it'd be one."

"What have you done to Adele?" Dylan asked.

Dylan's calmness was downright creepy. He didn't shake or seem panicked. Vanessa managed to keep a decent mask of not freaking out on the outside, but Dylan didn't seem to be acting. Easily, he stepped toward the two men, even as they aimed their guns at him.

Vanessa tried to swallow down the labored breathing that threatened to make too much noise in the quiet hall. She tried to move, but her body was still lead weight.

"Put the guns down and we'll make sure this ends well for everyone," Dylan said, still moving toward them, even as their fingers curled around the triggers. "Now, what have you done with my employee?"

Vanessa couldn't catch a breath. She and Dylan were going to die here in this hallway. Not just them, but their baby too. Her balance swayed and she had to squeeze her eyes shut and lean against the wall to find it again.

"Take them both?" one man asked the other.

The other seemed to consider it. "Only set up for one."

"Tricky business. Shoot her?"

Some awful sound escaped her throat, and she couldn't open her eyes or breathe. She was going to die. Her baby was going to die. Dylan was going to die.

Fight. You have to fight.

"Boss's got space. Rather take them both than get any blood on our hands till we know we can get away with it."

"Wasn't supposed to be two here. Boss's fault if we have to kill her."

Vanessa opened her eyes. She was still unaccountably dizzy, but she had to fight. For her baby. For herself. *Dylan.* "Are you seriously discussing whether or not to kill someone in front of said someone? What kind of criminals are you?" Vanessa demanded.

"Yeah, we'll take her," the bigger one sneered.

"Over my dead body," Dylan seethed, moving forward.

"I can arrange that," the sneering man said, jabbing the barrel of his gun right into Dylan's chest.

Vanessa went cold all over, even as she couldn't work out why Dylan was trying to save *her*. Just the baby, she supposed. Her teeth were chattering now, and she berated herself for being such a coward, but that didn't help give her the strength to push off the wall. To do anything. She could only stand here, shaking, falling apart, wondering why everything was spinning around her.

Except Dylan's profile. Something clicked off in his expression. It wasn't fear that overtook him, even though this huge, monstrous weapon was pressed to his heart. It was…determination.

"You should leave her. She's pregnant. You don't want to mess with that. I'm the son of the bank president. Think of the ransom you could ask for. You don't need her, and you don't need to hurt her." Then Dylan did the damnedest thing. He smiled.

"Dylan," Vanessa managed. The hallway seemed to be getting dim, and she thought maybe she was going to throw up. She tried to say something, warn somebody that it wasn't going to be pretty. But the world was moving. The walls. The floor.

"Pregnant, eh?" One of the men eyed her and she had to close her eyes again. She had to think of the baby. If she could get her brain to stop being a jumbled mess, get the panic to stop freezing her, she could barricade herself in Dylan's office and call 911.

These men would be able to shoot through the glass door though. She'd left her cell phone in her car. Did Dylan have his on him? He seemed like the type who wouldn't be parted from it. She opened her eyes, trying to study his pants to see if there was the hint of a phone in his pocket.

"She's a liability," Dylan said, still so damn calm while she was shaking. Had the lights gone out? Everything seemed so dark. "Any harm you cause her would come back on you tenfold. It's one thing to kidnap and demand ransom, another to harm a woman and her unborn child."

"Only if we get caught," the other man said, his smile going so wide half his mouth was hidden behind his black face mask.

Vanessa thought she could all but read Dylan's thoughts from the simple murderous expression he gave the man: *oh, you'll be caught.*

She'd never given Dylan much credit for bravery or having a backbone, but watching him face down two goons with giant guns, she realized she had to reassess her opinion of him.

"We need to get going. We should have been gone ten minutes ago. Stick to the plan, or the boss—"

"Yeah, yeah, yeah." The man holding the gun to Dylan's chest pushed him with it. "You're coming with us." He gestured toward the back door Dylan had led her through not that long ago. Dylan started moving toward it, the gun now to his back.

He didn't even look at her as he passed.

"We can't leave her, pregnant or not. She's seen too much. We have to take her with us. Come on, little girl."

The man not pushing Dylan reached out for her, but she flinched away. She wanted to deck him, but she couldn't manage to move her arms. She couldn't *move*, period. Bile rose in her throat.

"I'm going to…" But the room was something like black, and she wasn't on her feet anymore. Then something crashed against her head and painful stars burst in her vision, but it wasn't light. She heard Dylan say her name, but she couldn't seem to do anything but stay still—and then float away.

DYLAN'S FACE THROBBED in time with his heavy beating heart. He should have been able to fight them off, but he'd been trying to get to Vanessa to make sure she was all right.

Now his hands were zip-tied behind his back, and he was pretty sure his shoulder was dislocated from trying to fight that off. It was possible his jaw was broken from the butt of the gun being smashed into his face, but since he could move it, he'd hope for just a severe bruise.

He'd never be able to break the bonds on his hands or feet, or even loosen them, but he kept feeling around the back of the van, trying to find something sharp.

Trying to keep his mind off the fact Vanessa was unconscious on the floor of the van and carrying his baby.

They'd been in the back of the vehicle for at least fifteen minutes by his count, and Vanessa was still out cold. She was so pale. So…vulnerable.

He'd save her. He had to. His skills at survival had dulled somewhat these past few years of playing dutiful banker and protégé to his father. But he'd remember them. He'd bring them all back, and he and Vanessa would escape this mess.

Poor Adele. He hoped she was all right. Surely she'd have hit the alarm, even if they'd hurt her. But the two morons who'd abducted them had certainly taken their time getting out of the bank, and no one had shown up.

Well, someone would notice him missing. A Carson would surely notice Vanessa missing. Someone would notice she didn't come home and that her shop wasn't open. They'd see her car in the bank lot and know something was very, very wrong.

If he assured himself of those facts, he could concentrate on how they were going to escape. Because they *were* going to escape.

A quiet, gasping sound came from Vanessa's direction. Dylan scooted toward her. He wished he could maneuver himself to grab her hand, feel her pulse, but there wasn't enough room on the floor of the van.

"Vanessa."

She groaned this time, moving her head and then groaning again.

"Vanessa. Come on, sweetheart. Wake up." He tried nudging her with his elbow, but he couldn't lean that way without falling at every bump.

"Wh-what…?" She jerked at her arms, her legs thrashing wildly.

"Calm down. It's okay. I'm here. It's okay."

She jerked her gaze to him, all vicious anger hiding a little flash of fear. "Why would *you* being here make anything okay, Delaney?" she demanded, her voice rough. She looked around wildly.

"Just try to breathe. You fainted. Take your time to wake up. Then I'll help you sit up as best I can."

She sucked in a breath then let it out, eyeing their surroundings. The back of the van was all metal, and though the windows were tinted completely black, enough light shone through that they could make each other out. She moved her gaze to him.

"Fainted?" She tugged at the bonds on her hands as she moved herself into a sitting position—without his help—with a wince. "I've never fainted in my life."

"First time for everything. I'd imagine it had to do with—"

"How the hell am I tied up with *you* of all people?" She looked around, her expression one of panic with a steely disgust instead of that ashen terror from before. It was some comfort. "Where *are* we?"

"They took us both as hostages."

"Who's 'they'?" She pulled at the ties on her wrist again, then winced. She squeezed her eyes shut. "How did I get here? I can't…"

"What do you mean, 'you can't'?" He recalled that sometimes people with head injuries didn't remember what had caused them. Added to that, she'd fainted and suffered a trauma. Maybe she didn't even remember coming to see him at the bank. "You don't remember?"

"Remember what?" she snapped.

"What's the last thing you remember?"

She flashed him an impatient look, then her eyebrows drew together. "Man, someone did a number on your face." She seemed to finally understand he was tied up too.

"Yeah, yeah. We can talk about that later. Vanessa, what's the last thing you remember?"

She blinked, frowned. "I don't. Things are fuzzy around the edges. Fuzzy everywhere. I went to the grocery store this morning. Yeah." She closed her eyes and swallowed. "I'm not going to be sick," she muttered to herself, as if saying it aloud would make it so.

"That'd be preferable."

She frowned at him, but the confusion dominated her expression. "You look different. Your face is different."

"Must be the impressive bruising."

"No. You have lines."

"Lines?"

"Around your eyes. Your mouth. And that's some suit. Are we in Bent?" She tried to peer out the window, but she was still sitting and it was too black to see out of.

"You're supposed to be in college, aren't you? Somewhere out east. Yeah, that's what I heard."

"College?" Panic threatened. *College.* She was just a little confused. By over a decade.

"A fancy one, right? I certainly remember your dad bragging all over himself about it when I went to the store this morning. Dylan this. Dylan that. For my benefit. As if *I'd* be impressed."

"Vanessa. God." It was as jarring of a blow as the butt of the gun to his face had been. "What year do you think it is?"

"What kind of question is that? It's…" Her brow furrowed again, and she shook her head. "It's… I'm sure it's…" She looked up at him helplessly. "What's wrong with me?"

"You fainted. And you hit your head. Things are jumbled, but they'll clear up." He said it far more confidently than he felt it. She'd lost over a decade. That little trickle of panic turned into a full-on frantic clawing, but he ruthlessly shoved it down.

She'd just woken up. She was disoriented. The past ten years would come back. Everything with the baby would be okay.

It had to be.

"Got a phone on you?" he asked, his last hope at getting a message to someone.

"Why would I have a phone on me?"

Dylan swallowed down the bubble of hysterical laughter that tried to escape. He wouldn't panic and he wouldn't be hysterical. She'd be fine. She'd have to be. Surely pregnant women fainted and were fine, even with a little memory loss. Women had survived life on the prairie and what-have-you and had had plenty of babies.

Everything was going to be fine if he kept his mind calm, his body ready.

He'd been a soldier once. He could be a soldier again.

"Okay, no phone. Anything sharp?"

"There should be a knife in my boot, but I can't get it with my hands behind my back like this. Who took us? Why are we both tied up? I don't—"

"One thing at a time. Let's get free and then I'll explain everything." Hopefully. Maybe she'd remember once she fully woke up. He had to hope there really was a knife in her boot, and she wasn't remembering a knife in her boot from thirteen years ago. "Put your legs out."

She did as he instructed, straightening her legs out in front of her.

"Which boot?"

"Right. There's a slot for it behind the outside of my ankle." Dylan scooted forward, maneuvering himself so the hands tied behind him were close to her ankle. He'd have to kind of lean over her legs and brush up against her to get his hands anywhere near her boot.

It was uncomfortable and awkward, but the most important thing was finding the knife, if in fact she had one down there in the here and now.

She fidgeted just as he finally got his fingertips down the side of her boot. "This is weird," she complained.

"No weirder than what you don't remember," he muttered, concentrating on leaning this way and that and ignoring the sharp pain in his ribs where one of the goons had kicked him, and the fact his head was all but in her lap.

It took a lot of time, a lot of contorting and a hell of a lot of pain every time the van went over a bump, but he managed to pull the knife out of her boot.

He was sweating by the time it clattered to the floor

of the van, but he didn't wait around to catch his breath. The sooner he got them out of their bonds, the better. He leaned back, managed to grasp the knife. In a few swift movements, he cut the zip tie off his wrists.

Sometimes military training did come in handy in the civilian world. He wouldn't have guessed.

He didn't take a second to enjoy the feeling of freedom, however. He shook off the plastic and immediately cut the one around his ankle, and then freed Vanessa.

"Well. You move…fast," she said, as if that surprised her. "You better not have gotten me roped into this, Delaney."

"Quite the opposite."

"Figures. Always blame a Carson." She rubbed at her wrists, then delicately touched her fingertips to the side of her temple. She winced. "Some blow to the head."

"You folded like a card table and hit the ground before anyone could do anything."

She scowled. "I find that story very hard to believe."

"Well, I didn't knock you around and then tie us both up. But someone with guns *did* tie us up, so we need to be quick about getting ourselves out of this mess." But before they could do what needed to be done, she needed to recall one very important thing.

"You don't remember why you came to see me?" he asked carefully.

"I'm assuming these goons had a gun to my head, because that's the only way I would ever voluntarily go to see you. Unless you were being tortured. And I was invited to watch."

"Nice." Dylan sighed. This was going to make everything so much more difficult, but he didn't have time to get his nose out of joint about it. "I need you to understand something, okay?" He took a deep breath. If she really didn't remember years' worth of stuff, he doubted she'd believe him. He doubted a lot of things, but he couldn't let her go running around thinking it was just her. "You're pregnant."

She barked out a laugh. "Uh-huh."

"I'm serious. That's why we're together. You came to tell me."

"And why would I tell you… Oh. No. No." She shook her head back and forth. "You really expect me to believe I slept with *you*?"

"We were very drunk."

She shook her head, eyes wide. "I don't believe it. There's not enough liquor in the world."

"Okay. Don't believe it. But I need you to understand you *are* pregnant, it's thirteen years later than you think it is and bank robbers have kidnapped us to get a ransom. But I'm going to get us out of this, and when we escape you have to do everything in your power to keep the baby growing inside of you safe."

She went pale at that, but they didn't have time to keep discussing. The van had been moving too long, too far, and they had to make a serious jump-and-run effort here. She had to believe it, even if she didn't want to.

"It can't *be*," she whispered, pressing her hand to her stomach.

"But it is."

Chapter Three

Vanessa didn't believe him. Maybe things were all wrong—from the lines on his face to the nausea in her gut to the van they were trapped in—but she would have never slept with Dylan Delaney, even with a blow to her head.

And *he* would have never slept with *her*.

Dylan was fiddling with the door, looking serious and in control. He'd been beaten up pretty badly, but he didn't seem to pay it any mind. He wore a suit—and even though it was dirty and rumpled, she could tell it was expensive.

Her eyes stung, and it took a few moments to realize she wanted to cry. Everything was wrong, like a bad dream where only half the things made sense, no matter how real it all felt.

But cry? Not her. Not in this lifetime. She blinked a few times, and focused on the here and now. Not anything Dylan was claiming, but the fact they were tied up in the back of a van, and now Dylan was using her knife and his bloody hands to mess with the door.

"Can I help?" she managed to ask once she could trust her voice.

"Just sit back."

She scowled. She wasn't a *sit-back* kind of girl, but

she wouldn't have pegged Dylan as a take-charge kind of guy. Sure, to order people around maybe, but not to try and bust them out of a moving van.

How could this all be happening? She was about to demand he explain this and tell her the truth instead of his nonsense dream—lies—about her being pregnant with *his* baby.

She pressed a hand to her stomach, acknowledging that she *might* feel really off. But couldn't that just be the head injury? Couldn't Dylan have *caused* the head injury? Sure, he was all beat up, and he'd been tied up too, but…

She tried to remember. Tried to order her thoughts and memories, but the very last thing she remembered was flipping off Dylan's dad as she left the Delaney General Store.

Not her finest moment, but…

But nothing. The old jerk deserved it. She opened her eyes to the young Delaney jerk in front of her, still trying to jimmy the back door open. He didn't look right. He looked older. Was she really missing such a big chunk of time?

She looked down at her hands. There were pink marks and scratches where the zip ties had dug into her skin around her wrists, but otherwise her hands looked the same. Same rings she always wore… Well, maybe not exactly. She fiddled with a dainty-looking gold one in the shape of a mountain. She didn't remember that one.

She had to find some kind of center—both a mental one and a physical one. This weakness in both wouldn't save her, and it wouldn't fill in whatever memory blanks she had.

But the van chose that moment to rumble to a stop, followed by the engine shutting off.

Oh, God.

Dylan swore, then sat down on the floor of the van right by the doors. "Stand behind me," he ordered, like he knew what he was doing, like he could get them out of whatever this was. "Be ready to jump. On my signal, run as fast as you can for whatever cover you can find."

"What about you?" Not that she *cared* about Dylan, but…

He flashed her a grin so incongruous with the Dylan Delaney she'd grown up alongside, she could only gape at him.

The door made a noise, like a lock being undone. "Be ready," Dylan murmured, leaning back on his palms as he watched the door.

"What are you—"

The door began to open, and on an exhale Dylan kicked his legs out as hard as he could against the doors. There were twin grunts of pain as the doors hit something, but Dylan didn't pause. He flung the doors back open and jumped out.

"Go!" he instructed.

Because she saw one man on the ground, struggling to get to his feet, with a *huge* gun next to him, she did as Dylan instructed. She jumped out of the van and immediately started to run.

"Opposite way!" Dylan yelled. She turned, ready to do whatever Dylan instructed if it'd get her out of here, and watched in the fading dusk as his yell ended on a grunt as one of the large men landed an elbow to his gut.

Dylan Delaney, a hoity-toity Delaney who was getting a fancy degree and likely hadn't done an ounce of manual labor in his entire life, took the blow like it barely glanced off him. Then he pivoted, swept a leg out and knocked one large man on his butt. Dylan reared back a fist and punched the other guy in the throat, then whirled as the fallen man got back to his feet.

Vanessa blinked.

"Go!" Dylan yelled at her, and it got through her absolute shock at seeing him fight like he knew what he was doing. No, not even like he knew what he was doing. Like he was *born* to do it.

But there were angry men and guns, so she ran the opposite way she'd been going, toward the front of the van. It acted as a buffer between her and the men and gave her the opportunity to get away without them seeing exactly where she was going.

Dylan knew what he was doing—between the instruction to run this way and fighting off two men. What the hell? She shook away her confusion and focused on running as hard as she could. Her stomach lurched and her head throbbed, but the guns brought it home that she was running for her life here.

And your baby's life?

She couldn't think about Dylan's nonsense right now. She just had to get away. She ran hard, but the farther she ran, the darker it got. She had to slow her pace so she didn't trip. So she didn't throw up.

With heaving breaths, she slowed to a stop and pressed her hand to her stomach. She had a cramp in her side that felt like a sharp icepick. When she stopped, she was nearly felled by a nasty wave of nausea. Her head downright ached, and the stinging behind her eyes was back.

But she was in danger, and a Carson knew how to get herself out of danger. She swallowed at the sickness threatening, focused on evening her breath, then studied her surroundings.

She had run for the trees—the best cover she could find—but they were spindly aspens, and it wasn't ideal to be hiding behind even a cluster of narrow trunks. The van must have driven them up in elevation, but where? It was completely dark now, and she couldn't get a sense of her bearings.

Panic joined the swirl of queasiness in her stomach. She breathed through both. She could survive a night in the wild. She didn't particularly *care* to, but she could survive. As long as Dylan had taken care of those two armed men, she was safe enough. Anyone could brave the elements for one night.

And if Dylan didn't fight them off?

It was hard to imagine it. He'd moved like a dancer. A really violent, potentially lethal dancer. Dylan Delaney. She would have labeled him the prissiest of the four Delaney kids. Even his younger sister Jen had more spitfire to her than Dylan.

But he was claiming they'd slept together, that he'd impregnated her somehow, and then she'd watched him fight like a dream.

Touching fingertips to the bump on her head, where everything throbbed and ached, Vanessa had to wonder if the blow had caused hallucinations.

Either way, she was alone in the dark in the middle of the Wyoming woods. She lowered herself to the ground, leaning her back against one of the rough trees. It was uncomfortable, and a chill was creeping into the air.

It would be fine. There wasn't snow on the ground, and the leaves still clung to the trees, though they'd gone gold in a nod to fall. But they hadn't completely fallen.

Luckily, she was too nauseous to be hungry, though she wouldn't mind a drink of water. But she'd live. She was alive, and she'd live.

"There you are."

She would have screamed if a hand hadn't clamped

over her mouth. She turned her head to find herself face-to-face with Dylan. It was too dark to make out the individual features of his face, and yet she knew it was him.

"Shh. Okay?"

She nodded and his hand fell off her mouth.

"What happened? How are you… How am I… What is going *on*?"

Breathing only a little heavily, he scanned the dark. "I managed to incapacitate one."

"Incapaci-what?"

"I didn't have time to incapacitate the other," he continued, clearly not worried about how odd his word choice was. "Figured I had a better chance to catch up with you so we're armed."

And he *had* caught up with her.

He'd fought off two armed men like he belonged in some sort of action spy movie, run fast enough to catch up with her and now, in his rumpled, torn suit, was holding a giant semiautomatic weapon as if he knew how to use it.

"Who *are* you?"

He flashed her that incongruous grin again, just barely visible in the night around them. "Well, clearly not who you think I am."

THEY WERE IN TROUBLE. Dylan would be less worried about being stuck he wasn't quite sure where in the dark if Vanessa wasn't pregnant and sporting a hell of a head injury. He couldn't let himself dwell on that too much. All he stood to lose.

No, a good soldier focused on the mission at hand, not the future.

He hadn't had a chance to put his real talents to use, he thought bitterly as he looked at the gun. Knocking out the first guy and getting his weapon had taken more time than Dylan cared to admit, and when the second guy had hopped into the van and tried to run him down, Dylan's best choice had been to run, not shoot like the sniper he'd been once upon a time.

"I need an explanation," Vanessa said, and he knew she wanted to sound strong and demanding, but he heard the tremor of fear in her voice.

How had this day gone so far to hell so fast?

"I don't really have one," he said softly. None of this made sense to him. A bank robbery was foolish, but they'd gotten away with it. Except they hadn't taken any money. They'd taken him and Vanessa.

"More of one than I do."

Dylan sighed. He couldn't see well in the dark, but he was fairly the certain the other man had lost him in the trees where his van couldn't follow and headlights couldn't penetrate deep enough.

Still, Dylan needed to be on alert until morning. Maybe with daylight he'd be able to figure out where they were and get them home.

Surely someone knew something was wrong at this point, with both him and Vanessa missing, Vanessa's car in the bank's parking lot. Adele was likely hurt—he had to accept that more-than-possibility, and she didn't have anyone waiting for her at home. But maybe she wasn't fatally hurt and—

"Dylan. Answers." Vanessa gritted her teeth, and he wondered if it was to keep them from chattering.

"Still no memory, then?"

She was silent for a few moments, except for the rustling of her fidgeting. "No. I… No. My last memory is that morning in the store with your dad, but if I try to come up with a year or how old I am, it all jumbles up.

Some things make sense and some don't." Her voice trembled at the end, and she didn't say more.

"You seem to be missing about a decade. More than, actually. I've been home from…college for ten years."

"Why'd you pause all weird before you said *college*?"

"I didn't," he replied, irritated that she'd picked up on that. "Now, can we focus on the here and now?"

"I have *amnesia* and lost ten years plus off my life and you—"

"Just fought off two armed men who wanted to kick us around and use us for ransom. In the best-case scenario. Now we're alone in the woods with no supplies or help. Do you have any idea where we are?"

"It's too dark. It's too…"

He wouldn't let her panic, so he spoke over her. "The way I figure it we drove south out of town, and kept on that way since the sun was setting into the window when we left. That puts us close to Carson territory. Maybe."

"Maybe. But none of this looks familiar to me."

"That's okay. We don't want to be moving around in the night anyway. In the morning we'll have a better idea." One way or another. "How are you feeling?"

"Am I really…?" She paused, then audibly swallowed.

"Pregnant? As far as I know. You came by the bank to tell me. That's when these men came in. I hope they didn't kill Adele." He muttered the last to himself. "I was too hard on her. Sharp mind, abrasive attitude, sure, but she was always a stellar employee. I should have…" Not the mission at hand though. He blew out a breath. "You need to rest. Tomorrow might be a bit of a rough day. We'll have a lot of walking to do."

He moved from a crouch to a seated position next to her. He positioned the gun so he was able to hold it and wrap his free arm around her shoulders.

She tensed and leaned away. "What are you doing?" she demanded.

"Being your makeshift pillow, sweetheart."

"You think I'm going to sleep on you?" She sounded so horrified it gave him some semblance of hope.

"You may not remember, but you've done a lot worse on me."

She recoiled, and he couldn't help but chuckle. "If it helps, on that front, I don't remember either. It is no exaggeration that the night we were together was the drunkest I've ever been. Somewhere during the reception my mind goes black." Maybe he had a few flashes here and there of soft sighs or the silk of her hair, but she didn't need to know that.

She didn't lean into him, but she'd stopped leaning away. "I…"

"It's going to be a chilly night. We'll keep each other warm. Hopefully, you catch a few hours sleep. We move at first light. No ulterior motives. Just common sense and getting through this…ordeal."

"Are they going to come after us?"

Dylan wanted to lie, to reassure her. It was strange to want to comfort Vanessa, but she wasn't herself. She was pregnant. With a bump on her head. And amnesia. She was a mess, and everything in him had softened completely at that.

Still, it was important she knew what they were up against. "I have no idea. Which is why you need to sleep, and I'll keep watch."

"Don't you need to sleep?"

"I'll be just fine."

She leaned into him, slowly, almost incrementally. Eventually, her head rested against his shoulder.

It felt oddly comforting.

"Where did you learn to fight?" she asked, her voice thick with exhaustion.

Briefly, he wondered if he should keep her awake because of concussion concerns, but she needed rest. She was *pregnant*. And they had no food or water. Surely rest was better, and it wasn't like they'd get much anyway.

He didn't answer her question, and when she didn't push, he figured she'd fallen asleep.

Funny, Vanessa was one of the few people who probably wouldn't be horrified by where he'd learned to fight, by all the lies he'd told. She'd love it.

She'd also tell his family with relish and glee, regardless of the accidental pregnancy.

Why that made him want to smile in the middle of this mess, he didn't have a clue.

Chapter Four

Back in Bent

Laurel Delaney parked her police cruiser in front of Delaney Bank and glanced at the man in the passenger seat.

Deputy Hart didn't know it yet, but she'd asked him to be her second on this call because soon enough she'd have to disclose her pregnancy to her superiors. They might let her continue to do some light detective work but not in the field. Desk duty. *Ugh.*

Regardless of how she felt at having to sit things out for *months*, Hart would be a good replacement for the duration of her desk duty and maternity leave. Yet that didn't make it easy to accept someone else taking the role she'd worked so hard for. Bent County only had one detective spot, and she loved it.

Sometimes you sacrificed what you loved for who you loved. She may have only just found out about this baby, but she already loved the child she and Grady had created with everything she was.

Which was why Hart would take the lead on this case. Probably best regardless of her physical condition, considering the man who'd called it in was her father.

Dad stood in front of the bank, looking grave and irritated. His patented look.

He didn't know about the pregnancy yet—no one but her and Grady did at this point. Dad wouldn't be happy. But then, nothing about his children's choices of significant others lately made him happy. Dylan and Jen were his only hopes. Laurel and Cam had been relegated to black sheep at best due to their choice to connect their lives with Carsons.

It hadn't been a choice, falling in love with Grady. Though she supposed they'd chosen to center their lives in that love.

Laurel sighed and gave Deputy Hart a thin smile. "I'd ask you to take the lead, but my dad is only going to want to deal with me."

Hart grinned. Laurel knew he cursed his baby face, but she thought it'd often work in his favor as a detective. People underestimated the sharp mind and conscientious attention to detail underneath. "I'm counting on it," he offered cheerfully.

Laurel rolled her eyes but got out of her car. Darkness had settled around the bank, but the lights were still on. She took a deep breath of fresh air and shored up her patience to deal with her father.

"Dad."

"Laurel." He didn't even give Hart a cursory look. "Took you long enough."

"You said it wasn't an emergency."

Dad merely shrugged. "Have you heard from Dylan?"

"No, but I wasn't expecting to. Why don't you tell me what you think happened?"

"I don't know what happened," Dad snapped. He smoothed out his features, clearly remembering that it wasn't just her in his audience. He had to play the role of upstanding Delaney for Deputy Hart. "I was driving home from the airport after my meeting in Denver. I passed the bank and saw the normal lights on instead of the security lights. So I pulled in, thinking someone had forgotten to switch over to closing lights, but the door was unlocked and no one was inside."

"And you suspect foul play?"

Dad pressed his lips together, a sure sign of irritation. "I don't know what to suspect. Neither your brother nor Adele will answer their phones. The safes are all closed and locked, and nothing appears out of place, but the evening paperwork wasn't done, so I can't be sure if every dollar is accounted for."

"So it was just Adele and Dylan working?" She nodded at Hart to start taking notes, pleased to see he already was. He was going to be a good replacement. Just hopefully not so good she couldn't get her detective spot back when she returned from maternity leave.

But that was so far away. She didn't need to think about it now.

"As far as I know. Adele was scheduled to close. Dylan wasn't scheduled, but it's not unheard of for him to be here until close. Still, we didn't have any meetings, and he tends to check in with the foreman at the ranch before the foreman's done at five."

"Why don't Hart and I take a look around? Have you been home to see if Dylan's there?"

"No, but I called George and he hadn't seen him."

Laurel felt the first little tickle of worry at the base of her spine. "Hart, I'll take the inside. You take the outside. Dad, do you have security tapes?"

He puffed out his chest. "Of course. I haven't had a chance to look at them. I called you once I realized my bank had been abandoned and unlocked for who knows how long."

"Pull up the footage," Laurel instructed, stepping inside. She began to look around the front counter. Though she'd never planned on following her father's footsteps at the bank, she'd spent some time working as a part-time teller when she'd been in the police academy, since Dad had refused to pay for that.

She knew her way around, and nothing appeared out of place. It didn't look like your typical burglary. Surely it had just been someone's mistake. She couldn't imagine her brother or Adele Oscar, one of Dad's higher-up employees, being that careless. But maybe if there'd been an emergency elsewhere?

Yet there was the gut feeling that had gotten her through her years as a deputy, and now as Bent County Sheriff's Department's detective, that told her something was off. That this was more than an oversight.

Hart appeared at the front doors. "There are two cars in the employee lot out back," he said. "You want to come see if you recognize them?"

Laurel nodded and motioned Hart to follow her through the back hall that would cut through the bank to the back lot. She passed Dad's office and stopped when she saw him scowling and punching at the computer keys.

He looked up and, though his face was scowling and angry, she saw the hint of worry in his gaze. "I'm not sure what happened, but there's no footage today. It appears the cameras were turned off last night."

"Purposeful?"

Dad shrugged. "I don't know. I suppose it could be an accident, but whoever did it had access."

"I'll need a list of anyone who has access and opportunity to turn on or off the cameras. Hart, sit down with him and write down everyone who had access. I'm going to check out the cars." She moved through the back hallway briskly, that gut feeling diving deeper.

She immediately recognized the first vehicle, her brother's sleek sports car. It was enough to make her feel uneasy. Why would Dylan have left his car behind? Still, she could have come up with a few reasons. But the second car, parked farther down, made her stomach flip over in absolute police-level concern.

What was Vanessa Carson's car doing in the Delaney Bank parking lot? That wasn't just abnormal—it was unheard of.

Laurel immediately pulled out her phone. When the rough voice answered, the noise of his saloon a steady hum behind him, she couldn't smile like she usually did. "Grady."

"What's up, princess?"

The nickname didn't bug her anymore, but this feeling did. "Have you seen Vanessa today?"

"Van? Hmm. Guess not, but I wasn't expecting to." There was a pause. "What is it?"

"I'm not sure. Can you send someone to see if she's at her shop and give me a call back?"

"Laurel, do I need to be worried?"

It was her turn to pause. "I'm not sure."

"But you are. Worried, that is."

"Call me back, okay? Love you."

"Laur—"

She couldn't sit on the phone and argue with her husband. She marched back inside to her father's office. "It's Dylan's car and Vanessa Carson's."

Hart's eyebrows rose and Dad's face turned a mottled red.

"Are you telling me—"

"I'm telling you those are the cars left in the lot, and both people are unaccounted for. We need to find Adele Oscar. If she was working, and her car's gone, we need her story. If she won't answer her phone, we'll have to go find her."

Hart nodded. Laurel looked at her father. "Lock up. Go home. I'll let you know when I've got more information."

"I demand—"

"Go home, Dad. Let us investigate." She pushed Hart toward the front doors and to the police car.

She had a bad feeling Adele Oscar had something to do with this weirdness. Now they just had to find her.

Chapter Five

Vanessa awoke to a barrage of bad feelings. Pain, sharp and relentless, in her head and against her eyes. A roiling queasiness that seemed more familiar than not. Hunger. And a nasty crick in her neck.

She groaned in protest as her bed seemed to move out from under her. When she opened her eyes against the warm glow of sunrise, she realized she wasn't lying on a bed. She was on the cold, hard ground, curled around and tangled up in a very warm and comfortable Dylan Delaney.

He was staring at her, and she could only stare back, because if she moved she would throw up.

There was a prickle at the base of her spine, and a warm wave of…something low in her stomach.

His eyes were dark brown, closer to black. Had she ever noticed that before? He had the scrape of a five-o'clock shadow, which still didn't hide that sharp cut of his jaw. She had the insane urge to touch her fingers to his cheek to see if the bristle of whiskers would be as rough as it looked, if his cheekbones were really that sharp.

It was something elemental inside her, as if she simply belonged here and he belonged there. She should touch him because he was hers, looking dangerous almost. Like a pirate or an outlaw out of time. As if he'd whisk her away and she'd never fight back, because this was exactly—

Dylan Delaney? Dangerous? Her not fight back? What a laugh. She was clearly delirious.

"It's morning," she managed to say when he didn't move or say anything, just kept staring at her with dark eyes that seemed to go on forever, a century of secrets and longing.

Some bump on the head she had.

"That it is." Carefully, with a gentleness that touched her even though it shouldn't, he disentangled himself and got to his feet. Then he held out a hand and pulled her up.

She closed her eyes against the wave of nausea, tried to swallow against her cottony mouth.

"You don't look so good."

She wanted to be insulted, but she felt way worse than that.

"I want you to stay here," Dylan instructed.

Normally, instructions got her back up, especially delivered by a high-and-mighty Delaney, but there was something about his that made her feel safe.

"I'm going to find some water," he continued. "You stay put and look around and think about if anything looks familiar, okay? The gun is right there if you need it."

Again, some part of her brain insisted she argue with him, but it was buried deep underneath a fog of exhaustion. "Okay."

He nodded and headed off for the pines.

"Wait. How will you find your way back?"

His mouth curved, that ironic twist of humor she had yet to figure out. "I'll manage."

She wanted to believe he was stupid. That he'd get lost and she'd be left alone. That'd be preferable,

wouldn't it? Fending for herself rather than teaming up
with a Delaney.

But as he disappeared, panic bubbled in her chest. Just
about any company was better than no company in this
particular situation.

She tried to focus on the task he'd given her. Find
something familiar. But the aspens and pines and rocks
could be any in Bent County.

The sky was blue, the sun slowly warming up the air.
Maybe they weren't even in Bent County. Maybe they
weren't even in *Wyoming*.

She wrapped her arms around herself, trying to
squeeze away the panic.

Would she know where she was if she wasn't missing chunks of time? She closed her eyes, trying to work
through the years that were apparently missing.

But all she saw was Dylan's face. The dark whiskers,
his dark eyes. Something lurking behind them that called
to something inside of her. A certainty and a calmness
that steadied her when she wanted to fall apart.

She didn't want him to find his way back, or so she
told herself, but she knew he would. She was certain he'd
return with water and that enviable certainty.

She was hungry and thirsty and *insane*. She opened
her eyes, shook away Dylan's face and focused on survival.

He was going to find some water. Even if his crazy
story about her being pregnant was true, she could survive a few days without food. But she needed water.

She sucked a breath in, then out, finding deep breaths
helped the queasiness.

Pregnant. She placed a hand over her stomach, trying
to divine if there was any truth to it. Sure, queasiness
could be morning sickness, but couldn't it also be the af-

tereffects of the blow to the head? Couldn't that account for the exhaustion, as well?

Wouldn't she know on some deep maternal level if there was a human being growing inside her? She didn't know. She didn't feel certain either way.

But why would Dylan make up this ridiculous story about being the father of her supposed unborn baby? He wouldn't want that, even as a joke. Even if she was missing chunks of time, there was no way her feelings about Dylan, or his about her, had changed so drastically either of them would want to be parents together.

She gingerly touched a finger to the knot on her head, then winced at the pain from even the lightest touch.

Everything was so messed up, and instead of being her usual alert, tough, kick-butt self, she felt like a blob of uselessness.

She leaned against the tree, then went ahead and slid to the ground so she was sitting next to the gun Dylan had propped against it. What could she do but sit here and wait? Cry? She certainly wanted to, but she'd never let a Delaney see her cry if she could help it.

So she breathed. She kept looking around the small clearing trying to find something familiar, and she waited. She listened for footsteps and Dylan's return, but she heard nothing except wind and occasionally the faint sounds of scurrying.

Something puttered nearby. Wait. Was that a car? Definitely an engine. Slowly, Vanessa got to her feet. She began to follow the noise, leaving herself a trail to get back to the clearing, because she knew a thing or two about not getting lost in the woods or mountains.

It didn't take her long to get to what appeared to be a road. Dirty and bumpy. Clearly not used often, but similar to the one that ran up to the Carson cabin. Again, she looked around. She wasn't near her family's cabin, she didn't think, but they were definitely in the mountains. Isolated.

And then, almost as if she were walking through a dream, a car appeared. A sleek sedan, so out of place in the rough yet breathtaking Wyoming mountains. She *was* in Wyoming. Somewhere close to home. She had to believe that.

The sedan rolled to a stop, and the tinted driver's-side window slid down. The woman's face behind the steering wheel didn't look familiar. Vanessa squinted at her, searching for some kind of recognition.

"Hello there." The woman smiled, though it struck Vanessa as too sharp for friendliness.

"Hi."

"You seem…" The woman trailed off and looked around. "Lost. Alone."

"I'm not alone."

"Oh?"

Something about the way the woman jumped on that made Vanessa nervous, and really made her wish she'd thought to bring the gun. Silly. What could this woman do to her? She was help. Salvation maybe.

"We are lost though. Do you have a phone so I could call someone we know to come get us?" If she remembered anyone's number—the ranch. She knew the number to the ranch. Surely that hadn't changed, if it had really been years since she could remember. Noah or Ty would help her.

"I'm afraid it doesn't have any service up here." The woman's expression changed, but Vanessa couldn't read it. There was an element of sheepishness to the shrug, but it was too…pointed.

Vanessa took a step back from the car.

"I can give you a ride back to town," the woman offered. "If that's where you want to go. I was headed up to my cabin, but you look like you need some help."

Vanessa glanced back at the pines. She could take the offer, and then send someone back to get Dylan. Surely it'd be the smart, rational thing to do. Wasn't she positive Dylan could take care of himself?

"What town?"

The woman cocked her head. "Are you okay?"

"Could you wait?" she asked, wincing at her own idiocy. "I just need to get the man I'm stranded with."

The woman studied her. "You've got quite the bump on your face. You sure you want to get him, Vanessa?"

"He had nothing— You know me."

The woman's eyebrows drew together. "Of course I know you. I know we're not exactly *friends* or anything, but I've lived in Bent since I took a job at the bank."

Vanessa took another step back. Her instincts were all off, but this felt wrong. Of course Dylan Delaney felt right, which *had* to be wrong.

Nothing made sense. Nothing. The mention of the bank made her stomach clench—not in its normal disdainful way when faced with anything having to do with Delaneys either. Something closer to fear.

"You're hurt," the woman said, and though her voice itself was gentle, something in the tone was harsh, grating. "And scared. Let me take you into town. To Rightful Claim. Oh, wait, your brother doesn't live there anymore, does he?"

"I…" Grady. Grady didn't live above Rightful Claim anymore? The saloon he ran was his heart and soul. Where would he have gone? The Carson ranch, maybe. She opened her mouth to ask, but then decided better of it. She didn't know this woman, and no matter what she knew about Vanessa, she gave her an uncomfortable feeling. Vanessa had never been one for parading her weaknesses to strangers, and this weird memory loss was quite the weakness.

She might be all messed up in the head, but she'd always trusted her uncomfortable gut feelings before. Head injury or not, some form of amnesia or not, she had to trust her internal feelings of right and wrong.

"Vanessa!"

It was Dylan's voice. She wanted to run toward it, no matter how little sense that made. "Hold on," she mumbled to the woman. She walked back the way she'd come. "Dylan! I found a road."

It only took a few minutes before Dylan appeared, something like fury dug into the lines in his face. Until he saw the car. He rushed toward it.

"Adele."

That name rang some bell deep underneath the fog in Vanessa's brain, but the woman's face still didn't. But Dylan knew her. Maybe Vanessa should be relieved.

But all she could feel was regret he hadn't grabbed the gun she'd left behind.

"You're all right," Dylan said to the woman, coming to a stop just a few paces in front of the car. Surprise and then something like suspicion flashed over his face. He glanced at Vanessa, then back to the driver.

"We're just worried sick, Dylan," the woman said, suddenly sounding scared and just that. Worried sick. "What on earth happened?"

Vanessa frowned at the woman. She'd changed her tune now that Dylan was here. Put on this little panicked act. She hadn't been at all panicked or surprised before.

Vanessa didn't buy it for a second. "I—"

"You'll drive us back into town, then," Dylan said with

that commanding tone of voice that made Vanessa want to roll her eyes. *Men.* Delaney men at that.

But he hadn't grabbed the gun and this felt all wrong. He needed to know, to see something wasn't right. "Dylan—"

He was already opening the car door to the back seat. "Adele will drive us back to town." He took Vanessa's arm, pulling her to the car. "She works for me at the bank. She'll get us back."

"Dylan," Vanessa hissed as he pushed her gently into the back seat. "I don't think—"

He slid inside next to her. "To the hospital, Adele. Vanessa needs to be checked out."

"Of course."

Vanessa didn't trust the odd smile Adele flashed into the rearview mirror, but she kept her mouth shut.

DYLAN FIDGETED—SOMETHING he almost never did. But the fact Adele was safe and whole, and here, struck him as wrong. It had all his senses on high alert, waiting for trouble.

Beggars couldn't be choosers though, and Vanessa needed a hospital, enough so he didn't think it prudent to wait to go retrieve the gun he had left. Once he got Vanessa checked out, he'd be talking to Laurel about what had happened anyway.

Besides, what could one middle-aged woman do to the two of them? He didn't consider himself invincible or anything, but two-against-one odds were already in his favor. Add his military training and he was sure they were good, even if she had a weapon.

Weapon? Adele? This was ridiculous. What reason would Adele have to hurt them? She'd worked for Delaney Bank for over a decade and slowly worked her way up the ladder. She could be a little harsh and abrasive, but she did her work meticulously. She was devoted to the bank, which he'd always assumed meant she was devoted to the Delaneys.

"Lucky thing you two were on the road up to the cabin I rented for my vacation," Adele said. "Not sure what might have happened to you if I hadn't come along. Fate sure is a funny thing."

"You weren't scheduled for a vacation," Dylan said. Though Adele was technically in charge of creating the schedule, Dylan oversaw it. Knew it by heart. It was a habit he'd been taught by his father. *Always know who's in charge of what.* Dad did it to lord mistakes over people. Dylan had never been comfortable with that reason, but he made sure to know nonetheless. He never knew what that made him.

"Oh, I worked it out with your father," Adele said, her voice still overly cheerful. Not like her, and not at all appropriate for the situation.

Worse, as she drove she kept climbing the mountain. She didn't ask any questions about why they were wandering around the mountains lost, or why he had bruises on his face or why Vanessa had a bump on her head and needed a hospital.

Dylan realized far too late his worry over Vanessa's— and the baby's—health had caused him to make a very rash decision.

But this was Adele. He'd worked with Adele since he'd come back to Bent. It wasn't like they were best friends or anything, but he knew her. He and his dad had trusted her with all manner of bank business. Surely his instincts were going haywire because he was worried, because he was confused.

Because Vanessa Carson had dropped the bomb that

she was pregnant with his child minutes before they'd been kidnapped. Of course things didn't feel right. None of this was right.

But he couldn't convince himself this gnawing pit of doom opening up in his gut was something other than a premonition.

"Town's the opposite way," he noted. Not because he knew where they were, but because he knew going *up* the mountain definitely wasn't heading toward any town.

"Nowhere to turn around yet. Be patient." She flicked him a glance in the rearview mirror. "Isn't that what your father is always saying? 'Patience, Adele,'" she said, the last two words a low imitation of his father's voice.

Then she laughed.

Dylan didn't dare look at Vanessa, but with an unerringness that surprised even him, he found her hand and curled his around it. He could feel the tension radiating off her. She might not remember Adele with a portion of her memory missing, but she could feel how wrong this all was too.

And it was his fault. This whole thing from top to bottom. He couldn't even work up the righteous anger that Vanessa hadn't listened to him back at the bank and stayed in his office. He wouldn't have. How could he have expected her to?

Now they were in danger. No matter how he tried to convince himself he could handle Adele and that she wasn't out to get them, every cell of his being screamed otherwise.

She finally pulled up in front of a cabin. It looked like a fairly new construction and was completely isolated. It wasn't part of a cluster of cabins rented out to the odd tourist, and it wasn't like the Carson cabin, a ramshackle nod to the past.

"Adele. She needs a hospital," Dylan said calmly, clearly, keeping Vanessa's hand in his. He could overtake Adele. Drive Vanessa himself. He didn't want to hurt Adele, but he could, and he would if it meant getting Vanessa help. Getting their baby help.

Adele pushed the car into Park and then gave the horn a little honk. She looked over her shoulder at him, looking vaguely sympathetic. "I know. I really am sorry about this whole thing."

"Adele…"

But he trailed off when she pointed to the door of the cabin. His heart sank when the two men who'd kidnapped them stepped out. One still with his gun, the other bandaged and holding a rifle. Both unmasked this time around.

Hell.

Chapter Six

Vanessa could only stare at the two burly men standing in the doorway. This was bad. Still, with Dylan holding her hand in his larger one, she felt safe.

You are so very not safe, moron.

Adele turned around to face them, and this time her expression was one of pure contrition. Vanessa didn't know why she didn't believe it, but she flat out didn't.

"I'm so sorry," Adele said, keeping her gaze on Dylan. "I had to," she whispered.

"You had to what?" Dylan demanded, his voice sharp as a blade. It made Vanessa shiver. No matter how uncharacteristic this was of the Dylan she knew, or thought she knew, she wouldn't cross *this* man.

Apparently, Adele had no problems doing so though. "They told me I had to find you, and I had to bring you back to them. They threatened my life. I didn't have a choice."

"A choice? You were in a car by yourself! You could have gone to town and—"

She shook her head sadly. "You don't understand, Dylan. I'm afraid you're going to have to go along with this. Now, don't worry. They assured me they won't hurt us. A ransom is all they're after. We just have to do what they say."

"Why didn't they hurt you?" Vanessa demanded. Both Dylan and Adele blinked over at her. But the fact of the matter was, Adele was unscathed and she and Dylan were not.

"I went along with everything they said," Adele replied, a slight edge to her voice. It softened with her next words though. "If we all do, we get out of this alive."

"How can you be so sure?"

"So far, so good. Come on, get out before they drag you out." Adele looked at Vanessa. "We wouldn't want that, would we?" As if she knew Vanessa was pregnant.

How would she know? Surely she couldn't divine that simply from Dylan saying she needed a hospital.

Adele got out of the driver's seat and held up her hands as she walked over to the two men, as if in surrender. Then all three of them watched Dylan and Vanessa climb out of the car.

"None of this adds up," Vanessa muttered as they stood, almost in a face-off with the men a few yards away.

"No. It doesn't," Dylan agreed. "But for the time being, Adele is right. If we play along, they won't hurt us." He nudged her gently forward.

Vanessa gave a pointed look at all the wounds on his face as they trudged their way toward the cabin.

He shrugged. "A few bruises won't kill me. They'll have food and water. Shelter. A ransom requires keeping us alive. Right now, since we can't get medical attention, getting you food and water is the most important thing. If this is dangerous, I'll find a way to get us out. For the time being, you'll get to rest and be cared for."

It was very strange to have someone looking out for her. Oh, she had a big brother and two cousins who'd lay down their lives for hers. But they weren't the fussy sort.

None of the Carsons were. They'd protect and defend, but they wouldn't think to put getting her rest above their other objectives.

"Good job delaying the inevitable," one of the men said with a happy grin. "Welcome home, friends." He was covered in bandages, clearly the man Dylan had "incapacitated."

Vanessa didn't like the gleam in his eye. Not out of fear for herself but fear for Dylan. It didn't matter that she *hated* Dylan, and she was sure she did. Once this was all over and her memory returned, the hate would come back and everything would make sense. She wouldn't care about Dylan's well-being at all.

But in that car he'd held her hand. In this short walk to the men waiting for them with gleaming smiles and guns, he'd expressed concern over her well-being.

Because she was pregnant. Allegedly. And the baby was his. Supposedly. That must have been why he felt the need to take care of her. If it was all true, he was only protecting what was his.

Vanessa was unaccountably tired all of a sudden. She even swayed on her feet against her will. But Dylan held her up.

A Delaney held her up. She couldn't believe what was happening.

"She needs a place to rest. Water. Food."

"Don't recall you being the one in charge here, friend," the man with the bandages said to Dylan. "Best you remember that before we do another number on your face."

"Seems like he did a number on you," Vanessa muttered before she thought better of it.

"Boss didn't say anything about you pulling in a hefty ransom. You might be useless to us."

Dylan stepped forward, even as the barrel of both

weapons pointed at him. "You lay one hand on her, you'll pay in every possible way for a man to pay. I don't care how many guns you point at me."

Something poked through the fog in her brain. That same image of Dylan facing down deadly weapons but in a different place.

Adele laughed nervously, and the image skittered away. "Wh-why don't we all calm down? No one wants to get hurt." Dylan spared her a glance that would have melted steel. Adele cleared her throat. "What do we need to do to get out of here?"

Vanessa didn't trust the way this woman spoke to men with guns. It wasn't placating. There was no fear. She seemed in perfect control. A mask, maybe, but it wasn't a mask that made Vanessa comfortable.

"Inside," the bandaged man said. He took Adele's arm and nudged her in, then did the same to Vanessa.

She jerked her arm away from his sweaty grasp, but he grabbed her again and gave her a shake that had her teeth rattling against each other.

"I ain't afraid to knock you around, tough girl."

Fury razed all the confusion and exhaustion. Knock her around? She'd like to see him try. She struggled to free herself from his meaty grip. "I—"

Dylan's hand rested at the small of her back, a quiet plea to stop fighting. Even with her heart racing and anger starting to fire through her blood beyond reason and control, the slight pressure of Dylan's big hand reminded her that she wanted to stay alive, no matter how much her temper strained.

She took a deep breath and let her arm go limp against the hand wrapped around it. The goon gave her a good shove inside the cabin, and though she stumbled, she managed to stay upright. She skidded to a stop next to

Adele, and noted with more suspicion that Adele didn't even try to stop her skidding slide. Just watched.

Too clinical. Too detached. She was no victim here. Vanessa was almost sure of it.

"Now you, *friend*." The bandaged man grabbed Dylan by the shirtfront and tossed him inside, hard. Dylan fell gracefully, an easy roll that nearly reminded her of a dancer.

Seriously. Who is this guy?

He was up on his feet in seconds.

"Now, before we get settled, let's get one thing straight. I'm in charge here." The man pointed his gun at Dylan's heart. "You do what I say, or they die." The gun moved to train on Vanessa, but the man's eyes stayed on Dylan. "You're the only one worth anything to me, with your rich daddy."

"You have no idea who you're messing with."

The butt of the weapon hit Dylan's face with a sickening crack. Vanessa cried out and rushed forward, but the second man shook his head and tsk-tsked, his gun pointed right at her chest.

Dylan got to his feet. "Takes a little more than a pathetic sucker shot to keep me down, you worthless piece of—"

The man raised his weapon again, and Vanessa couldn't just sit back and watch any longer. Heart pounding against her ribs, but with a clarity she hadn't felt since she'd woken up in that van, she jumped forward.

"Wait!"

Everyone looked at her. She didn't know what to say. She'd dealt with violence her whole life, but she'd never been any good at defusing a situation. She was more the stir-it-up type. But things changed. Life changed. She *had* to diffuse this one whether she was any good at it or not.

"We all want to live." She stepped forward again, though she was still behind Dylan. She watched the guns pointed at them warily as she did exactly what he'd done to her.

She lifted her hand and placed it gently if firmly against his back. It was rock hard, like iron. He was tense and ready to fight, but as much as she didn't trust Adele or this situation, she knew two armed men were dangerous. They all had to play this with smarts more than muscle. And she'd had a lifetime of experience doing that.

Though she wouldn't mind finding out a little more about Dylan's impressive muscle.

Where had *that* idiotic thought come from?

"Let's all calm down," she said in a low, controlled voice, far more for Dylan than the bad guys in front of them.

Dylan's chin jutted out, but he flashed a glance at her. Fury. An edgy flash of violence that should have seemed incongruous on Dylan Delaney's perfect face. In this moment, however, it just felt right.

Dylan wanted to pound these two brain-dead barbarians to dust. He could too. They might be bigger, they might have weapons, but he had no doubt he could take them both out. He could even visualize it. A sweep kick here, use one goon's body to slam into the second. A quick gut punch, twist the rifle and use it to knock out the other. Blood. Bones cracking. Victory.

But what he could also visualize in his taking them out was them having an opportunity to hurt Vanessa or Adele. The two women were, very unfortunately, distractions and weaknesses he couldn't afford to ignore.

He let Vanessa's firm pressure on his back be a kind

of anchor. He had to think with his brain, not his temper. He even had to be careful not to let his instincts take over.

Because he wasn't surrounded by soldiers. He was surrounded by civilians. Their safety was paramount. Not his.

He turned to face Vanessa, ignoring the men with guns at his back. Her hand fell to her side and she looked at him with a whole slew of emotions in her dark eyes. Not the norm for her. Vanessa usually kept everything locked down.

But there were men with guns, a head injury, amnesia and the fact—whether she believed it or not—she was carrying his baby.

He couldn't lose his temper. He had to be methodical. Like he'd said to her outside, this was the best option right now. Get her taken care of, even if it was by hostage takers, and then he'd find a way for them to escape. No matter what they said or did, he had to be calm. He had to summon all that sniper calm he'd developed and use it here.

He glanced at Adele.

She stood a little behind both of them. He noted she was dressed in jeans and a long-sleeved T-shirt. Not what she would have been wearing at the bank last night. She watched Vanessa with a certain kind of speculation that made the hairs on the back of his neck tingle.

Calculating was the word that came to mind. Not exactly out of character for Adele. She was the calculating sort, but her high opinion of her intelligence often undermined her calculations.

Besides, maybe she was calculating how to get the heck out of the situation, same as he. As much as his instincts warned him something was off with Adele, his brain reasoned it away time and time again.

He was a man who'd spent a chunk of years living by his instincts and pure grit. Had that dulled in these last few years of doing what his father had demanded of him? Had all the fine edges he'd honed inside of himself—so he could live without suffocating in the box his name dictated—softened and been lost?

Now wasn't the time for an identity crisis. He had two women to save and two goons to fight.

He turned to the goons, calm now. Ready to *battle* rather than fight. Fight was instantaneous, with no real endgame. It was anger and revenge. A battle was all about winning. It was about getting these women safe, and making the world—even this tiny corner of it—a righted place.

He would win. Not just for himself, but for this future *child* that would somehow be a part of him. And Vanessa.

Who had to be taken care of at all costs.

"What's the plan, then?" he asked calmly. He'd treat it like a business meeting. They'd discuss what they wanted. He'd discuss what he wanted.

And when he had a good opening, he'd make them wish they'd never been born.

The two men looked at each other, and Dylan didn't have to be a mind reader to understand they weren't the designers of this little plot. They were here for muscle and muscle only.

But who was the boss?

"You two in that room," one said, pointing a gun at a door. "You—" he pointed to Adele "—in that one."

Dylan frowned. It was stupid to split them up. The glossy-looking doors to the rooms weren't at all intimidating, and surely there were windows in the room. He almost asked them if they were sure that's how they wanted to play it, then rolled his eyes at himself.

Adele shuffled off to her room, so Dylan took Vanessa's arm and led her to the other one. He pushed open the door to find what appeared to be an office. There were windows, but they were narrow and lined the very top of the wall. There was no way they could maneuver out of them, even if they could get up there.

One of the men had followed them inside. Dylan eyed him.

"Water. Food. You want me alive, I'll need both," he said, unable to soften the demand into something less abrasive.

"You'll get both. When I'm good and ready." The man slammed the door, the click of a lock echoing in the room.

It was clearly someone's office. Dylan wondered if they'd be able to figure out who if they snooped enough.

But first things first. He led Vanessa to the most comfortable-looking chair, a rolling, leather desk contraption that at least had some padding. He nudged her into it and, though she went willingly, he saw a flash of the old Vanessa in her expression.

She was still pale with exhaustion, and yet there was a clarity to her eyes that had been missing.

"Your employee is in on this," she said firmly.

Dylan hedged. *In on this* seemed a bit much, and yet… "Something is definitely fishy."

"It's her. All her. When I first stumbled onto her on the road, she didn't act worried or nervous at all. She was very calm and seemed to want me to leave you behind. I didn't know she knew me at first. Then you came and her tune totally changed. *'Oh, we've been worried sick,'*" she mimicked.

Dylan's jaw clenched. "It's off. But…"

"It's *her*," Vanessa insisted.

He nodded. "All right. She's mixed up in it somehow."

He could explain away almost everything. Except the change of clothes. If she was as much a victim as they, she'd be in her bank clothes just like he was.

He shrugged out of the now-tattered suit jacket and laid it across Vanessa's lap. "You need water, food and rest." What she really needed was a doctor. He'd find a way. He *would*. "We should look around. See if we can figure out who owns this place."

She looked up at the windows, and he could see her come to the same conclusion he had. There was no getting out that way. "We have to get out of here."

"We will. My father will pay—"

"The ransom business is crap. You know it and I know it. There's more to this than money, and even if Daddy Big Bucks would pay, I don't think Laurel and her precious police department would feel the same."

"I think the people we love would do anything to keep us safe."

"Keep *you* safe, goose."

Dylan wanted to laugh, but there was something vulnerable in the words no matter how sharply she said them. He crouched in front of her, took her hands in his and squeezed. He noted the surprise and suspicion in her eyes, and ignored both.

"No matter what you remember or don't, you know your brother would move heaven and earth to keep you safe. If he knows you're missing, he's out there looking for you. Noah and Ty too."

"They'd have to know I was missing."

"They will. Soon enough."

Chapter Seven

Back in Bent, Vanessa's mechanic shop

"She wouldn't."

Laurel looked at the firm, furious line of her husband's mouth and rubbed at the headache pounding at her temples. As much as she agreed with Grady's estimation of Vanessa not leaving town on her own, his lack of cooperation was grating on her nerves.

Grady had let them into Vanessa's place to look around, and while there weren't any cut-and-dried clues, her motorcycle was missing. Everything else was where it should be. Hart's supposition that Vanessa had left of her own accord on said motorcycle had not gone over well with Laurel's husband.

"Hart isn't asking if she *did* skip town, since we don't know," Laurel said, keeping her voice calm and no-nonsense. "We're asking what you think it would take for Vanessa to leave without telling anyone."

"It wouldn't take anything, because Vanessa wouldn't take off without a word to anyone no matter what was up." He lifted the bill from an ob-gyn's office in Fremont they'd found when searching her above-the-shop apartment. "Pregnancy wouldn't be a reason. She knows we'd support her. No matter what. She wouldn't be *scared* or running from anything."

Laurel had to keep her mouth shut. Since she'd been dealing with her own, there'd been a few times in the past few weeks she'd looked at Vanessa and wondered. Yet Vanessa had been with no man, and showed no signs of telling her family about her condition. So, *obviously*, it wasn't totally clear-cut knowing she'd be supported.

But Grady continued to thunder his irritation. Luckily, Laurel knew enough about her husband to understand that was bluster covering up his fear. She couldn't afford to be soft, but it was hard when she was worried too.

"She sure as hell wouldn't have disappeared on her *motorcycle* and left her car at the Delaney Bank of all places," Grady continued furiously.

"Easy highway access," Hart countered, impressing Laurel with how even and calm he was being in the face of Grady's notable temper. "Kind of hidden. If she didn't want to be—"

Grady growled and Laurel pressed a hand to his chest. He was angry, but that anger hid a deep worry and fear. She felt it too. It had been a long time since she and Vanessa had been friends. Even marrying Grady hadn't smoothed things over from their teenage years, though it had softened some of the edge.

The Vanessa she knew—thought she knew anyway—wouldn't run away from anything. And if Laurel thought about *Vanessa*, she didn't have to think about the fact her brother was missing too. Without thinking the move through she pressed a hand to her stomach.

She heard Grady's sigh as his arm came around her shoulders. Despite her uniform, and the fact she was here in an official capacity, he pressed a kiss to her temple.

"What can we *do*?" he asked.

It helped ease a tiny fraction of tension in Laurel that he asked it of Hart, and helped her anxiety even more when Hart answered, plainly and certainly.

"You trust me to investigate." He smiled a little sheepishly. "And Laurel, of course. If you find any hints of what might be going on with Vanessa, you tell the police. Give the same instructions to any and all family members. Work with us. We want everyone home and safe, same as you."

Laurel's phone trilled. She would have ignored it, but the Delaney Ranch's number gave her stomach a little jolt. She answered, stepping away from Grady's arm.

"Laurel?"

She frowned at the grave tone in her father's greeting. "What is it?"

"I was catching up on my email," Dad began. "I hadn't had a chance to check since I'd been driving home from the airport, then I was distracted last night, obviously. I have one from Dylan dated yesterday that says he'll be gone for a while. No explanation. Just that he had to leave town."

"Forward it," Laurel said automatically, ending the call to wait for the email.

"Dad has an email from Dylan dated yesterday saying he'd be out of town for a while. He's forwarding it to me."

"Maybe they ran off together," Hart said, gesturing to Vanessa's place.

Grady snorted. "Sure. I mean, maybe to murder each other. But definitely not *together*."

"Erm…"

Laurel stared at Hart, noticing the odd flush to his cheeks. "Erm *what*?" she demanded.

"Well, it's just…" He cleared his throat. "They didn't

exactly look murderous at your wedding reception. Quite the opposite."

Both Grady and Laurel stared at Hart with matching dumbfounded expressions.

"You know, I left early because I had the early shift the next morning, and I happened to see them leave together."

Laurel rolled her eyes. "Maybe they left at the same time, but not *together*. They were probably arguing on their way out."

"Oh, no. They were very much together and very much not arguing. Hard to argue when you've got your tongues down each other's throats. I gave them a ride back to Vanessa's because they were far too drunk to drive." Hart nodded at the medical bill Grady had tossed back onto the desk earlier.

"No." Laurel and Grady gasped in unison.

Her upstanding, somewhat-inflexible brother would never… He'd never… She glanced at Grady. There'd been a time *she'd* have never, but she'd never cared about the feud the way Dylan did.

"Seriously though, they were drunk as skunks," Hart continued. "Believe you me. Definitely on the road to a bad decision. Maybe even one with consequences. Could be they ran off together to deal with them."

Laurel looked up at Grady. It made a strange kind of sense, even though she couldn't truly believe it. Vanessa and Dylan. It had to be impossible.

"Impossible," Grady confirmed, as if reading her thoughts.

Her phone's incoming-email sound dinged and Laurel shook her head. She had to focus on fact, not supposition.

She pulled up the forwarded email and read the words with a frown.

Be gone for a bit. Don't worry. Explain when I get back. Adele can cover at the bank for me. —Dylan

She showed Hart, then Grady.

"Except Adele is missing too," Hart pointed out.

"Nothing adds up," Laurel said, staring at the email. While she could see Vanessa skipping town on her motorcycle, she couldn't see her doing it without tying up loose ends at her shop. And Dylan would never leave the bank so abruptly—especially unlocked.

But she felt a niggle of concern over the possibility Dylan and Vanessa had hooked up drunkenly at her wedding, conceived a child and were now both missing. They'd be embarrassed. Probably horrified. Enough to skip town?

But Adele Oscar was the thing that threw a wrench into all this. Laurel and Hart had been by her house last night and this morning. She hadn't been home. Everything had been locked and secure, and her car hadn't been seen, though they'd put out an APB.

"We need to find Adele Oscar," Hart said. "Search warrant for her house?"

Laurel nodded. Adele was the key.

Chapter Eight

A little while later, after watching Dylan meticulously search through everything in the room, then stalk around it, reminding her of a wolf—or some other dangerous predator—the door swung open.

The man she'd come to think of as Eyeballs, because his were the size of saucers, tossed a paper plate onto the desk. Then threw a bottle of water at Dylan. Hard.

Dylan caught it without a flinch, which made Eyeballs scowl. Without a word, Eyeballs closed the door and locked it again.

The heavy, almost chemical smell of the microwave pizza pocket made Vanessa dry heave, but she didn't throw up. That was a plus.

Dylan watched her with both concern and a kind of detached study. "You have to eat it," he said after a few seconds.

"Eating it won't help if I just throw it all up."

"You don't know that. Plus, vomit might be an excellent diversion."

She laughed against her will, but it died quickly when he crouched in front of her again, holding the plate with the offensive microwave meal in one hand. He held out the water bottle with the other.

"This atrocity is still frozen in the middle, but I'm

going to break off a small piece of the cooked edge. Eat. Drink. That should help keep it down."

"I don't need you to feed me." But she took the water, even as she eyed his movements warily.

He watched her with those steady brown eyes. Something in her chest fluttered—a light, airy feeling directly in contrast with their situation. With how she'd always felt about Dylan.

He disgusted her. He made her sneer. He made her *hate*. She had never had one positive feeling toward Dylan or one positive interaction with him.

But in the past twenty-four hours, he'd displayed a warmth she'd never seen and a resourceful strength she never would have believed. The man had fought off two armed men, and if not for her, and perhaps Adele, she had no doubt he'd be back in Bent, having happily dispatched all the bad guys.

Maybe it was just the beard that made her feel differently toward him. She was a sucker for beards, and his scruff was growing in fast and full and handsome.

She'd rather blame facial hair than her previous conclusions about him being wrong.

He broke off a piece of the gummy crust and held it up to her lips. Their eyes met, held. Something shuddered through her. She wanted to believe it was doom, gloom and hell, but it was lighter, sweeter, and some foreign part of her wanted to lean into it.

She could see him, clean-shaven and harsh-looking, in the dim light of another room. A flash of something. Hands on her face. He wasn't touching her, but she could feel him. She could remember the register of shock at—

"You have a tattoo."

He raised an eyebrow, slipped the food into her mouth.

She chewed and swallowed, so distracted by that odd flash of memory her stomach didn't even turn.

"Do I?"

"I couldn't make it out. It was dark. But you were shirtless. And you had a tattoo." It wasn't the first little burst of memory she'd had, but it was the clearest. And the most nonsensical. "Fill in the blanks for me."

He pulled off another piece of the crust, held it up to her mouth. "I don't know your blanks, Vanessa."

"Then fill in yours."

She could sense he didn't want to, but she could also tell he had taken responsibility for this mess. He thought it was his fault. He felt beholden to her.

She wasn't about to ignore the fact she could *use* that. She refused to take the bite and he sighed.

"Fine. You eat this, and I'll tell you as much as I can."

She nodded, letting him feed her small bites as she sipped water in between them. She realized he was picking off the heated pieces, and when he just had the frozen center left, he ate that himself.

It shouldn't surprise her he was noble. He *was* a Delaney, after all. Maybe the most condescending, high-horsed, snobbish Delaney of the bunch—next to his father—but noble tendencies ran in that clan.

What surprised her was that she was *moved* by the display of caretaking. She'd never wanted someone to take care of her. That made you beholden to them, and she would never let that happen to her. A Carson had to get by on their own wits. Sure, when she got in trouble Grady, Noah or Ty had stepped in and defended her. But no one had ever fed her and taken the crap ends for themselves.

That you remember.

"I have a tattoo," he said after his last swallow. "The only place you would have seen it is during our…"

She couldn't help the curve of her mouth. "Afraid to say the words, sweetheart?"

"See? You needed to eat. You're practically back to normal."

Except she didn't remember. Not really. Not in the way she needed to. She breathed through the panic that she might have lost thirteen years she'd never retrieve. At least she was alive to have more years.

"We had sex. I know that because I woke up naked next to you, also naked, the morning after Laurel and Grady's wedding. I don't—"

"Laurel and *Grady*?" she all but screeched.

He pressed his lips together, but his mouth curved anyway. "Don't worry. You made your outrage well known in the moment."

"My brother married… He couldn't have… *Married?*"

"Happily, even. Much as I'd like to deny it."

"But Laurel is such a do-gooder. She…she's a cop, isn't she?" Vanessa pressed fingers to her aching head. The food had helped her feel less shaky, but her brain hurt. "She always wanted to be. She'd have done it. She did. She helped…" But whatever fuzzy memory she'd been bringing to life faded. She swore.

"Easy," Dylan said quietly. "You're remembering bits and pieces. That makes me think it'll all come back, but we have some more important things at hand."

Vanessa scowled at the door. "Yes, we do. But tell me what happened. How we got here."

He recounted her coming to see him, the shooting from the front of the bank and their treacherous ride in the van. Vanessa didn't remember any of it, but she thought of Adele.

"She changed her clothes."

When she met Dylan's gaze, she knew he'd already put that together.

"And they separated us," Vanessa continued, working through all her suspicions, "because she's involved. If they had any sense at all, they'd put you alone since you're the money shot."

He winced at the term, which would have made her laugh if she wasn't so angry at Adele and her little farce.

"I bet a hundred bucks this is her place."

His mouth quirked. "A bet is what got you into this mess."

She racked her memory, but couldn't come up with it. So she focused on the here and now. "She works at the bank. For you and your father. She'd know your schedule." They had to figure out how Adele was connected, and if they did, maybe this would make more sense. Maybe they could find a way out.

"I would have been gone if not for you though."

"But you weren't gone. Your car was still there, right?"

"Right. But, she's worked for us for years. I can't believe—"

"What do you know about her?"

"She started as a teller. Moved from… I want to say Denver. Maybe Seattle. Some big city. She'd worked at a bank there and wanted the small-town life. Dad liked the idea of an outsider."

"That doesn't sound like your father."

"Better an outsider than a Carson or Carson sympathizer."

"Now, *that* sounds just like him."

"She had a kind of polish. She was a hard worker and moved up the ranks quickly. By the time I…came back home from college, she was second only to the assistant manager. A position Dad held for me."

"Came back. College. You say that so weird."

"Do I?"

"And you use that haughty tone to say 'do I' whenever something gets too close. Came back with your fancy finance degree."

"That's what they say."

Why was he talking in riddles about something so insignificant? It didn't make any sense. "What do *you* say?"

He shrugged. "Doesn't matter."

"Maybe it matters to me."

His eyes met hers, that same odd fluttering stirring in her breast, a little too close to her heart. But she didn't break his gaze, and she didn't back away. Maybe she'd lost her sense as well as her memory, but she couldn't bring herself to care.

POWER. THEY'D ALWAYS created powerful reactions in each other. Once hate. Now…the thing that crackled between them had altered. He wanted to touch her. His memories of that night were misty, probably like her memory of the past thirteen years, and yet he had images, odd feelings, like he could remember a rightness when their bodies joined.

He broke her gaze. He didn't believe in rightness or feelings. Reason mattered. Facts mattered.

Yet he was a man who'd shrugged off both and lived a lie for years, all so he could stand to live a different lie.

He stood, taking a few steps away from where he'd deposited her on that chair however long ago. It wasn't so much a retreat as a recentering. "We need to focus on—"

"No, don't brush me off. You're at the center of this. They weren't after me. I was a hapless bystander because we got drunk and stupid, apparently, if I believe that."

He raised an eyebrow and she huffed out a breath.

"Okay, *fine*. I believe we drunkenly hooked up, and I really hope I'm pregnant because I feel too much like crap to not have a reason. But, regardless, you're the center. Those men supposedly want a ransom for *you*."

"Supposedly." It didn't add up so clearly though, since he would have left the bank if Vanessa hadn't come. Since he didn't have a set schedule in the office that someone could have gleaned information from. Since it didn't seem like they'd taken any money from the bank—if money was what they were after.

Whoever those men were, whatever their purpose, it did have to do with him.

It would have been easy enough to see his car in the lot and act. But Adele had been there too.

Only one. But the men had three.

Adele had changed her clothes. He couldn't get past that one simple fact. He was still in his suit—dirty and tattered as it might be. Vanessa still had on the outfit she'd come to see him in. Yet Adele had changed into jeans and a clean shirt. And she didn't seem scared.

"If she's involved, the bank is involved."

"Which means money is involved," Vanessa supplied.

"I suppose."

"Did she have money troubles?"

"I don't know anything about Adele's personal life. Even if she didn't keep to herself, she's…"

"She's what?"

"It's hard to explain. She's perfectly nice, but underneath that is an abrasiveness. I wouldn't say anyone really *likes* Adele. Truth is, no matter how she tries to hide it—and I think she does try—she thinks she's smarter than everyone, a harder worker. She thinks she's better."

Vanessa snorted. "She must fit right in with the Delaneys."

He shot her a bland look. "But there's no tension. No

fights. She's never been demoted or scolded. She'd have no reason to hate me or the bank as an entity."

"What about your father? Would she have a reason to hate him?"

"I want to say it's the same, but…"

"But what?"

He rubbed the back of his neck. He didn't like parading his father's faults in front of anyone, let alone a Carson. "He isn't quite the stand-up guy I'd always assumed him to be." Dylan thought regretfully of what they'd found out last year about his father's extracurricular activities: an affair with a married woman. A *Carson* woman. It wasn't exactly murder or anything, but it had shaken Dylan's foundation of believing his father a good, if hard, man.

"So she could have had an issue with your father?"

"I suppose. But why not go after him?"

Vanessa rolled her eyes. "Don't you watch any movies? You don't go after the person you hate. You go after what they love."

It made sense. Uncomfortable sense, but sense nonetheless. "If that's the case—if this is some sort of revenge against my father—then I don't think she plans on me surviving. Get a ransom, kill me off?" He didn't shudder, didn't worry, because he'd like to see someone try to get rid of him. *Everyone* underestimated him. Even Adele.

Even Vanessa.

Vanessa watched him, consideration all over her face. "They made a big production about keeping you alive. Maybe it's to give weight to the ransom story, or maybe she's got something against you too."

"What would she have against me?"

"Same thing the rest of us peons do, Dylan. You're a jerk."

He puffed up, insulted even though he couldn't figure out why Vanessa's normal estimation of him would be insulting.

"Just like I'm a jerk. People hate us because we don't play nice. I say it like it is, and you ice out the world. Maybe it's not who we are underneath, but it's what people see."

"So what are you underneath, Vanessa Carson?" He hadn't meant that to come out sounding sexual, but it had. His body warmed, tightened. Because even if he couldn't remember the details of the act, there was a feeling he got when he thought about them being together. It was very nearly irresistible.

Nearly.

Chapter Nine

Heat flooded through Vanessa, and worse, a beat of arousal she couldn't deny no matter how much she wanted to. Her skin prickled and her core hummed with need.

Jeez.

She tried to swallow through her dry throat. Then, realizing she still held the water bottle from before, unscrewed the cap and took an unsteady breath. She could not have sexual thoughts about Dylan, period, but most especially when they were abducted by goons. And yet there those sexual thoughts were.

"We should focus on you," she managed, hoping she sounded stabler than she felt. "I'm an incidental."

He made a noise, one she didn't know how to characterize, though she thought it had to do with guilt. But he didn't press. Which meant *she* had to press her one advantage.

"And since I'm here because of you, we need to figure this out. Which means focusing on Adele. And you."

"Yeah. I suppose it's possible she wanted my position."

"Wouldn't anyone? I mean anyone who worked in that bank. Certainly not *anyone*." She'd rather jump out a window than try her hand at staid, businessy bankerland.

"Everyone knew that position was mine. He held it for me while I was…away."

"You're going to have to explain that." Why he got so fidgety every time his years at college were mentioned.

But he ignored her. "It'd have been pointless and stupid to think she or anyone else would get that position. I don't think Adele is stupid."

"No, but people are oftentimes foolish even if you don't think they should be." *We slept together.* It seemed the height of pointless and stupid.

"Stupid enough to kidnap? To send armed men after me? I can't believe it, Vanessa. I really can't. She might be a hard lady, but she isn't a psychopath."

Vanessa thought of her father and her uncle. No one had considered them *psychopaths*. Jerks, sure. Alcoholics, maybe. But the fact they liked to use their fists on women went mostly ignored, no matter how incomprehensible that act was to a normal person.

Noah and Ty had considered their father a monster when he'd been alive. Grady didn't know much about what their father had done in his absence.

She sighed. Old wounds had no place here. *She* had no place here, and yet here she was.

She felt a little bit better, a little bit steadier, now that she'd had water and food. Her brain didn't feel so foggy and her body didn't feel as though the wrong move would send everything inside of her rushing out.

"It has to relate to the bank," she continued, trying to muse through the problem aloud. "Maybe not you. Maybe your father."

Dylan's eyebrows drew together. "But I'm here."

"Sure. You're daddy's pride and joy though. So it could be you. It could be him. It could be about both of you. Delaneys in general."

"You'd like that, wouldn't you?"

"Probably under any other circumstances, but not

when I'm tied to you and in this mess. But you said we were abducted at the bank. Adele is somehow weirdly mixed up in this. It has to connect to the bank."

"They said they wanted a ransom," Dylan said, taking her threads and adding some of his own thoughts to it. "Maybe it *is* just a ploy to get a bunch of money from my father." He shook his head. "Doesn't sit right though. There'd be easier, smarter ways to do that."

"Maybe. Maybe not. Adele wants money, needs money maybe? She pretends she's a victim and no one ever knows she has anything to do with it. She gets off scot-free. Biggest problem is I got in the way."

Dylan seemed to consider, *really* consider her words. She hadn't expected him to. She was used to dismissal from a Delaney, especially *him*.

"If it's about the money, I feel like there were better ways to get it than kidnapping. Adele has access to all sorts of things at the bank. She could have embezzled, stolen, cheated. Carefully."

"But not easily."

"I hear kidnapping is so easy."

Vanessa ignored his dry comment. "Everything she could have done at the bank would have been traced to her."

Dylan's mouth quirked, causing that weird, annoying, unwelcome feeling to flutter in her chest again.

"You've got a sharp mind, Vanessa."

"Imagine that," she returned dryly.

"Considered robbing a few banks now and again?"

She wanted to be offended, but mostly the tongue-in-cheek way he said it made her want to laugh. *With* him rather than *at* him. "Oh, I've considered all *sorts* of things, Delaney."

That flash of a grin had unwanted lust pooling low in

her belly. She'd always thought he was attractive. She'd just hated everything about him underneath the physical. Now everything was getting muddled.

Head injury. She'd blame the head injury. And change the subject. "You fail out of college or something?"

"Huh?"

"You're squirrelly every time it comes up. Something happened while you were away. I want to know what. Maybe it connects."

"It doesn't."

"Maybe it does."

"It doesn't."

She huffed out an annoyed breath.

"I didn't fail. I—"

The door burst open. The goon she'd decided to call No-Neck stood there, holding that gun like it was some proof of his epic power. Vanessa wanted to sneer, but she held back the nasty look at the last second.

Now that she was feeling more herself, it was going to be quite the fight not to be *too* much herself and piss off the men with guns.

"You." He pointed the gun at Dylan. "Out front."

Vanessa jumped to her feet, even as Dylan began to move to go with the man. "You can't separate us."

No-Neck laughed. "I can do whatever I want, little girl."

Dylan gave her a sharp look. "Stay here. Stay put." He gave a pointed look at her stomach.

She brought a hand to it without thinking. For the first time, she really, truly believed him without reservation. She was pregnant with his baby, and he'd protect her—and it—at all costs.

The knowledge, the acceptance, shook her to hell and back.

DYLAN FOLLOWED THE muscle-bound idiot into the living room, noting everything he saw. There was a phone on the table next to the couch. He filed it away. Furniture, art on the walls, windows. He took note which way the sun slanted outside the blinds when he could tell.

When he got them out of this mess, he'd know how to lead police or anyone else to this place and make sure these men—and their boss—paid for what they'd done. That was a promise he'd make to himself, and he was not in a habit of breaking those.

The gun-toting moron shoved him onto a plush leather couch. Expensive, Dylan noted. Whoever owned this cabin had money, which meant they weren't likely *after* money.

He filed that away too.

"You're going to make a phone call. One of those Face-Time deals."

Dylan tried not to let his excitement show. Were they *stupid*? Even if they didn't let him say anything of importance, a FaceTime call would show a background. It would give Dad some hints, some ideas. A damn *lead* to hand over to Laurel and the police.

He fixed a disgusted look on his face and put as much sarcasm into his voice as he could manage. "Lucky me."

The man raised the butt of his weapon and Dylan forced his body to relax so when he took the blow it didn't meet resistance. It'd hurt like hell, he knew, considering his face was already throbbing from all the blows, but it'd help downplay whatever injury he got in the long run.

But the second guy came out of what Dylan supposed was some kind of kitchen area off to the side of the living room. "Remember what Boss said."

The guy with the gun grunted, lowered the weapon with a lot of regret. Dylan smirked.

Which earned him a meaty fist to the gut. Dylan wheezed out a painful breath, doubling over and seeing stars.

The goon in the kitchen sighed.

The one who'd punched him laughed. "Boss said no more messing with his face. That wasn't his face."

"Your funeral," the other one said.

Dylan sure as hell hoped so.

Slowly, he sat back up. Even though just about everything on his body hurt at this point, he wouldn't let anyone see it. Goons or Vanessa or…

"Where's Adele?"

"She's in her room, just like you two were in yours. She gets the nicer digs because she cooperated."

"She wasn't in the van with us."

"So?"

"Changed her clothes too."

The guy in front of him flashed a look to the guy in the kitchen area. Dylan tried not to react, but that hesitation, that look, told him a lot. Because they hadn't expected him to question Adele's place in all this.

Then the man in front of him threw his head back and laughed. "Yeah, sure. The blonde's the real mastermind behind this whole thing. You figured us out. Maybe I'll go turn myself in now, since I got this sharp detective on my heels."

The other man laughed too. Uproariously.

Dylan didn't buy it. It might have planted a seed or two of doubt but barely. Still, he let that doubt show. He wasn't going to take the smarter-than-you tactic or the dumber-than-a-box-of-rocks one either. He had to mix it up. Keep them off-balance.

"Go get the blonde to unlock her phone," living-room

guy ordered of kitchen guy. "She's got the old man's number on her phone."

Even though Adele would of course have his father's number in her phone, Dylan thought it was an odd request. FaceTime. Adele's phone. There was a convenience to their plan Dylan didn't trust.

Or was it smart? Use her phone, then there'd be no way to trace it to anyone besides Adele. Adele had access to his father, and having that kind of insurance was smart if they thought he was going to be uncooperative.

Maybe this *was* simply about money, and Adele was unconnected.

But she had changed clothes, hadn't been hurt in the initial break-in, and the men had distinctly said they were only supposed to kidnap one person.

Either way, if someone knew Adele was missing and they used her phone, it could be pinged. It might take some time—Dylan knew from Laurel there were all sorts of legalities to jump through before the police could access that information—but it was a chance.

The second man brought Adele out. She still looked put together, but her eyes were a little wide. Dylan almost believed she was scared.

Almost.

"C-can't I just tell you the c-code?" she stuttered, as the man with the gun held it out to her. Her fingers fumbled with it and it fell to the floor.

One of the goons nudged it with his foot. "Pick it up and fix it up for us," he ordered, gesturing toward a little tripod they'd set up. "Get him in the shot, then make the call."

"You could just record a video and send it," Dylan suggested. He doubted they'd take the hook, but it was worth a shot. A video could be watched, studied. A FaceTime call... Dad would have to know how to take a screenshot and have the presence of mind to do so.

The man shook his head. "Boss's orders are clear, friend."

Adele was shaking as she set up the phone on the tripod. Convincing nerves, and yet Dylan didn't *feel* convinced.

Still, regardless of her innocence or guilt, she had a phone. That phone was the best shot he had, as long as people knew they were missing.

Surely Laurel knew at this point they were all missing in a capacity that required police involvement. *Surely.* His sister was a good cop and a damn smart detective. He had to trust she was on this.

"Th-there. I think it's all set up. I just have to click the movie icon."

"Sit next to him. Don't speak."

Adele nodded and took a seat next to Dylan on the couch. She seemed to vibrate, and his first thought was nerves, but there was a look in her eye, a lack of tension in her expression. He wanted to believe she was scared and that she was being forced to do this.

But Dylan couldn't shake all the strange little pieces of this mystery.

One of the men shoved a piece of paper at him.

"You'll say that, and nothing else, or things won't end well for your friend in there." He pointed his gun toward the room Vanessa was in. "Read when I say go. Even if he talks over you, you read it once and then I disconnect."

Dylan looked down at the paper. The statement was simple: I'm in grave danger. Instructions on how to deliver money. No mention of Vanessa. Or Adele, even though she was clearly going to be in the shot.

Dylan looked up at the man, then the phone. He didn't

allow himself a glance at the door where Vanessa was. Didn't allow himself to think about the fact they might hurt her. He had to focus on any possible way to figure out what was really going on here.

If he knew the facts, the players, he could get everyone out with minimum fuss. He believed that.

"All right, friend. The minute Daddy Money Bags answers, you read."

Dylan nodded. He could still feel the vibrations coming off Adele next to him, and yet he forced himself to focus on his core. The deep steadiness within his soul. He'd learned to compartmentalize as a soldier. Learned to live within the mission and nothing else as a sniper.

When his dad answered, the small rectangle of his face showing concern and fear and hope before he even managed a word, Dylan felt nothing.

He looked down and began to read.

Chapter Ten

Back in Bent, at the Delaney Ranch

Laurel had her father go through it again. And again. She had him write down everything he remembered, and she wrote it down as he recounted his version of the phone call, as well.

She was worried for her brother, even for poor Adele, who seemed to be an innocent bystander now. Laurel believed she could save them though—had to believe it.

What made her sick to her stomach was that there was no mention or glimpse of Vanessa. She was going to have to go home to her husband and tell him that his sister may have run off without a word.

He wouldn't believe her.

She didn't believe her.

Vanessa's car in the bank parking lot was too much. If it had been found *anywhere* else, she'd feel the same as Hart—convinced Vanessa had run off to go have her baby far away from her family.

But even if Dylan was the father of Vanessa's baby—a theory Laurel had an even harder time believing—there was no reason, excuse or sensible explanation for Vanessa's car being in the Delaney Bank parking lot.

"It was new," Dad said, relaying that detail for the

fourth or fifth time. He sat at the Delaney kitchen table, looking pale and shaky and as disheveled as Laurel had ever seen him. He hadn't even been this upset when her mother had died or when he'd been mixed up in a threat to his life by Jesse Carson last year.

"I could tell the cabin around him was new. You could look at new cabins. Surely builders have records and…"

She tried to smile reassuringly at her father. "Hart's already on that from your first statement. We'll have the names of anyone who's built or bought a cabin in the county within the last year. It's a good place to start. And now we're trying to ping Adele's phone. We've got clues. Hard leads."

Dad looked at her imploringly. Apparently seeing Dylan on that video had eradicated his usual control. He was worried sick. It poked at Laurel's own sense of calm, but she was a cop. She had to be a cop now more than ever.

"What if they're not in the county?" Dad asked. "Or even the *state*?"

His words spoke to her own fears, but she couldn't show that to her father. "It's unlikely." A lie, but it was for the best for now.

Dad pushed back from the table and started pacing. "I need to send the money."

"You don't have the money. Besides, they'll only escalate and ask for more. You have to—"

He whirled. "I have the bank. I have access to all the money we need."

"Dad, you can't… That isn't legal. You know it and I know it."

"I could sell the cattle and pay it all back. I could sell everything if I had to. I could—"

"You could, but right now you have to sit down." She

took a breath and brought him back to his chair. She had to steady herself. If he'd been cold or demanding, it would have been easy. But Dad shaking, falling apart like this, made tears burn in the back of her eyes.

She wouldn't cry. She was a Delaney. Police officer. *Sister*. She swallowed at the lump in her throat. She could only be one thing here. The law. "You need to calm down, and let me and the rest of the police do our job."

"Laurel, your brother—"

Her heart cracked, but she didn't let it show. "I know. Trust me, I know. But we've called state, and they've got to look into this before I can let you pay off that ransom. It's rare a kidnapper gets the money and lets the abductee go. This whole thing is rare, but let's give state time to get caught up to speed."

"We should call the FBI."

"If there's a need, we will. State will. I can only do so much with my resources at county. But I'm doing everything I can."

Dad looked at her, and some of that cold disdain she'd grown used to since falling for Grady was back in his expression.

"Are you?" he asked coolly.

It hurt, even if she convinced herself it was his fear and temper talking.

She pressed her fingers to the table, taking a moment to steady herself when an unwanted wave of dizziness settled over her. She needed to eat. *Baby* needed to eat.

She glanced at her father, who still didn't know. And wouldn't approve. Bad enough to marry a Carson, but to procreate with one?

She almost smiled. If it was true Vanessa was pregnant with Dylan's baby, she'd get them home just to see the look on her father's face.

"Dylan is smart and resourceful. I don't know Adele that well, but she strikes me as someone who can keep her head in the midst of a crisis. I trust Hart to help me on this investigation, and I trust state to make the right call on when, if and how we should pay the ransom. You don't have to trust those things, Dad. You don't have to trust me. But it'd be a lot better for you, and Dylan, if you did."

"I'll never forgive you if anything happens to him," Dad said, cold and decisive. Yes, this was the father she'd known for the past year.

"Don't worry. I won't forgive myself either."

"You brought this on us. You've *cursed* us."

Her father's hatred of the Carsons had never shocked her, but this did. To the core. "Dad, you don't believe that."

"I absolutely believe this town has been in turmoil since you dared let that stain touch you. How many times has a Delaney been hurt since you—"

"I won't listen to this." She whirled away. It was too much. Too much blame when she was struggling with her own. "You'll sit tight," she ordered, striding away from him even as she barked out each word. "I've warned Jen to keep an eye on you. Don't make me bring in Cam." But she'd call her other brother nevertheless to make sure he kept an eye on the finances. If her father compounded this mess with a crime…

She couldn't think of it. She had a case to solve.

Dad said nothing else, and she let herself out. She stopped on the porch and took a deep breath of Wyoming air. The ranch was still, the quiet only interrupted by the breeze or an occasional cow lowing in the distance.

It was home, or had been. Now her home was with

Grady and this baby of theirs. The world was changing. Bent was changing.

Curses. She didn't believe in curses. She'd never believed in the Carson-Delaney feud that had kept two families sniping at each other for over a century. She wouldn't start now, and she'd never, ever allow anything to make her believe there was a curse when Grady was everything she'd ever needed.

But no matter how many certain, powerful words she told herself in her head, a flutter of fear beat against her gut.

Chapter Eleven

Not having a clock was sending Vanessa into a low-level panic attack. How long had Dylan been out there? How long would she be in here alone?

She'd never had trouble being alone before. In fact, it was her preferred state of being. At least, when she was in charge of her own life. Turned out, kidnapping was wreaking havoc with her sense of the usual.

Plus, she'd drunk the entire bottle of water. Which meant she really, really needed to get out of here.

But something held her back. No, not something. She knew exactly what held her back. It was just hard to admit.

Fear. She was petrified of what existed outside those doors. What if they'd killed Dylan? Tortured him? He might be some kind of secret tough guy, but two men with guns were with him out there.

Ransom. They were after a ransom. They wouldn't kill their star in the ransom show.

Except they were morons. And whoever was the boss—and in Vanessa's mind that was Adele—had this cabin, which had to have cost a pretty penny. It wasn't about money.

Unless it was. Money could dry up. A person could always need more.

Where was Dylan?

Vanessa squeezed her eyes shut. She wasn't a coward, and since she was feeling mostly normal, she couldn't even blame it on a head injury or this…pregnancy thing. She couldn't be a coward. It wasn't allowed.

She moved forward to the door and started banging on it. She didn't stop until it opened—though just a crack.

"Knock it off," No-Neck growled, his beady little eye visible through the crack.

"I have to go to the bathroom."

There were murmurs, grumbles, then after a few minutes of shuffling, the door opened the rest of the way.

One big hand gripped her upper arm and gave her a jerk, and then he had her other arm in his grasp so that both arms were pulled behind her back and he could guide her.

She immediately searched the living area for Dylan, though it only took a second for her eyes to be drawn to the figure on the couch. He sat, ramrod straight, in the middle of it. They'd tied his hands and his feet, and she got the impression—though she couldn't see it—that something was making him have that absurdly straight posture.

Then there was the strip of duct tape across his mouth. He didn't look at her, kept his gaze straight ahead, which again she wondered if it had to do with how they'd tied him up.

But through it all, even as the goon pushed her to a bathroom, Dylan looked…bored. No fear. No worry. Just like he couldn't believe he was letting himself be subjected to this.

Such a Delaney. For the first time in her entire life, that made her smile. And the smile made her maybe a little too brave.

"Where's your chick boss?" Vanessa asked of the jerk holding her arms.

The man didn't answer. He just shoved her forward by his grasp on her arms. Vanessa supposed he was leading her to the bathroom. As she passed Dylan, he inclined his head slightly to the other room, still not making eye contact. Apparently, Adele was still in there.

The man pushed her through a door, and she stumbled forward, catching herself on the sink when he let her go. She glared at him. He smiled his smarmy smile. "Three minutes. Time starts now." And he shut the door.

Irritated and furious, Vanessa quickly did what her body demanded. Washing her hands, she looked at herself in the mirror. Her hair was a tangled mess. She was pale and dirty. There were shadows under her eyes.

"One minute left," the man outside called.

Indulging herself, she stuck her tongue out at the door before letting her gaze sweep the small half bath she was in.

Another narrow line of windows she couldn't possibly slither out of, high on the walls. She crouched and opened the cabinet underneath the sink, pushed through rolls of toilet paper and hand towels, searching for anything that could be a weapon or a clue.

Nothing.

"Time's up!"

Vanessa straightened just as the door swung open. He didn't immediately grab her. Instead, he watched her, leaning against the doorjamb.

"You're lucky, you know."

She rolled her eyes. "Yeah, I'm a regular fairy princess."

"If I was in charge?" He let his gaze take a tour of her

body that had her stomach roiling. "Things would be *very* different for you, *fairy princess*."

She wanted to tell him things would be very different because she would have cut off his balls, but she bit her tongue and held his disgusting stare with a bland one of her own.

"Who hired you two apes? You don't have one brain between you," Dylan called out.

Her own eyes widened, even as No-Neck's did. How was Dylan talking? He'd just had tape on his mouth and...

"How the hell'd he get out of the tape?" the man grumbled, turning his back on Vanessa.

Vanessa had a flash of attacking No-Neck. Just jumping on his back and going at it. He might be stronger, but she was strong herself. Wiry and quick. She knew how to punch a guy's lights out with the element of surprise.

But he had a gun, and she was apparently growing a baby.

Then the moment was over. No-Neck remembered himself, grabbed her by the arm and jerked her out into the living room.

Eyeballs was standing over Dylan, fury and something like bafflement written in every ugly line of his expression.

"How'd you get it off?" he demanded, nudging Dylan's side with the gun he never seemed to put down.

Dylan smiled up at him. "Magic."

The butt of Eyeballs's weapon struck Dylan's stomach. Hard. Dylan bent over, even gasped out a breath, but when he straightened into a sitting position on the couch again, his expression didn't radiate pain or fury. He was just grinning.

Maybe *he* was a psychopath.

"How'd you get it off?" Eyeballs demanded, holding the gun upward again, readying for another blow.

Vanessa desperately tried to think of a way to intercede, but No-Neck pushed her forward.

"Let's get them both in the room before you kill him and Boss kills *us*."

Eyeballs grunted, then muttered something as he yanked Dylan to his feet. "When it's time to kill you—and, oh, there will be a time—it'll be my pleasure."

"Nice fantasy life you've got there."

No-Neck cut the ties on Dylan's feet but left the hand ones on. Then Eyeballs practically lifted Dylan off his feet. Dylan was launched forward, falling into the room they'd been in, and with his hands tied he had no way to stop the forward momentum. He crashed into the wall, falling to the ground with a loud thud.

Vanessa struggled against No-Neck's grasp, and when he let her go she rushed to Dylan's side.

"God. *God.* Are you okay? Are you…?" She struggled to move him onto his back so she could see how hurt he was. She didn't even notice the door close or the loud thud of the lock, so intent she was on helping Dylan.

He didn't groan as she rolled him over, and she might have thought he'd passed out, but his eyes were open and on her. His mouth was quirked as if this were a joke. Gingerly, she touched all the bruises and scratches on his stubbled face.

She shouldn't have done it—somewhere in the back of her mind the real Vanessa was losing it over the fact she was gently caressing Dylan Delaney's face.

But her fingers brushed through his hair of their own accord. Gently, she cupped his wounded jaw. "Are you okay?"

His gaze, so direct and serious, did some strange

things to the spaces inside her heart. She wanted to look away, but her pride was at stake. That's what kept her gaze locked to his. Pride. Nothing else.

"If I say no, are you going to kiss it and make it better?"

She knew she should jerk away or cuss him out, but she couldn't bring her fingers away from the silky texture of his hair. "You've got to stop pissing them off. You won't survive."

He leaned into her touch, and something flopped in her chest. "I'll survive. And keep you safe while I do it."

"I can handle myself, Dylan."

He made a noncommittal noise, then pulled his hands out from behind his back.

"Hey, how'd you get out of that?" she demanded, staring openmouthed at the plastic bindings that had fallen to the floor.

He grinned at her, and she saw the red marks around his mouth where the tape had been did nothing to dim the potency of that grin. "Magic."

HE WANTED TO touch her. Hell, he wanted to kiss her. The pain in his stomach was nothing compared to the gentle comfort of her hands on him. On his face and in his hair. Her hair fell over him, a tangled dark mess, and nothing about her was different from how it had ever been—tattoos, wary eyes, hard mouth.

Except her touch was light, and in this strange kidnapped world, he didn't feel like Dylan Delaney, where the eyes of Bent and his father fit like a suit two sizes too small.

She, and he, felt right. Together they had the power to weather this odd storm. For a moment, brief and changing, he *knew* she felt that too.

And then she pulled away.

Which was fine. What could be done during a kidnapping? Not much. He was grateful she seemed more like herself. Sturdier and sharper, instead of lost and hazy. Maybe her memory was still fuzzy, but the blow to the head hopefully hadn't caused any problems with the pregnancy.

He sat up, not at all perturbed by the fact that she watched him with frustration simmering in her gaze.

"You have to tell me. The fighting. The getting out of duct tape and ties and…you have to tell me how *you* of all people know how to be—be—"

"Fiercely lethal?"

She rolled her eyes, but she didn't offer another term.

He sighed. Not more than forty-eight hours ago, revealing his secrets to anyone—let alone a Carson—would have felt like life and death. But now he understood life and death in a way he hadn't even as a sniper.

Because it wasn't facing death that had changed him, it was facing *life*. The moment she'd told him she was pregnant, he'd been handed new life and everything he thought he'd known had flipped. All the things he'd thought mattered dissolved. He didn't care what anyone thought of him. Not even his father. Because he'd created a life…and whether he fully grasped that yet, he knew this child would be the center of his life. Part of him. Always.

So it didn't matter if Vanessa knew. It didn't matter if she told everyone when they got back home—and it was *when* not *if* they got back home, in his mind.

"Well, all that college bragging my father did to you in that last memory of yours…"

She pushed a finger to her head, near the bump where

she'd fallen. Her eyebrows drew together and he got to his feet.

"You remember?"

"No. Not exactly. But it doesn't feel like… Even though I can't put it all on a clear timeline, that doesn't feel as close to now as it did. I still can't believe Laurel and Grady are *married*, but it doesn't seem… I feel like I remember them together. Being irritated at them together. She's a cop. I remember the uniform. I remember her holding a gun, I think. Maybe."

"There's been some trouble the past year or so. You'd likely have seen her draw her weapon a few times."

"Trouble? What kind of trouble? Is everyone…?"

He could see the fear and horror chase over her features as she realized she might not remember losing someone she loved.

"As far as I know, every Carson you care about is present and accounted for."

She swallowed. "Right." Then her eyes narrowed. "You're trying to distract me."

"You're distracting yourself. I don't even have to try." He folded his arms behind his head and smiled at her.

She growled. "*How* do you know how to fight and escape bonds? Jump out of vans and incapacitate dudes with guns?"

He figured he needed to be straight and simple, so they could move on to far more important matters. Like Adele's possible role and the small plan he had for escaping tonight once he got some more info.

"I didn't go to college. I made everyone think I did. Took the money for tuition, told Dad I wanted to handle all my bills to learn how to be responsible. I forged transcripts and report cards and enlisted in the army and became a sniper instead."

"You…" She gaped at him like a landed fish. "You… That's a lie. That… You couldn't have. Why? Why go through all the trouble?"

"I knew I had seven years. Graduate high school early, take five years for undergrad, claim the need for a masters for another two, maybe three if I could stretch it. So, that's what I made them think. I knew if I did what I wanted in that short period of time, I could come back and be everything he wanted me to be. I just had to go be *me* first."

"Dylan. That's crazy."

"No. It felt like that's what I had to do. Cam refused the bank, Laurel was always meant to be a cop, and Jen didn't have the patience for finance. She just wanted to run the store. I was the only one left."

"Considering your father's going to live to be three million since he's evil incarnate, I'd say he was enough left."

Dylan shook his head. "No. I was the only true Bent Delaney left to take the mantle. The bank has been in our family since it began. Direct eldest son to eldest son. I'm not the eldest, but Cam wouldn't take it. You have to understand family pressure, Vanessa. Carson and Delaney pressure. We are what our names are." And yet, wasn't he sitting here thinking none of it mattered anymore?

Maybe it didn't. Maybe it did. The *now* didn't matter in the story, because it was the choice he'd made. It was what he'd felt then.

"You went into the army, became a sniper, falsified your *life* for seven years. That's *insane*. You're talking like it was the only choice."

"For me, it was."

"You could have told your father what you wanted to do."

"No. It wasn't an option. I was coming back. I was going to take on my responsibility. But I needed a few years to…" It sounded stupid to say *find myself.* But that's what he'd needed. He'd needed to know who he was outside of Bent. Outside of numbers and appearances.

Cam had gone to the marines, and Dylan hadn't been allowed to follow. So he'd found a different way. Maybe he should have stood up to his father, but he'd been seventeen.

The bottom line was, he hadn't. "I needed it to be secret. I needed to be someone not connected to this place. I can't explain why I needed it, only that I did. And it shaped me, made me, gave me the time I needed to be able to come home and take that…" *Noose.* Following his father's footsteps felt like a noose he couldn't escape.

"I had my me time, then I came home to fulfill my role as a Delaney. It was a little out of the box, but it wasn't insane."

"Army. A *sniper.* I…" She shook her head and paced around the room. "That's a lot of work for risking your life for your country. You faked your life to sacrifice yourself, to protect. I don't understand that."

He cocked his head and studied her. She didn't realize it, but she'd put her hand over her stomach. He thought she was finally beginning to believe the pregnancy was real. That he was the father.

"I think you're starting to," he said gently.

She looked down at her hand, then dropped it. She kept her back to him, and he couldn't read her posture so he crossed to her. Gently, knowing she'd probably fight him off, he put his hands on her shoulders.

When she didn't move away and didn't even tense under his fingers, he turned her to face him.

Her eyes were direct, though there was something in

them he couldn't read. Suspicion maybe. Or possibly just confusion. She didn't understand him.

That didn't hurt his feelings though. She was a Carson. He was a Delaney. They'd never understand each other.

But, God, he wanted to. Understand her. Have her understand him. He wanted to chase this *power* that arced between them. But it wasn't the time or place. Maybe it'd never be, but definitely not now. "Right now, we'll focus on getting out of here."

When the tension crept into her shoulders, he squeezed. "Don't worry. I'll protect you. I'm an expert."

She didn't laugh or even crack a smile, but the moment held. And in that moment he needed her to believe that he'd protect her with everything he was.

He placed his own hand over her stomach, nerves and fear of the future jumping through every part of him. He didn't let it show in his expression though. "I'll protect you both."

She took a sharp breath in, then slowly let it out. Then her hand reached out and cupped his jaw, just as she had when he'd been sprawled on the floor after crashing into the wall. His chest clutched, a metal fist squeezing against his heart and then his lungs.

Her dark eyes were rich and deep and fathomless. He saw something he'd never seen in her before. Warmth. Care.

You're losing it, Delaney.

"Protect all three of us," she whispered and then pressed her mouth to his.

Chapter Twelve

The kiss was a mistake. Out of place in every possible way.

But Vanessa wrapped her arms around Dylan's neck and took it deeper anyway. Her whole life had been built on out-of-place mistakes. She *was* an out-of-place mistake. Her philosophy had always been, why not embrace it?

So she lost herself in a kiss she shouldn't have allowed herself, and figured that was vintage Vanessa.

Until Dylan took control, his hands sliding over her cheeks and into her hair, fingers tangling there, changing the angle of the kiss as his tongue swept across her lips, then invaded her mouth.

Now she understood why his hands were big and rough and capable. Maybe it still didn't make sense to her, a secret life, a secret self, but she understood all the incongruous things about him now.

She knew something about him no one else did. In this moment, they were experiencing something together that no one would be able to share with them. They were linked. Connected.

And she wanted him. So why not take?

Slowly, oh so slowly, he ended the kiss. Pulled away just enough to keep their mouths apart, but her body was still pressed to his. Their heartbeats thudded against each other as their gazes met.

She'd expected to see...*horror* wasn't the right word, but something close to it. Regret. Disgust. She was a Carson and he was a Delaney. He'd only ever see her as a mistake. Even without all her memory, she knew that.

She had the flash of him walking out of her apartment above her shop, looking rumpled and angry. Disgusted. At the time she'd thought it was with her, but somehow in this moment, she realized it was with himself. With his loss of control.

Because his image was the gift he'd given his family, even when it wasn't him at all.

"Dylan." She wanted to kiss him again. Comfort him for...something. Offer understanding, maybe, even though her understanding was limited.

But then she realized she could picture her apartment. She knew what color her sheets were and that she lived there.

"Wait. Wait." She could't analyze why he didn't look horrified now, only the fact that she knew... "I—I run the mechanic shop, not just help out. I run it. I live above it." She struggled to keep that thread of memory, holding tight to him as if he was her anchor, even as she looked blindly at his chest. "It's mine now, because—because Grady helped me buy it after Jim croaked." She swallowed. She could picture some of the cars she'd worked on. Could feel herself walking down the boardwalk from her shop to Rightful Claim.

Where Grady didn't live anymore. Because he'd married Laurel. They'd gotten together when their stepbrother had been accused of murder and Grady and Laurel had worked together to clear Clint's name. They'd fallen in love and pissed off a lot of people.

She looked up at Dylan's dark gaze, amazed parts of her memory had returned.

"You should probably kiss me again," Dylan suggested, pulling her closer.

At her sharp look, he shrugged, a grin flirting at the corner of his mouth. "What? It made you remember. Might jog some more pieces."

Her mouth curved, suggestive words about to tumble out of her mouth, no matter where they were or what they were facing.

But the door flung open, and afterward, Vanessa realized there was something telling about the fact she and Dylan didn't jump apart. She didn't know what, but it meant, well, something that they held on to each other instead.

But it was something they'd have to figure out later because Adele was pushed into the room. Her hair was disheveled, and there was a trickle of blood coming out of her nose.

Dylan immediately rushed to her side. Vanessa stayed put.

Blood or not, she didn't trust the woman with the icy eyes. Because though she made odd, almost crying noises, Vanessa didn't see any tears.

"Got a call with the boss," No-Neck growled. "You three stay in here. Plot your escape because I'd love to break your kneecaps in the process."

Dylan ignored No-Neck and Eyeballs as they cackled and shut the door.

"Are you all right?" he asked Adele, gentleness in his tone, in his touch.

Vanessa scowled.

"I just…" Adele swallowed, her hand shaking as she brought it up to her nose. "I did everything they said, but they're so rough." She made another little crying sound. Still no tears.

Vanessa went over to the box of tissues on the desk and handed it to Adele. Adele blinked at the proffered box and then daintily took one.

"Oh, I…" She dabbed it at her nose and squeezed her eyes shut. "I get a little faint when I see blood."

"It's all right," Dylan assured her.

Vanessa barely resisted the urge to roll her eyes. She wouldn't have cared for the fainting-damsel act in the best of circumstances, but considering Adele'd watched Dylan get slammed by the butt of a gun repeatedly with little reaction, Vanessa was having a hard time working up sympathy.

Of course, Dylan was trained to get beat up and keep fighting. A secret soldier. Dylan Delaney.

And she was the only one who knew. Something about that felt important, and it softened her enough to crouch down and clean up Adele's nose for her.

"There. Good as new. Just tilt your head forward and pinch it right at the bridge. Should be right as rain in a few."

Adele winced and did as Vanessa instructed.

Dylan raised an eyebrow at her. "Bloody-nose expert?"

"I'm a Carson. Of *course* I'm a bloody-nose expert. My own. My brother's. My cousins'. It's like a virtual parade of bloody noses from getting punched in the face." Vanessa turned her attention back to Adele. "You weren't punched in the face though, were you?"

"Oh, I…" Her hand fluttered restlessly in the air. "No. They pushed me around a bit and I…"

"Looks more like an elevation nosebleed to me," Vanessa observed, ignoring Dylan's censuring look.

"Oh, but I fell. They pushed me and I fell."

Vanessa got to her feet and shrugged. "If you say so."

"They said they have some meeting with their boss," Adele said, clearly trying to change the subject. "And they needed that room. Do you think whoever is behind this is coming here?" Her voice vibrated with concern.

Vanessa managed to swallow what she wanted to say: *I think their boss is already here, liar.*

She didn't want to believe Dylan was falling for Adele's flittering fragile-female crap, but he was so gentle when he helped Adele to her feet and then led her to the chair he'd put Vanessa in not that long ago. He picked up the suit jacket he'd placed over her lap earlier, and put it on Adele's.

"Just take it easy. Whoever their boss is can't be that dangerous, or he wouldn't have hired two muscle-bound goons to do his dirty work for him."

"Do you really think?" Adele replied, eyes big and something like adoring on Dylan.

He patted her shoulder. "Yes, I do. Trust me. The only thing we need to worry about is the fact those two have guns."

Vanessa didn't care for the oily black slick of jealousy running through her. She was starting to think Dylan's gentle caretaking wasn't because he cared about her or even their baby. No, this was just who he was. Vanessa wasn't special at all.

Well, except for that kiss.

"You also need to worry about the fact Eyeballs has a penchant for kicking your butt," Vanessa said to Dylan. Because it was its own kind of pain to see all the physical evidence of their brutal way with Dylan, even if he acted as though it was nothing.

Dylan sent Vanessa a sharp look. "I'm fine. We'll all

be fine." He turned his attention back to Adele. "I promise you that."

Vanessa was not a jealous woman, or at least she hadn't been. But it burned in her now. Which pissed her off. At Dylan. At Adele. At No-Neck and Eyeballs out there. But mostly at herself.

Adele grasped for Dylan's hand, squeezing when she found it. "I feel so much better being in here with you two. It's awful being alone, not knowing what's going to happen."

"You don't have an idea or two of what they might be after?" Vanessa asked, hoping to sound innocent rather than sarcastic. "I mean, you've had more time with them. We escaped. Of course, you weren't in the back of the van with us." She smiled blandly.

"I was in the front," Adele said, letting Dylan's hand go and dabbing at her nose with the tissue again. "Tied up in the front seat. Only one person could fit, and they needed me to navigate. You were knocked out and Dylan was…uncooperative." She stumbled a bit over the words, and Vanessa thought it sounded rehearsed, but she had a practiced, simple excuse. Vanessa had to give Adele that.

"How'd you get in the van without us seeing you?" Dylan asked. There was speculation in his tone, but his voice was gentle.

"They took me out the front before they ever came into the back, at least that I can figure. I sat tied up in that van for I don't know how long before they returned and drove off."

It was a quick and plausible explanation. Vanessa scowled. This woman was a pro liar, that was for sure. Vanessa could tell Dylan was doubting her involvement, but Vanessa refused to entertain doubts. Sometimes you had to be hard and unyielding to get what you wanted.

She wanted her freedom and Dylan's safety.

Maybe you just want Dylan.

Well, maybe she did. But she couldn't get anything she wanted until they were home, safe in Bent, with only family curses to threaten them.

DYLAN WASN'T IMMUNE to Vanessa's speculative gaze. He understood it, even. The evidence pointed to Adele.

But was it too easy to put the blame on Adele? Dylan had the feeling something else had to be behind this. Maybe Adele really was being forced to cooperate, and since she was willing and not fighting, she was given certain things like a change of clothes.

Dylan knew Adele. He'd trusted her with the bank. He couldn't quite accept she was wholly behind this. Vanessa didn't know Adele personally, even if she was starting to remember more.

Something warm and very dangerous filled him at the thought of that kiss, of those memories. He wasn't foolish or romantic enough to think his kiss had unlocked her memories in a scientific sense, but it was nice to pretend.

Not the time or place though. Adele was shaking.

Well, if he sat back on his haunches and analyzed it the way Vanessa was, with some cynicism and suspicion, it was more that same vibration as when she'd sat next to him on the couch during the phone call. It reminded him more of excitement than nerves.

But people expressed nerves differently. He still had enough soldier in him to know he couldn't judge people's reactions by his own. Before he'd made sniper, there'd been a fellow soldier who'd giggled whenever they got into trouble in basic. Not because he was happy, but because nerves made him laugh.

That kid hadn't made it through, but remembering it

reminded Dylan that not everyone could control and hone their reactions to danger. More so, not everyone reacted in a way that made any sense.

Still, Adele's actions struck him as off, and he was still enough of a soldier to be wary of behavior that didn't make sense or follow a pattern.

Fear didn't always, of course. People didn't always. But he'd be wary until he found something concrete to believe in. Wary didn't mean cruel. It meant careful.

It wasn't like he could go by Vanessa's clear Adele-is-evil judgment. Vanessa had made a life out of distrusting people from the outset.

It irritated him that his own radar was compromised by knowing Adele for so long and not really ever *getting* to know her. She was Adele Oscar. Bank employee. He knew her attitudes about customers and the cleanliness of the teller station or her shared office, but nothing about how she'd act in crisis or what her background was that would inform her reactions.

Dylan couldn't let frustration lead him though. He had to focus on the task at hand, even if Adele was a wild card he couldn't pin down.

They needed an escape plan. And three against two was better than two against two. Especially when two on one side were armed, and one on the other side was pregnant.

"If they needed her to navigate, she knows where we are," Vanessa pointed out, not kindly. "We only need to find a way to have her make a phone call to get help up here." She sent Adele a challenging smirk.

Adele's eyes went wide. "I don't know where we are. Not really. Not enough to lead someone here." She grasped for Dylan's hand again, and he let her find it and squeeze.

"You could give them everything you know," Dylan said gently. "If we could get access to a phone, we can call my sister. Even with just some clues, the police would be able to track us down, if they haven't already pinged your phone."

"Pinged my...? Oh, maybe, but they made me turn it off. It's only been on when we made our phone call."

"Well, that doesn't mean we can't get a phone call in, and you can tell the police everything you remember seeing on the drive up here."

"It was dark," Adele said weakly.

"No. Not that dark," Dylan countered, extracting his hand from hers. She should be excited about the possibility of getting them out of here. Not shrinking away from it. No reaction to fear would make a person refuse to help them escape.

He stood and moved next to Vanessa.

"I don't know... I can't remember." She looked up at him pleadingly.

Dylan couldn't find compassion for her when she wouldn't even try to help. He narrowed his eyes at her. She swallowed audibly and even scooted back in the chair.

"Think," he ordered sharply. "Tell me everything you remember, no matter how insignificant it seems. But we'll start at the beginning. After they left the bank, which way out of Bent did they go?"

Adele blinked, her eyes darting everywhere. Her hands fluttered until she linked them over her lap. She took a deep breath. "I'm really not good under pressure," she whispered.

He'd seen her deal with difficult customers. Large, angry men who thought they deserved a loan, or a customer wanting a check to be cashed even if they didn't have the proper identification.

She'd never crumbled under pressure then. Either there was more to the story than she was telling them, or she was behind this. Either way, he'd be calm but firm. Until he knew for sure.

"All I'm asking you to do is describe what you saw, where you went. No one's going to blame you if you don't remember everything perfectly."

Adele nodded vigorously, twisting her fingers together. "Okay. Okay. I was afraid, Dylan. So afraid." She looked up at him, tears in her blue eyes.

They were meant to stir up sympathy, and it worked. He softened, even as he could all but feel Vanessa hardening next to him. Adele shrunk back in her seat, clearly intimidated by Vanessa's cold glare.

So Dylan stepped in front of Vanessa, a kind of shield. For both of them really. Vanessa could bore holes into his back, and he could hopefully find a way to get through to Adele. "You just take it easy and tell me what you remember."

Adele sniffled and nodded. "Okay. Okay. So. They started driving. Out of the front parking lot, but instead of getting on the highway, they drove down Ellington toward the back of town."

Dylan nodded. He'd figured that part out himself. He'd managed to pay attention to the turns in the back of the van, but measuring distance was harder since he hadn't been able to determine how fast they were going. He had a feeling he'd been lost the minute they'd gotten out of town.

"Then they went north, I think. I'm not good with direction."

"What road after Ellington?"

She pushed her fingers to her temples. "I-I'm not sure. I was just terrified. I wasn't paying attention. Those guns." She shuddered. "I never thought I was squeamish about guns, but they're so—so—"

"The roads, Adele. Let's focus on the roads. Ellington to the back of town then north?" He didn't think they'd gone north based on the sun's positioning when they'd escaped, but he'd draw out what she claimed to remember anyway.

"Country Road B maybe? Yes, I think that might be it. North toward the Tetons, maybe? It'd be isolated." She pressed her fist to her mouth. "We're *so* isolated," she whispered, a tear falling over and onto her cheek.

This time it didn't soften him. Everything she told him was the exact opposite of his own theories, his own gut reactions. He'd been paying attention. They'd gone to the back of town, then south. Not toward the national park.

Maybe he should trust the woman who'd seen it all, but Dylan couldn't bring himself to compromise what he *knew* in his gut to what someone he didn't trust claimed.

They *were* in the mountains though, and this nice cabin was more suited for Jackson Hole than anything south of Bent.

Maybe his instincts had been off. He had been beaten pretty badly. It could have messed up his sense of direction.

Hell. This was a mess. He didn't like second-guessing himself. Second-guessing got you killed in war, and this wasn't all that different from war.

"She's so full of it," Vanessa whispered into his ear.

Dylan gave Vanessa a sharp look. She returned it with a baleful one of her own. Because she'd been out of sorts—physically and in the memory department—and they were kidnapped and all, he'd somewhat forgotten her normal personality of doing the exact opposite of what anyone asked of her.

"Excuse us a second." He took Vanessa's arm and moved her to the far corner. They were all still in the same room, but if he kept his voice low, surely they could have a conversation Adele wouldn't overhear.

He huddled with Vanessa, lowering his mouth to her ear so he could whisper. "It isn't fair to hold her to our standards."

"What does *that* mean?" Vanessa retorted, crossing her arms over her chest. She kept her voice low, but she didn't whisper.

He kept whispering. "It means you grew up a Carson, and I was in the army. We're not exactly *normal*."

He could tell she took some offense to that, and probably wanted to argue with him that they weren't at all similar, but she didn't. She sucked in a breath and let it out, then glared over his shoulder at Adele. "She's fishy, one way or another." That one she definitely whispered.

He glanced over his shoulder at Adele. She was looking at them intently, but based on the confused line between her eyebrows, he didn't think she was getting most of the conversation.

"I agree with you on that, but that doesn't mean we can just leave her here. Any escape plan has to involve her, even if we don't trust her."

"There's too much goody-goody Delaney in you."

He managed a smile. "Some things you can't shake."

Her brown eyes met his, and he saw something venturing on soft there in the edges if he looked closely. Very, very closely. "Like feuds and curses?" she asked carefully.

He couldn't resist dropping his forehead to hers. "Like

who we are, underneath all that." And underneath all that, he thought they could maybe be something.

But first, they had to escape.

Chapter Thirteen

Back in Bent, Adele Oscar's house

"Nothing." Laurel couldn't keep the disgust out of her voice. They'd gotten the search warrant to go through Adele Oscar's residence and so far had come up with nothing. Meanwhile, the seconds ticked down and Dylan, Vanessa and Adele were still missing.

She hadn't slept last night. She'd convinced herself it was because she was anxiously awaiting the search warrant to come through or something from the phone company about a location hit on Adele's cell. She was worried about her brother and sister-in-law, so tension and sleeplessness could only be wrapped up in work and fear.

Surely it wasn't over the silent, stilted dinner she'd shared with her husband last night. That was just anxiety. They were both worried about their siblings. It was natural there'd be this wall between them. Grady and his cousins were probably breaking laws trying to find Vanessa, while she was toeing the law's line trying to find them.

But they'd gone to bed and turned away from each other, and it had eaten at her all night.

She closed her eyes and rubbed her hands over her

face. On the job wasn't the time to think about her emotions or her marriage.

"You okay?" Hart asked, a note of gentleness in his voice. "You're looking a little, as my mother would say, peaked."

She opened her eyes to give Hart a sharp, fierce look. "I'm fine."

He shrugged. "If you say so, boss."

"I'm not your boss," she grumbled, closing Adele's hall-closet door, which contained nothing but meticulously organized coats and shoes.

"No, but you're grooming me," Hart said conversationally, taking off the latex gloves he'd used to poke through the trash.

"I'm not," she protested, probably stupidly. She was irritated he'd figured her out but also impressed. She'd been trying to be subtle, though that had never been her strong point.

"You've let me take the lead on almost everything. Laurel, I've worked with you enough years. You never let anyone take the lead without a very specific reason, and this is your *brother*. There's no way you'd let me take the lead without a reason. You're grooming me."

She let out a sigh. It would have been nice for him to keep thinking he was just her help, but he'd figured it out. That was good, all in all. "Okay, I'm grooming you."

"Leaving us?" he asked, his voice devoid of any tell. Also impressive. He'd grown a lot in the past few years. She felt a kind of older-sister pride in that.

"Temporarily."

Hart raised his eyebrows. "Never thought I'd see the day you'd…" He'd need to work on his poker face, because when he finally figured things out, his eyes got a little wide as it all clicked.

"Oh. *Oh.* Well, I guess congratulations are in order."

"We've got a ways to go till congratulations are in order. It's still early and no one at the department knows yet."

He frowned. "They should know, Laurel."

"You sound like my husband."

"And you're irritated I do because you know we're both right. They should know, and you shouldn't be running yourself so hard. Pretty sure you should be on desk duty."

She might have gotten bent out of shape about Hart of all people scolding her, but there was one simple truth to this case. "My brother and sister-in-law are missing and in danger. I can't step back. I'm taking care of myself. You're here, aren't you?"

"I'm here. It's wild though. You and a Carson. Your brother and another Carson." He shook his head.

"What? You think the whole town is going to fall down around our ears?" She asked it too sharply and with too much of her own baggage weighing the words down. *Idiot.* She needed to get ahold of her personal ties to this case. Pregnant or not, family or not, she had to be the detective this case needed.

But Hart didn't flinch or evade. He smiled kindly. "Nah. Just crumble at the edges a little bit. Maybe a few more kidnappings and fires. Mob might come through and get me shot again. But eventually Satan and hellfire will get bored. Bent doesn't die."

She laughed a little at the Satan-and-hellfire bit, but it hardly felt far off. They'd had a lot of trouble over the last year. It had started before her and Grady but not by much. Most of the trouble happened after.

She did *not* believe in curses. Or feuds. At all.

On a deep breath, she repeated Hart's words to herself. Bent didn't die. Through all the trouble, even the trouble they were knee-deep in, Bent kept living, and so did its people. Even if there were curses, Bent would weather them all.

And so will we, she thought to herself, twisting her wedding ring on her finger.

"Let's get ready to go." But first she'd send a text to Grady. She pulled out her phone, surprised to find one from him already there.

Taking care of yourself & co, princess?

She smiled at the & co, and what she knew was a tentative peace offering. She decided to offer one of her own.

Doing my best. I'm going to knock off early. Take a nap.

Real nap or metaphorical nap?

Depends. What time can you be home?

I'll beat you there.

Simple as that, she was settled again, centered. She'd married a good man. He'd married a good woman. And whoever was crazy enough to kidnap a Carson and Delaney together was definitely going to come out with the raw end of this deal.

"Ready?" Hart asked.

Laurel looked around the living room. "Yes. We've been through everything, and I think I'm going to take the afternoon off. You can handle things for a while— call the phone company again and again if you have to. We've got to get something on that ping, but my brain's mush. I need a few hours." She started for the door, but then she stopped at a little desk in the corner. They'd gone through it looking for clues and hadn't found any. But she realized, now that they'd been through the whole house, the little stack of paint samples and fabric swatches on top of the desk didn't actually match anything done inside the house.

"Hart. Look at this."

"Yeah." He picked them up. "Paint samples and fabric swatches. You think she's planning on coming into some ransom money to redecorate?"

"Could be, but things have been marked off. Chosen." She didn't say anything else and instead waited, wondering if he'd come to the same conclusion she was coming to.

"But…" He looked around the living room they stood in. He took the time to walk around the entire house again, studying fabrics and paints in contrast to the samples he held in his hand.

"This isn't for here," he finally said, certain.

"No. She has another residence. Or had one built. Recently."

"A new cabin, perhaps? Like the one your father described Dylan sitting in the middle of, with Adele Oscar silent and scared next to him?"

Laurel kept pulling the thread. "Surely she wouldn't be so stupid as to kidnap someone to a cabin in her own name. And we checked all the new constructs in the area. We didn't see her name."

"But she put herself on camera. Made herself look like a victim. We'll expand our search now that we've got a name and a reason to," Hart said, sounding suitably in charge. "But there are other options here."

"Like what? If she's redecorating, it's *her* place." Laurel began to think of all the ways that could be untrue, but she waited for Hart to explain his own theories.

"Two possibilities. First, it's her place but it's not under her name—at least the name we have. What if she bought it under another name? A name attached to a bank account where ransom money couldn't be detected."

"God, that's far-fetched." And possible. So completely possible.

"It could also be under a boyfriend's name. Or a family member's. She could have a stake in it without her name being on the papers."

A boyfriend. There was definitely no evidence of one, and the people at the bank they'd talked to couldn't list any friends she might have spent time with outside of banker hours.

But the bank.

"There's a third option."

Hart snapped his fingers. "She works at a bank and handles home loans."

Laurel nodded. "Let's see if we can subpoena some bank records."

Chapter Fourteen

Vanessa wanted to escape this cabin because of the men with guns and whatnot, but at this point she also wanted to escape because she was going absolutely stir-crazy.

"Can't you just take them out?" she demanded irritably of Dylan as he went over the layout of the cabin with Adele again, trying to understand the full scale and find weak points for escape, or so he said.

Adele gave Vanessa a speculative look and Dylan gave her a censuring one. He still didn't want anyone to know about his secret. It made her want to scream. Partly because it was a stupid secret, and partly because they were kidnapped and who *cared*? Let everyone know that with a gun in his hand, Dylan Delaney could pick off anyone standing in their way.

"They have guns. We don't," Dylan said simply.

"We only need one," Vanessa returned.

"They'd still have one. We can't risk it."

Dylan's patient, indulgent tone pissed her off, even if he was right.

Right and protective and sweet somehow. It made no earthly sense that a part of her wanted him to bust into army-sniper mode, and another ached for the man who thought he had to hide himself because of his name and

Bent. She felt the second on a much deeper level than she wanted to.

She didn't have secrets. Bent and her family knew who she was…sort of. Maybe she'd cultivated a big-mouth, rough and dangerous, say-anything personality because she felt like she had to in order to survive being a Carson—especially a female Carson. You had to be hard and you had to be rough, or you had to leave. Hadn't her aunt disappeared and not talked to the family for years? She hadn't fit the mold—so instead of trying to fight that, she'd escaped.

Vanessa had done everything she could to fit the mold, even when she hadn't particularly felt as rough-and-tumble as she was supposed to be. She'd probably cut off some fingers before she'd willingly show any soft side to her family or to Bent in general.

"Maybe we should ask for food," Adele suggested brightly. "It might help everyone's mood."

Vanessa sent her the dirtiest look she had in her arsenal. Maybe she *was* hungry and irritable, but that didn't mean she appreciated Adele pointing it out.

"Good idea," Dylan said, striding over to the door. He began pounding on it until No-Neck appeared, growling and vicious.

"You need to feed us," Dylan demanded. "It'd be easier if you gave us some snacks and water to keep in here."

"Yeah, I'm real worried about your easy, pal," No-Neck returned with a snort, but he eyed Adele and then Vanessa. "Only because Boss's orders are to keep you alive and well. You'll come with me. I ain't your chef." He gripped Dylan's arm and yanked him out of the room.

Well, Dylan allowed himself to be yanked, Vanessa thought. He'd had that furious, violent look on his face, but then he'd tightened his jaw and banked it. She noted he couldn't seem to sweet-talk the guards, but he'd feign weakness for them.

She realized it was because he was used to one and not the other. He was always feigning weakness and never trying to sweet-talk anyone.

That flutter was back around her heart. Like she was impressed with him or something. Like he kind of amazed her and she wanted...

Well, it didn't matter what else she wanted right now. Just freedom. That was all that mattered at the moment.

Adele began to wander around the room in Dylan's absence. She touched a chair, poked at the wall. Her gaze went to the ceiling, the high, narrow windows.

It was dark, Vanessa noted. They'd been here two days now, with almost no sleep, and that was after their uncomfortable night in the woods.

She had to believe people were working to find them, but this was an awful long time not to be found.

"I didn't realize you and Dylan were so...chummy," Adele offered. A casual observation, or so Adele wanted Vanessa to believe.

Vanessa snorted from her seat in the desk chair. She was feeling a little queasy again, though not as weak. Adele walking in relative circles had her closing her eyes against the round of dizziness she could now remember was just one of her lucky pregnancy symptoms. "Chummy?"

"Is that not the word for it?" Adele chuckled. "There's certainly a connection between you two. An energy."

"Energy," Vanessa muttered with some disgust, opening one eye hesitantly.

Adele had stopped her prowling so she was standing in front of Vanessa. She leaned close, as if they were two girlfriends conspiring with each other. "It just crackles in the air."

"It's called hate," Vanessa returned flatly. Adele was fishing, and Vanessa wasn't about to be the trout she landed.

"You're pregnant," Adele said gently.

Vanessa gave Adele a steely look while she fought the urge to touch her stomach. "Not by a damn Delaney."

Adele rolled her eyes. "I never understood this town's obsession with Carsons and Delaneys. You're just people, like the rest of us."

Vanessa noticed she said *this town*. Maybe it was just the way she spoke, but it gave Vanessa a tingling jolt of excitement. Maybe they weren't that far outside of Bent if Adele was referring to *this town*.

"Besides, you two were wound around each other like vines when I was thrown in here. You can't tell me something isn't going on. Or maybe you just don't remember."

Still fishing for information. Assessing Vanessa's memory and relationship with Dylan with every question, every glance. Why would she need to know the nature of her relationship with Dylan or the state of her memory if she wasn't gathering information for something?

"It's an awful bump. Not recognizing people. Pregnancy. Quite a trauma."

"I'll live," Vanessa replied.

"Of course." Adele sighed gustily. "As soon as we get out of here."

"A shame you can't help that along."

"We can't all be like you, Vanessa. So strong and sure of ourselves. We can't all be Carsons and Delaneys in Bent. That would get a bit incestuous, wouldn't it?"

There was an edge to her voice and Vanessa wanted to smirk. She thought with the right attitude, the right throwaway comments, she might actually be able to break Adele into showing her true colors.

"And yet Carsons and Delaneys are all Bent seems to care about," Vanessa said with a sweet smile. "The world spins on and on, and all the citizens can seem to care about is Grady and Laurel getting married. Old man Delaney having an affair with a *married* Carson all those years ago."

Inspired, Vanessa blinked her wide eyes at Adele. "Oh, Mr. Delaney. I'd guess you worked more closely with him than Dylan, before Dylan came home."

Adele's face was perfectly blank, but everything about her was tense. Vanessa let her smile go sly and wide.

"I work with everyone at the bank," Adele said, in something like a robot voice. No inflection, no emotion.

"Sure, but Mr. Delaney is the boss. The head honcho. Surely there's some need to please the guy in charge?"

Adele's jaw twitched and her hand curled into a fist before she quickly released it. "I do my job. I've always done my job."

It was there, somewhere under the control—a breaking point. And it centered on that job. Vanessa only had to find it.

But Dylan returned just then with some food—more horrendous pizza pockets—and a few bottles of water.

Vanessa kept her attention on Adele. All that speculation, that intent staring and incessant questioning? Gone. The anger and tension melted away.

She was playing some kind of role, and Dylan was falling for it hook, line and sinker.

Men.

Vanessa couldn't even hate him for it because she knew it stemmed from that innate Delaney goodness.

He wanted there to be good in the world, and he wanted to believe the people in his life were that.

Vanessa wanted to blame it on arrogance and the fact he just couldn't believe someone who'd worked for his family for a decade was bad, because that would make his initial estimation about Adele wrong. A few days ago she *would* have blamed it on that.

But it wasn't that. He wanted her to be good because thinking people were bad was always his last resort. *Unless it has to do with Carsons.*

True enough, and yet he'd jumped to help Vanessa herself, taken care of her, protected her this whole time. Maybe at some point she'd convince herself it was just because of the accidental pregnancy.

But the kiss from earlier was too fresh in her mind. Dylan Delaney had fallen for *her* and was going to believe she was good regardless of all evidence to the contrary.

She swallowed, looking away from Adele to the man in question. He handed her a pizza pocket, wrapped up in a paper towel. This one was cooked through. He placed the bottle of water, already opened, on the desk next to her.

It was a gesture that, anywhere else, would have pissed her off. Why didn't it here?

"I think I have a plan," Dylan stated.

With that, Vanessa didn't have time to figure it out.

"Don't you think—"

Dylan already knew what Vanessa was going to say. Now, while he explained the plan, after the fact. She'd hate the plan simply by merit of her safety being paramount—and added to the fact he was going to tell Adele?

Yeah, he expected fireworks.

Hopefully, he'd learned how to deal with Vanessa's fireworks, because he was pretty sure he could pull this off.

"Those two idiots out there?" Dylan said, nodding his head toward the door and ignoring Vanessa's protests. "They *love* to talk to each other. They practically wrote down their evening routine for me."

"Just because we know their routine doesn't mean we could escape and then know where to go." Adele flicked a look at Vanessa. "I doubt a pregnant woman should be running around in the dark woods."

"You'd be surprised what a pregnant woman is capable of," Vanessa returned, her voice a low growl.

Dylan grinned at her. "*Very* surprised," Dylan agreed. "Plus, I'm not talking about escape exactly. I'm talking about diversions, redirection and calling for help." He gave Adele an encouraging smile. "With the information you gave me, I think I know where we are."

Adele nodded slowly. "Where is that?"

It bothered him she would ask that question. She should want to escape, not to check his theories. He could lie. He could tell her the truth, or he could avoid the question. He looked at Vanessa.

She was glowering at Adele, but she wasn't saying anything snarky. Dylan figured that was progress.

"Do you have any way to keep time, Adele?" he asked, ignoring her question completely.

She frowned. "Why are you asking me that?"

I could ask the same of you. Dylan held up his watch. "So we can make sure we act at the same time. Unless they let you stay with us all night, and I'm not sure that's going to happen. So we should have a way to act in the same moment. If you can tell time, we can decide on one."

"I don't think there's anything in the room, but I'm not sure."

Dylan shook his head. By trying to play it confused and uncertain, she was only proving herself to be in on the whole kidnapping. Still, he'd keep pretending that he trusted her, for the sake of his real plan. No matter how he could hear Vanessa seething behind him.

"That's okay. We share a wall. I'll come up with a signal. Two knocks, pause, two more knocks. That's how you'll know it's time to act."

Adele frowned. "Act on what?"

"The plan."

"We don't need to involve everyone in the plan," Vanessa said through clenched teeth.

Dylan looked back at her and held her gaze, trying to get across that he knew what he was doing. She remained scowling and infuriated.

"We'll wait until the middle of the night. Vanessa's going to ask to go to the bathroom. I'll knock on our shared wall right before she does. You'll listen for them to move around, open our door, lead her to the bathroom. Then it'll be your turn. You'll start banging on the door asking to go to the bathroom. Now, one of them sleeps on a cot in some room off the kitchen. So we'll have one guard confused by two women needing to use the bathroom. In the meantime, I'll slip out of our room and put in a 911 call off the landline."

"The door will be locked," Adele pointed out. "Even if you get around that, they'll hear you talking to the 911 operator."

He ignored the part about getting around a locked door. She didn't need to know everything he was capable of. "I won't say anything. I'll dial and leave the phone off the hook. By the time the guard notices, the dispatcher will already be tracing the call and sending someone our way. I'm sure of it."

"Well…" Adele chewed on her bottom lip. "Maybe it could work. But what if they realize the phone is off the hook because one of us dialed 911? Do we really want to risk them hurting Vanessa?"

It was a question that might have struck fear into him a few minutes ago and given him another reason to believe Adele had nothing to do with this. But he'd seen the evidence. Thank God for pizza pockets.

"No. We don't want to risk *anyone* getting hurt, but the fact of the matter is Vanessa isn't getting the care she needs here. We need to get her out of here. As soon as possible."

"I am right here and fully capable of speaking for myself," Vanessa said, a warning quietness to her tone that he knew well enough. Soon she'd go nuclear. He almost wanted to see it.

Instead, he chose to ignore her, because her being furious worked into his plans well enough for now. "I can handle anything those guards can dish out."

"Yeah, I bet a bullet to the brain would be *real* easy to handle," Vanessa muttered.

"Vanessa has a point. They don't want to kill you, Dylan. You're the one with the rich family. Vanessa and I? They could kill us with no compunction. Why don't we just wait until the ransom is delivered? I'd feel better. They've threatened my family, you know."

Dylan kept himself relaxed even though he wanted to tense. "No, that's not information you chose to share."

She shook her head and closed her eyes. "I've been so scared, so confused. Every step is a potential misstep and then my family is dead."

"I didn't realize you still had living family back in

San Francisco." He'd chosen the city because he knew she wasn't from there. He wanted to see if he could catch her in another lie.

"We're not close, but I don't want them to die." Her voice trembled, and she produced more tears.

Dylan felt no softening this time. Adele was a believable actress, and he could think of enough scenarios where she might have been forced or threatened into cooperating. Blackmailed into helping rather than violently intimidated into keeping quiet like the tactic the goons had taken with him and Vanessa.

But her family *didn't* live in San Francisco. He might not know everything about her, but she'd never spoken of family. She had spoken of going to Seattle or Denver on occasion over holidays, and the assumption had been for family visits. She never mentioned San Francisco.

So it was the final nail in the Adele-has-always-been-against-us coffin.

Dylan couldn't let her know there were nails or coffins. Somehow, despite his rage and disappointment, he had to keep it all under wraps. And he had to make sure Vanessa didn't blow their cover either.

So he whirled to face her, giving her the most murderous look he could manage while she sputtered and opened her mouth to certainly ask Adele why she hadn't mentioned this earlier.

She gave him a murderous look right back, but she didn't ask the question.

"Do you have a better plan, Adele?" Dylan asked calmly.

"Yes. We wait until the ransom comes and they let us go. They'll have to let us go."

"If you believe that, you're the dumbest human on the face of the planet," Vanessa spat.

Adele straightened and glared right back at her. "I beg your pardon."

"Do you?" Vanessa asked sweetly.

Adele returned the look. "I do beg your pardon. Because getting mad at such a trashy whore who doesn't even know the father of their baby is beneath me. So very, very far beneath me."

Vanessa straightened slowly, her hands clenching into fists and giving Dylan no doubt she'd throw a punch if given the chance. Dylan slid in between the two angry women and focused on Adele.

"Don't speak to her that way again, Adele."

"Hmm." She looked him up and down, cold, calculating disdain in her gaze. "Did that hurt your feelings?" she asked in a baby voice. "Because maybe she *does* know who the baby daddy is, and maybe it's you?" She pretended to gasp. "What would *your* daddy say?"

He took a step toward her before he remembered he was playing a dangerous game here. If Adele was the mastermind, he had to play it cool. He could wring her neck, and what would it do? He still didn't know what she was after, and the men out there with guns could easily kill them without Adele to play her little games.

No matter how his temper boiled, he needed to understand this better. More importantly, he had to get Vanessa out of the crossfire range before he attempted anything.

"You're starting to sound jealous, Adele," Vanessa offered from behind Dylan's back.

God, she wasn't helping.

"Let's all calm down. We're tired. We're hungry. We're lashing out at each other at the worst possible moment. We need to band together." Or at least he needed Adele to believe they had.

Adele took in a deep breath and let it out. She nodded.

"You're right, Dylan. Let's eat these awful things. We'll all feel better after."

Vanessa kept glaring, but she took a big bite of pizza pocket and chewed instead of arguing any more.

Chapter Fifteen

Vanessa hated to admit she felt better after eating. Too bad eating didn't cure the fact Adele was evil.

Was Dylan *really* this stupid? she wondered incredulously. She hadn't thought so. But he was going over the plan with Adele again as if he trusted her. As if he didn't see all the holes in her story.

Vanessa had stopped listening, stopped getting angry, because it was pointless. He was the dumbest man alive, and he'd deserve what he got when Adele turned on him and shot him through the heart.

Even in anger, that thought made her blood run cold, and she had to remind herself Adele clearly wanted Dylan alive for some reason. She'd had too many chances to kill him or have him killed.

It could be money. People had done less for money, but Vanessa didn't buy it. There was something bigger at stake here. If only she could figure out *what* before Dylan got his dumb self killed.

The door flung open to the sight of Eyeballs waving that butt of his gun around like it made him important. Vanessa barely resisted the urge to roll her eyes. He hadn't acted particularly quickly to use it as anything other than a battering ram against Dylan. Should they really be scared?

He grabbed Adele roughly by the arm. Adele whimpered and resisted, but Eyeballs squeezed hard enough to have Adele gasping.

Vanessa watched the whole thing as dispassionately as she might a play. Eyeballs could rough up Adele all he wanted, but unless he used even half the force against Adele that he'd used against Dylan, Vanessa wasn't buying this as anything more than a farce.

"Ransom time, and you're insurance, sweetheart." He pulled Adele toward the door. "I'd stop making all that noise before we start hurting that family of yours. We've got a man in San Fran ready to go."

"P-please. Don't…" Adele stopped struggling and let Eyeballs lead her out of the room, the door slamming shut and the lock clicking into place behind them.

"What a load of—"

Dylan held up a hand. Vanessa was tempted to punch it, but he put a finger to his lips. Quieting against her will, she watched him as he moved stealthily to the desk and began clicking keys on the computer.

He'd tried to get past the password protection earlier and failed, so she didn't know what he thought he was doing *now*. But after a few clicks where he seemed to just fiddle with the volume directly from the keyboard, he started to rummage through the desk.

He pulled out a piece of paper and a pen. Then he wrote in big fat letters: BUG.

She didn't understand what on earth he was doing. He'd seen a spider or a cockroach. Who gave a crap? "I'm supposed to be scared there's a b—"

His hand clamped over her mouth, sending the pen, paper and chair between them clattering to the ground. He gave her face a gentle squeeze, opening his eyes wider as if willing her to catch on. It took a minute, but then she finally got it.

Bug. Listening device. Had she fallen into some bizarre movie?

"They won't know what's coming," Dylan said cheerfully, slowly letting go of her face. "This 911 plan of mine is genius, and Adele helping us is huge."

Vanessa frowned at him. He didn't sound like himself, and wasn't he talking a little too loudly? But she couldn't exactly mount objections if they were being listened to.

He righted the chair and picked the pen and paper off the floor. He scribbled on it as he repeated the plan he'd made with Adele.

It was only now that there was a listening device and he was still going on about his 911 plan that Vanessa fully understood. He didn't trust Adele. He was setting her up.

She read the note he'd written.

I think the mic is in the computer. I didn't find anything earlier. Going to try to disable it.

Vanessa looked around the room. She tried not to think about the things Adele or her goons might have listened to or heard. Even though she hadn't revealed anything particularly telling, Dylan had. Because she'd made him.

A wave of regret washed over her. Whoever was listening knew who and what he was now. They wouldn't underestimate him anymore. They knew about the baby and that it was Dylan's. There were no secrets.

That was scary. Money could maybe buy silence but not forever, and Vanessa still didn't think this was about money.

"Dylan…" Except she couldn't talk because they were

being listened to, and he kept trying to hack into the computer to turn off whatever was listening to them.

Vanessa glanced at the wires coming out of the desk and snaking their way to a power strip. She walked over, studied it. One of them had to power the computer, and without power to the computer...

She stepped on the thick main cord that hooked into the outlet, dislodging it. The computer went off with a *pop*. She looked up at Dylan and shrugged. "Oops."

He shook his head. "I was going for something a little less noticeable. If they notice the feed just die, they'll come fix it. Or put in a new listening device."

"I doubt they have backup listening devices. Besides, this looks like an accident—not that we knew they were listening. If they come and plug it back in, we know. And we can keep doing it as long as we need to."

Dylan looked around the room. "*If* that was the only listening device. I searched before, but Adele could have added one."

Exhaustion washed over her. *Another* listening device? How were they ever going to escape if someone could hear every word?

"They could be recording to play later too," Dylan said as if thinking it all through aloud. "So it might not be getting to them immediately, whatever we say. I certainly haven't heard them listening to anything when I've gone to get food, and you didn't hear anything when you went to the bathroom, did you?"

"No. But Adele's door was closed. *She* could be the listener."

Dylan nodded. "Adele wouldn't do that," Dylan said, but he made a big production of rolling his eyes and mouthing, *"She darn well would."*

Vanessa couldn't help but grin at him. He wasn't stupid after all. He was simply covering his tracks, throwing Adele off the scent. Thank God.

"Still, we need to be careful," he said. Then he wrote something down on a piece of paper and handed it to her.

I'm going to search the room one more time with a better idea of what I'm looking for.

It felt like he took hours. He left no stone unturned. She almost nodded off on the chair, but then he made her get up so he could search the chair.

"You're tired," he said as he poked at folds in the fabric and pushed on the cushion—presumably looking for something hard inside.

"Exhausted," she returned.

"I'm tempted to demand some kind of bed, but if they're off pretending to collect ransom, maybe the best thing is to keep a low profile. I'm about ninety-nine percent sure there's no other listening device, and the fact they haven't busted in to turn the computer back on or tell us we'll never call 911 makes me think they're just recording, not listening in. So we'll take a few hours to sleep."

"I want to go home." She did, desperately. So much so her eyes were starting to sting.

He crossed the room to her, sliding his hands over her shoulders. That touch, the simple *care* in his gaze, just about had the tears spilling over.

"I know. I know. I'm going to get you home." A promise. A vow.

She hated that tears spilled, that something like a sob escaped her throat. But instead of being horrified or letting her wiggle out of his grasp, he simply pulled her to him. He held her there, putting gentle pressure on her head until she rested it on his shoulder.

He didn't say anything—nothing to try to make her feel better or stop crying. He simply let her cry there on his shoulder, rubbing his hand up and down her spine.

So she wept. In a way she'd never, *ever* done in someone's presence before. She let it all out, like she was alone in the shower or something. But she wasn't alone. She had Dylan. And he was holding her like he always would.

She really had to get ahold of herself. Crying was ridiculous, but thinking about *always* was the height of ridiculousness. She pulled away from his grasp, wiping at her face with the palms of her hands.

"I'm—"

"I know you're not about to apologize for crying after you've been kidnapped and had a major head injury that caused temporary memory loss, all while pregnant I might add. Because that kind of apology would just be stupid."

She sniffled, glaring at him, which she assumed had been his intent. Get her back up and a little irritated with him so she wouldn't start blubbering again.

"You need to rest up," he said gently. "We have to see what comes of this ransom thing." He looked at his clock. "I want the second guard fast asleep before..." He trailed off, still worried about the prospect of being recorded or heard.

"They won't be able to hear a sound if they're still recording," she whispered. She was too tired to wait around for him to write notes and then keep her eyes open to read them.

"We're not going to call 911. Well, we are, but we're going to escape in the process. We will not spend another twenty-four hours in this cabin, I promise you that."

"You really think we can escape?" she whispered.

"I'm going to get you home. It's a promise."

She frowned at the way he worded that—so it was about her, not them—but he walked away and started chattering on about finding a makeshift bed.

IT WOULDN'T BE a comfortable nap, but it was sleep and that's what was important. Dylan had stacked two rugs on top of each other, tilted the chair on the ground so the headrest could act as a pillow of sorts and found a drop cloth in the closet that could act like a blanket.

She watched him the whole time he worked, wary and speculative.

He ignored all those things in her because the quiet worked. He needed to slightly reformulate his plan, and being able to do it without her questioning or arguing was easier. "Here. It's not luxury, but it'll do." He gestured her toward the makeshift bed.

"You think I'm used to luxury?" She stood where she was, eyebrow raised at the sad attempt at a bed. "Where are you going to sleep?"

He gestured toward the door. "Against it. That way, if they come in, we're ready. I can sleep against anything." He forced himself to smile. "All that army training."

She walked over to the pretend bed and scrunched up her face, but eventually lowered herself into it. She leaned her head against the headrest acting as a pillow, and then studied him.

He didn't mind being studied by her. Didn't mind *her.* Life had changed in a blink. He was still trying to wade through what that meant, but he couldn't get a handle on it until he knew she was safe.

Everything else could be dealt with once that happened.

Eventually, Vanessa patted the spot next to her. "Come here. There's room."

It was amazing how much he wanted to—a physical need he had to beat back. "Better to be ready." Sleep on the door so they couldn't be taken unawares.

"Come here, I said. Aren't soldiers supposed to follow orders?"

There was enough steel in her tone to have him smiling. "I haven't been a soldier in years."

"You've done an impressive impression of one these past two days. Now, do as Captain Vanessa says and get over here."

"Captain, huh?"

"You're right. I'm really better suited to general."

He chuckled, and really, what was the point in resisting? He'd protect her whether he slept next to her or against the door. Besides, he probably wouldn't sleep at all. Though getting an hour or two would keep him sharp, and he was pretty good at sleeping when he needed to, he'd never been in the position before of protecting so much that was valuable to him.

On a sigh, he crawled into the fake bed, facing her. They were close enough he could feel her warmth, count each faint freckle on her nose and the long inky lashes of her eyes.

"When did you figure it out?" she whispered.

He didn't have to ask her what she meant. "I've been suspicious the whole time, but Adele's a good actress and I… It's hard to believe someone you've trusted is willing to hurt you."

Something in her expression shuttered. "Not for everyone."

He didn't know much about her childhood, but he knew enough. The Carson generation that had raised the current one was full of hard men, mean men. Violent men. He'd used that as an excuse to hate all Carsons, but the truth was…

Hell, Grady was an okay guy. Dylan had never had a problem with Noah. Ty…well, sometimes he'd like to knock that guy's block off, but none of them were like their fathers.

"No. I guess you're right." Unable to stop himself, he reached out and brushed some hair off her face. "But no one ever gave you a reason to trust them not to hurt you."

She shrugged jerkily. "Grady. Noah and Ty."

"That's different. Believe me. When it's just kids it's different. You need an adult who has your back. You guys never had that."

"You softening to Carsons, Delaney?"

"I'm going to be a father to half of one. I figure I better."

She held his gaze, and he saw everything he felt reflected there. Fear. Hope. Care.

"So, what sealed the deal? Regarding Adele?" she asked, her voice thick. He told himself it was exhaustion, but part of him wondered if it was emotion.

"When they took me to the kitchen to make the pizza pockets, I was trying to look around. See out windows, anything that might give me an idea where we are, and the door to the room she'd been in was open. There were two perfectly normal-sized windows. A computer. She's running the show, and the guys she hired to be the muscle don't have two brain cells between them."

Vanessa blew out a breath, sliding closer to him. Like this was their normal life. Nightly conversations in bed together where they weren't kidnapped and trying to sleep on the floor with office materials as bedding.

"I think it centers on the bank and on her job. When

you were out there, she was getting so angry with me. I kept poking at the bank, at your dad. It's something about that."

"Well, the bank is an endless source of money."

Vanessa shook her head. "It isn't about money." He noted she kept her voice at the lowest whisper yet. "I know it's not about money. You have to find the connection to the bank."

"She's off getting the ransom."

"It's a ploy or a lie." Her lips all but brushed his ear, and it was the absolute wrong time to feel the wave of lust and want coming over him.

"What's a bigger motivation than money?" he asked, trying to keep his brain focused on the task at hand instead of being distracted by the way she shifted closer, so their bodies pressed together.

"I'm not sure I can come up with anything," she said, rubbing her cheek against his jaw. "If you've got money, which it seems like she does, at least enough to get by on, why would you go through all this for more? It has to be something else. Too bad we can't ask your dad."

Dylan smirked. "He'd always take more."

"Sure. We all would, but this is about what you'd risk. Why risk everything for money if you've got it?"

"Secret gambling habit? A family member's bills for an illness? This cabin?"

"No. It doesn't add up. This is something personal."

"Or she's mentally unstable. Also a thought we should consider."

Vanessa closed her eyes. "I'm so tired of considering."

He brushed his mouth over her temple, wanting to soothe both her and himself. He wanted them out of this too. Wanted her checked out and safe and sound at home.

Home. Something they'd have to talk about, because

he'd be damned if she raised their baby over her greasy deathtrap of a mechanic shop, and he had no doubt she'd fight tooth and nail to make sure their baby wasn't raised anywhere near Delaney property.

He rested his cheek on top of her head and held her close. They had all sorts of challenges ahead. The predicament they were currently in. The baby. But something in this quiet moment resisted all need to figure it out. He wanted to breathe, and he wanted peace.

Vanessa sighed against his neck. "I know it doesn't make any sense," she whispered, and this time he didn't think it was because of the potential of being overheard. "But we fit."

"Yeah, we do."

She pressed her mouth to his neck and then his jaw, sliding her body sinuously against his.

"Well." He had to clear his throat since it was suddenly dry as dust.

This time her mouth touched his, light and teasing, and then she nipped, causing his grip on her to tighten, just like the rest of his body.

"And for about five minutes," she murmured, right against his lips, "I'd like to pretend that's the most important thing in my life."

"Five minutes?" he scoffed. "Really?"

She chuckled against his mouth, maneuvering herself on top of him. "I don't need more."

Dylan slid his hands down her sides, enjoying the sweet pleasure of the friction between their bodies, even with clothes on. "I do."

She flashed him a grin. "Wanna bet?"

Chapter Sixteen

Even though bets were what had gotten them into this mess—something she remembered around the time her clothes were quickly being removed from her body—this one felt right. He felt right. They fit together.

Maybe when they were back in the real world, she'd have to deal with that a little more head-on, but the real world wasn't here.

She took a moment to trace her finger over the small tattoo on his chest. She recognized it as the Delaney brand. It touched her. She had a quite a few tattoos herself, and some had heavy meanings, but she'd never branded herself with her family's legacy. It seemed both noble and a little sad that Dylan of all people had.

But she couldn't hold on to sad when Dylan slid into her. There was no world at the moment except them together. It was peace, and it was bliss. It didn't matter he was a Delaney, only that his body moving with hers felt perfectly right.

"Van," he murmured as she arched against him. He spoke her shortened name as if it was a precious, solemn prayer. He touched her like she was his to care for, and everything in her shimmered with a life she didn't know how to control or put her own impenetrable shell over.

"I want you. Us." *Us.* She wanted there to be a *them*.

Her brain couldn't wrap itself around that simple fact, but her heart had already made the leap. Maybe even before this whole mess. Maybe on that fuzzy night they'd conceived a child together.

She sighed into her release, holding him close as he found his own. When she drifted off, the sleep was deep, long and perfectly happy.

When she woke up—she wasn't sure how much later—she was somehow dressed and curled up in the makeshift bed Dylan had made. He was curled up behind her, arms wrapped protectively around her stomach.

She closed her eyes again, wanting to sink into this feeling of utter safety, no matter how uncomfortable the bed was.

But Dylan shifted, tightening then loosening his grip. She could feel him coming awake next to her, and the real world crashing back into them. She could tell his brain immediately clicked into gear, working out what the next step was.

Fear washed through her. Bone-deep fear that she'd lose him somehow.

"Are you sure it isn't safe to just wait? Surely someone's looking for you." A tension she didn't know how to label crept into her shoulders, and suddenly she felt… insignificant. "Do you think anyone knows where I am? I'm sure all of Wyoming has been rallied to look for Dylan Delaney, but does anyone know I'm a part of this?"

"Your car was in the bank parking lot. I'd wager there's an army of Carsons convinced *I* kidnapped *you*. They're probably roaming the mountains looking to take me down."

Vanessa laughed, snuggling into him. It was a nice feeling. Definitely new. She'd never considered herself a cuddler or a hugger. She got to sneak some cuddle time in with Noah and Addie's kid, but he was quickly turning into a toddler who squirmed and wiggled away.

She slid a hand over her stomach, and Dylan did the same. Their fingers brushed, both palms resting over the life they'd made.

"I know it's not the time to discuss it since we have to survive this all first, but how are we going to do this?" she asked, swamped with so much emotion she had to get it all out lest she fall apart again.

"I notice you've switched to *we* instead of cutting me out completely."

She turned in the circle of his arms to face him. "I guess you saving my butt a few times here and there during this whole ordeal softened me up."

"It's my fault you're even—"

"No, it's Adele's fault." Vanessa sat up and rubbed her eyes. There was a low-level queasiness in her stomach, but it wasn't as bad as usual. They could and probably should talk about not cutting him out of the future, but the reminder of Adele brought back the fact they had to survive first.

"Do you think she's back?"

Dylan pointed up to the windows. "It's still dark, but you can see dawn creeping in. She'd have to be back, wouldn't she?"

"There's one way to find out." Vanessa pushed to her feet and started for the door.

"Van—"

She looked over her shoulder at Dylan and winked. "Sorry, Charlie, pregnant women gotta pee and you aren't invited." She started pounding on the door even as he glared at her grumpily.

It took longer than usual for No-Neck to answer the

door. He looked a little rumpled, like he'd been asleep. Vanessa raised an eyebrow at him.

"Go to the bathroom. Try anything funny and I'll shoot." He led her out but didn't grab her by both arms. Before she even got to the bathroom, he let her go and trudged over to the kitchen area and began fumbling with a coffee machine.

Vanessa walked slowly toward the bathroom door, looking around the living room for signs of Adele. She didn't see the evil mastermind, but she did note that where there had once been a landline phone, there was now an empty end table.

Evil witch.

"Get on with it," No-Neck grumbled, waving his coffee mug at her.

She did as she was told and went to the bathroom. Since No-Neck was preoccupied, she took her time to paw through the cabinet under the sink, but there was nothing weapon worthy or helpful.

On a grunt of frustration she stood, just as No-Neck jerked the door open.

"Hey!" Vanessa protested.

"You're taking too long."

She sailed out of the bathroom past him. "You're cheery in the morning."

He gave her a shove, and only quick reflexes kept her stomach from slamming into the back of the couch. She turned to glare at him, but he was too busy gulping down his coffee and wincing, presumably at the scalding heat.

"Where's your buddy?" she asked.

"None of your business. You want another shove or you going to go back to your room on your own two feet?"

It was *so* tempting to say something snarky in return.

She briefly considered smacking the coffee mug so that it spilled on him. It would be enough of a distraction to…

What? Get to the door and be shot in the back?

Scowling, she sailed back to the room. She was going to grab the door herself, see if she could con him into forgetting to lock it behind her, but No-Neck was there in a flash, opening the door and pushing her inside.

She whirled and glared at him, which was good because she didn't look at Dylan standing right next to the door, pressed to the wall so he was out of sight from No-Neck.

As No-Neck grinned snidely at her scowl, he pulled the door closed. While he did it, Dylan soundlessly slipped something between the door and the frame.

"What—"

Dylan held a finger to his lips and shook his head. He led her over to the far corner of the room and then leaned down to whisper in her ear.

"Tape on the lock. Found some when I was looking for the bug. Not sure I got it on like I needed to, or that it's strong enough to keep the lock from engaging, but it was worth a shot." He shrugged. "We'll test it later. See anything out there? Adele?"

"Just No-Neck, but the phone that was on that table is gone."

Dylan didn't panic or frown or do anything she expected. He grinned.

"Why are you *happy* about that? It means we can't call 911! Our plan is shot to hell."

"Babe, that was never the plan."

She scowled at him. "Take your *babe* and shove it where the sun don't shine."

He grinned more broadly. "*And* it proves Adele is behind this."

"Yeah, because the giant window you saw in her room didn't," she returned sarcastically. "So, now what?"

"Now—" he took her by the shoulders, holding her gaze "—we plan *our* escape."

LAUREL COULD HAVE used a jumbo coffee. Instead she had to settle for water, because she'd inhaled her caffeine intake for the day by approximately 7 a.m. Now it was well after noon and she had been summoned to the Delaney Ranch to deal with her father.

She'd left Hart poring over the bank records they'd finally managed to get under subpoena. Still no cell phone ping to help them.

With a headache drumming at her temples, she knocked on the door and then stepped inside.

"Dad?"

"He's upstairs." Jen stepped out from the kitchen, where she usually was if she was home. "No word?"

Laurel shook her head and exchanged a quick hug with her sister. "State is setting up for a potential ransom drop-off, but they're having trouble getting details from the kidnapper. Apparently she's fallen off the face of the planet after her demand for money."

"Her?" Jen asked with a raised eyebrow.

"That's my theory." Which, much as she loved her sister, Laurel wasn't going to share more of. "Do you have any idea why Dad wanted me to come by?"

Jen shook her head. "He's been holed up in his office since he woke up. He wouldn't even talk to Cam when he stopped in." Jen looked up at the ceiling, worry lines creasing her forehead.

"Did Cam go out looking again?"

Jen nodded, wringing her hands. "I wish there was something *I* could do."

"Watching Dad is what I need you to do, okay? It's not fun, I know, but it's important."

"He's a mess."

Laurel nodded. "I'll head up. Thanks for staying with him while we work on this."

"You know you don't have to thank me."

"Yeah." Laurel thought briefly of telling Jen about the baby. She'd agreed with Grady not to tell anyone until she was further along, but Jen was her sister and her closest friend. Not to mention she'd had to tell Hart. "Listen…" Laurel chewed on her bottom lip. "You didn't see anything going on between Vanessa and Dylan at my wedding, did you?"

"Dylan and Vanessa?" Jen laughed. Hard. "You mean other than pure, unfiltered hatred?"

"Yeah, other than that."

"No. I mean… I don't remember really seeing them that much." Jen got a weird look on her face and then shook it away. "Do you really think they're together?"

"In more ways than one."

"That can't be," Jen said, surprisingly adamant.

"All evidence points to—"

"I don't care what all evidence points to. You and Grady are bad enough but Dyl…" She trailed off, squeezing her eyes shut. "I don't mean it like *that*."

"Yes, you do," Laurel said. Normally, it didn't bother her. Her family was set in their feuding ways, except Cam. She'd accepted that, moved on. But with being pregnant and Dylan missing, it stirred up…

Well, feelings she didn't have time for. "I'll be back," she murmured, heading away from Jen and her apologies and toward the stairs. She trudged up them, tired and dreading any discussion with her father while Dylan remained missing.

She knocked on the closed office door, only stepping inside once her father said come in.

"You wanted to see me."

"I've been sent another correspondence."

"What? And you didn't forward—"

"It was on the porch this morning," he interrupted, nodding to a manila envelope on the desk.

"How long ago?"

Dad shrugged.

"Dad. What's wrong with you? Why didn't you call me sooner? Why didn't you tell me you found a lead?" She was already pulling her latex gloves out of the pouch on her utility belt as Dad pulled a photograph out of the envelope. "You've got your prints on it."

It was grainy, but very clearly showed Dylan and Vanessa in a room that seemed to be a kind of office, arms around each other.

"Put it down. We could get prints off of it. We could—"

"Do you see what is happening in this picture?" Dad demanded, shoving it into her face. "And it isn't just this picture. The envelope is full of evidence my son has been lying to me for years. About everything. His education. His entire *life*, and now there's some nonsense about that *Carson* woman being pregnant and..." The rage on his face went cold. "You don't seem surprised."

"I knew Vanessa was pregnant as part of the course of the investigation," Laurel returned coolly. "Whatever other lies you're referring to, I'm in the dark on."

"And the baby being Dylan's?" Dad all but spat.

"It was a theory."

"How could you both be so—"

"No. No. We're not doing this. We're trying to find Dylan and Vanessa. You... How could you jeopardize them this way? You should have called me the second you got these. You never should have… How can you do this? All over something so insignificant."

"Insignificant? If he dared impregnate that scum—"

"What is wrong with you?" she demanded, temper bubbling over. "Dylan could be *dead* because of you."

He paled at that, but he still grasped the picture. "He's dead to me if this is true."

Laurel reached out and slapped him across the face before she'd even thought the action through. She expected regret to wash through her, but there was none. Dylan was in danger and an innocent bystander—a pregnant woman—was in trouble, and all Dad cared about was the family reputation.

"You're sick and twisted," she managed, though her voice cracked along with her heart. She ignored the tears of hot rage that spilled over. "Your son is in grave danger and all you care about is a *name*. A dusty old feud. You still talk to me and Cam, but this is somehow unforgivable?"

"You and Cam are not creating *children* with those mongrels. It goes against all our history. It goes against the very nature of Bent, Laurel. Carsons and Delaneys were not meant to be. Have you noticed what hell has gone on since you started your thing with Grady?"

She ignored the last part. She wouldn't let him put this on her. She wouldn't let him put this on *love*. "I am. I *am* creating children."

"I know you think that, but Carson will show his true colors before you—"

"No, Dad. I'm pregnant."

The picture in his hands fluttered to the ground and he sat with an audible thump.

"Your future grandchildren are all part Carson thus

far. I hope they all will be. And I hope to God you get it through your head that's something to be proud of."

Laurel refused to look at her father. She had a job to do. She pulled on the gloves so she could touch the pictures and envelope without adding her own prints.

"I don't know where I went so wrong with you children," Dad said, his voice faint and thready. "I taught you what was right, and this is how you've all repaid me."

"You did. You taught us the difference between right and wrong, justice and injustice." Hadn't he? Hadn't his four children grown up to be upstanding members of the community because he'd instilled in them a responsibility to do what was right? But the past year had shown her over and over again that her father didn't know what right was. "I don't know what happened to you that you can't see it."

"You're cursing us," Dad said, his voice sounding brittle and desperate.

Through this whole ordeal she'd wondered, no matter how stupid or utterly fantastical, if she hadn't cursed the town by loving the wrong man.

Except the man she loved was not wrong, in any way, shape or form.

"No. The curse all these years is this." She gestured at him. "This pointless, relentless hate. It's what you've all gotten wrong for over a hundred years. Hate doesn't solve a damn thing. It never has. It never will." She looked at her father, unbearably hurt. "But love will."

She'd believed in right and wrong, truth and justice, her entire life. She'd built her career and her soul on that very foundation, but the truth of the matter was that underneath that foundation was a base of love.

"I hope you change your mind in time to be the grandfather our children deserve." Because with love came hope and, hopefully at some point, forgiveness. "Now, while I'm busting my butt to get my brother home safe and sound, I hope you'll take some time to think about what you want to be the center of your life. Some stupid, pointless feud or your family."

She took the picture and the envelope and left her father silent and brooding. She sucked in a breath and let it out, compartmentalizing the hurt so she could do her job.

She left without saying goodbye to Jen, got to her car and bagged up the evidence. As she was backing up, her cell rang. She answered.

"I think I found it," Hart said, sounding breathless. "I called backup. We're heading out now."

"Address," Laurel barked.

"No way, Laurel."

"It's my brother."

"Exactly. I've got the manpower to handle it myself, and you've got the manpower to sit at a desk and wait."

She hated that he was right. She couldn't risk herself and her baby. She had to believe Hart could handle it. Which burned—enough that she said something she thought she'd never say.

"Fine, but I'm sending in my own backup."

"Laurel, I don't need Carsons."

"But you're going to get them." She always played by the rules, but if she couldn't be there to save her brother, she'd darn well send in a bunch of guys who would break every rule possible to save the people they and she loved.

Chapter Seventeen

Dylan could wait with the best of them. He was a trained sniper. He could sit in one uncomfortable position for hours on end, gun at the ready. It had been his life for a couple years, and his capacity for patience and control hadn't just evaporated the moment he'd reentered civilian life.

But waiting with an impatient pregnant woman who couldn't sit still to save her life was driving him insane.

"Babe, you've got to sit."

She glared at him. "This whole *babe* crap is getting real old, real fast."

He grinned. "Okay, no babe. Honey, you've got to sit."

She crossed her arms over her chest. "Real cute."

"I know." But because he knew her glares and irritation were really nerves, he crossed to her and put his hands on her shoulders. He gave them a reassuring squeeze. "Waiting is the hardest part, but it's the most crucial. Timing is everything."

"We don't even know if the tape worked. Shouldn't we check?"

"We have to wait."

She groaned and tried to wiggle away from his grasp, but he only wound his arms around her waist and pulled her close, dropping a kiss to her neck. "I could distract you," he murmured, enjoying the way her resistance slowly melted into him.

But she didn't relax fully, and she kept her palms on his chest for distance. She looked up at him, some attempt at skepticism keeping her mouth from curving, but her eyes gave her away. He was tempted to tell her how easily they did, but he figured she'd only make sure they didn't anymore.

The slight humor there faded though, and she grew serious. "If this works—"

"*When* this works," he corrected.

She blew out a breath. "Fine. *When* this works, and we're back home, we sure have a whole hell of a lot to figure out."

"Maybe. Maybe that's all just details. Bottom line, when we're back home, you and I do everything to build the best life for our baby."

Her eyebrows drew together. "We'll never agree on the best life."

Dylan shrugged. "I think you'll be surprised by how much we'll agree on. But, first and foremost, we need to get out of here. So let's go over it one more time."

She groaned again, and again he held tight when she tried to push him away. "Lay it out for me," he instructed.

She glared at him, but did as she was told. "We wait until four, which is when they start their evening switch-off. No-Neck takes his little nap, and Eyeballs makes his dinner. We see if the tape worked, and if it did, we slip out. Me first. Then you."

"And if Eyeballs sees, or Adele pops up from wherever she's hiding?"

"I say I had to go to the bathroom and they forgot to lock the door. If pressed, I admit you picked the lock and forced me as a sacrifice to try to leave. If they start moving for your door, I scream and say I saw a spider. You'll create a diversion, and I'll run." She looked up at him, and this time he was pretty sure she let him see all the emotion on her face on purpose. "I don't like that part, Dylan."

He rested his forehead on hers. "I know, but we have to get you out of here, and the bottom line is if you're not in firing range, I can take out those two nimrods."

He wasn't scared of sacrificing himself. The way he saw it, unless there was some big surprise waiting for him, he had an 85 percent chance of survival. As long as she didn't try to interfere.

Which meant he had to make sure she didn't. No easy feat when the woman in question was as contrary as they came. But they had more at stake than each other.

"Van, it only works if you run no matter what. No looking back. No trying to save me. It only works if you're off like a shot and leave me to deal with them."

"Dylan—"

"You have to run. You have more than just yourself to think of. Besides, I can handle myself."

"I'm not just going to—"

"Promise me."

"I want it to be clear the only damn reason I'm doing this is because I'm pregnant, and I promised myself a long time ago I would do whatever it took to be the mother my mom wasn't and put my baby first. That's it. The *only* reason I'm letting you do this. Carsons don't run. They protect what's theirs."

He smiled. "So protect what's yours."

"You're both mine," she said fiercely. And she didn't take it back or look away. She held his gaze, serious and determined.

It rippled through him, all that it meant, all that he felt.

The thing was, feelings were dangerous. They led to mistakes, and he couldn't afford any. His first instinct was to compartmentalize, put them away for later.

But he needed Vanessa to understand, to do what he asked. Which meant he'd use those feelings, *then* put them away.

He pulled back enough to frame her face with his hands, ignoring the fact they might have trembled just a little. "I never thought I'd fall in love with a Carson."

He ignored her sharp intake of breath and kept talking. "Or during a kidnapping. Or after I'd already gotten someone pregnant. But maybe it's fitting, all in all."

He felt the tremble in her own body, watched the way she swallowed. Hard. "Well," she managed on a shaky breath. "I'm pretty sure even a week ago I would have told you I'd rather drink bleach than fall in love with a Delaney."

"Lovely."

"But I think I felt that way because…well, not because I hate Delaneys."

"You sure about that?"

"I hate your dad. And sometimes I just want to punch Cam in his perfect face for no real reason. I've never hated Laurel. I…" Her shoulders slumped and she pressed a few fingers right under the bump on her head that was slowly lessening in swelling. "We were friends. We didn't stop being friends because I *hated* her. It's complicated. And with Jen I'm mostly just ambivalent."

"That's my father and my siblings, but so far nothing about me."

She took a deep breath and pushed it out. "There's been something between us for a long time."

"Yeah, there has." Something undeniable in so many ways.

"I wanted it to be hate, but maybe it never really was."

He pushed some hair behind her ears. So many pieces inside of him that he'd hidden or locked away or tensed eased suddenly. "Yeah, maybe."

"Maybe that's always what's gone wrong. People have seen hate where there was really love and…well, anyway. I guess what I'm saying is I love you too, and I'd say I don't know why, but I know. You're good, and underneath all that polish you're as tough as any Carson. You care and I… This isn't some goodbye, is it? Because I'm not letting you out of this. We're riding back into Bent together. Screw their curse."

He smiled, because it was so her. Because he hoped they could make that happen. "No goodbyes. I just want you to know what's at stake. So you can promise me you'll run. You'll run and you'll protect that baby. And if you get a chance to call your brother and cousins to help me out here, I wouldn't say no."

"You don't want me to call Laurel and the police?"

He eyed the door, considered that. "I'd take both."

She took his wrist, tilted the watch to her gaze. "Looks like it's show time."

But he didn't release her. He held her tighter. "Promise me."

She shook her head, but she looked him in the eye. "I promise. I'll run. And I'll trust you to fight your own battle." She took his hand and placed it over her stomach. "But remember what you're fighting for."

He nodded. Kissed her once, hard, and then put it all away. Tied it up and shoved it out of his brain. It was a shame he couldn't, just for the next few minutes, shove it out of his heart.

He released her and a breath. "All right. Here goes nothing." He moved to the door. With care and patience he could all but feel made her bristle, Dylan twisted the knob. It gave, slowly and silently, and he ignored the excitement pounding in his chest.

He twisted the full way, then pulled. The door gave for a second, but then caught. He wanted to swear, but instead he kept his mind clear, calm.

"I need something to wiggle in here. Something thin enough to fit through the door crack. Like a credit card or a hair pin. Find me something." He held the doorknob turned all the way, ignoring the impulse to jerk the door open. They needed quiet.

And a metric ton of luck.

Vanessa hopped to work, pawing through the things on the desk. She found a spiral notebook and ripped the cover off. She held it up to him and when he nodded, she ripped it in half.

"Smaller," he instructed. She ripped it again and again until it was the size he wanted. She handed it to him, and he slid it into the space between door and frame. He wiggled the light but firm cardboard cover against the lock partially engaged by the tape.

It worked. He eased the door open.

The living room was empty, and as suspected, he could hear someone moving around in the kitchen.

He motioned Vanessa out, and she followed the plan, moving quickly and quietly to the front door while Dylan scanned the room for weapons he could use if they were caught. There wasn't really anything, but he trusted his fists—and his wits.

He didn't dare watch Vanessa since he had to observe the opening to the kitchen to make sure no one popped out. At one point he heard the faintest squeak of the front door and winced, then readied his body to attack.

But no one came.

Heart thudding with too much hope to contain, Dylan

began to back away from the living-room opening and toward the door. It couldn't be this easy. It couldn't be, and yet...

He made it to the door where Vanessa was poised in the opening she'd made, just big enough for her body. He nodded to her, then took the doorknob from her grasp.

He'd need to make the opening a little bigger to fit himself out. As he did, the door squeaked. It was faint, but he knew they would hear it.

Dylan gave himself one precious moment to look Vanessa in the eye. "Run." He gave her a little shove, shut the door and prayed to God she listened.

VANESSA RAN.

Tears threatened, some mix of anger and fear. What an idiot he was, shoving the door closed so he had to handle it all himself. That was not going to fly if they got back to Bent and got to plan their lives together.

"When. *When* we get back to Bent," she whispered to herself, running for the trees. Dylan had instructed her to run there first. Deep enough she couldn't see the house. Then she was supposed to stop and listen. If she didn't hear anyone coming after her, she was supposed to slowly inch her way back, using as much cover as she could, then follow the road back down the mountain.

If anyone came out of the cabin, she was supposed to run as deep into the woods as she could, and trust he'd be able to find her once he took care of everyone.

It was a desperate, stupid plan and she wanted to punch herself in the face for ever listening to it. But she stopped, deep enough she could just barely make out the faint color of the cabin far off in the distance through the trees.

They didn't come after her. For as long as that was true, Dylan was alive.

Unless you don't matter and they only wanted him.

She choked on a sob, but she got out of the crouch and slid slowly and carefully between trees, getting closer and closer to the tree line until she could make out the road.

She noticed there were two cars in front of the cabin and tried not to let that worry her. Nothing could worry her except getting the baby inside of her back to safety.

Another sob escaped her mouth, but she bit her lip to keep the rest in. She kept behind trees, moving forward quietly and carefully through the woods parallel to the road.

After a while, the sobs stopped and tears dried, and all she had was a grim determination to keep walking no matter how badly her feet hurt or her head throbbed.

When she reached a fork in the road, tears threatened again. She didn't know where she was. Should she try to cross the road and follow the opposite path? Or follow this one under cover? What if it wrapped back up into the mountain? What if she crossed the road and someone started shooting?

She couldn't take the risk of stepping into the open. One way or another, either fork would lead her somewhere eventually. She stayed on the fork that allowed her to keep in the tree line and trudged on.

On and on, until she had to stop and lean against trees for support every few minutes. Her head was spinning and her mouth was too dry. She was wrung out and dead on her feet.

But Dylan was back there somewhere fighting two armed men, and she had to save him. Somehow, she had to save him. She needed to get to a town, to a—

She stopped abruptly at the sight of a car parked on

the other side of the road. Someone was leaning against the hood.

Vanessa held very still, squinting through the trees. It was a tan car, with some kind of logo on the side. A logo she knew. And the person in baggy clothes and a puffy coat leaning against the hood was—

"Laurel." When Laurel didn't move, Vanessa realized she hadn't really said it. She'd gasped it, afraid it was a mirage. But as she weakly stepped forward, the police cruiser didn't waver and disappear. Laurel's serious profile didn't morph or change. She wasn't hallucinating. She wasn't.

Vanessa kept moving for open air and the road, still waiting for the image to disappear. "Laurel," she said as she stumbled through the tree line.

Laurel's head whipped around, and it didn't escape Vanessa's notice that her hand went straight for her weapon, though she didn't draw.

"Oh, my God. Oh, my God." Laurel dropped her hand from the weapon and immediately rushed across the road.

She was at Vanessa's side in a flash, and for a moment all Vanessa could think to do was hug her and sob. It was real. Laurel was here, and Dylan had gotten her out. She leaned against Laurel's shorter frame, squeezed her as tight as the strength she had in her body allowed and sobbed.

Laurel pulled away, though she held Vanessa upright, which was about the only thing doing the job at the moment.

"Dylan," Laurel said, eyes searching and scared. "Where's Dylan?"

"He's still there. He needs help." Vanessa swallowed, summoning her strength. "He's back there. He's back there. Come on." She grabbed Laurel's arm. "You've got a gun and a badge. I'll lead you."

But Laurel didn't budge. "We're not going back there, Van."

Panic and fear skittered up her spine. "What the hell is wrong with you? He's back there fighting off two goons with guns and a crazy woman. You have to get to him."

Laurel closed her eyes as if against some great pain, but still she didn't let Vanessa pull her toward the trees. "My men are handling it."

"Your *men*? Since when do you let a bunch of Podunk deputies save your flesh and blood?"

"Vanessa. Calm down." Laurel used her free arm to pull Vanessa's hand into hers. "Are you all right? I should call you an ambulance. Come on." She started leading Vanessa a few steps toward the police cruiser before Vanessa skidded them to a halt.

"No! I'm not going anywhere until Dylan is safe and sound. You have to find him, Laurel. You have to save him."

Laurel nodded. "We are. They're surrounding the cabin as we speak."

"It should be you."

Again, Laurel looked incredibly pained, but her voice was level and calm. Her cop voice. "It can't be me. For the same reason Dylan got you out of there."

"You…" It took a moment, or a few, to connect all the dots. Laurel knew. And she was… "You know."

"We had to search your place. Hold on." She lifted the radio on her uniform to her mouth and started using codes and police blabber to explain Vanessa was with her. "Two men with guns, and one woman? Adele Oscar?"

"Yes. You knew?"

Laurel led her to the passenger's side of the cruiser

and opened the door. "We figured some things out." Gently, Laurel nudged her into the passenger seat. "So, it's true. Dylan is..."

"The father of my baby? Yes. I surely hope Grady is the father of yours."

Laurel gave her a baleful look, then gently closed the door. She marched around the front of the car, then took her seat behind the steering wheel.

"We can't just sit here."

"We have to." Laurel shook her head. "You have to know it's killing me too, but...sometimes a woman has to make a sacrifice a man never has to make. We're making it. If it makes you feel any better, I gave Grady the address. It's not just my deputies up there."

Vanessa relaxed into the seat. "Thank God. Someone with some brains." And all the people she loved were in danger. "There has to be something I can do," she whispered to Laurel.

"There is. You're going to tell me everything you know about who's in there, what the layout is and what dumb plan got you out and is no doubt about to get my brother hurt, while I drive you to the hospital to get checked out."

Vanessa's eyes flew open and she reached out and grabbed Laurel's arm. "I'm not going anywhere until Dylan's out. I'll tell you everything right here, and once they get him out safe and sound we go up there. He's hurt too. Not bad, or at least it wasn't bad before. I'm not going anywhere without him."

"You love him," Laurel murmured. There was shock in her voice, but not censure. Then again, of all the Delaneys to censure it, Laurel didn't have a leg to stand on.

"Maybe I always did," she muttered.

Laurel smiled gently, taking Vanessa's hand off her

arm and then squeezing it and interlocking their fingers. "I know the feeling. Now, tell me everything."

So Vanessa did.

Chapter Eighteen

The fight was a brutal marathon, but Dylan was still alive. He figured that was something. Now, if he could just get his hands on one of their guns, he'd be home free.

But he'd knocked No-Neck's across the room and, considering the man currently had his meaty paws around Dylan's throat, there wasn't much hope of getting to it.

Luckily, Eyeballs hadn't fared so well. He'd been the first on the scene, so to speak. When he'd lunged at Dylan as he was closing the door, Dylan had decided to use the door as his best weapon. He'd swung it open as Eyeballs lunged at him. The corner of the door had cracked right against Eyeballs's forehead, and the man had dropped like a deadweight. He was bleeding and moaning now.

But then No-Neck had come out to see what the commotion was. Dylan had considered running, almost sure he could outrun him. But he might lead the guy straight to Vanessa, and he couldn't risk that. Especially if No-Neck had some kind of vehicle.

So he'd fought instead. He'd managed to land a few decent kicks and get the gun away from him, but it had clattered out of reach. Then No-Neck had used his considerable girth to knock Dylan off his feet.

There'd been a moment of panic, which was why Dylan was in his current predicament of having the air slowly choked out of him. If he'd held it together like he had when he'd been a sniper, he would have been able to break the hold.

Still can. Still can. He chanted that to himself even as his vision grayed. He tested the mobility of his legs, feeling the pressure build and build in his head without the ability to take in new air.

One slip of his hand in the right place and he'd—

A gunshot rang out, and No-Neck's body jerked, eyes going wide and then blank as he lurched to the side, lifeless.

Gasping for air, relief coursed through him. Enough that he even closed his eyes. He'd been saved. Saved in the nick of damn time too. His throat ached, his head pounded, but God, he could breathe again and someone…

He opened his eyes, ready to be pissed as hell if Vanessa had come back.

But it wasn't Vanessa.

And he certainly hadn't been saved.

Adele gestured with the gun. "Get up."

Dylan couldn't follow orders because he couldn't make sense of this. "You killed him."

Adele glanced at the lifeless body. "Wasn't as hard as I thought it might be." She glanced at Eyeballs, who was still groaning. Then, before Dylan could even move, she shot him too. Not very cleanly, so she pulled the trigger again. This time, Eyeballs went still.

She turned the gun onto Dylan. She paused there though, not shooting like she had the other two. She watched him, consideration all over her expression.

Dylan didn't let fear enter. He focused on what he could do. She was just a little too far out of reach to knock off her feet, and it would take him a few seconds to regain his clear vision.

"Why are you killing your own men?" he asked incredulously. Surely she wasn't actually saving him.

"My own men are stupid and useless. How many times can they be overpowered by some second-rate unarmed soldier saddled with a pregnant woman?" She cocked her head, still studying him. "You're rather stupid, but you aren't useless yet. Get up."

Slowly, gauging every move she made, every potential action to grab her weapon, Dylan moved to his feet, but before he could fully straighten from his crouch—which was from where he'd planned to lunge and dislodge the weapon—the gun fired.

The searing stab of pain in his gut had him falling back to his knees. He bit back a howl, his body involuntarily shaking at the unbearable pain in his stomach.

He could feel blood seeping into his shirt, his pants, gushing out of the wound. Gritting his teeth, he sat back on his butt and pushed his hand over the hole. He needed a bandage. Hell, he needed a miracle.

"Sorry. Men with bullets in them are less likely to overpower a poor little woman like me." She shrugged. "Hope I didn't hit one of those internal organs."

Dylan could only hold his hands to the wound, hoping to God she was right. But the blood...

His vision grayed again, so he pressed hard and focused on the pain.

"This would have been easy, Dylan. Simple. But you had to complicate things," Adele said, walking in a circle around him. "No one would be dead if you'd done what you were supposed to. You certainly wouldn't be shot. Don't you always do what you're supposed to?"

"Guess not always," he managed to say between gritted teeth. He needed to get the gun away from her. Preferably before he passed out from blood loss.

"Your perfect daddy knows. About all of it. The sniper nonsense. Vanessa." Adele laughed. "God, I wish I could have seen his face. His precious prince knocking up a Carson. I never *dreamed* I'd get something that good, but you keep *ruining it.*"

"Adele. Please, I—"

"Oh, don't patronize me. Don't try to mansplain my life to me."

She waved the gun around, enough to make him nervous. He could maybe survive this bullet wound. He wasn't so sure about another one.

"I'm smarter than you," she said, her knuckles going white on the handle of the gun. "I've always been smarter than you, but somehow you keep ending up on top. Not this time. I'm better. I've always been better."

Dylan fought off a wave of nausea. "If you kill me... Adele, it's over. You don't get any job, any life. *Yours* is over just as much as mine."

"Because you ruined it! I had a plan and you ruined *everything*!" She huffed out a breath and Dylan realized that in this moment in particular she'd lost it. Before, she'd been controlled. She'd had a plan, and he actually believed it hadn't been to kill him.

Now? All bets were off.

"That woman wasn't supposed to be there," she muttered, tapping the gun against the palm of her hand. "You weren't supposed to know how to fight. I rolled with the punches as well as I could, but these two fools were the last straw."

"You can't kill me, Adele."

She raised an eyebrow, and cold, bone-deep fear settled itself in his soul.

He cleared his throat, tried to focus his vision, his brain on anything except the constant wall of pain assaulting him. "Of course you *can* kill me. I'm suggesting it wouldn't be in your best interest."

"And you, of course, would know my best interest. Being a man and all."

He tried to make an argument, but the words sounded jumbled in his head. Everything around him was dim. Had someone turned off a light?

He tightened his grip on his stomach, but he was fading fast.

"I could let you bleed out." She pretended to consider it. "Killing you wasn't in the plans, Dylan. But plans change. Your father told me to be patient. He told me if I proved myself, the job would be mine. And you know what I did? I proved myself. Again and again. Above and beyond, and still *you* got everything."

"What does that have to do with me?"

"You got it. Killing you means you don't have it anymore. And your father suffers. Though I was hoping you'd suffer right along with him when he realized you were a lying, Carson-impregnating disappointment and kicked you out. But death works too."

"You'll miss out on your satisfaction," he managed to slur.

"Maybe. I didn't plan to kill you, Dylan. I just wanted to ruin you." She held the gun up again, this time at his head. "Turns out, I get to do both."

"Like hell." Though he knew it was just as likely to get him killed, he let go of the bullet wound and used his hands to push himself off the ground in the most fluid movement he could manage.

He'd thought to grab the gun, but mostly he just crashed into her. She fell backward, and he fell on top of her. They howled in pain at the same time, the gun clattering to the floor.

Dylan tried to fight, to think, but everything was going black. Pain. So much pain. It was so hard to remember what he was doing or what he was fighting for.

"I'm going to kill her too," Adele screamed, narrowly missing kneeing him in the crotch.

Her. *Them.* Van and his baby. He summoned all his strength, all his focus, shoved the pain away and made a grab for her arms.

His hands were slick with blood from pressing on his wound, and he couldn't manage to hold on to her wrists as she landed blows against his face and then—worse— right where the bullet wound was.

His body went weak and everything became a particular kind of black. Adele made some sound of triumph as she managed to slither away from him.

Dylan couldn't let her win. Couldn't. He struggled to his feet, his balance wavering as Adele rushed over to where the gun had fallen. Using his side that didn't have a bullet wound weakening it, Dylan grabbed the lamp off the table he was standing next to and heaved it at her as hard as he could.

It crashed against her, and she wailed in pain. She began to sway and fall. Or was that him?

A few seconds later, he realized he was on the floor. And someone stood over him.

It wasn't Adele.

It was Grady. And Ty. Carsons. "Am I dead?" Dylan managed to ask. "And in hell?"

Grady swore viciously. "He needs an ambulance. Yesterday." He nodded at Ty, who disappeared from Dylan's wavering vision.

"Adele?"

"If you're talking about the blonde, you knocked her out with that lamp business."

"Where are the police?"

"Setting up they said. They told us to wait. Aren't you lucky we didn't?"

"Grady." He could make out the man's face. Sort of. "Van?"

"Laurel's got her. They're probably on their way up."

"No. Don't let her..." He groaned at the wave of pain, the threat of pure oblivion—or was that death? "Help me up. Get me a clean shirt."

"You need a hospital, moron."

"Yeah. That too. Don't want her to know it's this bad, okay? Just help me... She can't know. Not until a doctor looks at her, okay?"

Dylan didn't really hear Grady's response, but then there were cops running this way and that. Someone ripped off his shirt and pressed a bandage to the wound. He wavered in and out of consciousness, but fought back every time.

He thought he heard Adele screaming, but the most important thing was Vanessa. She needed...

"Come on, tough guy," Grady muttered, pulling a T-shirt over Dylan's head.

"Get me on my feet."

"Ambulance will be here soon. Just sit ti—"

Whatever the cop was saying was cut off by Grady hefting him to his feet. "She's not going to buy this," Grady muttered.

Dylan breathed, letting his body lean against Grady's. "She'll believe it." One way or another. "I want her checked out and good to go before she knows how bad this is."

Grady shook his head, looping his arm around Dylan's waist. Dylan felt another arm helping him move forward. Ty.

"You're going to be dead before she knows how bad this is," Ty said disgustedly.

"Well, you just make sure she doesn't find that out either until she's talked to a doctor."

"He's got it bad," Grady said.

"Bad? He's got it terminal," Ty replied.

If he lived, yeah, it was damn well going to be terminal.

THE RADIO CALL for an ambulance made Laurel's blood run cold, but she forced herself to smile reassuringly at Vanessa. "They're out." She flicked off the radio, because if they started describing things... Well, as much as she wanted to know what had happened, it was more important to keep Vanessa calm.

She was too pale and even shaking, though Laurel had a sneaking suspicion Vanessa didn't realize her body was reacting to the shock and worry.

"Can we go? I need to see him. I need to be sure..."

"We'll drive up, just as soon as someone gives me an all clear."

"Laurel. If they called an ambulance, doesn't that mean there's an all clear?"

"Not necessarily. Listen—"

She was interrupted by the sound of her phone chiming. She pulled up the text and frowned at Grady's words.

I don't suppose you'd just take Van to a hospital and let us handle all this?

"We're going up," Laurel said. She kept her voice detached and her expression calm, but dread pooled in her stomach.

Surely if Dylan was dead someone would just come

out and say it. Surely. She swallowed at the bile that rose in her throat. She'd been a cop long enough to know how to deal with being sick with fear and appear untouched.

She drove too fast up the road toward the cabin Hart had told her about. Two police cruisers, one motorcycle and Grady's truck were parked along the road out of sight, but Laurel drove right up to the cabin.

There were two officers with a handcuffed Adele Oscar. She was bleeding from her head, but clearly yelling at everyone around her. Laurel hoped like hell the cut on her head was the only reason they'd called for an ambulance.

Laurel pulled to a stop. Hart, Grady, Ty and the other deputy Hart would have taken were nowhere to be seen.

"Stay here and—"

The cabin door opened and, before Laurel could stop her, Vanessa was out like a shot. Grady and Ty appeared, Dylan between them.

Vanessa rushed to him, but Laurel held herself back. There were a few things she noted about her brother. His face was a mess, but underneath bleeding cuts and blooming bruises, he was deathly pale. He was wearing what he'd probably worn to the bank the other morning, except for the shirt, which she recognized as one of Grady's T-shirts he often left strewn about the back seat of his truck. Lastly, Ty was all but holding him up.

But if Vanessa noticed any of those things, it didn't stop her. She flung her arms around Dylan and clung tight.

Laurel tried to get ahold of herself as tears stung her eyes and she felt the weakness in her muscles. Dylan's eyes weren't focused, even as he wrapped an arm around Vanessa and murmured something into her ear.

Slowly, Laurel approached, trying to gauge anything from Grady's expression, but it was infuriatingly blank.

"He's hurt. Let's give him some room," Laurel managed to say gently.

Vanessa sniffled and unwound herself from Dylan. "You need an ambulance."

"Getting one," he said, his mouth curving.

But everything about Dylan was wrong. Faded and weak.

"Van, let me take you down to the hospital. You've got your own knock on the head," Grady said.

He moved away from Dylan, who now leaned even harder on Ty.

"Why can't I just ride in the ambulance with him?" she demanded, pulling her arm out of Grady's grasp.

"You'll have a smoother ride with Grady," Dylan said. His voice was thready.

He was hurt way worse than he was acting, and no one wanted Vanessa to know. Laurel thought about demanding they stop, but Vanessa was a mess herself. Added stress wouldn't help.

"I'm afraid it's procedure," Laurel improvised. "We'll want your statements separately and without the other's perceptions clouding it. We want to make sure Adele goes away for a long time." She touched Vanessa's arm. "You go with Grady and get to the hospital. I'll follow in a minute to get your statement, and Hart will ride with Dylan in the ambulance to get his. Once we've done that, you'll be free to see each other as much as you want."

Vanessa frowned, but Laurel had a sinking suspicion time was of the essence.

"Go on now. We'll get this all sorted ASAP."

Grady managed to lead Vanessa away, though she kept

looking back. Dylan managed a smile, but Laurel didn't see anything other than a blankness in it.

"What is it?" Laurel hissed.

"Just wait," Dylan muttered.

His gaze stayed on Vanessa's retreating form until it disappeared around the corner, then his whole face went slack. He swore weakly.

"What *is* it?"

Since Dylan looked like he was in the middle of passing out, she turned her glare to Ty.

"He was shot. In the gut. That ambulance of yours better be quick."

"Get him on the ground," Laurel barked. "What the hell is wrong with you? Letting him stand up? Are you stupid?" Her voice cracked on the last word, and she helped Ty lower Dylan to the ground.

Laurel kneeled next to him, berating him the whole way. "How can you be this stupid?"

"Don't cry, sis."

"I'm not crying," she retorted, even though the tears were rolling big and fat down her face. "What are you doing getting yourself shot? That's my job," she managed, hoping to keep him talking, keep him awake. As long as he was awake…

"I'll be okay. Probably. Tradition, right? You, then Cam. Now me. Someone better get Jen a bulletproof vest."

"Not funny. Stay with me, okay? Stay with me." She took his hand and squeezed it. "You've got an awful lot of explaining to do, so you can't go."

He didn't squeeze back and his eyes were closed, but he kept talking. "Damnedest thing, Laurel. I love her. I don't know how it happened. It was like…there. Just there."

"Yeah, I get that." *Keep him talking. Keep him talk-*

ing. "One minute you think they're the bane of your existence and then you realize they were just…meant to be part of your existence."

"Meant to be. I never believed in meant to be, but I believed in a feud. How backward is that?"

"Nothing's backward if you right the ship." She could hear the faint sound of sirens and prayed they'd hurry. She pressed Dylan's palm to her cheek. It was bloody and beat up, and she couldn't hold back the sob that escaped her mouth.

"Laurel. Don't worry so much. It's going to take more than a bullet to stop me from being a father. Better one than ours."

It shocked her to hear Dylan say that. He'd been Dad's staunchest supporter, and he certainly didn't know about Dad's outburst earlier.

"Better than ours," Laurel agreed. "And you'll have to work on your uncle skills too, okay?"

"Uncle. You too?" He chuckled, though it sounded more like a wet wheeze that had Laurel crying all over again. "That's a trip. That's a—"

"All right." Laurel looked up, relief almost making her pass out as the ambulance came into view. "Time to show us how strong you are."

"I'll be okay. I'll be okay. Tell Van I'll be okay, yeah?"

Laurel got out of the way of the paramedics and turned away from watching them work. When she felt a hand squeeze her shoulder, she turned to see it was Ty.

"Come on. Let's get to the hospital."

She nodded, pulling herself together bit by bit. There was still a lot of work to do.

Chapter Nineteen

"Definitely a nasty bump, and the short-term amnesia is concerning, but it's probably more a response to trauma than head injury. Though you'll want to pay specific attention to headaches, vision problems, anything that might point to an underlying issue."

Vanessa nodded at the doctor and bit her tongue so she didn't say something like, *"I don't give a damn about me. Tell me about the baby."*

"Baby's heartbeat is strong. I don't think you'll have anything to worry about there, though I'd make a follow-up appointment with your ob just to be sure they don't have any concerns."

"So the baby's okay?"

"Seems to be."

Vanessa slid off the exam table. "So I can go?"

"Your blood pressure is high. I'd like to keep you here and see if it levels. So let's have a seat and relax."

Vanessa glared at Grady. "Did he just tell me to relax?"

"Come on, Van." Grady nodded the doctor to the door, and the doctor did the first intelligent thing since he'd opened it—he left without a word.

Grady ushered her back to the exam bed. "Listen to the doctor," he said gently, urging her back onto the bed.

She went, but she folded her arms across her chest and glared. "I want to see Dylan."

"He's getting checked out, same as you."

Now that she had time to think, there'd been something very wrong in that whole scene outside the cabin. Dylan hadn't been himself. But he'd been standing there, talking to her.

She *hated* this feeling that she was missing a piece. Laurel had questioned her earlier, looking pale and distracted, and informed her Adele was being treated for her injuries and then would be released into police custody.

But she couldn't tell her Dylan's condition or what he'd said in his statement or what would happen to that awful woman.

"Where's Laurel?"

"She told you. She went to check on Dylan."

"*I* want to check on Dylan."

Grady gave her his patented raised-eyebrow look. "Funny thing, that."

Vanessa looked away. She wasn't embarrassed. Not after everything she and Dylan had been through, but there was a certain discomfort over the fact she'd given Grady such a hard time about getting together with Laurel and now she... "How did it happen?"

"How did what happen?" Grady asked, scooting the too-small chair he was balanced on closer to her bed.

"Us. How did we... How are they...?" She shook her head, feeling overwhelmed and emotional. "I love him. I don't know how. I don't know what did it, but I love him. So much it's scary. A *Delaney*."

"Yeah, kinda hits you over the head like that." He took her hand in his and gave it a squeeze. "I couldn't tell you why. I can only tell you if it feels right, it is."

Vanessa nodded, blinking back unruly tears. "I need him to be okay."

"Then he'll be okay."

"Because I have such a great track record of getting what I need?"

"Because he's a Delaney, and they do." He touched her hair gently. "You gave us quite the scare."

"You should have known I'd kick my way out of it." All those emotions inside her wanted to lean into her big brother and just sob them away, but she felt trapped. Until she knew for sure Dylan was okay...

"Something's wrong."

"It only feels that way because you've been through this crazy thing. Time's only going slow because you're waiting. But you aren't getting out of here until that blood pressure comes down, so why don't you try to rest?"

Because she wouldn't be able to. She couldn't *rest* until she was out of this claustrophobic room and she could hold Dylan again.

Something wasn't right. Something hadn't been right for a while, but she wasn't going to get answers until that doctor let her out of here, so she closed her eyes and breathed.

She was more than grateful Grady didn't drop her hand. He held it the whole time, and it became an anchor.

Time passed interminably, but no matter how many times she asked, Grady didn't have any information. When the doctor returned what felt like a million years later, her blood pressure had gone down enough that he felt comfortable releasing her.

Which took another million years, with paperwork and instructions, warnings of headaches and blah, blah, blah. Her baby was fine and she needed to know why the hell she hadn't seen Dylan yet.

"I just need to use the bathroom. You want to wait here?" she asked, pointing at some chairs in the lobby.

Luckily, Grady was distracted enough by texting with Ty that he didn't look at her to see the lie.

"Sure." He took a seat and kept typing on his phone.

Vanessa walked casually toward the restrooms but then kept going. She found a map, tried to decide where Dylan would be. He'd come in an ambulance, so Emergency probably. She started backtracking to where she'd been treated in Emergency, but before she made it there she saw a cop going in the opposite direction. She knew him. Something Hart. He worked with Laurel a lot.

He didn't see her, and she made sure he didn't. She turned, waited, then casually started tailing him at a reasonable pace.

At one point he looked back, but there was a large gentleman in front of her who blocked his view.

When he pushed open the doors for the surgery wing, Vanessa's heart dropped and she didn't bother to keep her pace slow or calm herself. She ran forward, then came to a stumbling stop at the row of chairs occupied by Delaneys.

"Oh, my God."

Laurel jumped to her feet, swearing under her breath as she came up to Vanessa. "Don't jump to the worst conclusion."

"You're all here."

Jen's face was blotchy, and so was Laurel's. Hilly, Vanessa's long-lost cousin and Cam's girlfriend, was dabbing her eyes with a Kleenex.

"You're all crying," Vanessa accused, pointing wildly. *God, no. No.*

"Not all of us. Cam isn't crying," Laurel offered hopefully. When Vanessa only looked at her in horror, Laurel hooked arms with her and continued. "Look, Dylan's in surgery."

"For *what*?" Vanessa demanded, wrestling her arm away from Laurel's grasp.

Grady stormed through the doors, face etched in furious lines. "Damn it, Van. You told me you were going to the bathroom."

"And you told me everything was fine!" She whirled back to Laurel. "Why is he in surgery?"

"He was…shot."

"Shot? *Shot?* When? How could he have been…?" She swayed on her feet but Grady grabbed her and pushed her into a seat next to Hilly. It dawned on Vanessa why everything had been wrong since that moment. "He was shot before we got there. He was *hiding* it from me."

"Yes," Laurel agreed.

"Why?" She looked up helplessly at Laurel, then Grady. She'd give Dylan a piece of her mind once he was out of surgery. Oh, boy, would she. "How long? What are they— Tell me what you know."

"Let's just—"

"Tell me what you know." She grabbed Laurel's arms, trying to get it through the woman's thick skull. "I don't care what he wanted kept from me. I don't care about anything except knowing what's going on. I *need* to know what he's going through."

Laurel softened, but her eyes filled again. She ruthlessly blinked those tears away, putting on that cop face Vanessa had to admit she envied.

"He was shot in the stomach," Laurel said, and she might have sounded like some detached cop if her voice wasn't so scratchy. "Unfortunately, it did hit some organs, which means he could be in surgery for a while. Right now, all we can do is wait for the surgeon to do his job and then let us know how it went."

"He might die." It slammed through her, the understanding. Why he'd been trying to shield her from knowing. He might legitimately *die*.

"Van, listen—"

She looked up at Laurel, fury and fear causing her to shake. "He might *die*. Don't '*listen*' me. It's true. He might die."

"It's true," she said, though her voice was an unsteady whisper.

"But he might not," Hilly said, taking Vanessa's hand in hers. Her voice was calm and collected. Soothing. Not detached like Laurel's. "No use focusing on the worst-case scenario when it's not the only option. Focus on—on—"

"Healing thoughts," Jen supplied. "Prayers, vibes, whatever you got."

Vibes. Prayers. Thoughts. Vanessa wanted to scream. None of it mattered. None of it helped. "It's a curse. It's true. I didn't believe in curses, but here we are."

Grady crouched in front of her. Her brother who'd happily talked about feuds and being better than Delaneys for most of his life. He took her hands in his, looked right at her, certain and sure.

"There is no curse. Love is never a curse. New life is no curse. This is a challenge, but not a curse. And if we beat all these challenges, can you imagine what we'll have?"

No feud? Carsons and Delaneys all intermingled? Not so long ago she would have told anyone who listened that that was her worst nightmare.

But somehow it had become her brightest dream, so she did what Jen said. She prayed. She thought about healing. She sent all the energy she could muster into the universe.

And in a waiting room full of Carsons and Delaneys holding hands and murmuring encouragement to each other, Vanessa waited.

THE DESERT WAS never ending. And why was he wearing all these clothes? A cowboy hat, of all damn things? He was riding a horse through the desert and all he wanted was a drink of water.

His body hurt everywhere, rivers of fiery pain. He looked down. Bullet holes, but no blood.

He tried to make the image go away, since it couldn't possibly be real, but the scene just kept playing out. He could see it, like a movie, and yet it was him. He could feel the cowboy hat. The weird scratchy pants and boots that fit like a second skin.

But he was full of bullet holes.

When he looked up, there was another horse. Another rider. He was in white. She was in black.

She.

"Vanessa?"

The black flowed around her as she rode toward him—the fabric of her clothes, the long strands of her hair. The wind whipped her skirts and scarves and she had a hat. A bright, shiny skull glinted on her hat. It looked just about perfect.

Her horse pounded through the sand, closer and closer and yet not close enough.

A choice. Somehow he knew that somewhere, there was a choice. Take the bullet holes and go to her. Doomed.

Turn away and everything would be fine. He could turn his horse in the opposite direction and the bullet holes would heal and all would be well.

Except she wouldn't be his. He was alive, maybe? Bullet holes and all, but no blood. Pain, yes, but you had to be alive to feel pain.

Why would he turn away?

He fell off the horse into the sand, but it didn't feel like sand. It felt like a bed.

He blinked his eyes open and…the desert was gone. He still needed a drink of water, desperately. But everything was dim instead of blinding. All he could think was she was gone. The horse and her swirling black costume.

"Van."

"There you are."

Her voice. God, he thought he might cry. But he didn't. He couldn't seem to move his head toward her voice. "You were all dressed up," he muttered, realizing somewhat belatedly it had been a dream. Just a silly, weird-as-hell dream.

"Can't even have a sex dream right?"

"I can't…move."

"That's okay." He felt her hand on one shoulder, then she moved into his line of sight. "They said you'll be out of sorts and they've got you hooked up to all sorts of things. Just lie still."

He drank her in. She looked good. Healthy and sturdy. Not pale. She wasn't swathed in black layers, but instead wore jeans and a T-shirt. Still, she looked so good and so *his*, he didn't think it could be real. "Am I dead?"

"Not unless the dead can speak. And all those doctors and nurses prodding at you day and night seem to think you'll recover. I guess you don't remember waking up? You've been in and out."

"I don't remember much of anything since Adele shot me. Except that I felt dead there for a while."

"Yes, well, speaking of that. You're lucky you're laid

up because I'd like to kick your butt to Toledo." She slid onto the edge of his bed, studying his face intently. Her dark eyes were hard to read, but he thought he saw relief.

"I don't have much interest in going to Ohio, so I guess that works, all in all." He closed his eyes, feeling unbearably exhausted. "Are you going to touch me or what?"

She made a sound that was almost a laugh, and then he felt her shift next to him, stretching out in the small amount of bed space available. "They're going to come in and yell at me, but I don't care."

"Good, I don't either."

"Dylan Delaney, you always care about the rules and what's right."

"Nah, that's just what people think." He nuzzled into her. "I want to hold you."

"Well, you'll have to settle for me holding you for now." Her arms came around him and he sighed into her. Because one arm was close to her, he managed to inch it toward her belly. He touched her stomach, fitting his hand over the softest swell.

"Baby's fine," she murmured, her fingers feeling like heaven against his hair.

"What about mama?"

"Mama." He felt her whoosh of breath against his face. It felt like heaven. "You know, it's funny, I hadn't really thought in terms of *mama* yet."

"Well, you've got some time to get used to that. And the fact you're going to have to marry me."

She was quiet for a while. He worked up the energy to open his eyes. She was looking at the IV hooked up to him, and all the other machines that seemed to keep beeping at him unnecessarily.

She met his gaze. "Never really figured I'd get married. I'm not much of a traditionalist."

"I am. But I can be flexible. We'll hyphenate our names."

Vanessa snorted. "You want our child to walk around Bent, Wyoming, with the names Delaney and Carson together?"

"I do," he returned. "You can keep your name. I'll keep mine. Baby will have both. You'll keep your shop. I—I don't know what my position is at the bank, but I can get a job at Cam's security business if I have to."

"Mr. Secret Sniper."

"I was thinking more along the lines of accounting. I think my sniper days are behind me." He gestured helplessly. "I don't know if you noticed, but I got beat to hell back there."

She closed her eyes, an expression of pain taking over her face. "Yeah, I noticed." She held him a little tighter, though he could tell she was being exceptionally gentle. He wished he didn't feel like he needed it.

"So, your plan is…you're going to marry me?"

"Damn straight."

"In front of your father and the rest of your family, in front of Bent citizens, you're going to promise to love and cherish a Carson?"

Though it felt like flaming hot needles in his side and shoulder, he lifted her hand to his mouth and pressed a kiss to her palm. "Till death do us part."

"Are you sure you don't have a head injury?"

"I might have several for all I know." He sighed, letting his arm fall back down, his eyes drifting closed. "But I'm sure I'm going to marry you. If you want to wait to decide until we make sure my body's in working order again, that's fine. But I can tell you right here, right now, I love you. And we're going to get married. Bullet holes or no."

"Holes? Pretty sure you were only shot once."

"I dreamed there were bullet holes all over the place. But I had a choice. Live through them with you, or walk away. I didn't walk then. I'm not going to, ever."

"You aren't making any sense."

He muttered something and slid back into dreams. There weren't bullet holes this time. No horses or desert. Just a quiet porch.

He awoke a few times, mostly to nurses poking and prodding him. Once Laurel was there with Grady. Twice it was Jen. A few times it was Cam and Hilly. And always, every single time, Vanessa was there too.

The next day when he woke it was dark, and it wasn't to a nurse poking at him. He just surfaced naturally. Vanessa was curled against him, fast asleep.

Unable to resist, he brushed some hair off her face. She hadn't left him. Maybe a hospital wasn't the real world yet, but it was real enough. This wasn't going to evaporate. They were going to make it work.

She stirred, blinked open her eyes and yawned. "You're still too weak for sex, buddy."

He didn't laugh because he knew it would hurt his side, but he smiled. "Noted. They let you stay in here?"

"Tried to kick me out. Even threatened to call security. I just snuck back in."

"Mmm, have I mentioned I love you?"

She snuggled closer. "Not enough."

He managed to move more than he had yet. He turned his head and kissed her temple. "Decided to marry me yet?"

She shook her head. "You're relentless. I thought the bullet hole and massive blood loss might slow you down."

"Your family and mine both donated blood. I'm just filled to the brim with relentless now."

She laughed at that, and he couldn't get over being

able to lie with her, make her laugh. The pain didn't matter. The circumstances. She was his. And they'd made it through.

"You going to move in to my shop?"

"No."

"You think I'm going to move onto the Delaney ranch?"

This time he laughed, then winced at the wave of pain. "No. Not in a million years." He frowned, realizing something he hadn't quite put together till she'd mentioned the ranch. "My father. Everyone has been in here except..."

Vanessa stiffened, then slowly exhaled. "Well, you know he has a lot to clean up at the bank."

Dylan maneuvered so he could look down incredulously at her, but it hurt so he ended up just kind of flopping around. "Are you defending my father?"

"No. I think he's a dirty rotten bastard." Vanessa blew out a breath, rubbing her hand over his shoulder. "Let's not talk about your dad."

"He really hasn't been by, has he? He..." Dylan couldn't wrap his head around it. He'd almost died.

Well, he supposed it told him all he needed to know. No matter how much it hurt, his father wasn't the man Dylan had thought him to be. Dylan closed his eyes. His body hurt. His head hurt. His *heart* hurt.

"So where are we going to live if I marry you?" Vanessa prodded. "My answer depends on that."

She was trying to distract him. Why not let her? "Well, I'd consider your shop except I'm pretty sure there's no way on earth to baby proof it. We need some room. A house to build our family in." He thought about the cabin they'd been stuck in, then chuckled a little to himself at the fact it'd likely be on the market eventually. "I know a cabin that's going to be up for sale."

She laughed. "Yeah, let's buy Adele's cabin and live there. How much of your blood are we going to have to scrub out of the floorboards?"

"It *is* where we fell in love," he said, warming to the idea. "Isolated and away from Bent. Even if we didn't live there full-time, it could be our vacation home. I'd miss ranch life, but being outside of town would be good enough."

"It's only a twenty-minute drive to town. We'd both be able to get to work." She gently slapped his chest. "No. What am I saying?" She laughed again, and it was like heaven to hear her laugh. Soothed all the rough edges, the pain and the disappointment.

Maybe he didn't have his father anymore, but he had something bigger. Greater. A family who cared. *Family.* Love. No more feud nonsense or pointless bitterness. He was going to embrace the good.

"We're not buying Adele's cabin," Vanessa said firmly.

"I don't know. Something to think about."

"You go back to sleep. Wake up with an ounce of sense in your head."

He kissed her temple again, since he could, and then decided he would go back to sleep. But he wouldn't make any promises about sense.

Chapter Twenty

Vanessa was exhausted. Sleeping in a hospital wasn't exactly restful, fighting with nurses and doctors even less so. But Dylan was getting released tomorrow and…

He'd have to go back to the Delaney Ranch for a while. She couldn't take care of him in her shop, much as she wanted to.

She'd made a promise to herself back in her teenage years that she'd never, ever step foot on the Delaney Ranch again, but she was going to have to break that promise to herself. For Dylan. For their future.

Which meant she had to clear some air. She'd left Dylan after his meeting with the doctor to discuss rehabilitation. Jen had planned on spending the day with him while Vanessa did what she had to do.

First up? Something long overdue.

She knocked on the door to Laurel and Grady's house, knowing Grady would be at Rightful Claim getting ready for opening.

Laurel opened the door looking bleary-eyed and miserable.

"Oh, so I see it's hit you too."

Laurel groaned. "I felt fine. Maybe a little tired. Dizzy sometimes. Then this morning? Barf city."

"I'd love to tell you it gets better."

Laurel groaned again, motioning Vanessa inside.

Weirdly, the shared morning sickness both put her at ease and somehow made this harder. "So, um."

Laurel waited patiently, but all Vanessa could do was stutter. Irritated with herself, she decided some things didn't need to change. Including her *go-for-it* attitude.

"We used to be best friends," she blurted.

Laurel blinked, then nodded slowly. "Yeah, we were."

"I haven't really had one since. A best friend."

Laurel's confused expression softened. "Me neither. I mean, there's your brother, but his eyes glaze over when I want to discuss the romantic overtures in a movie."

Vanessa managed a weak laugh. "Hey, my eyes used to glaze over too."

"No, you pretended, but you watched all those rom-coms right along with me."

Years ago. Something like a lifetime. How was Vanessa expecting to go back to that? Of course, how was she expecting to marry Dylan Delaney? Life just didn't make sense. "I guess I was hoping we could be friends again."

Laurel grinned. "Van. We aren't friends."

Vanessa frowned. Why was she grinning at that? Laurel wasn't *mean*. But that was a mean thing to say. "Well, screw y—"

Laurel rolled her eyes and stepped forward. "We're *sisters*." She held out her hands like it was as simple as that.

For Laurel, it was. And Vanessa was beginning to realize, after coming through the hardest, scariest, most complicated moment in her life, that sometimes simple was the best way to go.

"Do you really believe all that stuff Grady said in the waiting room about no curses, just challenges? Do you really believe that?"

"I do. I'll admit when you and Dylan were both missing, I wondered. I doubted. But…" She shook her head, then placed both hands over her stomach. "How could I ever think this was wrong? Cursed?"

Vanessa put her hands over her own stomach. It wasn't a curse. The baby had never, ever felt like one, even when she'd been certain she'd write Dylan out of their lives forever. "Us both pregnant at the same time? Kinda feels more like fate than a curse."

This time, Laurel gave her a hug. "Fate," she said, squeezing tight. "I like that a lot."

Vanessa squeezed her back, uncomfortable with all this baring of her soul and whatnot, but she wasn't quite done. "Listen." She pulled away. "There's something else I wanted to talk to you about. Your dad hasn't been by to visit Dylan."

Laurel blew out a breath then made her way over to the couch and sank into it. She gestured for Vanessa to do the same. "No, he hasn't."

"Dylan wants to go see him when he's released tomorrow. I don't want him to go if your dad's going to be a jerk."

"Then you'll have to stop him, because the bottom line is my dad's going to be a jerk."

"I don't get it. I mean, I always hated your dad but he didn't whale on you. I figured…you know, that meant he was a good dad at least, even if he was a snobby jerk."

"I don't get it either. That's not the man I knew. Sure, the feud was important to him, but his family was the *most* important thing. But…"

"He came to your wedding."

"Yeah. I thought that meant something. Turns out he thought I'd come to my senses before I started popping out babies."

"That's awful."

"It's sad. He's sad." Laurel reached over and took Vanessa's hand. "I know you want to protect Dylan. I do too. But he's going to need to face him. Talk to him. If it ends badly, you'll be there to support him. Trust me. It won't make it not hurt, but it helps."

"You know, I think you're good for Grady."

Laurel raised her eyes. "Are you sneaking Dylan's painkillers?"

Vanessa rolled her eyes. "He needed someone to depend on but not another Carson dude. You. You're… I've been awful and I think it's because I knew…" Vanessa pulled a face. "I'm about to be barf city too."

"Yeah, because you're talking about your feelings, not because you're having morning sickness."

"I guess you've still got my number."

"Well enough, anyway."

"It's just… I knew you were better for him. I resented that. I resented you and him both getting over all that crap they've been feeding us since we were babies. The feud was safe. No one got hurt with it."

"And no one got any better either."

"Yeah, I'm figuring that out. I don't want your father to hurt him."

"I know. He probably will. You won't be able to shield Dylan from that hurt any more than he'll be able to, say, give birth to that baby for you, though I know he'd take all that pain on himself if he could. Love, I've discovered, doesn't really solve all our problems."

"So what *does* it do?"

"Gives us a hand to hold to get through the problems with. Which actually works out a lot better than just avoiding pain."

"If you say so," Vanessa muttered. But much as it

sounded like a load of crock, Vanessa had no reason not to trust Laurel. And that felt pretty damn good.

DYLAN MIGHT HAVE kissed the ground if he wasn't in a world of pain. Still, he was free. Free. Walking of his own accord out of the hospital, not to return.

Except for rehabilitation and checkups and blah, blah, blah. But he'd focus on his freedom.

And what he had to do. The sun was shining and the sky was a vibrant blue. It felt like a fresh new start.

It would be, once he dealt with this one cloud over his head. First, he had to get rid of Vanessa and preferably one sister. In an ideal world, he'd get rid of all of them, but he wasn't cleared to drive just yet.

"I've never had so many females fluttering over me in my life. Remind me never to get shot again."

"Remind yourself, hotshot. I wasn't the one playing Mr. Hero and shoving me out the door, then pretending like you hadn't been shot. You'd probably be in better shape if you'd owned up to it."

"The ambulance would have gotten there at the same time either way. Besides, your blood pressure was high enough."

Vanessa crossed her arms over her chest as they stopped outside the hospital doors. "I can't believe Grady blabbed to you about that. Besides, I was *fine*."

"We'll go get the car. You two sit tight." Laurel smiled and pulled Jen away.

"They're giving us privacy to argue."

Dylan tilted his face up to the sun. "Yeah. Or themselves privacy to gossip."

"I want to go with you," Vanessa said firmly.

He didn't need a translator to figure out her abrupt subject change. "It's just not a great idea."

"I'm not afraid of your father."

"I'm not afraid of him either. That's why I'm going to talk to him, but you being there is only going to irritate him."

She glared. "Good. A man can't visit his on-death's-door son in the hospital, he can stand to be a little irritated."

Dylan tried to hold on to the contentment he felt over being out of the hospital, but tension was creeping into his shoulders. "It'll be better for all of us—"

"No. We're done with that. I'll let you handle the crazy lunatics with guns since you know how to handle yourself, but you're not deciding what's right for us. That's not how this goes."

"You're exhausting."

"Get used to it."

"You have to know some of the things he's going to say, and I don't really want an audience for how awful he can be. I don't want you to feel—"

"What? You're not really afraid I'll have second thoughts?"

Laurel pulled the car to the curb and Dylan started to move for it, but Vanessa stopped him.

"Babe, I ain't ever cared what this town or your father thought, and I'm not about to start now. In fact, I think I'm going to take out an ad in the paper and make a big old banner that says 'PREGNANT WITH DYLAN DELANEY'S BABY AND PROUD OF IT.' I'll hang it above Rightful Claim so everyone can see."

He took her hand, brought it to his mouth and brushed a kiss across her knuckles. "I love you."

"And I love you. Which means I'm not leaving your side no matter how many Delilah references your father makes."

Dylan looked at her. Really looked at her. He'd accepted he'd fallen in love with her despite previous incidents. She was strong and brave and awe-inspiring. He wanted to build a life with her because she fit, perfectly, like she'd always belonged at his side.

But he'd never fully grasped the simple fact that Vanessa Carson would be *good* for him. He'd spent far too long caring what people thought—not enough to capitulate always, but enough to lie or cover it up when he didn't.

Vanessa wouldn't do that, and he didn't think she'd let him do it either. He knew she wouldn't let their kid grow up feeling like they had to be something they weren't.

"Why are you looking at me like that? Your sisters are waiting."

"You're right."

Her eyebrows rose. "Well, I know I am. So, you're not going to fight me coming with you?"

He linked his fingers with hers and moved to the car. "No. No, you're right. We're a team. No more lone-wolf stuff."

They climbed in the back seat of Jen's car and chatted casually on the way over to the Delaney Ranch, but the tension that crept into the car the closer they got didn't escape Dylan's notice.

"Can you guys let me and Van do this on our own?"

Jen nodded. "Of course. We'll go down to Hilly's, and you just holler if you need anything."

"Appreciate it."

Much as it grated, he had to let Vanessa help him out of the car. Even though it had been a mostly smooth ride, he felt jostled and achy. This whole recovery thing was not going to be a walk in the park.

But walking up to the door with Vanessa's hand in his

was a soothing balm to that pain, and he had to believe that would always be the case.

He opened the door and led her inside. He called out for his father once, but it was soon clear he wasn't on the main floor. Must be upstairs in his office.

Dylan was exhausted. He lowered himself onto the living-room couch. "Need a minute before we head upstairs," he muttered.

"I'll go get him," Vanessa said, already striding toward the stairs.

"Van."

She gave him an arch look.

"Teamwork, remember?" He patted the spot on the couch next to him.

She wrinkled her nose then huffed out a breath before she plopped herself next to him on the couch.

"Man, you got some fancy digs, Delaney."

"It's no above-business apartment, but it'll do in a pinch."

She smiled at him, then brushed her fingers over his hair. "You're wiped."

"Yeah. I'll live though."

"I'll make sure of it." She kissed his cheek. Her random acts of gentleness never failed to move him.

"I love you, Van."

"I love you too."

Footsteps sounded on the stairs that led into the living room. "Gird your loins," Dylan muttered.

Dad appeared at the base of the stairs. There was a moment of shock in his expression, then something more like pain. He cleared his throat. He looked...rough, Dylan decided. There was no wave of sympathy though, because he'd been in the hospital for *days*, and not once had Dad been by.

Didn't that tell him everything?

He'd had a plan to ask his dad how things were. To be calm and kind when he asked where they stood. But that plan evaporated.

"I'm only here to get my things," Dylan announced. A man who'd made the mistakes his father had and still refused to see his son in the hospital wasn't worth an attempt at civility.

"Dylan."

"No. No, I can't stay here. Not under this roof. I thought I could be reasonable, but I just keep thinking of Adele telling me she'd been promised my job and—"

"She was a good employee, but she needed motivation. My handling of the situation hardly made her kidnap you and—"

"Shoot me? Try to kill me? Maybe it didn't *make* her do that, but it certainly didn't help. Your manipulations and lies…all the hurt they caused." He pushed himself into a standing position. "I won't be a part of it. *We* won't be a part of it. I'll get my things and we'll find somewhere else to—"

"Perhaps we can come to an agreement where you both stay here," Dad interrupted, his businessman-negotiation tone of voice firmly in place.

Dylan sank right back onto the couch, all his energy whooshing out of him with that bombshell. "Excuse me?"

"You certainly don't *have* to, but the offer is open if it might help your rehabilitation. I'm sure you could make room for Vanessa in your room. She'd be welcome."

"Okay, we'll take you up on that."

Dylan looked incredulously at the woman who'd once said something like she'd rather drink bleach than live at the Delaney ranch. "We will?"

"Temporarily. Until you're recovered enough to do it

all on your own." Vanessa looked imperiously at his father. "Thank you."

"It's settled, then."

Vanessa nodded firmly. "Settled."

Dylan pushed his fingers to his temple. "I think I'm hallucinating."

"No. Your sister said some things to me that…" Dad blew out a breath. He was clearly flummoxed and irritated, but instead of retreating or putting on his usual cool disdain, Dad ran a hand through his hair. "I've made mistakes. I don't regret all of them. But I've been…wrong a time or two. It isn't comfortable or joyful for me that you've all decided to…"

Dad shook his head, trailing off and then pacing. He stopped, looking at Dylan and Vanessa. He drew into that ramrod posture that Dylan was used to seeing precede a lecture. "I've been working with some lawyers about setting up trusts."

"Trusts?"

"For your child, and Laurel's. That's simple fact, and regardless of circumstances they will be my grandchildren. My grandchildren will have the best."

"Your grandchildren will have a choice," Vanessa replied.

Dad clearly wanted to say something to that. But he didn't.

Dylan was pretty sure he was hallucinating. Maybe Vanessa had slipped him one of those painkillers that made him loopy.

"Family is the most important thing. Which isn't the same as our name, I suppose."

The *"I suppose"* almost made Dylan smile. But he wouldn't put Vanessa through his father's behavior. "There will be rules."

"Of course. As long as Vanessa is the mother of your child, I'll treat her with the amount of respect that entails."

"Now I think *I'm* hallucinating," Vanessa muttered.

"I've made some mistakes and things have gotten out of hand these past few years. Everything, really. Well, that won't do. We're still Delaneys. So instead of falling apart, we'll—" Dad made a face, but Dylan gave him some credit for continuing "—work together. Make adjustments and a few compromises. Maybe…maybe Laurel was right and that's been the answer for this town all along."

Vanessa's hand curled around Dylan's and squeezed. "I think working together is just what we need."

Dylan squeezed her hand back. He'd spent most of his life hating Carsons and everything they stood for. He'd never imagined himself here…being part of a linking of the Delaney and Carson names.

But he'd never been prouder of anything in his life.

Epilogue

Two months later

"You guys know this is the most insane thing possible?"

Vanessa swung on the porch swing Dylan had installed yesterday, while their families helped move furniture and boxes so neither Vanessa nor Dylan would overexert themselves in their move from the Delaney Ranch to their new place.

"Are you talking about *us* or the cabin?"

Laurel eased onto the spot next to Vanessa. They'd both gotten much bigger recently. Once Vanessa and Dylan were all moved in, they were going to have a joint baby shower. Then in no time at all, their babies would be born just two months apart.

It felt like it was taking forever.

"I suppose you heard about Adele's insanity plea," Laurel said softly.

Vanessa shrugged. She'd had to let some things go in her life. Anger toward Adele was one of them. She'd never forgive that woman for the hell she'd put them through, but she wouldn't waste her energy being angry over it. "Long as she's locked up, I don't care if it's a jail or an asylum."

Laurel looked at the cabin again and shook her head.

"I can't believe you want to live in the house you were basically held prisoner in."

Van smiled at the gleaming wood, her brother and cousins hefting in couches and bed frames while Dylan's brothers surreptitiously handed him only the lightest of boxes.

"I fell in love with your brother here. Why wouldn't we want to raise our family here?"

Laurel only shook her head again. "If you say so."

Dylan crossed the porch, eased himself next to Vanessa. "I think that's it."

Vanessa studied his face. She'd been worried he'd overexert himself. He was mostly back to normal, but still working on endurance and range of motion, and he tended to push himself.

But she didn't see signs of extra fatigue or that awful gray note to his complexion he sometimes got. He'd held up well, and it allowed her to relax.

"Cam and Hilly are going to get the pizza. They treated me like a damn toddler when I suggested I could get it myself."

Van patted his shoulder. "You get toddler status a little while longer."

Dylan rested his hand on the rounded mound of her belly, and they both sighed contentedly. Home. They were home. And about to be a family. Whatever hell they'd been through, it had been worth this moment right here. Them. Their families. A future.

Vanessa nodded at Ty, who was standing by the moving van looking standoffish and moody. Then Jen, who was all but hiding behind Grady as she chatted with her cousin, Gracie. "Have you guys noticed those two act like they have a magnet repelling them at all times?"

"No," Dylan replied, frowning.

"Oh, totally," Laurel said. "I'm almost *certain* they had a thing in high school."

"Jen and Ty?" Dylan demanded incredulously. "No way."

"Way. Then he went off into the army. I don't think I've seen them exchange more than two words in the year he's been back."

"Maybe they just don't like each other." Dylan patted Vanessa's belly. "Not everyone falls in love with the enemy," he said with a wink.

Vanessa shook her head. "There's something there, and at some point? It's going to explode. Happened to us. Don't know why it wouldn't happen to them."

Dylan studied his sister, and then Vanessa's cousin. He shook his head. "No way."

Laurel got up off the swing as Grady sauntered over. "Mark me down in the *something-is-there* column," she offered, walking to meet her husband.

Vanessa looked at *her* husband—a term she surprisingly loved, as much as she had their simple courthouse wedding and raucous after-party at the Carson ranch—and grinned. "How much you want to bet those two hook up by the end of the year?" she said, nodding back toward Jen.

Dylan rubbed his hand over his chin, studying Ty, then Jen again. He named the same astronomical sum he'd named at Laurel and Grady's wedding. The night that had changed both their lives for the absolute best.

She leaned over and kissed the scar on his eyebrow, a parting gift from No-Neck, he liked to say. "Delaneys always love to flaunt their money," she murmured.

He linked his hand with hers. "These days, I hear tell, Delaney-Carsons love to flaunt their love."

She rolled her eyes, but she leaned into him, content to

swing on the porch swing with her husband, watching their family—all those intertwined Carsons and Delaneys—interact and love and laugh.

Yeah, that was definitely something to flaunt, enjoy and nurture.

Forever.

* * * * *

COMING SOON!

We really hope you enjoyed reading this book. If you're looking for more romance, be sure to head to the shops when new books are available on

Thursday 16th May

To see which titles are coming soon, please visit

millsandboon.co.uk/nextmonth